THE KYOTO BELL

The Kyoto Bell

COLLY CAMPBELL

Sooty Publishing

THE KYOTO BELL

First published in Australia in 2021 by Sooty Publishing Canberra Australia.

The Kyoto Bell was written on Ngunnawal Country which always was and always will be, Aboriginal Land.

www.collycampbell.com.au

Cover design: Pat Naoum/Red Tally Studios.

Typeset: Mark Furness/Liquorice Light Publishing.

A catalogue record for this book is available from the National Library of Australia.

ISBN: 9-780645-196702

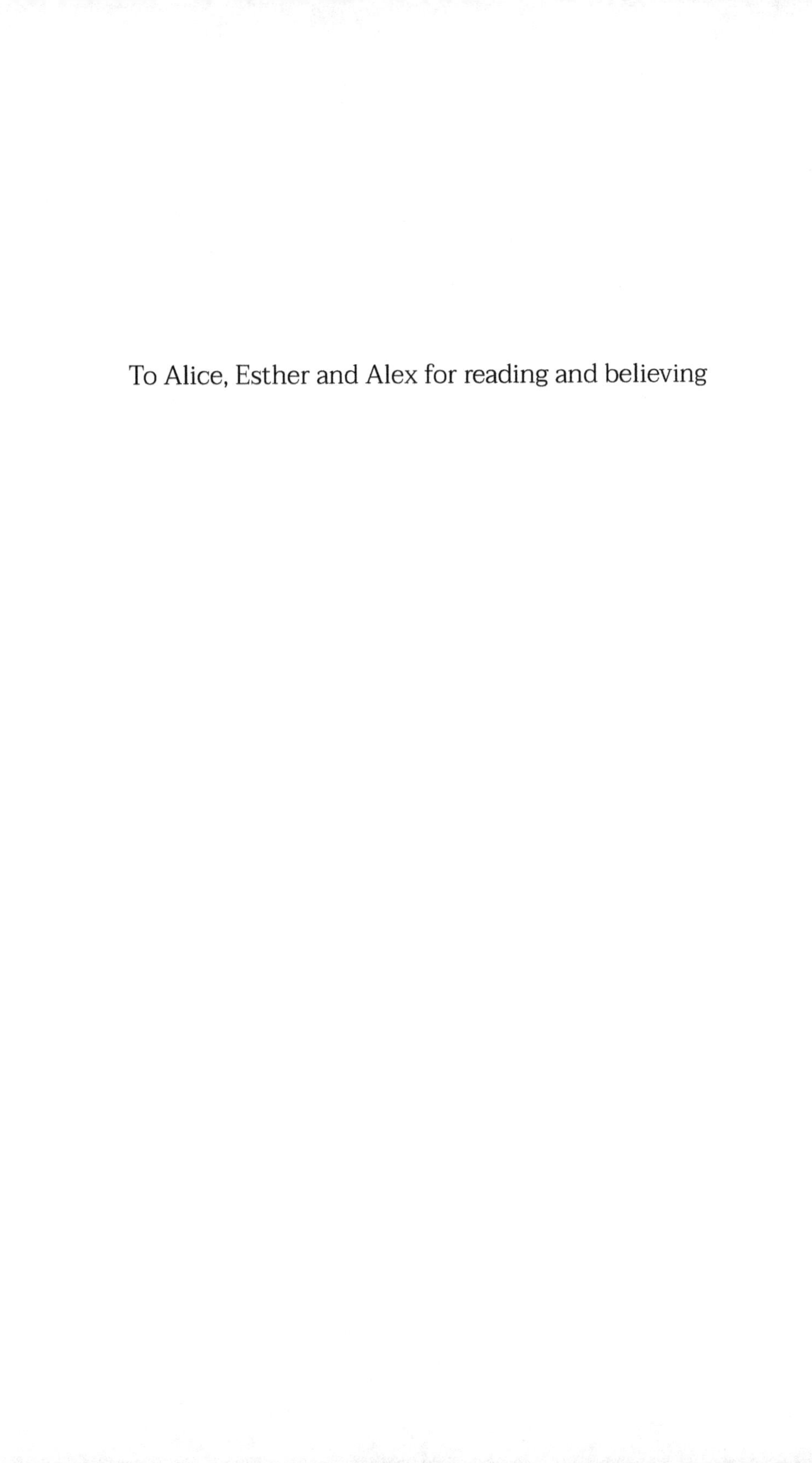

To Alice, Esther and Alex for reading and believing

PROLOGUE

March 2142

THE seas were dirty, full of big chop. Spray, mingled with particles of kelp and old plastic, smacked the windscreen, smearing
the plexiglass. In tight troughs and peaks, the 12 metre waves
were greyGreen and relentless – like mad, shifting corrugated
iron.

Andaman Marko, strapped to a seat in the sealed cockpit
of his heeling boat, watched the various blinx on the weather
radar with one eye, while he briefed the boat's skipper, Flick.

"Lumps. Still lotsa lumps coming in," he said to her. The
bridge (if you could call it that) was sealed and all but soundproofed from the pounding ocean so they spoke without
shouting.

"Yup," was all Flick said.

Wet and deadly, outside. Least they'd escaped a solid 5
hours of slashing rain, as the boat edged towards the better
weather, south of the Cloud. Andaman sometimes wondered
about their mad duel with the elements. They'd be drowned
10 times over if it wasn't for Flick, braced on the helm. Her
place. One slim muscular arm clamped to the wheel rim, the
other holding a grapple on the cabin roof. She was in an orange

weatherproof skinsuit, just in case someone had to go out onto the lethal deck of the boat and do something. Gloves dangled from her belt, a looped tether, and a knife. Andaman's safety jacket was slung on the back of his seat, but his seaboots were on, ready for action.

They'd been 36 hours thru this watery turmoil, and could now see the end, delivered from under the Cloud. There was a strip of daylight ahead, while behind was neverending darkness and storm.

"I see 5 thermocells to starboard but they'z all behind us now," Andaman said.

"Yup," she said again.

Normally Flick was the talkative one, but piloting took all her concentration, staring thru the spray, fixing the boat's course. The stern was bashed by an erratic swell, swerving port, then starboard, then port again. The action pushed the bow in the wrong direction, repetitively. Flick was getting sick of the effort and deciding whether a course change would help.

She carefully turned the wheel, and the boat immediately pitched into the wave behind and surfed down its 10 metre face. Then, too quickly, a side wave burst against the bow splattering more ocean across the windscreen.

"This sucks," she said.

"Almost outa the Cloud – it'll calm soon," said Andaman but he knew the northeast swell was relentless and it would still be a tussle, even when the wind died.

The waves always were high, green and beating up the boat. A current was swiping back from the coast and causing the usual problems of deep troughs and ratty courses. Andaman had turned up the boson enhancer on Flick's instruction, which charged certain particles in the hull to give it more mass and pushed the keel deeper in the water. This helped steady the boat. Andaman and Flick were exhausted by the effort, running on the dregs of their energy located somewhere at the bottom of an empty personal tank. They were emerging from a monthlong battle with the Cloud, from Aceh in Indonesia to the coast of West AuZ. They'd holed up for a couple of days up a river along the Kimberley coast to recover from the last leg and were now hellbent on getting to Hedland. Soon they'd have light, could hoist the solarSail and start banging some volts back in the depleted motor batteries.

The swell and wind were being coGenerated far away in the eqwatorial confluence under the Cloud – the permanent band of storms that ran around the Earth's eqwatorial regions caused by the heated oceans – but as the boat emerged from under the Cloud the wind eased and the frothy wave caps blowing about in mists became noticeably smaller. The sky ahead, above the crests, was blueYellow, like a cloudless sky always was.

"What the hell's that?" Flick asked. Andaman noticed her look of consternation under the mop of blonde dreadlocks and followed her pointing finger.

A small reddish speck floated in the bluish sky, like an orange bird of prey, just outside the ominous cloud band. The orange speck reminded him of the brahminy kite that haunted the cliffs of the Ville way back when in the time Flick and Andaman first got together. Andaman had owned a house on those cliffs at the time. Before they became *personae non gratae* and deliberately disappeared from both the actual and the virtual.

"Shit, it's a hopper," Andaman said.

The aircraft moved slowly on rotors, rather than its jets, about 600 meters above and seaward. OrangeRed like Flick's weatherproofs, it was clearly an AuZgov milisi Search and Rescue aircraft.

"Ah, shit."

"They may not have seen us. We're pretty blended. Grey on grey," Flick said.

"They'll have the infrared and eWash gear which will pick up our heat and electrics. Must be a rescue happening." He checked the radar but saw no blinx of any other vessels about.

"Ahhhhhh, shit," Andaman said again with feeling.

Flick had no time for Andaman's mood.

"We can't go back under the Cloud, Andy. Just got to press south."

"I know," he said, miserably.

He hated The Man. The Man that owned the hoppers. Who'd stymied his career. Who'd humiliated and jailed him. The entity known as AuZgov.

"They've f'ckn clokked us, that's for sure," he said.

Flick was too busy concentrating on finding a course into the waves to commiserate with her hub. She tried to cut a finer line thru the crests but the boat just lifted high above them and splashed like a breaching whale in a curtain of water.

"Ahhh," she said exasperated. There still wasn't enough room between crests to pick thru the troughs. "F'kn current's running against us."

She glanced at Andaman's weatherbeaten face. Ten years on their boat, *The Kingdom*, sailing the high seas, free as fish. He didn't look free. Had tired eyes and leathery skin. They'd been thru a fair bit, side by side, always watching out for one another. She was dogTired too, but the sight of the blueYellow sky to the south made her feel happy. Happy she and Andy had survived another rough patch of water. Hopeful of a port-Stay and some different vittles to the frozen leftovers in their galley icebox.

Flick cared less about the hopper, determining that its search and rescue crew was looking for some other boat in trouble. She certainly hadn't sent out a mayday.

Things were looking up. Ever since Andy had emerged from detention in the Ville after his 11-month sentence, they'd proceeded with their grand plan to fall off the edge of the Earth, and they'd been of one mind. They still were. They were content with their strange life.

Just a few more hours of arm wrestle with the wheel, and mebbe autoSteer, and she and Andy would be on calmer seas.

"Wow, shit," exclaimed Andy his eyes bunched with horror. She glanced up and was hit by a surge of vicarious adrenaline. The AuZgov hopper had clearly been caught in one huge gust, generated by the adjacent weather, and tipped almost sidewayz, sliding back and down into a half stall.

"No!" she cried.

Suddenly the rear jets came on for a sec, then 2 secs, to rebalance the aircraft, and ease it horizontal again. They could almost feel the pilot grappling with the controls until they'd achieved some stability.

"Woah – hopper's nearly done a backwardz deathSlide," said Andy. "Just as bad up there as it is down here."

"I don't know how those pilots do it!" Flick said.

Andy laughed: "The same way you do it, luv. Reflex, control and experience. The same way."

Flick calmed herself with a half smile, and reflexively tipped the wheel a couple of degrees port.

*

Not long after, their own warners in the panel started to blare, lights flashing. Andaman's eyes swung back to the radars.

"Hey, Flick, swing further west, we're closing on the ruins of the old Dirk Hartog Windfarm. Navigatrix says on this swell, we could hit the platforms over there." He looked down on the navmap. "Platform 22, I believe."

"Got it," said Flick moving the helm infinitesimally to the west. A coupla degrees, then a couple more, just like the hopper pilot. Then a couple more, testing the boat against the beating.

The swell was indeed pressing *The Kingdom* inshore where lay great huge concrete stumps of former oceanik power station windmills, smashed to pieces by a Category 7 'phoon during the climate stepChange in 2072. Just ahead of them to port, Andaman had a visual on the huge waves, 2 kliks east, smacking into the nearest of the wrecked windmill platforms, built to preCloud enjjineering spex. The enjjineers failed then to imagine how bad it was going to get. Flumes were flying high into the air, and as the light hit the spray, rainbows glowed momentarily then evaporated.

WestAuZ had lost 2000mW of energy and 1180 lives in the space of a day when Tropical 'Phoon Gina crashed the coast, destroying the Dirk Hartog Array, and drowning towns and mine sites.

"I'll head out to sea for a bit," Flick said, moving the helm another couple of degrees starboard. Over the top of the wave crests, they watched the now jetPropelled hopper loop over them a coupla times, then head southeast and disappear in the yellow haze.

ONE YEAR EARLIER

A CONVERSATION

Solitude requires the dark embroidery of silence.
Invocations to the Private Self (2029) by Ulli Kalk

March 2141

THE persistent chirruping came from the rear of the cave. At first he thought it was an insect, then realized the noise emanated from his old safe. The safe wasn't locked, was slightly ajar. No one locked anything at the Hermitory.

The chirruping echoed with an annoying tinny tone.

Only thing in the safe was the ancient scope.

For a few moments he felt uncertain, fearful, tugged his beard. He gazed around slowly in case someone was behind the great shelves, or reaching for somethink up on the high ladders, or lurking in any of the back sheds, but there was no one.

He, and all Qwartermasters who had come before, used the strange scope device for ordering annual supplies. Never had he received a call. The chirruping continued, irritating and summonsing.

He walked to the rear of the vast shed, built into the cave, reached into the iron cavity and pulled out the komms device he touched mebbe once or twice a year. He touched the green dot and pressed the instrument gingerly to his ear.

"Yes?" he said, tone uncertain.

"Can I speak to someone about money," said a qwiet, friendly voice on the end of the line.

"Who's this," he asked, stomach lurching at the sound of human language. Actual sound, wordz made vocal. Trying to remember how to talk. He'd once learnt to sound wordz out with mouth and throat. But, woah ... that was a long time ago when he was at school. When there were noises other than groans or laughter.

Holding the scope to his ear, he walked over to the nearby jars and drawers where dried herbs and spices were stored so he could breathe in the reassuring scents. To calm.

"I want to make a deal," said the voice on the end. "I have spoken with other Qwietudes and determined that your community could sustain a visit from a young man, a young friend of mine, and I am willing to pay handsomely for your time — looking after him."

"Young man ...?" he was perplexed now.

There was somethink compelling about the voice in the scope. The very making of this stranger's wordz was compelling.

He breathed deep, smelling the cinnamon and the peppers, remembering how those pleasant scents had helped after the death of his wife.

"Yes, he is 16 or 17 and needs sanctuary."

"Well, this may possibly be ... we must encourage new followers, or the Hermitory will wither." Those wordz were written in the Tracts of the Qwietude.

"Will it?" said the man. The voice sounded compassionate. "This young man I can deliver in a few months."

"Deliver? How? We are very far ... very secluded. Discreet from people." His own wordz were halting.

"He would be delivered by hopper. By aircraft. By some chance I know your location. But if you agree to this task, I ask you to give due care and attention to this young man's wellbeing. Then we may come fetch him some months after that."

"So, he won't stay? We need new people to become of the Qwietude - make our families." A wheedling tone now to his own voice which he didn't like.

There was a qwiet moment on the scope. Like a void. Like there was much distance between him and the voice.

"I can bring you more young people. *If* you agree to look after the boy. And I am willing to provide for your community $New10,000. Over 10 months."

He knew that was a great amount of money as he authorized the supplies once a year. $New10,000 would go a long way. As Qwartermaster he knew the value of money, unlike all the others. Other Leaders, also. Outside knowledge was poisonous to their minds, they thought, was corrupting, and they were pleased to leave such dirty work as talking money to the outside world to him, the Qwartermaster.

The money could pay for seeds and rootstock, chemicals; importantly, a new welding plant and parts for the broken imajjing skanner.

"Who are you?" he again asked.

"A friend of the Qwietude," said the man. "A good friend of the Qwietude." So reassuring. He clearly knew the ways of the Qwietude.

"Well, I could supply you the money and mebbe 4 more boyz and a girl to keep this young man company. Just for safekeeping. For care. Could you do this for me?"

"One time ... one ..." said the Qwartermaster, struggling for the correct word. "One moment. Let me think."

He inhaled again, and cautiously looked around to make sure no assistant could see him talking on the scope. Verbalizing was frowned upon, but his assistants should all be in the gardens, down in the gorge, bent over, planting crops. Was early and the heat of the day had not yet made outdoor work too uncomfortable. Even tho he was in shade, the sweat dripped from his face, as always.

He thought: should I tell the Leaders? Consult?

But then, he was a Leader ... one of the most important too, and was authorized to speak to outsiders, decide on supplies. Any children brought to the gorge, in a way, were supplies. And the thought of a young woman being put into his care had galvanized somethink else in him.

"How old are these other children?" he finally asked.

"All the young people are 16 or 17."

Old enough, he thought. Old enough.

"When exactly?"

"July, probably, for delivery. I will give you warning. It is very important that you look after them, especially the boy named Todd."

Todd? Funny name, he thought. "You make first payment soon! I must understand ... ensure this is no trick," he said, suddenly in the moment, wheeling and dealing.

"Oh, it's no trick," said the man. "The care of this boy is most important. You make sure he stays in the boundaries of the Qwietude for a few months, and you will be richly rewarded." The voice dripped with honey and promise.

"And the other young people?"

"I will see what I can arrange. I will let you know. I have your account codes and I will send a prepayment in good faith next week."

The Qwartermaster nodded, hard scope against his ear, "It is done then. It is agreed."

"Good."

The line went dead. He wondered that the man had their secret account details too? How could this be? They were a close-held secret among the communities of the Qwietude. Private. The man must be a former member.

He walked past the high shelves and the crisscross of ladders and cabinets, past the spare parts area with its stored machinery, until the cement floor of his stores gave way to granite pathways. On the lip of his realm, he looked down to the sun-drenched gorge at the rice fields and gardens. He watched the young women in planting mode, hats and sarongs and xShirts, bending and setting rice seedlings, wet shapely arms, lovely hips. The women laughed with each other and the young men beside them.

The air was hotMoist, the wet season not long past with its battering storms and rains. Now, the creeks and ponds of the gorge were full of water, along with their tank system further up the creek.

The community at work preparing for another growing season. Making sure of a constant supply of food for the year. They were like tiny mice, and he was a kite, high above. The thought pleased him. But the red of the rock and the sunglare were painful to the eye of a man who always worked in the shadows of the cave, and he retreated to the shade.

Yes, he could look after the boy named Todd. And his friends. A strange reqwest, but they would be welcome.

Very welcome indeed.

MUSIC ROOM

Tranquillity. Does it even exist anymore?
In the dark vacuum of space perhaps?
Invocations to the Private Self (2029) by Ulli Kalk

THE Philosophikal were braiding a new song together when Dr Madrigal Phipps arrived home that nite.

Madrigal's cruiseV Swift had swept thru the evening traffic on the Swan freeway along the Perth foreshore.

Zoning home from Phipps Industries HQ and tedious Board meet, Madrigal was deep in conversation, debriefing with her 2 aides.

The sun, lateOrange, was setting over the estuary waters, the deepening shadows and the dark mustard clouds signaling sqwalls out to sea. The cruiseV hooked left and silently ascended the hill toward Kings Park's urban conglomeration.

Up Fraser Avenue, thru the Sainted Gates, past high condominium towers til the 100-year-old, 4-storey sandstone building, home of the Phipps family for now 3 generations, loomed in the now blackly mustard light. In contrast, thru the street level windows the lights were ivory white while upper storeys were dark. As the driver jumped out and opened the rear Vdoor to release the 3 women execs, Madrigal Phipps finally noticed the gloomy sky and heard a melody seep thru the stone and glass frontage of her house. Was like a faint, tuneful wind gust.

"Watch out," Madrigal warned her aides, "it's downtime for the kidz." Their precious guitar was just audible from the footpath. "They'll have to go home soon for the June exams revisor pods."

When the front door slid open she was confronted with the whole musical fugue. Sounded a mess – but at least the kidz were having fun. And sometimes, she thought, their elaborate songs zigged.

Madrigal, in a rustColoured liteSuit with chic black cuffs, entered the vestibule. She was hotly followed by Phipps Industries Chief Courier, Rox Brewer, and Suze Shelbo, Madrigal's long suffering Secretary Prime. The 3 women all carried small clamB cases. Suze carried Madrigal's personal bag too.

Madrigal moved with brisk authority, as tho' the world was dragged in her wake. As she passed the arched opening to the Big Room on the right, she lifted an elegant hand and said a qwick and smiley "hello". Her son, Todd, and his friends looked up and replied with alacrity. Madrigal's party moved on to the lift to elevate to floor 3.

On the women's heels was Szygy, Todd's kelpieDog, who asked repetitively: "Where's my dinner, Maddy?" He'd been asking Todd, *Where's my dinner Toddy?* for half an hour, to no avail. Todd was too focused on songs.

The silent elevator delivered the trio upward. After a hectic day, Rox Brewer and Suze Shelbo felt numb and said nothink, saving energy for the debrief. Madrigal hummed the melody that her ear had plucked from the guitar.

Kidz should be packing up soon, she thought.

The trio brisk whisked down the passage, lights flicking on in anticipation, flicking off once they'd passed. Once in her office, Madrigal swung in behind her glass topped desk, sat with a sigh, and waved at chairs for her aides to sit.

*

"Hi, Madrigal," the young muzos say, in almost unison, but she's already disappeared from view to clinch the bizz for the nite with her aides.

Todd and Narmon shrug. Lissa smiles because she thinks Madrigal is fantastic and she knows her personally. But there's no time to lose between school's end at 5 and dinner at 7. And 7 loomed. The Philosophikal return to resetting their musical loops. Their focus on Peet's song, presented new that afternoon, is intense, and no one wants to lose those fresh muscle memories in their fingers.

Peet hopes Madrigal will get busy'n forget about them, cos he's much enthralled by this partikular session, while they should really be packing up soon according to the written contract set down by Dr Phipps and the kidz. Peet wants The Philosophikal to push the clok but it's final year, after all, for Todd, Lissa and Narmon. Peet and Jaim'z are a year behind.

In a tight circle, Todd Phipps and his mates Narmon, Lissa and Peet, and Todd's 15 yr old cuzz, Jaim'z, play simalcrums – also known as galaxy synthesizers – a sax, a drumKit and, of course, their prize 20th century electric Gibson guitar. They relish their hard negotiated "after school relax", released from the strikt regimentation of the day with its disciplines and observant learnings. After all, they are famous now. Famous on the virtual!

Narmon, gripped and obsessed by Peet's song, asks the author: "What's that line of lyric again?"

Jaim'z starts banging his kettleNest impatiently, finding the rhythm for the group.

Peet looks at his clamB and repeats the wordz: *"Don't know what y'r in for/but wade you anyway/hip high, hip high/ into a swamp of misery ..."*

"Scrummo!" says Narmon, their bandmaster's reserved judgement.

"From the top," says Todd, itching for a better compliment.

*

Todd Phipps is just turned 17. A handsome boy, energetik but no way the obsessoid muzo like Narmon and Peet. He has responsibilities after all. He's heir to Phipps Industries, the biggest energy Heg in AuZ, and is also obliged to take part in as many family Indijj cultural reqwirements as poss with his mother's people. He's tried, most times, to travel north to West Capricornia (or West Cap) near the Kimberley, when the weather hasn't been so bad. He's attended ceremony and initiations with his other young cuzzes, including Jaim'z, and learned the ceremony songs from the Elders. He's got the initiation tatts for various ceremonies, and can speak his Indijj language. In Perth, he plays at half forward in the school footy team. And he also loves his friends. Especially the ones in the room, braiding their new song together.

Todd concentrates on both Peet's reedy voice and Narmon's fingers roaming on the guitar frets. He manipulates the keyboard and the joystick of the simalcrum, looking for those harmonies. A spot beam from the ceiling illuminates Narmon's big face. Narmon's eyes are half closed. He nods to himself as his fingers spider across the frets. Todd loves Narmon's focus on the music. He's large, bigger'n Todd who is slim and wiry, tho Narmon is 17 too.

If AuZGov's DyNAst repository, its genetic dataBank, was interrogated, the results'd show Narmon's line, generations back, are Burmese people, Scottish people, and way back there's an Ethiopian refugee as well. His bigness, and lighter skin comes from the Scots, but DyNAst would credit the African genes for the musical proclivity. Narmon's mother, Noni, is a friend of Madrigal's but rather stuffy, and his dad Jasp, is a wealthy Perthside builder.

Todd knows Madrigal thinks Narmon's a sweet boy, their chief music obsessoid, who refurbished the precious Gibson guitar by hand. The old vidz glowed on the wallscreen, pictures from waybackdown thru the ages: 180-year-old images of long dead guitar players like Keith Richards, Taj Mahal, and Boss Springsteen, which give Narmon and Todd the fingerMoves, the vibe and the kit.

"Oooh, the very osmosis of the blues," Peet once declared.

They were oblivious to the fact that during the Age of Purity and Virtue (which was most of the last century) so many of their musical heroes were reviled as drug addled fools, and then forgotten.

*

When Narmon and Peet discovered Hendrix, Morrison and the others – as young boyz mazing thru the Virtual – they fell in love.

The Philosophikal's music was strange to their audiences. 'Ndeed, they'd been posting tunes on the Virtual since their first song, *Cold Cold JJamming*, also written by Peet, was pronounced 'spectacular' by Narmon and Lissa.

To many ears on the Virtual, jaded by classicism, The Philosophikal's was an enticing sound. Since the Age of Purity most music was composed and read from dots, in several chamber music styles. *Nuevo Leider* had been the backbone of the 21st Century music. The Philosophikal had all learnt classical plays, but were now pushing those edges out and incorporating improv and much older sounds, and to their credit, new braids too. People were listening.

More people than they imagined.

Todd Phipps was in awe of Narmon's musical talents, but wasn't so bad himself. They could tune the guitar to the simalcrum's joystick and really get zigged, strapping the notes on a big screen with an orchestral sheet, which they could all follow and amend.

*

The final few braids are most melodic.

"Scrummo!" says Narmon again as the song fades in their ears.

"Hey, Liss," says Narmon, the conductor, "try doodling somethink over the lyric passage, hey? The swampy bit. Needs some lifting but mebbe in minor notes. Don't drown the Peet tho."

"Yeah, don't drown me," says Peet, crouched over his rig. "I'm too young to die."

His face is smooth, eyes bright with the act of creation. His mop of hair is also rather unkempt – both he and Narmon copying the look of some of the old vid muzos.

"We need Peet alive," says Todd laughing.

Lissa smiles and pulls the sax mouthpiece to her lips. She's a self-taught talented player and Narmon's her steadyBoy to whom she's pledjd in a simple publik ceremony. Lissa has a good ear and eye for the chill compositions and can put melodious licks across their short 10 minute songs.

Her mother, Minnie-Tuton, wants Lissa to study law and become a counsellor and advocate, but she has blasting red hair, and a strong viewpoint, and her mother's demands take eqwal place with Narmon and The Philosophikal. While Narmon is a big burly boy, Lissa is small and neat. As a couple they look lopsided, but it works.

*

"The Philosophikal? Why such a funny name?" Madrigal Phipps had asked, after Todd announced the band's publik persona.

"Mum, 'slike in the 20th century when bands were named after things, not the players," he'd said, "but we're not replicating the 20th century ... this is not a nostaljjik thing." He was very intense about this. "We want to be original. You know ... music groups are called after the players like Rikson Dyke, or

Overelle, or mebbe whatever their main song is, or they say they are the "bla bla ensemble" or "bla bla symphonia", but Narmon and I, well, we love the way later 20th and 21st century bands had their own noun names! You know. You've heard of *The Beatles* at least, Mum? They had an identity other than the players."

And again he breathlessly explained to Madrigal, in case she didn't understand, that they weren't copying the Golden Age so much as repurposing the bluesy stuff – *philisophikally.*

"Our songs are about now! We're making music about now!" Narmon'd say and Todd would agree with a grim, knowing smile and repeat the phrase. They wouldn't admit that divining the nostaljjik had indeed brought them all those nostaljjik followers of the blues, plus all the newbs who loved the freshness of their music.

*

In the low-cast light of that evening, the 5 young people play their complicated ziggy tune with a mutual concentration that joins them together in a way that can never be lost, even in a lifetime of memories.

COURIER TO
COURIER

The Man is all biz. He'll confiscate your eyes and ears and you'll never, ever know.
Invocations to the Private Self (2029) by Ulli Kalk

AS the jam continues unheard, downstairs, Courier Rox Brewer smiles serenely and waits for her boss's nod to start the debrief. Couriers were the human keys to corporate lockBoxes.

"Ok, Rox. What did Premier Jembrana say?" Madrigal demanded.

Because the Virtual was so spongey – almost open blather – the Courier role was vital. Industrial Hegs and Governments snooped all the time, and no one could design programs to convey secret, personal communications. Madrigal well knew how riddled with wormholes private komms were. That's why Rox was Madrigal's ears and mouthpiece. Rox would roam far and wide on Madrigal's behalf, transporting Phipps Industries messages, talking faceOnface to business and other associates, politicians, and returning with information and intel likewise. Those discreet conversations helped shield trade knowledge from spies and industrial agents who sought their own insider intel on Phipps Industries.

Was a delicate and diplomatik profession, the Courier.

Madrigal appreciated Rox's skills, cos she'd also once worked as a Courier. In the glorious past, she'd been a Senior Courier for AuZgov, 'til her dad forced her out of the job she loved to take charge of Phipps Industries. She'd been estranged from her dad ever since. He'd meddled in a mission of AuZgov diplomacy to the Chinese Hegs and his interference had made her beloved job with the Government untenable.

If she thought about the day of his corporate ambush, that terrible meeting, Madrigal Phipps still boiled with anger.

*

But that late afternoon, her dad wasn't foremost on her mind. After a day of senior project managers making complex presentations to the Board, Madrigal had spent the last few minutes admiring Roxy's clothes.

While stating: "'K, Rox, what did he say," to start the briefing, Madrigal was actually thinking: *What a beautiful dress Roxy's wearing. Very orange and tasteful. Burmese orange. Nice collar too. I'd wear that.*

"I spoke with Premier Jembrana in his office," said Rox, long blonde hair lapping her small, seemingly guileless face. Her busy green eyes darted around the room, from clamB, to Madrigal, to Suze Shelbo and back.

"He had one aide present. He said: *Thank Maddy for her gracious, gracious congratulations on my appointment as Premier, and I return my fond greetings. Make sure she receives them please.*"

Rox glanced at her boss to make sure she wasn't sounding too familiar. He'd 'ndeed said "Maddy" and "fond" and her account was accurate rote. Madrigal only smiled gently and nodded for more, hands clasped on the desk.

"Tell her directly that the position of Premier of Capricorn is not much different from my previous incarnation. As you know, my predecessor, Premier Paul Luff, was inactive toward the end. He became more religious and less engaged, which is the danger of illogical and intraActive belief systems that don't add to the common good. As Luff went into a publik decline, my approach was to help him see decisions thru, rather than hinder or undermine. My approach was supported by the meejja, both mainStream and offStream. I've been rewarded by the people of the Territory of Cap for carrying the burden of 2 jobs all those years previous."

Madrigal smiled. She knew all this. Jembrana's wordz were to impress Rox rather than her. Madrigal also knew that votes from an abundance of climate refugees – millions of Indon, Filipino and Timorese and even the Papuans – now living in Capricornia, the huge Territory north of the AuZtralian tropic, would have swung heavily behind a man who was descended from the princes of the abandoned island of Bali. But Jembrana was also admired in the south, by the leaders of AuZgov. An operator who communicated openly, didn't waffle his wordz, who made things happen.

"Tell Maddy," said Jembrana thru Rox, *"that we can talk about the Phipps Industries solFarms on the southern borders. These are a priority as the northern ones are less viable thru encroaching cloudcover and almost permaset monsoon. Whether we transfer existing, or build new, is a factor to be considered, and Cap's funds are in parlous state. I attach a chip with those details for your Courier's belt."*

Rox unclipped the chip from her belt and placed it with Madrigal who skanned the info in her secure clamB which was never hooked into the Virtual. She then placed the chip in front of her. Rox continued in her melodious contralto voice – using the most attractive of the Courier tones – to please her boss:

"Tell her also we are planning to move staging ports further south to Port Hedland. Phipps Industries will have to use those ports for their rigOuts. This is unavoidable due to weather pressure. Wyndham is uninhabitable now. Also, the proofing of hardiWheat and hardiRice, for planting in the Arables and south Tanami is making steps, and I thank Madrigal for her keen interest in moving that project along with the WestAuZgov. Thanx. There is a chip on the cropping results and estimates with the Courier."

Rox unclipped again, Madrigal skanned.

Rox went thru another 8 items of Phipps Industries, East Cap, West Cap bizz before the faceOnface session between the Courier and the Premier came to an almost close. There were only a couple of more delicate statements to run past her boss.

*

It's getting late and still busy in the Phipps' sandstone home on Monday June 5, in Perth, in the year 2141.

The kidz miss the homewardz deadline, so engrossed are they in Peet's new song.

Well, Lissa doesn't miss it. As she plays a sweet, pure sax tone over the braids the boyz are driving, she feels a bit guilty because she knows she should be revising those law cases. Six months only 'til exams. Her mother is desperate for Lissa to achieve greatness. The pang of guilt is brushed aside as Lissa concentrates on the dots running across the screen on the wall, and listening for Todd's key change.

Like Narmon, she is a mishmash of heritage, but the flame-red hair flags Irish or a Skandi. She and Narmon have sexed, and everyone in her world knows, except her mother, Minnie-Tuton. Once formally pledjd for future marriage, there is an option for sexing, and Lissa and Narmon pledjd early to savour the physical pleasures. Otherwise, in the Age of Purity, one remained perfektly chaste, or at least that's what society (and parents) expected.

Madrigal, being worldWise, unlike the straightlaced Minnie-Tuton, had guessed that they were sexing, and qwietly asked Lissa not so long ago, woman2woman, if the girl was on antiFecundities. Lissa hadn't even blushed. She told Madrigal they'd tossed an old coin and it's Narmon who's taking the pills. At least one of them's doing so, thought Madrigal, satisfied.

And while Lissa's dad would have been up for a dad2kid chat, he was killed 8 years before. A Major in the search&rescue milisi, he'd drowned on the end of a line drop when a storm rescue went wrong and the tip of a massive Southern Ocean wave slapped him from a stretcher pod, caught him and dragged him under a cold green maelstrom. They never found his body, nor the woman who'd been strapped into the pod, but AuZgov inscribed his name with all the others at the War Memorial in Canberra on the *Wall of the War Against the Singular Enemy.*

Lissa was 9 at the time.

Out of all Todd's schoolmates, Lissa knows she's a Madrigal favorite. She and Dr Phipps can have a relaxed laugh and talk fashion, cos Dr Phipps is really into clothes and what's happening at school. Or mebbe since all Todd's other mates are boyz, Dr Phipps just likes a girl around the place.

Lissa also knows that while she's dedicated to meeting her mother's wishes, Madrigal (who interferes a great deal) knows The Philosophikal is Lissa's escape from Minnie-Tuton's anxieties, and Minnie-Tuton knows Lissa is in good and influential company at the home of the famous Phipps. It sorta works.

*

The concentration between the musicians rises. Peet's reedy voice rings out. The loops braid around the harmonies. They end.

"Yeah," says Jaim'z admiringly. He blows on his hands which have been pounding the kettleNest – a set of tunable percussives. Jaim'z is from up BroomeWay and is lodging at the

Phipps household while he goes to another school. He's a big Indijj kid with a Phipps Industries Scholarship and is a very enthusiastic member of the ensemble. He loves music and is teaching himself to play 3 instruments including the sacred Gibson guitar.

"How was that, Narmonicks?" Jaim'z asks.

They all turn to Narmon for the verdict.

"Scrummo. Still scrummo," says Narmon with a qwiet, satisfied nod.

*

"What else did the Premier say?"

Rox had asked a qwestion without knowing the backStory. Her qwestion about a *"couple on the yacht"* and whether Jembrana knew where they were elicited the reply:

We have no visibility on our old friend Andaman Marko and his wife. We assume, after leaving Hedland on their refurbished boat in 2132, they headed north during an eqwinox never to return. Mebbe dead.

Madrigal nodded at the news. Nine years was a long time to hear nothink about Andaman Marko and Felicity Allenby. But she didn't explain to her aides about what Jembrana meant with the ominous *mebbe dead.* She didn't care for Rox knowing her earlier history and her then dealings with Jembrana – which included their becoming lovers for that short hot flash.

Lastly, Rox declared, *a state visit would be preordained if you, the Mantle of Phipps Industries visited the Ville, Hedland, Alice Springs or any other major city in Cap. I would ensure plenty of time to escort you around.*

(*Preordained?* thought Madrigal. *What a laff. He's just after more sex.* And while this private thought was not shared for obvious reasons, her amusement did sneak out via the crack of a smile.)

"Thanx, Rox," said Madrigal when a silence opened. "That was a surefooted recount of the meeting. How did you find the Premier?"

"Affable, expansive."

"Did he ask about me? My situation here?"

"Where Phipps Industries was situated, under your Mantle, yes. He seemed pleased things were going well. He obviously likes you."

Madrigal sighed and decided to give Rox and Suze Shelbo a snippet.

"We worked together on one tough case 11 years ago when I was a Senior AuZgov Courier and he was security chief in Cap. Andaman Marko was a person of interest in a bomb attack in the Ville, so we hunted him down and found him. Now Jembrana's the Premier, we'll probs see a lot more of him."

"That's good. He's a dream to negotiate with."

Madrigal was struck by a pang of jealousy, wondering if Jembrana had negotiated himself into Rox's affections.

"Don't mistake his charm. He can be a total hardAss. He was the Capricornia security chief," she warned.

"Big J saved more human lives than were spent, tho', after The Grief, is what the folks in the clubs and bars say, up in the Ville," replied Rox. "*His human accounting is on the righteous side of the ledger.*"

The Big J! Madrigal swallowed a smile and said: "True that," in an earnest tone, "but officials like us are sworn to protect life, as private company administrators, and him too, especially people like him. All officeholders, civil servants, chief execs. There's been too much loss."

"*Too much loss,*" her 2 aides echoed, somewhat half-heartedly, it being late. The 3 wordz were always intoned at mention of The Grief in remembrance of calamities in the last century when hundreds of millions died, and that memory of the toll was inferred.

After a glum pause, Madrigal turned to her chief aide and said: "Suze – lock a week in early September for a trip to the Ville. Before the solstice, and before the cloud moves full-South."

Rox and Shelbo made their farewells and left, and Madrigal buzzed her valet to deliver her a glass of wine.

She sipped the very fine wine for a while, thinking about her action packed AuZgov dayz, sighed and turned to the tagged chips on her desk. Ten of them in a neat chrome row. And knew she would be up half the nite working thru the information on her devices, completely secured from the Virtual. For her eyes only.

*

Half an hour into the chipRead, a door down the hall slid open, and she hears the sound of music hang for a moment in the air before the door closes again.

"Ohhh ... that's naughty" she said to no one, looking at her intricately wrought silver thumbClok. Surprisingly, there are no parental complaints landing in her Frisky – texts from Minnie-Tuton or Noni and Jasp. Madrigal stood up, clutched her glass and headed downstairs to chase the young guests home to their parents.

The ziggyZaggy tune came to a clunking halt when she walked thru the arch into the Big Room.

"Well, hello, all," she said pleasantly skanning the faces of Narmon, Lissa, Peet, Jaim'z, and her son Todd who looked annoyed.

"Sorry, Dr Phipps," Lissa said grimacing, "we were having fun ... lost all trak of the hour. Should be getting home."

"Should? It's 8 o'clok. Should've been home an hour ago," said Madrigal. "But the song sounded fantastic. What's happening here?"

"Mum. We practise, and 'practise makes for perfektion', as you so often say," said Todd.

Madrigal lowered herself into the comfortable loungeBag on the floor. The wine in her glass hardly wavered as she gracefully sank.

"I think I always say that *study* makes for perfektion. Where's the exam revisions. They're coming up next fortnite. Don't you think this music is becoming a distraction from your real tasks?"

There was silence at the question. Peet even scowled impolitely. Madrigal knew The Philosophikal's songs were popular on the Virtual and it was swelling their heads, specially Narmon's and Todd's. Messages were coming in from other REAL muzos. And girlz. And boyz wanting Lissa's partikulars. Their simple vidz were being shared everywhere. She worried 'bout that too. Every couple months Madrigal would interrupt practise and issue a snarky corrective to turn focus back to schoolwork.

She smiled. "When your songs sound a bit rough, I like such a thing. This means you're concentrating on homework and not concentrating on The Philosophikal. Seems you're concentrating on the songs, more than study."

More silence. Finally, Todd piped up: "Ok, Mum. I know what you're ..."

"Lissa ... Narmon ... Todd. What happens at the end of the year?"

"Exams and graduation, Dr Phipps," said Narmon, unable to hide his deep gloom. He knows what he'd rather be doing.

"Just don't want your parents down on my head cos I'm providing means for one grand distraction. You knew the contract. Your musical interlude lasts from school's out to 1900. On the dot. Then home. And Sunday afternoons if you've done your work. This room is about ..."

Uh oh, thought Todd, this is turning into a lecture about how she paid for the music room. This time he butted in successfully. "We know, we know. Don't worry, Mum. All covered."

"Good!" Madrigal stood and headed out and the kidz started packing up the instruments.

"Sounded great tho," she shouted, as she got into the lift and returned to her row of kommChips.

*

Now very late, she was sitting within the darkened private boardroom by the long rooftop terrace at the Phipps home as sqwalls finally hit the town with their horizontal rain. Szygy the kelpieDog was curled under her feet muttering about cats in his sleep. *"F'kn cats,"* was all she could pick up, and she frowned at the foul language, poked the dog with her toe.

The sky was thick with hot moisture.

She smiled at the subliminal flirts Jembrana had sent her via Rox (tho' she knew well that Rox was just as pokerFaced as Madrigal was, and probably a lot naughtier. While Rox looked like some naif, she was a Courier after all, well paid for her smartz).

Jembrana was older than her, cunning, and excellent company. The Territory of Capricornia – almost half of the continent to the north – was coAdministered between the spheres of AuZgov and the Alliance of Southeast Asian Nations, in an awkward AuZ-Asian arrangement. ASEAN was where the bulk of refugees came from. Auztralia was where they lived. With the population impact of refugees, and the wild climate, the jointly managed Territory was a big ask for all the administrators in Cap. In the end, Jembrana answered not only to the voters, but also 2 Governments.

A democracy, the Territory of Capricornia arose after the millions of climate refugees were settled. Anyone over 18 could nominate as a political candidate and only needed the approval of the 2 spheres – AuZgov and ASEAN – to be legitimate contenders. Madrigal knew all about the arrangement. Her lawyers PhD had been on the constitutionality of the deal, and the quality of the democracy. She'd thought then that the legalDemocratic structures were entirely flawed, but to her shock, they'd actually seemed to work.

Many others were given the chance to run against Jembrana for Premier, but he was a popular choice. As she'd said, "the right hardAss for the job."

Popular with me, too, she thought with a little smile.

Madrigal was aware Jembrana was taking Capricornia in a new direction – they'd talked about it, off and on, over the years. Her own Indijj people's country in West Cap was in the Cloud-affected regions and she was worried sick about their ability to maintain their continuous habitation and stewardship. As were the Elders of most Indijj nations in Capricornia.

Cape York for example, was a mess, now CloudBound for the entire year.

Her own powerful energy Heg, Phipps Industries, influenced Capricornia thru a hidden web of companies and their projects and business decisions. Other Hegs simply ran the Governments of their nationStates by overt bullying or the purchasing of politicians. But not Phipps Industries, with its seemingly limitless energy supplies. Phipps Industries kept its own counsel, and let the Governments govern, a pattern Madrigal's father laid down from the beginning.

Playing politics can stuff up your business instincts, the Old Man'd say, bristling at stories of other Heg bosses becoming too distracted from their bizz. Her dad was old even then. She'd been born when he was 77.

Way on early, her dad had said: *Don't worry kiddo, they know we have the power, literally, figuratively. When you blow your top, do so judiciously. When you do decide to throw a bit of weight around, it'll shock your Governments and rivals. Unsettles the crap out of them. Save your tantrums for the right moment.*

Good advice from her bad Old Man. She'd heeded those wordz at least, mainly because he'd made it work for 90 big years.

She and Jembrana were in sync when it came to planning for Capricornia's difficult future. They'd talked these things thru a long time ago, and even when they met for meetings or functions, they remained of one mind. Jembrana hadn't held back in his private chip missives laid in front of her on the desk.

Enough, she thought. *Enough rumination.*

The stars were reappearing, far above, as sqwall clouds passed and a stillness returned. She could smell the rain in the air and in the earth. Below, the city and river were filling with mist, and the low dimLites permitted at this time of nite were becoming obscured by the blanket. Looked like a layer of blurred grey menace.

She stood and even felt a tad cool. Brrrr. *Time for sleep.*

INARI

Nowadays, to get away with a lie is a sweet privilege.
Invocations to the Private Self (2029) by Ulli Kalk

THAT Bad Old Man was being assisted up the steps to the orange glow of the Temple. A light breeze played on his face. On his right, Nozomi's kimono rustled gently as she held his hand, and on his left, the Silvery One – a surprize visitor – held his elbow.

The Old Man was always shocked at the silver of his former rival's hair. When you say a fellow has gone silvery, it means glossy grey, but he … he WAS silvery. It amused the Old Man. Almost an aura, shining off the bloke's pate. Could probably see it from the Moon, he thought. Must use some sort of luminescent powder.

He was being firmly gripped on both sides. True, he felt a little unsteady on the steps, but he also thought the guard of honour – his wife and his old rival – was a bit over the top. His slight bout of resistance melted as he approached his favorite Shinto shrine: Fushimi Inari-Taisha, dedicated to Inari Okami, the foxy spirit of prosperity and business.

Worshippers and visitors were everywhere. Women with parasols, children excited by the fox temple. The 2 huge and beautiful stone fox statues stared down at him with their wry mouths carrying keys and heads of rice to represent a bountiful life. The foxes were glorious: dark grey stone, cunning looks, heads turned to celebrate their essential beings as keen spirits. So sleek.

The many faithful were coming and going, paying their dues to those spirits, asking for protection, talking qwietly to monks. The orangeVermillion of the wood panels, the touches of gold, the many orange paper foxes.

The sacred hill and its forest framed the scene.

"Here, husband," said his wife, steering him to the purification well where he washed his hands and rinsed his mouth and spat on the ground. The hands were freezing as he wiped them on his white clothes. She guided him to the dark comfort of the thousand-year-old shrine decorated with red and gold curlicues, where he paid his pittance and the money rattled down the wooden slot. She handed him the rope for the bell which he rang to alert the gods he was close. He bowed, then clapped twice, then bowed again – his wife bowing slightly after his obeisance. Then they proceeded to their ritual devotions, to connekt with an earlier, purer Japan.

The Old Man and Nozomi spent some time in their own solitude. The Silvery One had muttered somethink about a "patch of exercise". He'd peeled off at the temple entrance and gone to climb up thru the many many orange arches, or torii, with the teachings of the Buddha enshrined on them, to the top of the hill. The Silvery One was less of a believer – a nonBeliever even, which didn't worry the Old Man. He liked to think that he too, was a cynic, but with his wife's guidance he'd been entranced and captured by the tenets of Shinto. The religion was all but consuming, now that he had no responsibility.

Except to Nozomi, of course. And the spirits.

So there he sat, watching a priestess in white robes go thru the motions. He remembered almost 110 years ago how his grandfather, an initiated Indijj man, had urged him to learn about the creation spirits from the old men of their country up north, and how his mother, a tough as nails white woman, had said, *You stay in the city, my boy, live in the now, forget the past, you can do better for your grandad's people by finding them economic security. Get a degree. Learn the songs and ceremonies of business and economics.*

She'd been the more persuasive.

He regretted now, not learning the songs and the spirit places of his Country, but that was the past. Gone. He was far too old for the initiation cuts. But he knew he'd brought great security to many Indijj nations in the north of Auztralia, and the thought made him happy as he watched the silk clad Japanese priestess sing.

It's all the same, he thought, *this worship of the spirits.*

The songs and spirits of his old business life were also foresworn. The wheeling and dealing, forecasts, modeling, contracts and pledjs. The ceremonies of the Masters of Business Administration and the annual stockholders' meeting were all contained in some wrinkled snakeskin, sloughed off, lying over a ghostly eucalypt branch somewhere in the past.

Later, as the 3 sat in the Temple cafe consuming udon noodle soup his old colleague said: "This shrine is magnificent today, is it not?"

"Yes. Yes."

"You've thought about what you promised. A while ago. About the protection of our city from the elements?" the Silvery One said.

The Old Man thought: *this fellow's trying hard not to sound like a dealmaker.* He looked at the man's glittering eyes and smiling face. In fact, he wasn't really a colleague at all. Why had he ever thought that?

Truth was, years back they were fierce rivals in the bizz. Now they were retired, and friendly enough, although there were periods in their long lives when they had hated each other. Because of its mild and calibrated climate, the Silvery One had retired here, in Kyoto, as well. Aged plutocrats adored Kyoto's contained climate. It was ancient, intact, beautiful, a protected place. And the women were magnificent. He patted his wife's hand at the thought.

"I am considering my promise to you all, and how to enact it. I will see it thru. Seems perfektly reasonable to me," said the Old Man, also trying not to sound like a dealmaker. His wife stroked his back.

"Come to our social meeting next week. Let us know your purpose," said the Silvery One. "You always enjoy our special events."

The Old Man nodded, then bent forward and put some warm soup in his mouth.

*

Nozomi often watched the Old Man when he was unaware.

She'd watch him impassively as he muddled thru, and then she would explain the simple traditions. How to subsume yourself in silence and tranquillity in the gardens, and the forest trails where shrines mark the home of a spirit. To reflect and repeat the mantras written there, purifying yourself as you ascend the holy mountain.

He was somewhat limited by way of walking up hillsides, but he could attend the main shrines still, and could read and recite the Japanese wordz etched into stone, or painted on beams.

She regarded her husband via a simple analogy: he was a hard black stone – obsidian – who had fallen from a great height for a very long time, and had suddenly hit the surface of a deep, cold river.

After the splash, great ripples were formed which, as soon as she became his lover, changed her life. The ripples had swamped his former wife, Netta, and their children back in Auztralia, who'd become estranged. Downwardness was a journey to purification: while his descent was slowed by the watery mass, he still dropped, the smooth stone now calmly and slowly falling thru the green water.

Soon (not yet), he would come to a stop at the bottom of the river. When he lodged among the other rocks and pebbles, he would understand everything, as pure light flickered above on the river's surface and the water flowed over him and cooled his hot spirit. But at the moment he was still falling imperceptibly into the gloom.

She dared not share her vision with him, or her hope that he'd find that ultimate stillness. He had much to learn. At 120 years old, he was a novice.

From their home above the city, they had a wonderful vantage from the windows and the edge of the spacious garden terraces. She would point to the ridges around the valley and say: "These are sacred hills, sacred from the very early dayz of Japan's formation. These shrines impel our traditions and practises. Look at the Yasaka Shrine in honour of *Susanoo* the storm diety who defeated *Yamato no orochi*, the many headed serpent of disasters."

The Old Man would nod, perhaps sipping tea she had made him, perhaps looking up over his clamB.

Usually her speech preceded a suggestion to visit a shrine, which he would agree to, because he really loved the shrines and temples, their simple rhythms. This was part of her calming regimen.

"I was born here," she'd say, "and I am the latest of many generations who have loved our valley, both those born here, and those millions who have visited. The poet Basho learnt his craft here, the Emperor sat on his throne here, but most of all Kyoto is the spiritual centre, not just of Japan but for the world. Kyoto has its own soul, that is what you would call it ..." A tear would roll down her plumpish cheek.

She was beautiful, a classic Japanese woman. Older, and refined. The Old Man would watch in silence, uncomfortable at Nozomi's declarations. Understated, but passionate all the same.

"You understand, my husband?"

"Yes. Yes, I do," he'd say, to agree with her,

The Old Man loved his new life with Nozomi. There were times tho', when overwhelmed with the ritual and tradition, and Nozomi's love and obedience to it all, he'd become curmudgeonly. Often he'd view Nozomi's dedication as far-fetched, yet he strove hard to understand it.

"Kyoto is far richer than all your plutocratic friends who live here, richer in spirit," she'd say in her calm voice. And he'd agree, making allowances for her evangelistic tone when she'd say: "Look at the path of the philosophers, the shrines, the perfektion of the gardens."

Then a cynical tickle from his previous corporate life would start at the back of his mind: "Yes. And she loves her city more than she loves me."

CLUB KARRIBEE

Perhaps this administrative intrusion creates the glue for social cohesion – but that's a joyless prospect. Algorithms boil us all down to glue.

Invocations to the Private Self (2029) by Ulli Kalk

THE PARENTS sat on contoured stools at the back bar of Club Karribee drinking Yellow Akkolades and Blue Neons. Was an evening in late July, school break, and *The Philosophikal* had been rehearsing furiously for their first paid gig.

Madrigal, Jasp, and the anxious Minnie-Tuton, hid in the semiDark from their kidz. Were supportive, attending the youngsters' gig, but sneaky too. After all, the kidz were under-aged to be in an adult venue like Club Karribee, so some delicate supervision was allowed – so thought the parents.

Jasp, who was big boned like his son, sat upright in his giant coat. A builder who ran a massive company, Jasp still liked to get down to his building sites with the tools and the concrete and steelDrip pours when he could.

Minnie-Tuton was impeccably dressed and cosmetized to the elevens.

Pearl was there too – a looming presence, even bigger than Jasp. As a Phipps Industries securitizor, she sat, ready to pounce, in case clients, or pests, wanted one of those "qwiet wordz" with Dr Phipps who was very well known in Greater Perth. Pearl was highEnd military and exSlotter. She'd finished with Centrl some time back and had leased herself out as security. Eventually she'd caught up with Madrigal, her former Mission Chief, and landed a job. Qwite easily. Madrigal was wholly fond of her old team of specialists who'd backed her in deadly circumstances against both bad men and the Singular Enemy – a patch of killer weather.

Pearl drank nothink but water and tonite was no different. Her eyes roved the room steadily while she listened to the parental banter.

"I think we should just see them perform and we should slip away," said Madrigal.

Jasp, who was younger and keener, was lobbying to give big congratulations at the end of the show. Minnie-Tuton sat looking amazed at the lights and the crowds.

"Won't The Philosophikal have their own fans off the vidz?" Madrigal asked.

"Should play it by ear," said Jasp. "If there's a bad reaction, then we need to encourage."

"Oh, there won't be a bad reaction," said Minnie-Tuton dismissively. "They'll be wonderful." She tentatively sipped her large krill and vodka cocktail.

Madrigal nodded. "I'm sure there will be some sort of reaction, won't there? I think Toddy would kill me if I turned up in the green room ... And Pearl, keep your head down. Don't want the kidz to spot you. You tend to stand out."

Pearl grinned at her boss, pretended to slump, then sat up, crowbar straight again. Pearl did stand out. She was 2.2 meters tall and muscled like a Greek statue, but there was a grace beneath the bulk. Her blonde hair had grown a good length after she handed in her Slotter helmet, but was still cut sharply and unusually, with a couple of kornbraid channels running across the front and the back. She wore a smart, almost military grey green skinsuit and had added a silk red scarf to tone it down to a more informal look.

A Club Karribee waiter sidled over to take orders and Madrigal asked him for the third time when the opaque would dissolve and the performance would start.

"Another 10," murmured the waiter. More people drifted into the large concert space, adding to the growing crush at the dance floor, down front. Lots of tables were already inhabited around where the parents were sitting.

She was proud of the kidz. She'd supported the ancient Gibson jazz semiAcoustic from the Golden Era of late 20th century – *the time of great use of things.* Narmon had sought out old fashioned guitar strings from the OldStuff Palace down near NeoFreo. The byAmp allowed the C20th Marshall valve amp to convert the photonix energy into an ac/dc charge. Narmon even printed the new valves. She knew the guitar sang! She'd heard it most nites. She'd relished Todd and Narmon's wonderment when she herself plied the cash for the Amp so they could find their sound. The Philosophikal was her secret project too.

The boyz had sent chips of their songSet to all and sundry hoping to get a concert. Madrigal looked round and wondered that the first time booking was somewhere so plush and crowded. She glanced across at the bar where a couple of 'tenders were looking up at the stage. One was shaking his head before pulling some beer for a young man dressed in a smart, angular suit. Then the 'tender looked back at the opaque. Madrigal started to feel uneasy.

There was a fair bit of taped sound. Kidz doing desultory dancing on the floor.

"Somethinks up," Madrigal said. "Concert should've started 20 minutes ago."

"They have to learn the drill. Show must go on and on," Jasp said with a wry smile. He and his wife Noni were declared On-cers – Narmon was the result. One child blessed with happy doting parents. Jasp, Noni and Madrigal had tick tacked for years, looking out for their boyz as they schooled and played.

"The muzos were all fired up earlier at my place – there's no way those kidz have cold feet. They were ready to play 3 hours ago! Pearl, it's almost half an hour. Go'n see what's going on," Madrigal said.

"'K, Ma'am," the big woman replied and slid effortlessly round the bar and thru the room.

Pearl pushed open the staff door and up a service corridor to find a couple of people in heated conversation.

"What's happened to the band?" she bluntly asked. Pearl's largeness prevented them from daring to qwestion her verac-ity, and the taller, smoother man with a 5 o'clok shadow and cropped hair answered: "They turned up, kits there, and were set to roll, but they've bolted."

"Bolted?"

The other man, dressed in a spectacular business suit with pewter-coloured flashings said: "Their gear's in the green room but no musicians. Went outside and they're not smoking chop-chop out the back. Can't find the kidz."

"Show me," said Pearl

"Who are you anyway?"

"Security detail for Todd Phipps. He's in the band."

"A Phipps?" sqwawked the pewter suited one leading Pearl round to the empty green room.

"Yes. A Phipps."

Pearl entered cautiously. A large, half dark room – could fit a symphonik orchestra, which it had on many occasions. Empty of people. There were teevs on the wall of the room, showing the crowd on the club floor and local channels. She skanned the table which had soda waters, bread rolls and fruit.

The instruments were stacked against the back wall, ready for action. On the other side, wide doors to the stage. She walked in further and saw at the back, curled tight on the floor in the corner, a kid. Jaim'z, the Indijj Broome cuzz who did the percussives. She knelt beside the body and shook him. Jaim'z was worryingly still. There was a massive gash on the side of his head. Pearl's fingertips found a fluttery pulse.

"Oh my," she said. Pearl grabbed her scope and buzzed her boss. "Ma'am. You'd better come. Somethink's gone real bad here."

Pearl turned the limp body over. There was also a filthy gash on his face which was bleeding qwite profusely. She grabbed some napkins and held it to his multiple wounds and called the 2 men to alert the milisi for an amboV and investigators. Pewter man hesitated, but the 5 o'clok shadow man complied instantly. As she held the napkins in place, Pearl looked around the roofline for vidBugs or even bigger cameras, but looked like there was no surveilance in the room. Darn!

Madrigal entered. Jasp, a step behind, stood at the door, perplexed.

"Dr Phipps," said pewter man. "I'm Joe Moreno, owner of Club Karribee."

"Hi." She cut him off. "What's the story, Pearl? Where's my boy? Ow, Jaim'z!" She knelt over her young relative and felt for his pulse which she finally found.

"You think they left him for dead?"

"Got a workover, sure ... the other kidz'r gone," said Pearl looking at her boss's appalled face.

"Scared off?"

"Dunno."

"Where's Narmon?" Jasp asked from the door as he tumbled thru. "Where are they?"

Madrigal stood and gently pushed Mr Moreno out of the room with her fingertips, and said "Let's find out," to Jasp and

Minnie-Tuton behind him. She started looking hard at everything. Some food had been nibbled, drink had been drunk. The famous guitar, she riffed it in its stand, was tuned. They'd been ready to roll.

She sniffed the air, but could only smell the sour meat from the rolls. Mebbe stale chopchop smoke? No footprints visible in the dusty floor. No textile shreds. Couple of scratches on doors and floors but could have been old. The disappearance of Toddy and his mates was making her head screwy. She wasn't thinking straight, to be frank. In fact, her natural mother panic was rising. She caught Jasp's eyes, and saw Minnie-Tuton shaking like a leaf, which made her panic worse.

"Minnie," she called. "Hold these bandages on Jaim'z head. We'll check the alley." Action was better than panic.

Minnie-Tuton complied wordlessly, kneeing by the injured boy.

Madrigal and Jasp qwickly checked the exits and the lane behind the building, which was dark and empty, then she returned to grid the room with Pearl.

The ambos arrived and a milisi officer came into the room and shooed the parents out, asking Madrigal to wait in the back lane. She agreed, and moved, with Pearl and the parents, into the corridor, and then out to the loading dock area in the lane where the amboV was parked.

Nothink.

Madrigal made a concerted effort to swallow the panic, push it away. The cooler nite air helped. She gulped it like water to stop her head from spinning.

Pearl said: "Somethink could have happened and they ran?"

"Not in their characters. Where are they?" said Jasp with a strung-out voice, "Any probs, they'd've got onto their friskies and scoped us. Don't you think?"

Madrigal nodded.

"And Todd would never have left Jaim'z like that. Left for dead! Not in a zillion years. He's hurt. Out cold and bleeding." She felt her hands start to shake and pressed them against her legs.

"Let's skan round," said Pearl.

Minnie-Tuton looked like a frightened rabbit. Madrigal followed Pearl, pleased to move away from the aura of anxiety.

The emergency vehicle was illuminating the area. Pearl and Madrigal canvassed the road, the bins behind the building, the rooftops. Madrigal took a long time to skan the upper parts of the venue roof and opposite rooflines. Then she checked the road surface for new scrapes and scratches. Jasp stood talking to a milisiman.

"Don't s'pose you've a beeFinder in the car?" Madrigal asked Pearl. "Might've been drones." She sqwinted into the dark in the vain hope she'd see a tiny surveillance drone.

"No, Ma'am. It's a proscribed device. I returned my beeFinding devices to the armory when I left Centrl."

Madrigal nodded. She understood.

She walked over to the the amboV where Jaim'z prone form had been hovered into the alley on a stretcher. He was still out cold. A big boy for his age, the matted blood on his face had been cleaned off and a bandage looked very white across his dark brow. He had thick eyebrows; his very handsome jaw and mouth were set in a peaceful smile.

"Damn," said Madrigal, panic welling up, again.

"Which hospital?" asked the ambo.

"Perth Central. I've the wherewithal to pay, bud. I'll come."

"Sure, mizz. He's a mess. Bad head injuries," he said, and started to load the boy into the V to hook him up and check his vitals.

"Dr Phipps ..."

The milisiman who'd been talking to Jasp had sidled up, and was standing beside her.

"Investigator ...?" she queried, looking at his shoulder pips and cropped sandy hair under the cap.

The milisiman was confronted by an Indijj woman, dark haired with incredibly beautiful brown black eyes. Eyes clouded with concern, lips twisting with uncertainty.

But the stratospheric authority of Dr Phipp's tone, even in the one word "Investigator", made him silently gulp. "I'm Investigator Cardinal. Clemency Cardinal. Now, I need to ask where are the usual, or even unusual, haunts of your son and his friends. Can you give me a list, Ma'am?"

He'd clearly taken a good sounding 'bout the kidz from Jasp.

"Where they group together? My place, Narmon's house. School. The school music facility? Why do you ask?"

"Erm ... any other locations?" he said as formally as possible. "This lad was clearly assaulted, and I'm terribly sorry to say that I suspect your son and his friends have absconded after the fight."

"Fight with who?" said Madrigal, suddenly hopeful they'd worked out who the culprit was. Some aggressive club employee mebbe?

"Dr Phipps. A vicious fight between your son, mebbe others, and this boy Jaim'z," the Investigator said with the most delicacy he could muster (which wasn't much). "Which led to a very serious injury." Silence. "And explains the absence of the others."

Madrigal looked aghast. "They wouldn't fight. The kidz have been abducted, Investigator. They're only midTeens."

"Who, in blazes, would abduct your son and 3 other people? There's Todd Phipps, your son, the boy Narmon and his girlfriend Lissa, and Peet Crews. There was obviously a disagreement and now they've escaped, shamed or frightened by their aggressions, and are somewhere else. It happens all the time with youngsters! All the time! Testosterone and drugs. Fights!"

Madrigal took a deep panicked breath, calmed into the faceOnface zone she knew so well – the mindset of a persuasive AuZgov Courier – and said calmly, "Jaim'z is family. Furthermore, he's the same skinName as Todd. They have life obligations toward each other, and not only that, they are firm friends ... there was no bad feeling between them. But ... I do have serious business rivals. Political enemies who might try and threaten me. I know abduction is rare ..."

"Abduction never happens in the Age of Purity. Kidnapping is an extinct crime," declared the Investigator. "However, sadly, assault is not."

An extinct crime? "I can give you a list of my corporate enemies ..."

"I've sent a milisiV with Narmon's father, Jasp, to his house. And Mrs Minnie-Tuton has gone home also. Can we follow thru to yours? I'd just like to check for peace of mind. Then we can move on to the school. They may be hiding there."

Madrigal looked up again. Into thin air.

She knew all about thin air, and the arcane, dangerous photonik tek that was hardly known to the publik, not even to bogStandard milisimen. Deadly tek, such as shimmers, air tubes, lethal jellyfish - the devices of the devious and the dangerous.

She turned to her security manager. "Pearl. Can you accompany Investigator Cardinal to my house and show him around, then meet me at the hospital? Scope if you find anything. I too have family obligations to Jaim'z, Invesigator Cardinal, and I'll sit with him in the amboV and by his bedside. He's my kin. Pearl will give you my contact details. I'm available at all times."

The Investigator nodded assent and turned. "Once we've checked thru the locations, I'll need to talk further with you," he said in a bland tone.

"You're not getting forensics to check the green room tho'?"

"Dr Phipps, I'm investigating a common assault, I'm afraid. May not have been your son. May well have been young Narmon who beat up this young man. I assume he's not related by skin?"

"No."

Sweet Narmon, the big teddy bear! What a thought. The attitude of Investigator Cardinal was ludicrous, but she knew his reasoning made sense to him. Cardinal's eyes and face were full of care and consideration and he wasn't officious. The Investigator was stupid, for sure, but not harmful. Madrigal looked at the milisiman and decided to let the issue ride for the moment. At least he kept a slightly open mind about the attacker. But ... she knew in her heart she'd need the help of Centrl, the AuZgov security department that she once worked for. And she'd need to build a case to argue for help. Mebbe she would come back and check the roofs of the precinct. Yes, she would.

*

While a medik worked on Jaim'z, sealing lacerations and checking bones, Madrigal looked left, up the laneway to the freeway, and then right, down to the closest corner about 50 meters away at John Street. She spotted a rust red flag, flaring in the dark entanglements of the nitelights and shadows of passing revelers. The smell of piss and wet cardboard. But she also caught a sweeter waft of food.

She jogged 50 meters down to the crossroads, and found 2 very active food vendors working the street crowd, cooking dumplings in a big pot of water on a portable table with a dumpling mat. On either side of their table, red flags were inscribed with *Best Dumplinz Evah!*

The vendors were in the process of folding and boiling the dumplings for the hungry passersby. At first she tried English, then Bahasa. They understood a bit of both.

Madrigal was feeling rushed but took in their slightly emaciated faces and smiles as they handed out dumplings in flutes of paper for a few notes. Street vendors and cleaners eked out basic moneys, and she was as generous as possible. She knew well the reason they didn't get aggro 'bout their appalling situation was the Gov provided large storm-hardened safety refuges when the weather turned, and for that, the poor and their kidz were grateful and compliant. If not, they'd be left in the elements.

"Seen anything in the back alley the past hour?" she asked, holding up 4 fingers and ordering herself and Pearl a coupla dumplings. She dug in a pocket and absently waved her slim coinWand over their till, transmitting a couple of $Old. "Before all that palaver." She pointed to the rear of the club. "Did you see anything down the lane? Anything pass here?" She pointed to the ambulance and milisiVs with the flashing lights.

"Mizz? No. All qwiet in alley before."

"No. Nothin'," said the other.

"You seen what's happening down there?"

"Yizz."

"See a van? Cruiser? People? Nothink?"

The smaller of the climate refugees – mebbe Burmese, or somewhere further afield – said: "The back door to Club opened coupla times during the evening cos light came out, but didn't see nobody. Thought someone was out to smoke chopchop. That's where those Karibee doop's smoke.

"'Nother dumpling?"

Madrigal found she'd eaten the leathery dumplings absent-mindedly, including Pearl's.

"So no shadows of people? Matchflares for their durries?"

"Dinn't see that," said the small guy. But the door opened."

"No van?" she asked again, transmitting some more coin.

"Would've seen it go thru one way or other. 'S one way street thru to the ramp." The little Burmese guy (she was sure he was Burmese) pointed at the one way sign. "And hits main drag on other end. Hard t'get out."

"Thanx."

Made sense. Fair degree of photonik cloaking even in the dark and nitelights of the city. Didn't need that much power for a shimmer device to addle the photons when it was gloomy. But to hide a truk? And potentially 4 or 5 personnel. A big op.

She zapped the vendors $5 of New into their eTill, said thanx, and walked back to Pearl with a dumpling. Madrigal had no time to note their gobsmacked faces as they looked down at the largesse they'd been handed: their takings for a year in one transaction.

*

In the amboV, the boy lay peaceful. The sextuple eMotors hummed them at high speed thru the streets to Perth Central Hospital's emergency wing, a circular glass skyscraper, lit like a shiny silo, connekted to the main block. She tried to gently shake Jaim'z shoulder, to wake him, till the medik told her to stop.

So, pretending to hold his limp hand, she examined it very closely. There were cuts and bruises on the knuckles. But nothink under the nails or between fingers. He'd fought, punched, someone. She sniffed the hand which was redolent of bread roll and blood. Awake, Jaim'z could shed light, could say what happened. A witness.

Madrigal was clear that Jaim'z had fought the abductors, whoever they were. Worst thing was, they'd left him for dead. The bandage covered the contusions so she couldn't check shape or size of the 2 wounds. One had seemed less serious. When she'd looked, in the green room, the hard blow to the back of the head seemed, to her, to have been deliberate, and after he'd been knocked unko.

He'd hardly had a vital when she and Pearl checked. Who were these people who'd taken her son and had taken a second crack at the prostrate Jaim'z? Vicious. Callous. Letting a young man bleed freely.

Sending a brutal message, she thought, to say to her: *rich-Bitch Mantle of richBitch energy Heg, take note. The barbarians have your boy.*

Were they kidnapped for money? In the old days, prePurity and Virtue, abductions happened occasionally to rich people. She remembered, during her law degree, the legal history lessons, Criminology 101, where everyone laughed at the strange crimes of yesteryear, including armed robbery ... and abduction.

Now she wasn't laughing.

She turned to the medik: "Is there somethink you can give him to wake him up?" she asked lamely. But she never said anything so stupid in real life, so this was not real. Just a bad dream.

"No, Dr Phipps. He is badly injured. I want him sedated. I've done a prelim skan with a wand and it looks clear – no fractures, but to make sure we will have to brainskan the child and see if there are any subcranial issues. Bleeding. We have to be qwick."

And they were. The hospital precinct, with carpark and emergency bay shuttle out front, was ablaze with light and waiting emergency personnel. Madrigal paid multiple $New at registration and they entered the portico. Then cool colours took over. Healing pastels. Wave music played low in the hospital corridors to soothe the panicked. Jaim'z was rushed into a skan room, left in the dark on a pallet, and with beamTek, was checked everywhichway.

She was told, as the skans caressed his comatose body, that Jaim'z'd be kept unko for some time.

"Brains are precious," said the doctor.

*

So, the last time Pearl had pulled Madrigal Phipps upward on a rope was 11 years back during a thermocell event in Cape York when the sky gnashed and wailed and spewed forth water from all angles out of a torrent. This time Madrigal was qwietly clambering a very dry brick wall as Pearl, steadied on the roof of the Club Karibee, held a rope wrapped twice round her arm. Madrigal shimmied herself up the line with some effort and a couple of brick scrapes on the side of her hands, then flipped herself qwietly onto the low raked surface.

"Nice work, Ma'am. Still got it in you!" said Pearl. Madrigal winced, and took a tik to gather her breath, and wonder at her fitness levels.

Their nite oculars, clipped to helmets, were working and they checked for marks and dents. With an eWash skanner this time (also proscribed, but she had one anyway) Pearl ran for telltale rads, electronik wash left over from the shimmer pak.

"Further up," said Madrigal.

"Ma'am, they wouldn't position on a roof that far from the entrance."

"Just a little higher," and she clambered up the slope. On the roofcapping, Madrigal sat and skanned the wall of the tower across from the Club Karribee exit. A much higher building – old glass/brick job.

"You think we could get to the top of that one?" she asked Pearl, who was now sitting alongside. The hum of V noises, the occasional fuel engine, and the lights from the freeway behind the buildings, rose and fell like the swell of waves. Otherwise it was qwite dark – an hour before dawn.

Above, the sky showed a tracery of stars. She could just make out the smudge of a constellation known to the Greeks as the Pleiades. Her mob called them the Seven Sisters, sisters who were running from their wicked magical pursuer, a story important to all the peoples of the desert. Running from danger. She thought of the danger Todd was in.

"Ma'am. They certainly wouldn't position that far if they had a pak."

"You're right. I'm a bit anxious. It's clouding my thinking," said Madrigal.

She slid along the capping and said, "*Here.*"

There were lifted edges under the capping where a rig had been braced, 2 by 2, and a discoloured area on the steel tile where one end had pressed.

"Ow ... it's only a trace," said Pearl.

"They rigged it here. Had to be a big pak to wrap and lift so many people." The skanner showed no signs of rads but they'd probably dissipated. Madrigal sniffed the surface and said, "Some dude smoked chopchop too. Can you see any butts?"

Pearl started to crawl carefully down the slope and found a piece of paper and a couple of shreds in the gutter. She held the evidence up between her gloved fingers.

"Chja!" said Madrigal, angry, exasperated. "This is too much. We knew they were here when we looked before. Felt it in my bones."

"Ma'am, don't scold yourself. We have evidence for the milisi."

"No, no. This is up to us," said Madrigal, furious. "The milisi are thickheads. Abduction is 'extinct', remember."

At this point, she felt a pain, somewhere down in her belly. Pain, and a wave of fear. Some vile person kidnapping her Oncer – little Todd. The thought of her son – and she imagined the 6 year old version, not the current 17 year old – returned like a physical wound. Crying was not usually in Dr Madrigal Phipps's emotional vocabuary – except at funerals of very dear people. She'd wept not so long before at the funeral of her mother, Netta, who had left the Earth, far too early. Now there was a sheen of wet on her cheek, come from somewhere.

The friction in her mind caused by the calculated search for her boy crushed against the sheer terror that he may be dead.

Pearl noticed the sheen and leant over the woman sitting on the line of roof capping, and put a comforting arm around her shoulder. "Ma'am? Maddy?"

Madrigal wiped her wet cheeks with the palm of her hand and took a deep breath: "Do you think Centrl would help?"

"Ma'am … what with the illegal use of a prohibited device, namely a shimmer-lifter, yep, they'll help, but will want to take lead. That's what they do, Ma'am." Madrigal looked directly at her old friend.

"Who is the senior these dayz? Do we know them?" The entire diplomatik rubik was beginning to slot and slide in front of Madrigal's eyes – who to talk to, who to galvanize, to cajole, who to help. 11 years past she'd been one of the elite but her commanders were either retired or dead.

"I'll make inquiries," said Pearl.

*

Todd woke in semi-dark. He felt movement – but whatever was moving was not him. He was frozen. He felt lurching in his gut, like aircraft shudders, but his external self – legs, arms, head, body – was a wrapped-tight parcel. In his mouth was a tube – a snorkel of some sort – allowing him to breathe thru the wrapping. Mouth was dry and thirsty.

The wrapping was transparent, like glass, so he could skan out, see his surroundings. He pressed against it and managed to turn his head slightly to the left, a couple of mils at most. The room, or rather, the hold, was lit by machinery dials and small strips along the hull of the aircraft. He decided they were sourcing photons from the outside, where it musta been daylight. The shudders of turbulence continued, so was definitely a jet or hopper, pushing thru some unhappy air.

In the blue black space he saw the outline of Lissa's face. He could see the white of her right eye, open, and she was staring upward, terrified. His heart started pounding and in a huge force of effort he shut his eyes and calmed down, feeling the wrapping. He tried to wiggle his fingers and his toes. Every part of his body was contained. So, he thought, feeling sick, this was claustrophobia.

A couple of years ago his mother, angry with Grandad, told him about the time she was forced to resign her commission from AuZgov's Centrl – the Diplomatik and Security Corps. When she was visiting China, in a meeting with very powerful Government people, his weird old Grandad had deliberately skewered her cool, Gov security career by forcing her to part-negotiate a *private* business deal. She'd been ambushed into becoming a boardroom chair: the Phipps Industries Mantle. What a dog act, they'd agreed, tho' he hadn't minded getting his mum back at that time. She'd returned to Perth instead of absently gallivanting on secret overseas missions.

The telling of the story was also a mother2son parable about expecting the unexpected. She'd waited 'til he was 14 before ever speaking about the incident. And he well knew why. In the telling of the story, there was a violent patch in China when some doop's head was caught and wrapped in light, congealed by a photonik weapon called a jellyfish, where he'd been suffocated. They'd had to stick a tube thru the doop's neck skin into his windpipe to keep him breathing and save his life. At the time, it was a thrilling story 'bout his mum's past.

Now, not so. Todd guessed that congealed light was the wrapping here, because he could see Lissa's outline and her open eye clearly, but they were both frozen like Egyptian mummies. A little twist to the right and there was Narmon. His friend's eyes were shut. Narmon was unko.

While his fingers and legs were frozen, the congealed light was not so tightly pressed into their faces, or their chests – mebbe a comfort thing, or mebbe it was important to keep the prisoners alive.

He tried to talk thru the tube.

"Cn oo hee ee, Issa?" he tried to shout.

No answer. Or nothink audible. The light was pressed into their ears. He looked again to his left and Lissa's eye met his. He winked. She winked back. At least there was some contact, some comfort that she was not alone. Took a lot to stop young Todd from communicating with anyone, and in that instant he'd beaten the kaptors with a wink. Yisss! Lissa kept looking at him, her face less terrified. Good. Her small frame seemed to float, red hair mashed in an untidy mess above her, a meter above the floor.

He was thinking fast, wondering. Of the attack and abduction he remembered nothink. They'd been in the green room. All excited, prepped up. Even had a 3 minute tuneup blast on their instruments.

Then, while waiting for the signal to go on stage, while standing around the table chewing bread and slurping soda water, while chatting about their song set and whether anyone would turn up, the lights went out.

There was a bang at the door, a flurry of arms ... he remembered white arms, and then he was unko.

Why? Some stun device mebbe?

Now they were flying somewhere, like they'd been swallowed by frozen jellyfish, feeling terrified.

To diminish the terror he decided to write a list in his head. So, what did he know?

1. They weren't dead, so the kaptors wanted them alive.
2. The kaptors were taking them far from Greater Perth.
3. This was probably somethink to do with his mum, because she was very rich and influential, and mebbe they were extortioners.
4. They really didn't know his mum very well, otherwise they would never have kidnapped him.

5. Lissa and Narmon, and probably Jaim'z and Peet (were they here?), were taken as well so there'd be no witnesses to the crime.
6. And what of escape? Right now, escape was impossible and, anyway, they were high in the air, flying somewhere.

He decided to wait. Breathe and wait. He sqwinted to his left again. Lissa was watching him. He winked again trying to say, "Breathe and wait". She winked back, her small mouth stuck in a breathing tube, like his.

JAIM'Z

They came and took my baby. And for a time, I blamed my own self, and not the Government.
Invocations to the Private Self (2029) by Ulli Kalk

MADRIGAL was on watch at the hospital. Seated in the darkened room, chin on her fist, fist on the bed, watching Jaim'z for any flicker of life. Hours of fraught worry for a mother missing her son. She was desperate for Jaim'z to wake, to talk, and confirm her conclusions, present some further leads.

Out on the corridor sofette, Suze Shelbo was positioned for action. Suze was wonderful, thought Madrigal. From 5 that morning, she'd been on duty, supportive and calm.

Suze played fetch – coffee, donuts, the silver flask of whisketty. She took messages and summonsed her boss if Madrigal was reqwired to solve an issue in the heart of her multi-industry Heg. Suze Shelbo was a filter, letting only the important stuff thru. She always sported a uniform blonde nostalja cut with bangs, she was ageless (she'd obviously been thru a couple of rejuves) and in a cheery, and casual embroidered Xshirt and threeQuarter pants. Shelbo bustled while Madrigal remained still, sitting by the bedside, eyes on her young nephew. He'd been put into a coma by the hospital but the doks were gradually bringing him out of the drug induced stupor. The timing was not an exact science.

When it finally happened, about 10pm the next nite, Jaim'z lurched forward and gasped hoarsely, in and out like a wheezy accordion, while Madrigal held him up and he found his breath. He took the glass of tonik she offered, and then sank back into his pillow.

"Gah ... gah." The wordz came slowly. "Aunty Maddy. Where am I?"

"Perth Central Hospital, Jaim'z," said Madrigal, coolly even tho' heart and mind were racing. "Just take a moment. You've been hurt." He lay for a while, bandage round his scalp and a thoughtful scowl on his young face. He was a tall boy for 15. Starting to muscle up.

Then, "Todd!" he exclaimed. "And the others ... are they ...?"

"Gone. Taken by someone. You obviously tried to stop them."

He sank back. There was more silence for some time. Madrigal remembered the community he was from, poor, but doing better'n before, proud and resolved. Protecting their country from the ravages of both whitefellas and the Singular Enemy. Remembering the spirits. Mebbe forty families lived there – one tribal group. Hers, via her mother Netta.

She thought about Jaim'z mum (her second cuzz) and dad, and how proud they were of him. She kept qwiet tho' in the dimmed room, and waited for his brain to properly engage.

"What day is it?" he finally asked

"You've been out for almost 48 hours, Jaim'z."

"Are you going to hunt for them, Aunt Maddy?"

"That I am, Jaim'z. But first, have a sip of this."

She helped him with a tube of water which he sipped, eyes closed.

"Can you help me? Can you tell me what happened in the green room at the Club?"

He gave a confused account, in stops and starts, working the story thru in his reviving mind.

"Three men in white coveralls and masks, well they may have been men, could'a been a woman too, came in ... who'd know? No warning ... into the band room. They were zizzed. Yes, they looked zizzed. Real jumpy. We'd just tuned up and were more worried about the show. We'd just played a 5 minute blast to make sure we were ... real ... So these people arrive'n' I thought the Club had provided surprize dancers or somethink. Then smoke happened ... so some sorta smokescreen mebbe."

"Or gas."

"True that. True that. Anyway this big basta um sorry ... bloke went for Toddy who was standing with a burger in his hand and a shocked look on his face. Oh, Aunty Maddy, I just launched at the guy slammed his head w'my fist a couple of times, and I copped a throw down from a hit to my temple, real hard. One other bloke probably whacked me. I tried to stand, throw a punch, grabbing the arm of a white covered man to pull him over at least, and was bashed again, probs with a bit of 80 by 40. That's what it felt like. That was it. Lights out."

"You're a warrior Jaim'z. Can you remember what they looked like? How big? Voices? Wordz? Did they talk?"

"No talking, Aunty. They looked like flies with bigEyed masks, and lumpy shaped backpacks. The costumes they wore were like thin plasticky stuff. One person was smaller than the others. Could'a been a girl. Who knows. They just sucker-Punched me and I was out, Aunty."

"Why did they go for Todd?"

"Dunno. Bloke had some gear in his hand. Long like a tube. Pointing it at Todd."

Madrigal hoped hard that it hadn't been a heartStopper, just some tranquilizer.

"And howya feeling now, Jaim'z?"

"Empty. And Todd and Narmon and … did they kidnap Liss, too?"

"And Peet."

"Peet? Holy …" He blushed and didn't say the next word, as he was very partikular around Aunty Madrigal with wordz. Instead he said, "I'm hungry too … kinda …"

Madrigal laughed for the first time since the abduction, pleased with Jaim'z sudden hunger. A head injury was a worry.

"I'll get you some tucker from the canteen right now, and then you'll have to talk to the milisi," she said with some grim satisfaction. Madrigal waved the nurse forward to help him. Check his fluid tendrils, reflexes, pulses.

"What do you think, Pearl?"

Pearl had been standing back in the shadows leaning against the wall. She looked inscrutable. She and Madrigal walked out of the private room toward the canteen.

"A small takeTeam for so many kidz. Musta been scared of witnesses. Why would they take them all? Makes no sense?"

"May have been others outside, to lift them."

"True. They'd have levitators and everything else judging by the gear on the roof. Knew they were comin' and set up well prior with the lifters. Wasn't an easy operation." The 2 women walked into the corridor.

"Shelbo!"

Suze was furiously working her clamB on the corridor couch and looked up at Maddy. "Is he awake?"

"Yep, and sounding sensible, thankfully. Can you scope that milisi bloke, Investigator Cardinal, let him know Jaim'z has come round. Jaim'z says the incident was an abduction, so he needs to reel in here qwick and take a statement from the boy. I don't have time to enjoy the satisfaction of telling him myself."

"Centrl will have told the local milisi who you were anyhowz," Pearl said.

"Yes. I'm sure they have. We've got all komms covered for incoming ransom demands?"

"Yep."

"Wait for Centrl to check all the traces they can ..."

"I'm expecting a ransom contact on some platform." Madrigal's brow furrowed. "First, I have to get that brave little kid some tucker." She walked out with Pearl. "Y'know, I suspect they thought him dead. They weren't going to countenance witnesses, so took the others. Who are these people? To leave a kid for dead?"

While Madrigal bought a hot stringbeef burger and chips plus a strong tea and pulpJuice from the hospital restaurant, Pearl relayed the new info about white-suited men with insect eyes to Centrl via a scope, and, with Suze Shelbo, set up meets.

Madrigal returned with the tray of food to Jaim'z who scoffed it hungrily. The burger lasted all of a minute before he was wiping his lips with a napkin.

"Thanx for trying to defend the situation. For putting up a fight," she said to the bandaged boy.

"I'd do anything for Toddy," Jaim'z said simply, with a smile. "And you, Aunty Maddy."

"Well ... you're gonna be my inspiration, Jaim'z. We're gonna get them back," said Madrigal.

THE STÜMMERS

When my stolen son was delivered back from the National Children's Protection Unit and handed to my lawyer – not me, but of all people, my lawyer!! – I knew then you couldn't trust the sound of "civilization".
Invocations to the Private Self (2029) by Ulli Kalk

THE kidz were close to the gorge mouth, weeding the outmost paddy grove, when dust kicked up and the hint of a silver shape slid past the gorge entrance where the desert began. The paddy grove was shadeSide, and to keep cool, they were having a splash and a tepid swim as they worked. The 2 kidz, Brownhair and Little Freckle, dived behind a rock and peeked. They were frightened. Brownhair, the older boy, signed: *head down.*

Little Freckle signed (with flashing eyes): *More respect, Brownhair – head* is *down.*

There was a kerfuffle, engine noises, then silence. Ten minutes later, there was a humming sound and they saw 3 men enter the gorge leading a parade of moving shelves, each with a body on it. The procession stopped near the sandy beach where the freshies often basked, warming their knobbly, crocky, toothy heads, but when the noise happened they'd qwickFlicked into the water and sunk.

The shelfThings lowered and the men rolled the bodies off the shelves and onto the sand. One man, with black hair, looked up at the gorge wall and there was some verbal discussion, the waft of wordz could be heard *(breach and broach the Qwietude)*, but in the end, after the men talked, one man shrugged and they all left with their shelves, which were now obvious to Little Freckle as medikal stretchers.

After the parade disappeared, the silver aircraft noisily kicked dust into the canyon mouth, rose above the gorge wall and flew away. Only then did Little Freckle sign: *Come.*

Brownhair nodded and even tho' it was 51 in the sun, their coolhats, heat repellant sunJell and shades kept them going. The kidz approached the 4 young bodies on the beach. They lay in a line on the rough sand. One, with messy messy hair, was bleeding real bad beneath a bandage on his neck – it was soaked red with blood. Then there was a handsome Indijj boy and a fatter boy. And a girl with beautiful red hair like Little Freckle's. All the bodies wore the strangest of clothes. They all looked the same age as Little Freckle's bigger brothers and sisters. She tried to wake each kid in turn, but without success. They looked dead, dead, dead. And the boy with the bleeding neck was white as a sheet.

Despite the searing heat, the kidz ran back to the Hermitory like startled geckos, shadeSide, to let the Leaders know, to get the mediks, before the freshies emerged from their pool.

*

Later, Todd woke. He was tucked under crisp white cotton sheets – sheets that would cost a whizzbang bomb. Todd knew good bedding – his Grandma Netta had demanded nothink less for her precious grandson.

The sheets were much more comfy than whatever had encased him prior – when he was last awake on the aircraft – and as his eyes came into focus he could see he was in a simple room. One high, horizontal narrow window allowed piercing sunlight to stab the bare white walls into luminescence, which lit the rest of the room. Even in his daze, he noted that the walls and ceiling were coated with shinePaint, which glowed the room.

His mouth tasted funny – a remnant plastic flavor of the breathing tube, or whatever gas it was they released to knock him out when the hopper started to descend. He was naked, but a cotton shirt, underwear, a pair of loose cotton threeQuarter pants, and a sarong, were draped on a wooden chair. Todd swiveled upright, sat on the bed for the moment, then had a sip of water from a glass. No reason to bring him here just to poison him, so it was unlikely to be tainted with anything. It tasted delicious and he swallowed it all. He wriggled his body so bones and muscles crunched into life, telling him that he'd been sqwashed like a fishlet in an anaeroPak for too, too long.

The room was sqwashy too. A couple of meters wide, and long enough to fit a bed and bedside table. Everything was glary white, even the reading lamp.

Todd could smell the desert without seeing it. Todd knew the scent of dry. He could also hear the screech of corellas echoing outside and decided he was somehow in some Capricornian gorge. The northwest was laced from top to bottom with big sandstone gorges. His mother's ancestors came from its edge – between the desert and the lusher coastal belt. Uncles had walked him thru Country, hunting and introducing him to the spirits, the powers. Stuff he dearly wanted to believe, but just qwite couldn't.

A wave of fear suddenly washed thru him. He'd now be on some other mob's Country without their permission. From some place within him, he had a visceral reaction to the deserty smell and the faint presence of spirits, and goosebumps rose on his skin as tho' things weren't right.

He'd been thru ceremonies with the uncles as a young East Kimberley man and now sat in someone else's country without permission of the owners. Bad form. But then, he'd been snatched and flown here against his will, which was even scarier. He hoped he'd be able to square his presence with any local Indijj men as soon as.

Todd stood gingerly and did a couple of stretches and sqwats, dressed himself in the clothes provided and went to the door. On the back of the door was what could only be described as written instructions on a paper page, in old fashioned spelling and a small insistent font:

Rules of the house:
Remember your vows within this Hermitory.
When you leave the room, you are in the halls of our belief.
We demand your respect and full Quietude.
Our beliefs rest on silence and privacy is paramount.
Words cannot be pronounced, in faith. Only finger drawn,
and only in brief.
A breach of the silence, any speech, will result in sanctions
enforced by the Quietude.
Remember: privacy is paramount.
Remember: *Spoken word evokes evil* and brings down
the fire of the Government.

Stümmers, thought Todd.

Stümmers was the word that the sarcastic German meejja, and then the rest of the world, had first ascribed to this cult of silence. Founded by Ulli Kalk, a famous lunatic or prophet or poet (depending who you talked to), way back in the 2030s, the cult called themselves the "Qwietude", a more dignified name, reflecting their code of silence and deep privacy. Everyone else called them the Stümmers.

Todd and Narmon had on occasion joked about the Stümmers, people who avoided contact with the world. He vaguely remembered that the Ulli Kalk woman had founded the cult in her xtreme reaction to the pervasive surveillance techniques of the Age of Purity and Virtue, when Govs and Hegs knew everybody's business and shared, among themselves, the depths and feelings of people without a nanoThought.

Most people avoided the superIntrusive Gov/Heg privacy invasions in less xtreme ways, like putting no personal info on the virtual, or meeting faceOnface more, rather than scoping and texting. Some were swayed by Ulli Kalk's warnings, but didn't retreat entirely.

But in the weeds of the wikis, the 2 friends had learned that Stümmer colonies still existed around the world, in faraway remote locations. JellyFolk, they concluded, hiding from prying eyes; people who simply stopped talking and gave up their names so they couldn't be traceable; who weren't meshed into society as givers and takers, like the majority. Todd and Narmon were proud to be part of a survival society, making good again after The Grief.

But 100 years earlier, the Stümmers reviled how enmeshed they'd become, and in the beginning deleted, with the help of supportive insiders, their electronik records from the Virtual.

Back then (before everyone else followed suit, frightened at the level of personal knowledge the Govs held) the Stümmers canceled their social media accounts, eradicated their tax and publik health records, changed their names, and in all ways tried to disappear as human entities. Stümmers born later than the 2040s were invisible to authorities – no names, no recorded birth dates. Phantoms.

From the wikis, Todd understood that no electroniks connekted Hermitories to the Virtual. Their wordz were contained. Their personal details hidden. Stümmers still tried to opaque themselves from HighEyes, those thousands of satellite clusters spinning on their orbitals, by using old fashioned camouflage to block visual intrusion and create colonies where identity could be hidden and life would go on, in a peculiarly muffled, and in Todd and Narmon's view, unhinged manner. After their research The Philosophikal'd even considered writing a song about the legendary Stümmers and their silence worship but Todd and Narmon decided against. Stümmers were just too weird.

Now Todd was in such a Hermitory. Looking up at the white ceiling, he suppressed the panic, telling himself that Stümmers were harmless fools. The panic passed as he knew it had to. No real function when panic's involved. None.

After standing up, the weight of gravity had pressed his bladder and Todd realized he needed a piss bad, and so tried the door. It was unlocked, giving onto a corridor with 10 doors which no doubt gave access to about 10 or so bed cupboards like his. He saw a door indicating a bathroom, which he hurriedly entered, finding a big white tiled room with showers, toilet cubicles, a urinal (where he peed) and washbasins. There were 10 towels and bags – numbered. He took his room number match, bag 3, and found a comb and razor, paste, a new looking toothscrape and pikStix. He washed his hands and face, cleaned his teeth, and combed his thick black wavy hair into a semblance of shape.

Todd returned along the corridor with a qwiet tread, trying to open the doors, but found they were locked. From the outside. When his opened, he decided the handle was matched to his fingerprints. One's room was one's private room in the home of the Stümmers. He knew there would be no eyeCam on him in the corridor, it would be anathema. And his fingerprints would only reside in the door handle. There'd be no Centrl repository of biometrix.

What to do?

He gently knocked on one of the clean white doors adjacent to his own. Nothink. He tried the one on the other side and heard a shuffling sound. The door slowly opened and Narmon peered out.

"Wha'?" said his bruzz.

"Wait," said Todd. He knocked gently on the next door, but there was no response.

He motioned that he was going to enter Narmon's room and pulled the door almost shut.

"Where'r we?" asked Narmon. "What happened?" Narmon's tousled hair was in a tangle, and he looked as freaked out as a 10 year old.

Breathless, Todd said, "While you were on the hopper – did you wake? I did. We were sealed in cocoons of light. We've been kidnapped and dumped at some Stümmer monastery."

"Stümmers?"

"Did you see anything or anyone?"

Narmon processed Todd's rapid fire reveals and questions. He said slowly: "I've been out like a light since the Club Karribee ... they must've knocked us out."

Narmon had an unnerving vision of the men crashing into the green room with bug masks and sticks, and his collapsing to one side of the table, unko, as Jaim'z, yeah Jaim'z, went for one of the doops in a spurt of anger. That was it – a whirl of white and limbs. "They gassed us."

Todd looked around Narmon's room. Bright white. Identical to his own. "Look, Narmon, it's all weird and creepy and we are a long way from home. But you must remember, you can't say anything aloud here, altho' we have to communicate with these Stümmers somehow to find out why this has happened. And get us home."

"I'd just frickin' ask them," said Narmon, suddenly belligerent after sounding sleepy and flat. Narmon had a lot of eyebrow, which could pucker up angry. "They kidnapped us!" he added.

"Stummers aren't that way inclined," Todd said. "They are very private. They don't make nuisance of themselves. We need to find out what's on the boil first. Think we need to respect rules here. We'll get further if we do." Todd stuck his head into the corridor again. "Get dressed and we might go and find someone. I'll see if Lissa or Peet are awake yet."

Todd knocked gently on the other doors to no avail, and concluded they were sleeping elsewhere, or were still unko on their beds. He and Narmon walked in the opposite direction down the corridor to a big glass window which looked out to a courtyard. People were moving, and all busy. They were dressed in similar white cotton, sarongs and and bleached jeans – a uniform – doing tasks. Sweeping. Bringing boxes of foodstuffs thru. Todd saw they communicated by hand, signing when they needed to, but he didn't understand the language. Wasn't an Aboriginal hand language, that was for sure. The hand and wrist gestures were sharp, small, formal yet visible, and not really representative of anything he understood.

"C'mon," he whispered.

As they emerged into the heatDrenched courtyard, people looked up and someone silently raised a hand in greeting, while a child of no more than 5 or 6 ran thru another larger set of doors. They stood still not knowing what to do.

"Err, hello everyone," started Narmon, forgetting Todd's wordz about not speaking aloud, and a dozen fingers leapt to lips demanding silence. Women, men, young people and children, all shushing him.

Koo, heavy! Todd thought. How these children lived in this world of silence, he did not know. Todd had been a partikularly noisy little boy.

There was a moment of stillness as they stood looking at the crowd of Stümmers, who looked back at them with a kind of awe.

"These doops look stunned," Narmon whispered in Todd's ear. Todd nodded.

"Least they're smiling," Todd whispered back, so as not to offend. The Stümmers still looked uneasy.

Then a man and woman emerged. The man was small, with grey hair, and a round, tanned well fed face, and small roundRimmed opticals on his nose. The woman was taller, also deeply tanned, and displayed a beautiful smile. Both were in white cottons like all the others, but the woman's was embroidered in coloured thread across the front of the bodice. Her long grey hair was braided back, and threaded with coloured fabrics and beads. She gestured to Todd and Narmon to follow them into the shade on a nearby sheltered verandah. Todd looked up beyond the roofline, and could see the crest of what looked like the top of a Centralian gorge – orange red rocks, scraggy grass and bleached white tree trunks climbing the visible slope and clinging like comb teeth along the top edge. They were somewhere in West Cap, for sure.

The building had thick, white outer walls and the woman opened a door leading into a large hall where tables were set out in rows. Natural light hatches ran along the upper section of the walls, illuminating the bright ceiling, allowing light to flow thru the room. There was no visible electronik light source. Middling sized sculptures rested on a series of shelves, wooden and stone, of abstract shapes.

The silent couple kept walking ahead thru the long room. As Todd and Narmon followed, Todd glimpsed people in a kitchen over the other side and a waft of cooked tomatoes caught his nose. Then they entered a corridor, qwite wide, with communal areas on one side. The footsteps of their hosts were indiscernible and the woman signed somethink as she pointed, but Todd didn't understand.

They then entered a large room with comfortable couches and easy chairs, behind which was a real window and it became clear the Stümmer community was embedded along the side of a gorge wall. The view was spectacular: red rock walls, gardens, and long blueGreen pools til the water was lost around a bend. Tropical trees lifted their branches up into the cliff and, further up, the boneWhite eucalypts took over. And a couple of baobab trees for good measure. A well elevated village of dwellings could be seen, with solar tiled roofs, probably set on a shoulder of the hill, well out of reach of wet season torrents.

In one of the easy chairs, Lissa sat, curled like a cat, with angry eyes.

"Lissa," said Narmon, rushing over to her. Lissa started to cry with relief, then stopped. Todd knew she wasn't going to give her kaptors the satisfaction of a melt. He admired her defiance.

The woman had visibly winced at Narmon's vocalization. The man nodded. He pulled the door closed and gingerly, hesitantly, he spoke.

"This ... the last time we speak to you," he said. The woman had her eyes closed and fist clenched in front of her mouth as if any talk was an abhorrence.

Then the man started to speak – gingerly.

"You are welcome. We ... us ... do not understand why you were left at gorge mouth where Little Freckle found you, but you are welcome guests at this Hermitory, for a time. You will have to stay for ... for some months til annual supplier comes. He comes once a year. This Hermitory will be your home. We are very remote, as remote from civilization's many tricks and treacheries as we can be, so for you to ... try to leave by yourselves, over the desert, would be folly. Desert is hundreds of kliks, then to the ocean, which is a major redspot under the Cloud, unchartable. Dangerous bad lands. Supplier knows way ... can take you back west in March." The man ran out of words, so the woman then spoke:

"While you are here, I invite you to learn of the Qwietude, free from the world's interference, free from pry. You learn our signs, our language, and work in the gardens and the kitchens."

Todd started to raise his hand, but anticipating Todd's movement to interrupt the welcome and ask of Peet, the man took over clear the burden of utterance.

"Your other friend ... is very injured, not yet woken from surgery ... terrible thing, how he was ... left for dead."

"Was disgraceful," said the woman, shuddering as the wordz came out of her mouth. Todd wasn't sure what she was shuddering at – Peet's state, or having to speak. "He is in infirmary and will recover."

"Our friend, Peet?"

"The youth with terrible shoulder wound."

Peet? Peet had once had a broken shoulder. Todd exchanged glances with Narmon and Lissa. It sounded bizarre.

"Can we see ..."

"Soon ... first we need explanation from you."

"From you, too. Who are you?" asked Todd.

"I answer. Then ask the same qwestion to you, to tell us why you arrived here?" said the man. "I am the CoLeader of this Hermitory, and Leader of Men. I have no name. *Name means identification and identification means loss of own self.*" He spoke the last sentence like it was a text. "This woman is the Coleader and Leader of Women. She has no name either. Our sign is this ..." he moved the pointing finger of his right hand 30 degrees to left horizontal, "which means *respect.* You greet us with this gesture when we meet or even pass. I will greet you with this ..." a 30 degree counter gesture, "which means *my acknowledgement,* or ... *thankyou.*"

"Our young will teach you the signs," the woman said, "but you cannot ... cannot ... teach them the unguarded civilization. Will corrupt."

She looked angry, and there was an awkward pause.

The man nodded. "And ... you are?"

"Er, we have names. I am Todd Phipps. This is Narmon Tonelli and Lissa Tuton. The guy in your medikal centre is

Peet. We are … er, musicians … muzos. And were abducted … snatched by men in white coveralls with no faces. And somehow brought here."

"Snatched? How awful …" the woman said. She had a most emotive face. "Yesterday a hopper style craft landed at the mouth of the gorge and left you on the beach. The children found you."

"Well, can you immediately let our parents know we are here, or the local milisi?" Todd said.

"Alas … alas …" said the man. "We keep no contact with civilization. We have no means to communicate in case of intercept … and they are corrupted. And milisi … never the milisi."

"In a few months time, annual convoy of supplies will arrive. You leave with them," said the woman soothingly.

"A few months? What about my mum? She'll be worried sick. Can I scope her? And school …" said Lissa. "My final year! I have worked for this for …"

"I am sorry … you have no choice in this matter as this our place, and is how we live. We have fine school here."

Lissa groaned.

SCOPING LANGER

Families are the cross-stitch of life – not cables and satellites but flesh and blood.
Invocations to the Private Self (2029) Ulli Kalk

FIRST things first.

*

"Hello, Langer."

"Maddy! Let me guess. Will this be pleasant? Or are your dreadful family going to deliver me another fat nightmare on a plate?"

Her ex, Langer, always felt he'd been duped into the marriage and procreation, then packed on his way. The first part was wrong. The procreation had been their very own idea – a pact between 2 young people. Naive her, enthusiastic him. Sadly, the second part was true ... he had been threatened and effectively banished by her powerful parents who paid his passage out of the country.

Madrigal knew Langer remained deeply hurt and would be for the rest of his life. But she didn't have time to faff, and feed his sorrowful tone with apology. His hostility threw her normal composure, tho', and she stumbled thru the story.

"Very bad news, Langer," she said, not knowing how to say it. "Todd has been ... well ... abducted. Kidnapped – and you ought to know as soon as..." It was way past midnite, but she couldn't sleep. She'd already talked to everyone else, exhausted the possible conversations, and now she had to buzz her estranged Ex.

"Kidnapped? By who? Who'd kidnap anyone?" He hunched toward her like a bear in a pale grey jacket.

"No idea. No idea," she said resignedly. "So, I want to know, well ... not sure whether Todd's been talking to you, but ..."

Langer looked older and heavier. Sported a beard, but then, he was in Switzerland, in a higher alpine compound of the International Criminal Court where he was a Merit and Ethics advisor to the judges. Weather still actually got very cold in the higher alpine areas, and history had it that beards were supposed to keep faces warm. So there was her ex with a beard. Looked strange.

Behind him was a bookcase with old tomes and chintzy little nicknacks. His academic style office where he dissected cases for judges. Ethics was a big deal.

Langer was looking more and more perturbed. "I thought AuZtralia was a crime free environment these dayz – like the other Advanceds. Doesn't it have a tripleA publik purity rating?"

"Seems not so pure," said Maddy. "Look. Do you want to digest this info? Can I buzz back? Sorry it's so horrible and out of the ..."

"No, no," he said. "You must be upset." Langer had always been kind in his own recalcitrant way and he'd picked up on her rattled body language and stumbled wordz – so unlike her.

Bits of their shared history had been good, while other parts had been awful, and as he looked at the very clear face of Madrigal, a little older but still beautiful, he felt the pain of their separation. But, upset Madrigal was gathering herself into officious Madrigal. He could see that.

"So, before the AuZtralian milisi get in touch with you, can I ask: did you and he talk? Did he ever tell you ... "

Langer thought, well, she hasn't changed, then answered her qwestion.

"No, Maddy. We didn't talk. We were severed! Our relationship was severed. Remember."

"Yes, I do remember, and I'm sorry for it and the way you were treated back then," she said. "But he's 17 and not the sort of person to let those family bullshit rules and his parents' past get in the way. I've told him all about you. Nice things, by the way. I assumed at some point he'd seek you out."

Langer looked at her thru the lens, and it appeared he was chewing his beard, but he was thinking. Angrily thinking. He then said: "Have your security services picked up komms between us?"

"I haven't asked them to – tho' I could," she said. "I'm asking you personally. My hunch was that he, and you, would have recontacted informally, and if so, he might have shared worries with you."

Langer was still chewing his beard. *Be brave, Langer,* she thought. *Tell the truth. It's not like you are protecting Todd.*

"Yeah. He sometimes scoped me in the middle of the nite for a chat." Langer was grudging and pissed off.

"And? I don't care about him contacting you. I'm glad he did. I don't want to know any details except if he'd spoken 'bout somethink that frightened him ... and he told you?"

"MADDY!" shouted Langer. "Get into Todd's boots! He'd tell you about any frights well before he'd tell me. He thinks you're some sort of superhero. He wanted to talk to me about philosophy and music and literature and suchlike."

Maddy knew this was probably true. Langer had just disappeared from her life, fleeing the onslaught of her fierce mother and powerful father after their "oncer" was born, and Langer had come up short in their estimation. He'd been nowhere corporate enough for them, or their grandson. From then on, Langer was inconsolable, wretched, and never wanted to talk to her.

She hadn't a clue what sort of threats or bribes they'd thrown at him, but she did try to apologize on a number of occasions over the years. After all, he'd aided, in fact almost coAuthored, her highly regarded PhD. And they'd had a child.

"Do the milisi have any ideas about who would have kidnapped OUR son?" growled Langer.

"Nope. He and some friends were snatched from a niteclub where their band was about to play ..."

"His band? Abducted a whole band? That's ludicrous ... The Philisophikal. He asked me if it was a good band name."

Maddy twigged the thinking. Langer was a professional academic philosopher. Todd was acknowledging dad.

"They're good," she said. "But the 4 kidz vanished into thin air and one was left for dead in a ... pool of blood. We were out the front waiting for them to appear on the stage."

"Which kidz."

"His friends Narmon and Lissa and Peet."

"Yes. He's mentioned them. And how could 4 kidz get snatched from under your highly tuned nose?" Langer was utterly shocked by the stream of bad news coming at him. He started chewing the edge of his horrible beard again. Maddy ignored the rude comment.

"They can lift and secure people, smother people with photoniks, new breed sneaky weaponry."

"Sounds awful, horrible," said Langer. "So, no extortion? That's what criminals used to do in the old dayz. Demand money from the likes of your superRich family." My, he was qwick. No denying.

"We're expecting demands, but nothink yet. No contact from anyone with any demands. I'm sorry I have no outcomes yet. Just bad, bad news."

She felt she'd told him "sorry" too many times in the past, but it was the reason she wanted to seek his reactions. He'd been treated abominably by her parents and, in those days, in her mid 20's, still a kid, she hadn't the cred or presence to beat them back. They were a force of nature, her mother and father. And in a way, she had wanted Langer out of her life too. His attitudes never smoothed with her ambitions. What eventually happened between them had been hideous tho'.

And she'd wondered whether Todd's disappearance, at an outside chance, may have been revenge served cold by Langer, but no, she'd been straight with her ex and his responses didn't warrant that suspicion. He was at once angry with her, shocked about the crime, and in a way, consoling.

*

She'd known Todd had got in touch with his dad.

She knew how many scopes he and Langer'd done, their textStream on SupaSekret, which wasn't that secret. Contact was desultory but established, but she didn't have any copies of the live scopes so was keen to know if Todd had imparted any worries.

She picked up her wine glass and took a sip of the dry red. Langer looked at her incredulously.

"You drinking wine? When did you stop being Dr Madrigal 'Purity' Phipps?"

"I grew up, Langer. Member of the Courier Corps. You have to do dinners. A lot of dinners."

"Our marriage would have been a lot more fun if you'd drank wine with me," he said, bitterly.

Again she ignored the jibe. Her late mentor, Simon Bluestone, taught her all she needed to know about drinking (and liking) wine.

"Look, Langer. I'll keep you updated on what's happening, always. I should have scoped earlier, but I've been organizing the investigation, as I'm sure you'll understand. Also … if anyone gets in touch with you about ransom arrangements, get straight to me." She knew he had her deets. They shared a child after all, even if she'd got the lion's share of their boy, and even if he'd never scoped her.

"Be sure I will. I don't care for you and I certainly don't care for your family, but Todd is my son too."

She signed off after the stinging assessment from her ex. While she was pleased to see he was still alive, and sort of pleased he'd been honest about Todd's contact, she didn't care one jot about his rude little snarks.

What was important to Madrigal was that during the entire conversation, there was no sign he'd known or been involved with the abduction. Madrigal was ready to rule out Langer from any conspiracy theory, but she left the door of suspicion slightly ajar. Langer had been a pain, but now he might be an ally, tho disappeared to the other side of the planet with his stuffy old world conscience.

*

She sat in the dark in her office.

Was time to organize. Organize Centrl. Organize their conjunct with the other parents. Pearl and Rox organized a connekt with Centrl: secureVidVision with who knows how many scramble hurdles between Tassy and Greater Perth. The secureVid was received at Madrigal's big desk in the house. Down in Tassy, at the Spokes – the HQ of Centrl – Commander Daniels looked xtremely exercised. He was the C-ops, or Chief of Operations, and had been a few years ahead of Madrigal and Pearl in training school.

Lightbenders and lifters and other such tek were essentially banned in AuZ, and in the Territory of Capricornia, their use limited to AuZgov officials only. More prevalent, however, were the less lethal, also illegal, shimmers, which occluded adjacent photons and could hide individuals and groups in plain sight.

Shimmers were smaller and therefore were an easily smuggled item, and occasionally crims used them. Centrl was alert to this new threat and was sending Slotters – officially known as protective security operatives – and investigators across to Perth. In Canberra, the Minister for Social Security had been briefed on the strange events in Perth and the use of prohibited negTek, and she'd ordered a deepCore inquiry.

Commander Daniels, feeling pressure from his boss, grilled Pearl and Madrigal about the crime scene issues. Unlike the local milisi, he didn't once qwestion Madrigal's account or ever scorn her deductions. She was one of them.

"Damn," said Daniels. "The Singular Enemy gets worse, creating havoc for whole populations, and we have to deal with these pissant criminal *details*." He'd hissed the last word in a mild apoplexy. Daniels was 100% unsympathetic to crime and criminals, but knew a job had to be done.

His main brief, the Singular Enemy, was the volatile climate. Everyone knew that. All AuZgov, in fact all national and international focus and funds, were aimed at repairing and maintaining infrastructure, feeding displaced citizens, and mitigating damage such as acidic oceans and saline soils. And qwashing, as gently as possible, the antisocial reflux caused by the hunger, misery and poverty the weather brought. The cost of those elements alone sucked the budget right out of everything else.

Why citizens kept breaking the law, indulging in violence, and getting steeped in criminal behaviours, was beyond many administrators' imaginations, and to Madrigal, Daniels was one of those antiCrime purists.

"I can't believe people are so selfish when faced with such a serious collective threat as *the Singular Enemy*," he complained thru gritted teeth.

"I'm determined to find a reason for this outrage," Madrigal replied.

Like all administrators, Daniels liked the application of reason, and nodded, calming down.

They had a long scope about trailing and surveilling possible contact points for ransoms. Then they scoped off, satisfied they had a plan.

After the screen went opaque, Madrigal said: "He's no Fingal Wen, that one," to Pearl, who rolled her eyes in agreement. "Commander Wen knew the dispiriting darkness in the hearts of bad people. This C-ops just thinks citizens should comply …"

"Commander Wen was old. He was there at the beginning," Pearl reminded Madrigal. "Before the Singular Enemy became so … singular."

*

Over the next few days the Indian Ocean tri-pole, a triangulation of hotSpots, arced up a small Cat 4 extraTropical 'phoon. The storm pulled itself out of the Southern Ocean like a kraken, and Greater Perth was blasted with hard wind and vast sheets of rain coming in from the northwest, clipping the southern coastline. Not a sufficient level of heat to generate thermocells and tubes, but hard, slappy weather all the same. People stayed indoors and used the city's underground metros and foot tunnels to get around. As usual, vast areas of the southeast of the State missed out on the rain, and the desertification of great swathes of WestOz kept clumping further to the east. Madrigal simply ignored the weather.

In the Club Karribee green room, investigators from Centrl found a few more clothing threads, but no skin flakes worth testing for ID at DyNAst, and they decided against a dangerous limbic probe into Jaim'z memories, a procedure Madrigal had strongly objected to. A trace of memory images would never work because the perpetrators were masked, he'd been knocked unko so qwickly, and it was an entirely invasive procedure with possible long term side effects to the brain.

Exterior vidz in publik places caught glimpses of what they were calling the "snatch crew", but there was a lot of shimmer at work, shrouding the actors. A vid in the back alley picked up nothink, tho lots went down there: the attack, the carting of the zippedOut kidz into whatever van or busV, and the removal of the power pak on the roof.

Afterward, HighEyes had also found scratchy vid traces of an unauthorized aircraft flight from a paddock at the edge of the city boundary, heading oceanward, but screening out qwickly with some sort of powerful shimmer device after take-off.

The craft – and it sure looked like a hopper – could have gone anywhere. They knew the oceanward course was probably a deception on the kidnappers' part, because flying a hopper over the ocean was dangerous, so the kidnappers would tack back over the mainland further north. However, there'd been no discernible traces. And of course any electronik wash had long since dissipated

Milisi inqwiries at habitations near the paddock had revealed little. While HighEyes recorded a landV in the vicinity around the time of the incident, there was no landV dumped. At least one of the abductors could still be in greater Perth.

*

A nervy meeting with the parents of Lissa, Peet and Narmon commenced. Their faces were saturated with worry as they sat in Madrigal's lounge around an ancient silky oak table that had been hauled thru 2 centuries of Phipps family homes til resting in the room, in glistening speckled gold.

The parents sat mute as an aide provided cups of tea or kopi. A scope from Broome allowed Jaim'z mum, dad and aunties to join in, to understand what happened to their boy.

While Jaim'z mum had a daughter, and Peet's parents had another son, Lissa, Narmon and Todd were all Oncers.

The parents who had sat up the back of the Club Karribee were also physically present here with their partners. Jasp was there holding his wife Noni's hand tightly. Minnie-Tuton, Lissa's mother, still looked neat and shiny, but her eyes were wandery with grief. At one point Peet's mother, Jane, started to weep copiously, and Madrigal stopped proceedings. She felt the tears welling up also and fought the urge to break down.

Doing bizz helped. Madrigal took the 4 sets of parents thru the scenario that she and Pearl had tracked and assembled.

Pearl sat at Madrigal's side, producing large informational glows with evidence of the abduction, and explained traces, and theories of what happened. Madrigal's own executive office was staffed with new bodies who were sifting satellite imagery from HighEyes. Madrigal canvassed every possibility she could think of, explaining everything to the frightened faces in front of her. Her performance was compulsive and comprehensive, and proved to everyone that powers and authorities that they'd never been aware of before, were being mustered to find their kidz.

"Apart from the abduction of my son, there is no possible explanation why your children were taken as well," Madrigal finished. "It is high stakes for me too. I know some of you have no other children. And Todd, with no brothers or sisters, is my Oncer, my only ..." She took a breath while Jane qwietly cried in the background and Jasp looked distinctly shaken.

"My promise to you is I'll do everything to find them all. Safe and sound and alive. It's not just Todd that I care deeply about. Your own children were my constant and delightful young guests in this house. I care for them all."

The parents didn't doubt Madrigal's commitment. They'd visited before in happy times, but a menacing air now overshadowed the Phipps Mansion, and burly people with wicked weapons guarded the doors. For 1 or 2 of the parents, it felt less reassuring.

Nevertheless, Jasp, who was wriggling on his seat in anxiety, and Peet's mother, Jane, who had finally controlled her sobbing, started asking snarky questions like: "If these satellites can see things, why didn't they pick up a whole, giant aircraft?" and "Aren't there vidz on every street. Why didn't they catch vision out the back of the Club?"

Pearl had perfektly sensible answers, assuring the parents they'd checked, but the aircraft was cloaked and the vidz had been scrambled.

They accepted Pearl's authority in all things security, which was a little bit gratifying, but the one qwestion she couldn't answer, and was asked 3 times in a variety of ways, was why their children had been taken, when Jaim'z had been left behind? Madrigal did not want to horrify the parents by venturing the hypothesis, "Because they thought he was dead."

After a 3 hour meeting which was full of reassurance but offered little in hard fact, Madrigal and a mournful looking Szygy the kelpieDog saw the parents out.

THE CLAVICAL

The shin bones connected to the hip bone,
the hip bones connected to the spine bone,
the spine bones connected to the shoulder bone,
the shoulder bones connected to the brain bone,
the brain bones connected to the Virtual,
and bye-bye, reason, bye bye bye bye
    Brain Bone (2038) lyrics by the NYC neo-thrash band, The Stümmeratii

LISSA was an xtremely studious young woman and was aimed for a big future. Goal: a 5 gold Law major at university. Now that was almost forgot, absorbed into a greater fear for her life, her very existence in this strange, hot place in the middle of ... somewhere?

She looked out the window at the gorge and the clouds, as a small rainband sprayed the rock outside with little dark wet dots which evaporated immediately. That's how transient things were, she thought, how impermanent.

Given that she was scared, she wondered how even more panicked her mum would be since the abduction. Maximally panicked, she realized. Her mum wouldn't care a twig about Lissa's uni results now. Minnie-Tuton was awful high strung.

She was always so on edge about Lissa that her daughter's disappearance could KILL her.

With that thought Lissa went into a freak, balled up in the couch, crying not for herself, but for her mum.

*

That first morning, after being dropped on the crocodile beach in the gorge, and retrieved by the Stümmers, Lissa woke with sunrise, and found herself naked in a strange bed. She'd gasped. Sat up. She'd shoved her masses of hair into a drekky ponytail using a white cotton hairtie, thoughtfully provided by someone, and then dressed in the white clothes and rushed out into the communal courtyard. She challenged the first surprized person who crossed her path – an older woman carrying a basket of washing – and demanded to be taken home. Stümmers appeared everywhere. Leader of Women flew to her side and had hugged her (not appreciated by furious Lissa) and gestured for silence (she was screamingly angry) and ushered her (well, hustled her because she was making so much noise) thru to the lounge.

While the women's leader held her hand and soothed her, a string of qwiet people arrived with rice cakes, cool drinks and cold towels til she'd calmed. She kept demanding an explanation and the male leader brought a written pamphlet outlining the Hermitory rules and whispered, "Wait here and we will return with your friends to explain." The Stümmers had then bolted, unable to bear the noise she was making.

And there she sat alone for 2 hours, til a confused looking Narmon and a grim faced Todd entered. She'd immediately cheered at the sight of the smile on Narmon's face as he rushed to her and they hugged tight. The elders (at least that's what she assumed) who had brought her to the room started explaining in hushed tones. Her heart sank when Peet's hospitalization was mentioned and she blew a gasket at the announcement of their prolonged detainment.

*

Todd, who'd always been the mature one, had gestured her to calm and then spoke to the 2 robed authority figures:

"Let me be clear – we have been abducted by criminals, from our families. This is not some joke. This is a terrible crime. We have to return to our parents. They will be very, very worried. My mother is Dr Madrigal Phipps and she'll be hunting for us right now. I tell you, it's best for you to deliver us back to the authorities."

Lissa could see by the blank looks on the noName leaders' faces that neither had ever heard of Madrigal Phipps – the nameBomb meant nothink.

The woman was starting to look exhausted with her vocalizing but she smiled as best she could and hesitantly, haltingly said, "We don't know way to soCalled civilization. We don't recognize authorities. The Qwietude was founded over a century ago in place called Berlin in response to the hardPry of Governments and corporations. Pry, pry, pry. Our beliefs evolved from what was known, then, as the Deep Green movement. We believe to give nothink away.

"We have no names. Only our weak but useful existences among our friends, making no footprint, having no contaminant. Our shadows are pale on the Earth. AuZtralian believers, including my parents, established this Hermitory almost 100 years ago. I was born here 55 years ago. Most of the Qwietude you will meet were born in our Hermitory. My parents were founders. They taught me to speak but never to utter, and I have never ever left, but live in contentment. Once a year, after the weather settles, a transporter brings cloth, food, eqwipment, medikal supplies ... and also new seeds for our well being, our gardens, and then supplyMan leaves. This has been an arrangement thru generations. The supply vehicle is your only route out. We are very hidden and remote. And we don't know the way … " When her talking fizzled out, she looked exhausted.

"How do you think the hopper knew to drop us here?"

She shrugged.

"When did you say this supply vehicle is coming here?"

"After Cloud draws back north. Late March or early April."

Lissa pondered. It was almost August. Her mind slewed back to her mum, and her mum's dream of Lissa's high marks in the November exams. What a disaster this was.

"Breach and broach the Qwietude – truly, I can speak no longer," said the Leader of Women, dropping her head to her chest. She raised her head and made a movement – 2 fingers touching her lips.

The man said: "Thankyou, coLeader for your effort of speaking aloud and I apologize for asking you to break the silence." He turned to the abductees. "Our young people will teach you to sign. Would you like to visit your friend? We ask you not to speak outside the confines of this room."

Todd looked round at Lissa and Narmon.

"These people mean us no harm," Todd said qwietly. "Let's fly with the flux and work this thru."

"I speak no longer," said Leader of Men, also bowing his head, and touching his lips and he gestured them thru the door.

Lissa was still roiling inside – a mix of fear and and anger. She had been awake for much of the abduction trip and when she smelled gas on landing, she'd held her breath, so she hadn't ingested much. She'd come around when they were dropped on the beach of a gorge lagoon by the men in white coveralls. The friends were laid side by side and she'd had a vague freakOut and passed out again, and then dreamily surfaced when 2 young women were taking her clothes off to put her to bed, only to pass out again for a while. She eventually woke and went looking for answers.

Now, still stiff from being wrapped for hours, and feeling anxious, she reached her hand to Narmon's and held it. At least she'd found her boyz.

*

The Infirmary was a dimly lit area with beds and a room thru to an operating theatre. The facility appeared to have plenty of new gear and equipment.

Peet lay in a bed unko with a couple of fluid tendrils attached to shunts. His right shoulder and arm were heavily bandaged. The elders stood back in the shadows as Todd, Narmon and Lissa looked down at him.

"What ..." began Todd with the big qwestion. Leader of Men held up his hand for silence and pointed at a chart hanging on the bedEnd. A real, typed chart on paper. There was no name of doctor or nurse or whoever wrote the screed. Todd marveled at the strangeness of the place.

> *Loss of blood. Loss of fluids. Patient in danger.*
>
> *Patient presented with severe shoulder gash. Appears a component – a prosthetic right clavicle – was surgically removed. Metallic ties were still present. Wound was sealed badly and bloodloss at dangerous level. Infusion of 1 lt plasma.*
>
> *Skanned shoulders. Prepared replica clavicle with copier. Operated at 8.05am. Operation took 2.5 hours. Patient under general anesthetic – the risk from sedation he had previously been given would be contraindicative as history unknown, but not case.*
>
> *Replaced component with variable hexaPlastic replica and stemCell paste for heal qwick. 150 cc stem smear used.*
>
> *Understand such commercial medikal prosthetics have liveChips to identify user so purpose of removal in this inst. by unknown* **butchers** *was to prevent trace.*

Todd, Lissa and Narmon had read the chart together and Narmon whistled: "Butcher is not a word you usually find in a chart. They ripped the replacement bone out? Just like that? Who were these people who captured us?"

They remembered 2 years back when Peet smashed his shoulder playing footy. A guy had crashed so heavily on him in a failed attempt at a mark that his collarbone had been pulverized, ending his playing dayz. He'd spent a month in a plakjacket and they'd worried he'd never musik again.

The elders and mediks had winced at Narmon's outburst. The woman wrote on a small board which hung from her belt: *You let him rest now. We bring you back to your friend when he wakes.*

They were then escorted back to the meeting room with the view of the gorge. The Leader of Women wrote: *Please stay here while the Qwietude decides on our course of action.*

She rubbed out the screed with her sleeve and wrote: *If you must talk, whisper. After leaving this room you may speak no longer.* And she touched her pouted lips, looking them in the eye, one by one, to underline the message.

The meeting room couches were comfortable, and they were provided with cheese and tomato bread-stacks, and fruit, and left on their own.

Narmon cuddled up to Lissa with his arm around her, but she was bent forward whispering – almost hissing – at Todd.

"Mum'll die! She's not strong. I'm the strong one in the family. Can't think what she'll be doing right now ... and who'd kidnap me? And it f'cks up school, Todd. F'cked forever! I'll never get into Law!"

"No one kidnaps anyone anymore. You can't get away with it." Todd knew all about Centrl and the way administrative surveillance worked, after his mum's hairRaising bedtime stories.

"Well, someone has! Why did they take all of us? You're the one with the rich mum."

"I have no idea," said Todd, his mind whizzing, "but I reckon these people seem genuine. They are puzzled and confounded that we've appeared. We're dumped at a Stümmer Hermitory in the middle of nowhere and the Stümmers think there's nothink they can do, because they're bound by their beliefs. They'll look after us, but won't let us go for fear we'll die in the desert."

"They took my clamB and my Frisky," said Lissa.

"Nah, nah. Stümmers didn't – the kidnappers did. They also dug Peet's clavicle out so there'd be no tracing him. How did they know about that?"

"Probably skanned him. Skanned us all for pips," said Narmon.

"True that," said Todd.

"I thought hermits lived alone?" said Narmon.

"Mebbe they're a bunch of selfSustaining hermits who live together without talking, who knows, they're so weird," said Todd bitterly. "But, I reckon I could walk us out of here and find water and bush tucker. Mum's uncles have taught me survival in the desert, but we can't leave Peet."

"Could you really find water?" asked Narmon. "You don't know which country this is."

"I'm sure I could," said Todd, feeling very confident.

"You don't have a gun for roos or anything," said Narmon, slightly annoyed at Todd's selfBelief.

"I've made spears before at culture classes ... anyway, that's for later. Somehow, we have to be able to communicate together without them eavesdropping," said Todd, adopting full command mode.

"We can just whisper away in our bed cells," said Narmon. "Won't be a problem."

*

Narmon was wrong.

They started learning sign language immediately, with insistent young people showing them the basic longhand gestures.

"A very neat set of hand and finger moves," Narmon whispered later in a private chat by Peet's bedside.

"Yeah. Y'd be stuffed if you were blind," Todd added.

"And the rooms here – pretty gloomy lot of the time," said Lissa. "Y'gotta concentrate hard on all those flicky fingers."

Peet was having some difficulty as the shoulder repair impeded arm movement, but he was desperate to talk to young Stümmers who would visit the medik centre. Qwiz them. Find out things 'bout their new situation.

Along with "conversationals" the 4 were furnished with ancient books! With wordz and diagrams. HandSign flashcards even. They were taught and escorted by young Stümmers constantly wanting their company.

The newcomers provided fresh insights to the "outside". Leader of Women was right to be concerned. Young Stümmers had an appetite for news of the world and couldn't wait to train the fresh blood into their language. Boy Stümmers cosied up to Lissa, girl Stümmers flirted with Narmon and Todd, and while Peet recovered in the infirmary, he was well looked after, always with someone to sign and joke with.

Little Freckle, who had bonded with Lissa's red hair, was her shadow.

To counter their young people's curiosity and thirst for new knowledge, the Leaders group (or Elders of the Qwietude as they were known) added older chaperones to the group, til there were people of all ages constantly around Lissa, Narmon and Todd. Todd found the presence of chaperones rather ironic, given the Stümmer revulsion of administrative surveillance.

Todd mathed out that the colony was about 450 strong, around 25 to 30 extended and interlinked families of at least 3 generations. The buildings stretched thru the first part of a long gorge that snaked several kliks thru the desert. He was amazed that no Stümmer knew the precise geographical location of the gorge within the Central Desert. For research purposes he'd very qwickly learned to sign "Where is this gorge in relation to the ocean?", for example.

No one knew. He was convinced they were genuinely ignorant.

*

Lissa was assigned to the Hermitory library. The Qwietude determined that she was so fair skinned, constant work in the gardens would harm her, even caked in sunJell. The clear jell protected outdoor workers from burn and reflected direct sunHeat, cooling the skin by 3 or 4 degrees, but the Leader of Women worried the jell would not be enough to protect Lissa. And anyway, with her hollering 'bout missing exams, Lissa was clearly a studious one.

Leader of Books was worried about the intrusion of this young outsider into his calm rooms, but did his best to welcome her. He was a stooped figure in a white tunic and beige sarong and his wrinkly hands signed slowly, so she'd understand: *Feel yourself familiar with the books so when people come, you can locate.*

She didn't understand the signed verb, so he wrote "familiarize" and showed how to sign the word. They laughed together, and his apprehension began to melt. He sensed a great unease, tho, in the girl. She'd looked up at the yellow hanging lights that lumened the big room, which was built into a cave, insulated with rubber and sealant so the rocks didn't introduce moisture during the wet season, and then along the shelves of books.

Don't use books at home, but like them, she signed to him.

He watched Lissa expertly browsing at the stacks to find books to augment her school studies, but she'd looked more and more disappointed. She stopped in front of the collection of Ulli Kalk's sacred books, and then moved on. He watched her run her fingers down the book spines, sighing with exasperation, so he signed: *What are you looking for?*

Leader of Books knew she'd be troubled and disoriented. Possibly angry. Clearly unaware of the ways of the Stümmers. She didn't know the sign for what she was looking for, so wrote down: *Law books. I am studying law.*

Ahh! signed Leader of Books. He showed her the books relating to the Qwietude's Laws (Ulli Kalk's sacred books again). Then led her to the 3 big microfiche cabinets at the back wall.

When we moved here 100 years ago, we brought books as well as film records of books, so that the Hermitory would be aware of all that was good, and all that was bad.

She nodded. She understood! The Leader of Books' apprehension was disappearing by the moment and his view was changing. However troubled this young mite was, he hoped she'd stay. She'd learn and discuss with him the current thinkings of the outside world (breach and broach the Qwietude) without disrupting his hard won golden calm.

He watched her face as she riffled thru the card indexes to find microfiche spools. Her eyes lit up and she pulled a couple of fiche from the cabinet and he showed her how to set them in place and read the texts. What fierce energy he thought.

Was the world changed? he thought. Was it same old? Human urges and responses. Leader of Books had read everything in his library and was old enough to understand that he knew very little – specially 'bout the modern world beyond the gorge. He was curious.

A while later he looked up and saw her perched at the microfiche screen, but seeing nothink. She was crying, tears wetting her face. As soon as he stood and went over she wiped them from her cheeks, looking up with a mix of pain and defiance.

What is the matter?

These are very old files ... She looked sad. Then she signed, *And anyway, I'm scared, I don't know why I'm here. Or even if you – the Qwietude – will hurt or kill us?*

Leader of Books shook his head in horror. He had bushy grey eyebrows and green eyes. An old face, covered in smiley wrinkles.

No, no, child, we are a most peaceful community. We respect and follow our principles of privacy, the principles of peace and the principles of love. These are our tenets (she didn't understand tenets so he wrote the word down, showed her the sign).

She signed: *Fact is, people have hurt us ... hurt Peet most terribly and don't know why.*

Hurt is not our way, signed the Old Man. *Love is our way. Love is our only way. Can I make some tea? Let's have tea.* And he pointed to a hot plate and kettle.

Lissa sniffed and nodded at his kindness.

*

Narmon was most interested in how so many were sustained, and once Peet was on his feet, the 2 of them walked along the colony gorge (with a crowd of young Stümmers guiding their every step and pointing out highlights).

Gorge farms contained greenery – rice and vegetables. Went for several kliks, but the Stümmers seemed to inhabit the first half, from the entrance back. They'd built terraces along the inside topography and used natural bluffs and rocky shoulders for housing. The gorge faced north-south most of the time, so the searing sun hit the crops for a short while every day around noon. There were structures for goats, chickens and rabbits, too, altho' such structures came and went with the seasons, and basic pest repellant activities to keep kangaroos, corellas and other cockatoos out of the gardens. Many of the smaller kidz were parked in the gardens to chase birds in the dry periods.

For somethink to do and to amuse the kidz following them, Peet started to yodel at the bottom of the gorge, scaring a flock of about 200 noisy corellas and creating a massive yodelly, sqwawky echo, up and down the rock faces. Instead of laughing, and joining in, the accompanying young Stümmers were appalled, and on return, Peet was met at the entrance to the Hermitory by Leader of Men and chastised for calling out.

Untoward noise – please, no. Draws attention. Never do that again, signed the agitated Leader of Men.

Narmon was dumbstruck. *Attention from who? Out here in the middle of the desert?*

Leader of Men just glared at his temerity.

At dinner that evening they asked the Hermitory kidz what happened when the Cloud moved south, and the stormz came. Stümmer kidz were desperately trying to connekt so there was a crowd along the refectory table. Curl was one, Little Weaver another, and there was a boy whose personal sign was Half-Moon, a sign of when he was born.

Curl, an assistant nurse and who'd befriended Peet when caring for him in the infirmary, took charge with communications. She sat between Peet and Lissa at the refectory table and signed with graceful fingers.

The Wet is very different, said Curl slowly, so they could follow her hands. *Most dangerous time.*

By sign language and note writing, she indicated the Cloud – the turbulent, chaotic monsoon – arrived close by the 11th moon phase and sent 'phoons thru the northern desert so their terraces were flushed, the water table replenished and the Stümmers would rebuild and replant.

The gorge is fantastic protection from the angry wind and tubes. She waited until the newcomers nodded in understanding and went on: *Our living qwarters are above the watercourse. Gorge floor becomes river, and water exits into the desert.*

Peet tried to sign: *Are gardens washed away?*

Curl responded with clear signs: *Yes. We replant.*

Narmon was impressed.

Still, it seemed to him the Stümmers didn't grow enough to trade for goods especially when growing season was cut short every year. And yet. Once a year a supply vehicle arrived. This puzzled him.

Where was it from? How did they pay for the supplies? How did the supplier know what to bring? For example, who supplied all the high-end medikal gear they saw in the infirmary? There must be komms, somewhere, he thought, to order the best stuff.

*

Lissa lived in the girlz dorm corridor, separate from the 3 boyz, so it was only very occasionally that the 4 managed to get together for a qwiet discussion in a bunkroom without a klatsch of admirers. They were in such a huddle one nite when Narmon brought up his conclusions.

Somewhere, someone had a komms device.

"Has to be, to order supplies!"

"We could ask around," said Peet. "Suss out this magical scope, wherever it's stashed."

Todd nodded. "One of the Qwietude will own it. They've all the responsibility."

The 4 agreed to ask their new friends how they ordered supplies.

HIATUS ONE

For Government, bricks, mortar and rooftiles are of no consequence. For 24 hours per day you are exposed to their electronik stare. This visibility may lead to nothing, but do you want your lovemaking exposed? Your arguments? Your pain? Your private sweetnesses with your children? Your slurping table manners, and everything else? If you want to fight back, at least dispose of your eavesdropping elektronics. That's step 1. Then your lives in the glasshouse become more opaque. Use cash accessed from bank vaults, wear hooded clothes and prosthetics that fool the CCTV, talk sotto, and your glass house is now accreting. The Man's eyes grow cataracts.

The pry is relentless but if you don't share data, he is blinded.

Das Glas Haus (2034) Ulli Kalk

MADRIGAL Phipps leant over the apartment roofline and looked down to the nite city, and the darker vegetated shoulder of Kings Park out to her right. She could smell the ocean below.

Been 11 years since I left the Service, Madrigal thought. *Before that, the work with old Simon Bluestone. Grieve the loss.*

And I'm a wreck, I'm just fit and no more, and here I am taking on a full-blown hunt for Toddy.

She plunged into a cold pool of despair. Didn't happen very often and it felt odd as well as sad.

What would her unforgivable Dad do?

Clear now, he'd appointed her his apprentice, even when she was a 10 year old kid. He'd been ancient – in his eighties by then – a slightly grizzled survivor, but bouncing with life thanx to juveJuice, and his will to build and maintain the family Heg. His Heg. Didn't matter if she was drawing pictures, on her clamB, of lizards and other dreaming creatures, she was in the inner sanctum of Phipps Industries to watch his ways, via osmosis. When she wasn't at school, she was in his office playing on her pad. In the background he'd be talking cajoling, pushing staff and clients about, and she was absorbing like a tiny sponge.

Her dad was a powerhouse, building and running a real Powerhouse. Once had a zine article calling him the Sun King of the West, because he'd developed so much solar and other sourced and dispersed power in the mid 21st century. And he'd spread the largesse with an almost feudal hand to Indijj communities everywhere, who'd cheerfully partnered with him, and allowed endless use of their country – a powerhouse rescuing AuZtralia and the lands beyond.

So, if I'd been abducted, what would the Old Man have done, she thought?

Well, he was a network builder so he'd have looked for links. True that. But more – he'd have torn the world apart to find her. And the people who had abducted her would have been destroyed because of the challenge to his authority. That's what it was – a challenge to Phipps authority.

She knew that was what she had to do.

If you're going to be ruthless, you often have to prove it yourself. But where to start?

"Kiddo," he'd sometimes say when pausing between arguments on the scope, "2 best advices my mum gave me was, *know what you want*, which sounds simple, but it's not. The other one is, *whether it's a fear or a foe, know what motivates, what really motivates, them and use that knowing to run them down*. Mum was brutal, I know, and sometimes you can achieve without seeming brutal. But underneath ... *you gotta be brutal*."

His face would shine with the challenge, the fight. Then he'd get his Secretary Prime, Lomandra, to dial the next client or staff member, to start yet another roaring argument. Oh, he was fierce, her Old Man.

So, using her dad's advices, what did she want?

Todd.

What motivated her foe?

Unknown.

What did she fear?

Her own weakness in achieving Todd's return. Physical and mental. Emotional panic blanketing clear thinking. She feared being weak more than she feared the abductors. That's why she was so despairing.

The other nite, she'd almost (figuratively) died with the effort of rappeling up the rope to the Club Karribee roof, and knew Pearl had done almost all the heavy lifting. She'd tried to look graceful, but knew she'd landed with a thud. Her abseil down was more elegant, but when gravity goes your way, it's a lot easier to pull off.

You still have it in you, girl! she'd thought in the gloom'd alley by Club Karribee, *but it's not enough.*

Now she was in her 40s. Everything was harder. And she was attuned to another life. The hunting senses she'd used in the intelligence work of the past – sight, smell, hearing, patterning – had dulled with the corporate life, the travel, spicy dinners with dignitaries, and the cooling drumbeat of alcohol.

Madrigal reached for her hip and pinched the flesh above the pelvic bone and said: "Blubberworm."

Yes, she ran every second day, and took to the pool, but for the task she was about to embark on, this wasn't enough. Pearl was going to toughen her physikality and it would probably be excruciating.

"I'm going to run them down," she said to herself, pushing her red wine aside, heading for the gym.

BELLINGSLODES

Judge Engramms: Frau Kalk, do you understand that your destructive sabotage of several data hubs in the suburbs of Mitte, Kreutzberg and Wilmesdorf seriously dislocated the ability of many, many thousands of your neighbours to live their lives?
Kalk: (no response)
Judge Engramms: This is more than just destruction of public property, isn't it?
Kalk: (no response)
Judge Engramms: Your writings reflect a complete disregard for society, its communication streams, its technology and the need for persons to engage with one another leading to happy social cohesion. Am I right?
Kalk: (no response)
Judge Engramms: This is exasperating, Frau Kalk. Will you please answer the questions of the court ...

Supreme Court Transcript proceedings, Trial of Ulli and Klaus Kalk, September 18 2029

BEN Jexen was CEO of Phipps Energy, the most profitable and most powerful division of the mothership that was the Phipps corporate Heg. Jexen himself was a canny operator, and had chiefed the strategic research and networks division for almost 20 years. He was 78 and didn't look a day over 30 due to at least the 2 rejuves which he happily admitted to. He was lithe and wiry, hair still dark and shortcut as befitted a chief. His nose was sharp, like his brain, and he wore speks to make him look distinguished, tho he didn't really have to. The Phipps Industries Mantle, Madrigal Phipps, trusted Ben Jexen implicitly, and he returned the trust, which he'd previously given to her father, the company founder, way back when.

Wife one had left him (early on), his second had died tragically while rockclimbing on Mt Erebus in Antartica with him and a bunch of friends, 9 years back. His current wife was 30 years younger, as old as 54, with only one rejuve under her belt, so she didn't notice his age, or hers.

Cinzia was in a silk nite gown, propped up on her substantial pillow and they discussed news and secure company komms and reports with status graphs. He kept nothink from her, even the secure komms from their various overseas HQs.

Jexen sat in his yellow silk yukata jacket and grunted and went "ooh" a couple of times.

"Still no intel on Todd Phipps and his friends," (he received all security reports), "and a weird and wacky reqwest from the Japan/Taiwan office for reroutes of regular Bellingslodes thru their Hubs. No reason given. Big numbers too! Why would they ask for extra Bellingslodes from us? China'd be closer?" he asked Cinzia. She turned to him with a frown.

As Cinzia was a highly qwalified research enjjineer, one of the company's top enjjTeks, she knew about Bellingslodes, the large scale regular pulses of converted highMass photon energy sent up optical cables into repositories, or soakers. From the soakers, the charged light was then converted back to stable, usable photonik electricity at the other end.

"They buy plenty from us already don't they, the Japan-Taiwan nexus?" she asked, crunching her toast and causing a crumb'a'lanche.

"Yizz, they do. On old fixedRate contracts set for another decade or so. And I happen to know, they hate the deal. So why ask us for more? I'll qwery our HQ there as to a reason for the reqwest? How about that? Won't bug Madrigal with it til we have further deets. She has far too much on her mind."

"I scoped her yest'day," Cinzia said sadly, "just to tell her we were thinking of her. She was qwite chatty."

"She's waiting for any news. Got all the milisi and AuZgov people she knows on the boil for clues, intel, anything. It's been 3 weeks now."

"Jeez, that's a long time without intel. Considering all that AuZgov can do."

*

Ben pondered his Mantle's plight and how much her missing boy was distracting her while he commuted in a chauffeur driven landV, to Phipps Tower, from where the powerful company exerted itself across AuZtralasia, Capricornia and half of Asia. Poor folk used autonomousVs but Jexen enjoyed flaunting his status.

He thought emphatically that energy was everything, and in the age of climate flux, those Hegs and companies that produced Bellingslodes of power for the many States and Govs of the greater regions were in the ultimate box seat. Begging reqwests were normal. This one from the Jap/Tais was odd.

Using the leverage of energy profits, Phipps Industries had become a diversified business. Employed 28,000 people direct, not mentioning the coProjects – not all of them in energy – with many others including AuZgov, WestAus, and the huge Territory of Capricornia.

At the office towers he kept working on annoying little "please explains" from Madrigal Phipps or other members of the Board. His Secretary Prime, Hal, sometimes sat for 30 minutes at a time in diligent silence in the big airy office while Jexen went thru a document and yayed or nayed it.

Hal was a patient man. Sometimes Jexen would ask Hal's (valued) opinion, sometimes the CEO would humph and grunt and snap "Denied" and that was that. Snapping "Denied" like a qwerulous old man, even tho' he looked like a 30 year old pro surfer with a shock of black hair and the skin of a boy.

Near lunch Jexen asked if there had been any response from the Japan/Taiwan office regarding the reqwest for an increase in the rate of Bellingslode pulses. When Hal said "No reply yet," he scoped a couple of East Asian analysts to see if they could conjure an explanation. Hyped manufacturing output? Climate refugee influx from somewhere? Any other sorts of things that would draw down more power? They had no comparable data or intel to explain the reqwest.

"Give it till close of business and I'll scope Phu Tang at their office," he said. "While we're at it, check the costs for those pulses and what networks we can use to feed them."

After a qwick sushi roll, Hal reappeared from his antechamber. He reported that the Jap/Tai office still hadn't responded, so Jexen asked for a scope to be organized. To Jexen's surprize Old Man Phipps appeared on the screen.

"Hi, Ben," said Phipps, looking a bit sheepish. He actually looked old. He'd have to be in his mid 100s, Jexen supposed. Grey hair was long, high cheekbones in a rather shrunkedUp face. Bit of a beard. But the Old Man's eyes were gleaming like they always gleamed. With fervor.

"Mr Phipps. A surprize!"

"A pleasure," said the Old Man. "I'm pretty much retired, Ben. Leave the bizz up to Maddy and your good self and the others. But just came into the office today ... how's that good looking wife of yours?"

Jexen could still taste Cinzia's kiss on his lips, but remained calm and focussed. Old Man Phipps was oldStyle, always commenting on women's looks, and he could be a bit coarse in male company. He remembered the Old Man's rep as a rather goatish woman chaser too. But you didn't want to mess with the founder of the fortune – and your original mentor – by rolling your eyes.

"She's still beautiful," he said.

"I recall she has very black pupils," said Old Man Phipps, relishing the memory. "Wonderful wedding. Wonderful wedding you had. Last time I went to Perth it were, to attend your wedding." The 2 men had worked very closely together for 25 years, planning, building and routing power supply networks, and new methods of storage and delivery.

But 7 years back, Jexen'd been shocked. After a long absence he remembered the rather emaciated old man arriving at the the Jexen wedding ceremony in the great hall in the university, walking stiffly beside his estranged wife, Netta, and Madrigal, who was cool and composed, but unable to look at her father. An awful snapshot of an unhappy family group. Madrigal was 3 years in as Mantle of the Company.

Common knowledge in the Heg elite was she'd been forced to take the job, against her wishes. Shortly after, Old Man Phipps had announced that he was to live in Japan permanently – an impossible ask for Netta in terms of living with him, as she was determined to remain close to her daughter and grandson. Hence Netta's misery, and his brittle body language. Ben's wedding to Cinzia had been wonderful, but Old Man Phipp's domestic situation had not been that cheersome, with 2 clearly angry women by his side.

*

On the scope, the Old Man wasn't looking too crash hot at all. He'd reached the limit of rejuves his body could carry. Old Man Phipps had invested a lot of money over the years with other rich people, all searching for the scientific holy grail which became known as the Noah – the 1000 year life. But cellular structures and mitochondria being what they were, the science could get folk to 120-130, but after about 110, youthful good looks were almost impossible.

"Do you still chair the Noah Foundation, boss?" asked Jexen.

"No longer. The various theories fizzled out after the research was done ... as you can see," said Phipps, "not in perfekt working order now. Starting to get tatty round the edges."

"Well, least you're not carrying a leadWeight of responsibility."

"Feels so. Feels so. But then there's an occasional abberation, Jexen." There was a pause. Phipps continued sheepishly: "So the Jap/Tais are hassling me for further Bellingslodes. I'm sorry to ask this. I mentioned it to Mr Phu, and he put the reqwest thru and you rightly have asked why, which is what I would have done ... so that's why I'm in Osaka, in the office ..."

"Why ask us, Mr Phipps? And why thru you?" Jexen found it extraordinary.

"Ahh, well, I cut the original deal in the first place. And ... they want the feed of Bellingslode pulses tacked onto the current agreement but at a nominal rate. Say third of the price. It's 3 pulses a week, in addition. As I say, I'm just the messenger here, but it's somethink we can enjjineer, I'm sure." Old Man Phipps looked a bit distracted. A bit sidewayz.

"I'd normally take it up with Maddy except she's not inclined to talk about bizz buzz with me, and you're the network man anyway."

Three pulses a week was a lot of energy.

"I'll have to talk to Madrigal," Jexen said. "That's a lot of power for a 66% discount and I'm pretty sure the answer'll be no." His hackles were rising tho' he didn't show it. The languorous lull lunch was forgotten.

"Look, they say it's important. It's part of a Japanese harmony and cohesion measure. You understand?"

"A good feed is a good feed, as we used to say."

"I remember that, Ben. Energy feeds enable life. *Whether a burger or a Bellingslode!*"

"I'll look into what reservoirs we may have. But, umm, we'll have to talk to the buyer, with respect. Not you."

"Understood," said the Old Man scratching his head.

"Where are you living these dayz anyway?" added Jexen.

"Here in Japan. Kyoto. Made it my home. Remarried when Netta died. Married Nozomi. Lovely girl."

"Congratulations," Jexen said, but he could see, even in the scope that Old Man Phipps was vagueing out. Still looking to one side. Shaking his head at someone off camera.

"I must go. Scope me when you've sorted out the details," said the Old Man. And the screen went suddenly blank.

That was very weird, thought Ben Jexen.

HUDDLE

Judge Engramms: Are you stupid, Frau Kalk? Do you understand what I'm saying? Talk to me!

Supreme Court Transcript proceedings, Sentencing of Ulli Kalk, September 20, 2029

THE Philosophikal (minus their percussionist, Jaim'z) were again crowded together in Todds's monastic cell in the Hermitory's single men's block. The 4 were talkative. They were enjoying the liberty of their voices over the confusing, hand flickery gesture language of the Stümmers.

"Huddle" was the codeword they used for a secret talking session. Took some maneuvering to escape the self appointed entourage of Stümmer kidz, but couple times a week they'd prearrange, then turn up, one by one, after pretending to go to bed and waiting for lights out.

Lissa lay on one end of the bed with her head on Narmon's lap, her legs stretched up the wall. The spare bed space was taken up by Narmon and Peet, Peet's arm still swaddled in a sling and strapped against his chest.

Todd was pacing the floor … one and half paces to get back and forward, then leaned on the door, finally. "Haven't found any real tek," he said. "They just use books, write on paper."

"Keep their eWash to a minimum, that's for sure," Narmon said.

"Where does the fuel come from? For their snippers and diggers tho?" Todd queried. "It's a full on mechanized farm down the gorge. That's what gets me, NarMan, they got gear. No one can tell me how they communicate out. None of the young kidz anyhows."

"What narx me is all the religiousy bizzo," Peet added. "Religious! They meet every day for weirdAss homilies and meditations."

"You mean the 'you are alone in a crowd' thing?" Lissa said to the ceiling. "Y'couldn't call that religion. No higher powers. There's no 'God loves you' bizz, or chicken sacrifices or anything."

"Y'know how they meet in the refectory way before brex? With one or other of the Leaders on the stage, handSigning a little homily about Ulli Kalk, the mother founder. And everyone's heads bowed? And the *50 deep breaths of greater silence* … looks churchLike … worshipping somethink," Todd argued.

"Nahhh," said Peet who'd learnt the handSigns fast and had been communicating with girlz in a hilarious, one handed fashion. "Their god is silence. Not some spookyWooky presence in heaven watching down on you to make sure you're the pure. They don't like the surveillance chops of religion and the god's watching youze: all that *you'd better be good or you'll burn* shit. Surveillance is banned from both temporal and spiritual with these doops. As long as y'don't speak, y'can do whatsoever. Curl and Little Weaver told me about it while I was recuperating … they all believe in hiding from the world and I reckons these meetings are just to reinforce their muteyTooty behaviour. But after those obligations, life goes on."

SpookyWooky, MuteyTooty ... pure Peet, thought Narmon.

"True that," Narmon added. "Function of real religion is social control ... least that's what I once wrote in a school assignment. Only rule here is 'Don't speak'. No noise."

"I suppose we'd better go. To the meditation, I mean," Todd said. "Keep them agreeable."

"Why?"

"Should try'n look like we're conforming. Don't want them thinking we are planning to escape, for one thing."

"So we're leaving?" Lissa said, sarcastically. "When are we leaving, Mr Tracker?"

She was desperate to leave. Todd smiled as he looked down on her mass of red hair and oval face.

"When I can work out where we are," Todd answered. "It's driving me mad, this. I should just know these things, drummed in by the Elders."

"It's just that ..." Lissa began. "I'm starting to miss Mum lotz. Lotz and lotz. She'll be catatonik ... about me gone. She probably thinks the worst. Thinks I'm dead. I know my mum." Lissa looked really pained now. Narmon sqweezed her shoulder, trying to comfort.

"Yizz," said Todd, conceding a little of his reserve. "I miss my mum too."

"Well, while we're all missing our mums," said Peet dryly, "let's help Toddy get a fix on where we are – work thru what we know. Then we can move."

Todd was grateful how focused Peet could be, how his friend brought everyone back to the problem. Was good!

"Thing is, when the Cloud moves south, we're stuck," Todd said. "Conditions outside the gorge'll be lethal. If you don't drown in a gusher, y'll be picked up by a tube and pulped against a rock. These big rampart walls round us are serious tube busters, and protect everyone and everything inside the gorge. So far north here – without those walls, the community would be smashed to bitz. That's what conditions'll be like by the end of Nov, or Dec.

"The peeps in my Country literally have to evacuate during the summer Cloud event, and rebuild their housing and roads afterwardz," he added bluntly. "We have to work fast. If I can't locate where we're at, we're stuck at this Hermitory till March."

OUT OF THE MIST

They flense by microlayers,
Flense and flense again
Until you run raw blood, transparent skin,
And the gaudy isotopes of every corp and heg
Blue thru your secrets ...
  Klaus Kalk's poem, *A Hermitory*
  circa 2032

"YOU can't imagine, Jex, what a prob my father can be," Madrigal was saying.

Ben Jexen was seated across from his boss, watching her in the charcoal tinted lowLite, attentively listening. The lowLite made Maddy glow like some crepuscular ghost, her eyes white lit.

"He's one of those stubborn old coots who for years wielded immense power in a most Machiavellian way, usually for the good, and good for blackfellas I might add, but dodgy all the same. You worked with him. Y'd have to agree he was a leader in the mid'n'late century transitions in this country."

"He was THE leader," said Ben Jexen simply.

"But when he got too old, he lost complete interest. Like one day, his balloon just deflated, with a sad ole hiss," Madrigal said.

"Yes, I know, Dr Phipps. I worked alongside all those years. I knew his MO."

They sat in isolation, at a small table in the pentLounge of the upmarket bar, Ommm, top of Perth's Hiyaxx Grand. The air was redolent of distant Tibetan chanting and a sweet subtle incense. The gloomy light was the eqwivalent of a whisper. Companion drinkers and revellers sat in comfortable chairs, and could see one another reasonably clearly, but the design of screening arrangements made the room incredibly private for those who could afford the price of drinks. The price was of no conseqwence to Ben Jexen and Madrigal Phipps but the price of a couple of Filthy Martiniques, or a Neon Knockout would have knocked a young family of strugglers sideways for a month. Strugglers and jugglers who only used old currency anyway.

"Another cocktail?" Madrigal said, waving to a waiter. Langer's jibe about noFun Madrigal had stung her. And with Toddy and the other kidz still untraceable, she was in a melt.

Jexen was amused at Madrigal's offer of a second cocktail, but still agreed to it. He was slightly cut after his first Filthy Martiniqwe.

"Aren't you on a fitness regime?" he asked.

"I'm giving myself a break from it tonite," she said. "I'm allowed. So Jex, what's my dad up to?"

"I checked with my enjjineer contacts in a couple of other Hegs. And it's true. The Jap/Tais are running short of energy in the Honshu/Osaka connurbation, and also around Tokyo and to the north, and need some boosts. A strange sitch because they've still got a few legacy nukes, and tidals, a couple of nascent gamma generators and a bunch of remnant gas burners, plus the big photonFeeds from us and from Central

Asia too. Thing is, they've had their decadal election recently. There's a new economic sweep happening. S'pose they're re-assessing needs."

Most Govs went a decade between election these days. So hard to organize with the climate - and voting could last up to 6 months, like in AuZ. No one trusted electronik, and voting by ballot paper was tricky.

Madrigal considered the stark change in Japan. "Well, the new administration could be doing a whole energy audit as Govs do, but still, this is speculation. Dad always said *data+intel eqwals the reason, and never trust whatever comes after the plus sign anyhow.*"

"Huh?"

"The Old Man only believed in data."

"Yeah, I know that."

"So there's no hard explanation for the reqwest? But we know the Jap/Tais are chasing more power?"

"Remember that 11 years ago, in one of his last acts as the Mantle, your father locked us into a tremendous 30 year deal for Phipps Industries. Your previous career was a direct casualty of that. I've been looking at recalibrated costings for when the deal ends 19 years from now. By then, we'll be competing for the bizz with Central Asia Energy, which is pulling lots of cheap energy from solar and methane reserves now, and with some of the Chinese Hegs – like your old friends from White Lady."

There was a pause as they sipped their drinks. Madrigal qwite enjoyed the background chanting. Soothing. *Ommmm ...*

"But the White Lady's onside with us. They get $New from distribution networks, don't they?"

"Yeah, but they're still a Heg. They'll deal with a better bet in 19 years possibly? May have the Bellingslodes themselves," Jexen replied.

"Can we price our power so we keep providing?"

"Currently, with the White Lady, we've got the cheapest power and cheapest delivery networks, so probz Mrs Soong won't go anywhere. She's a timeless soul and will probz be around in 19 years still. But whatever happens, gonna be a dumpling fight down the track."

"And so … and so … my dad parps up this morning, wading in with his cut price, almost freebies for the Jap/Tais. He wouldn't by chance be working for …" Her face suddenly looked perturbed, brow furrowed, mouth turned down. For the first time in Ben Jexen's life he thought dear Madrigal looked … well … older.

"Madrigal – let's be clear. Your father would never jump to another Heg or work for the Japan-Taiwan Nexus. Eleven years ago he played that dirty trick to force you back to the business because we desperately needed you. He'd lost focus and knew it, and wanted a tough successor. Was, and is, always about Phipps Industries."

"Jex, he never "forced me *back*" because I was never in the business in the first place. Let's be clear on that, too."

Madrigal looked miserable. She sipped the cocktail which had appeared out of a patch of mist at her elbow.

"You see, Jex, everything that happens now, that's unusual. I'm jumping round'n'round facing down the unusuals. Asking myself – is this about Todd? 'N I don't know. I'm stuck in this horrible waiting spiral."

"Understandable. But what I'm saying is Phipps Industries was always his reason for being." There was a pause. "Mind, he wasn't alone in the room this morning when he spoke to me – he kept glancing across."

"Yizz, I know. Saw the scope vid. Kept looking at other or others unknown. He looked sheepish."

"Like he wasn't qwite with it," said Jexen.

"He's very old, you know."

"Yes. But not too old to be that stupid."

Madrigal sipped her Martiniqwe and thought awhile.

"Where's he living now?" Jexen asked.

"Last I heard he was with Madam Nozomi ... in Kyoto. In some traditional house. I've never checked it out."

"The Old Man loved working the Jap bizz," he said. "East Asia was where it was at. Was always up in Tokyo, or Osaka."

"He was chasing the women up there – they were the attraction'n my mum knew it. And he's married the Geisha, as my mum used to call her. He seems to be happy with the Geisha. Hmmm ... I'll swallow my pride, I think, and scope him. A daughterly chat. There's no known way he'd have anything to do with the abduction of his only grandson, but he may know somethink that points the direction."

Jexen looked relieved. During their lull session that day, Cinzia had said, *Family should take care of family*. Ben'd immediately sent a note to Madrigal after the scope, plus the vid itself, and she'd dropped an urgent late evening meetBomb in his diary. At least they were in a cocktail bar.

Cinzia had said: *Jex, it's all about her little boy. Why should you have to deal with Old Man Phipps? Maddy needs to take care of her dad.*

His wife was correct.

But again, Ben Jexen well knew he was expected to keep business zinging. That was his job.

"So there hasn't been a ransom demand?" he asked.

"Not as yet," said Madrigal. "No one has surfaced, cos they know it'll be bleak for them if we can catch their trail."

"The gang that took the kidz ..."

"Knew what they were doing." Madrigal started looking gloomy again, and tapped the olive stick against the glass.

"What will you say to your dad?" asked Jexen cautiously.

"I'll let him know Todd's gone. Should have let him know a while back, when it happened, but I just can't bear talking to him. I'll say we're doing everything to track the culprit, and ask if anyone suspicious gets in touch, he tells me. Like I did with Toddy's dad, Langer." She twirled the stick between her fingers. "And I'll ask him how he is, and whether Kyoto is nice at this time of year."

"Autumn. But all that 4 season stuff is over, isn't it," said Jexen. "That part of Japan gets huge rains now. All tropical."

"S'pose," said Madrigal, distracted. "I don't know what it was like before."

*

Last time she'd scoped her father – last year – they'd had a fight. They'd battered each other with wordz. In the end he'd snarled at her, in an entirely unpleasant manner, showing teeth. She'd called to tell the Old Man that his wife, her mother Netta, had died, peacefully but prematurely. A stroke. Netta'd been way younger than her dad, by 30 years, but she was still an old Indijj lady with a heap of pride. Dad looked grim and upset, but not grim enough. She could see he was feigning sadness. Madrigal knew he'd marry Nozomi straightaway – Netta had predicted it. But Madrigal felt that after a 40 year marriage, he should attend his wife's funeral and at least talk thru some of the Sorry Bizz up north with Netta's remaining sisters and cousins. She said they'd delay so he could attend.

But the Old Man apologized, said he couldn't travel anymore. That was that.

She put the screws on him, just like he'd put the screws on her, 10 years before, forcing her into replacing him as Mantle of the company.

"Don't you make demands of me, Maddy," he'd snarled. "No demands. I've handed you the Mantle. The Mantle. The only gift you can present to me is your gratefulness and thanx!"

The Old Man clearly didn't give a glowing blue shit about Netta.

"How dare you just ignore the death of your wife of 40 years," she said with a growl in her tone. "This is nothink to do with the company. This is about enduring loyalty."

"Don't dictate at me about loyalty. I was loyal to a fault with Netta.You can just f'ck off, dearie."

Loyal to Netta? What a lie!

"And f'k you, Dad!" she'd bellowed, and cut the scope and fell backward, head spinning. She'd never been so angry in her life.

Before that argument was a worse one. Worse, because there was no scope to cut. He'd been standing in front of her, in person. They'd had a blistering yelling match and she accused him of destroying her chosen career. That was 7 years ago – at Ben Jexen's wedding. The first time she'd seen him in the flesh since his dirty f'king trick with the White Lady group in China.

She didn't create a scene at the wedding itself, but afterward she went for his jugular and upset her mother, who had craved the chance of reconciliation. Fat chance!

"You're my favorite," he kept shouting at her. "You're the smart one. The talker. The listener. The thinker. None of the others can carry this complex can of bickies. The bizz is yours. Aren't you happy about it?"

"Well, no, Dad. There are others of us who've been in the bizz for years!"

After all there was Djuna, Madrigal's half sister (Netta's first daughter), and Willem, a half-brother (the Old Man's first child) who were inheritors as well. But they were much, much older, and set in their ways. After all, Dad was in his late 70s when she was born and Netta was 45 then – an old mum.

Old Man Phipps wrote Djuna and Willem off from early on, while he saw somethink special in his youngest daughter. Derek Phipps couldn't understand that Madrigal would be anything but ecstatic.

"You have the Mantle. You're the only one with the flair and finesse. Don't you understand?" he'd said in complete bemusement. Sometimes she thought she'd been specially bred for the job, prepped and groomed from birth. That he'd picked Netta, a smart woman to marry, for one last crack at a competent heir.

The halfSiblings, who were present, were both unimpressed that, while wearing the Mantle of the business, Madrigal had been so rude to their father. They'd also objected 4 years prior when she was passed the Mantle. The sibz hadn't spoken to her for months, and in Djuna's case, almost a year. This further unintended conseqwence had hurt Madrigal deeply because Djuna was a darling – one of those softSpoken, hard working Indijj Elders whose leadership of the Phipps philanthropik activities made her the toast of WestOz and increasingly across Cap.

When the Blend happened, and millions of climate affected Papuans and Southeast Asians were permitted refuge in Cap, Djuna had found ways to feed, house and integrate them, and negotiate concensuses between them and the traditional owners, the TrOws. She was a dynamo, but she was also slowing down. Because of the Old Man's poor calibration of family dynamics, Djuna sent Madrigal to the dogBox for months, just when they had to work together.

Willem ran an entire Phipps Industries division, but again he was getting older and the Old Man had clearly written him off too. Willem had been xtremely hurt, but at least kept talking to Madrigal in a pleasant tone, aiming the blame more at their father.

*

No, Madrigal thought, Dad has interfered shockingly. She still hadn't forgiven him. She was so used to fighting him.

She took a big deep breath before banging the intejers into her scopePad.

But the Old Man was very calm. Wrinkled and calm.

"Hello, favorite," the Old Man said in a dreamy voice. He was obviously stoned on somethink.

"Don't call me that."

"Ok. Then, hello Maddy, my dear, did you get my message?"

"Jex let me know. But I was going to scope you anyway."

"What? Not send that pretty young faceOnface courier girl like you usually do? That Roxy is beeeeuuuwwwwtiful." He smacked his lips. He was behaving very badly for someone who was 120 years old.

"No. Dad. Can we be serious, please. This is between you and me, this scope, this convo. This is family bizz. I've very bad news. Toddy has been abducted by criminals. He's gone."

"What? When?" Her dad suddenly looked a little agitated. Snapped out of his dream stupor.

She didn't answer his qwestion, because it'd been a while back. She was trying to hold her composure. Her dad looked ashen. "I've been following leads, getting a process going, but nothink ..."

"Oh, that's rough, Maddy. That's rough."

He looked shocked and discomforted. "He's a good little lad."

"He's 17 now, Dad. Not so little." She tried not to inflect annoyance. Keep it civil.

"Of course."

"So I gotta ask you. You are the sort of very wealthy person a criminal could make ransom demands to – so, has anyone put the screws on you for anything in return for Todd? Have they? Any untoward demands? You'd tell me if they ..."

"Course I would. No weird 'outa the blue' calls ... and I'd tell you if someone called with demands about your boy. Course I would. But Maddy, you are remiss not telling me about this abhorrent sitch sooner."

"I know, Dad. That I am. I was just trying to ..."

"You're trying to sort it out by yourself. I've warned you about that!"

"Yizz, Dad." This was taking all her self composure, as the Old Man started to bristle up. "I'm letting you know now. Now. Please calm down."

He blew out of his mouth as if he was blowing away the agitation. She could just see his neck with some sort of Japanese coat collar. In fact, he was actually looking a little bit like an old Japanese man. Was he paying a surgeon to mess with his eyelid lines? At his age? Astonished at the thought, she waited for him to speak.

"What can I do?" he finally asked.

"Let me know if anyone hassles you for money, or for info about me, or any strange ransom demands. We're on it here: Centrl and their formidable tek, the milisi, me. All following every lead."

"Did he just disappear?" her dad looked upset now. "Fail to turn up to school or somethink?"

Madrigal took time to explain the chain of events, imprints of gear, hopper traces, everything. Todd's grandfather deserved to know. He looked very uneasy, muttering somethink about this being a big deal, and commenting the whole op would have taken massive criminal resources, and she agreed.

"Why isn't it in the news?"

He still called it "the news".

"Milisi ordered a gag. Probably some meejja outlets know, but the risk of copycat crime is too much – don't want anyone else getting fresh ideas. So, no reporting of this one. Suits me."

"Good," said the Old Man.

The conversation wasn't as bad as expected. Her dad was concerned and thoughtful, but looked tired and upset toward the end of the scope. So she broke her own news.

"And I'm getting my old job in AuZgov back – just for the interim. Until we find my son."

"What?" asked the Old Man, perplexed. "You need to delegate, girl. Let the authorities ..."

"Dad, I was the authority. I'm one of the few people in AuZ qualified to lead this sort of rescue. Do you understand that?" Her dad looked really confused now. "You don't understand, do you?"

He shook his wrinkled head. The definition was so high, she could even see the misted sheen in his old eyes. She suddenly felt sorry for him, in his selfExile, away from his family and people, vulnerable with age. Why was he there? she thought. Couldn't be for the sex with the Geisha – he's far too old. She'd snap him in 2, she thought.

"Anyway," she reassured him, "I'm back in the Phipps hot seat as soon as Todd is secured."

"So you're having a busman's holiday," he said, a little bit amused.

"A what?"

"Look it up, favorite," he said. "It's a very old saying that goes way back to the days of bus travel."

He asked Madrigal to keep him posted with every little breakthru, and she promised she would.

At the end he asked: "So you'll obviously be too overwhelmed to worry about the Jap/Tai matter I raised with Jex?"

"Oh, that – Ben is pricing the reqwest. We'll let the Jap/Tais know when we have an offer."

And that was that.

WAVE MUSIC

TWO weeks on, still before they got a full handle on the hand-Sign language, the kidz musical talent was brought to bear by Leader of Men, he with the twinkly friendly eyes. He'd been trying hard to make them feel welcome.

The young Stümmers had been desperately tutoring the 4 muzos, but their signTalk was still rubbery, loose and undisciplined, and progress was accompanied by a lot of laughter.

"Laughter is not a banned substance in StümmerLand," Narmon had said qwietly to Todd.

"Naw ... it's a universally positive, binding, social noise. If you ban laughter, then you're f'cked," Todd had whispered back. He'd discovered whistling, sobbing and making positive slurping noises at mealtimes were also permitted. Wordz, however, were not on. Or attention attracting yodeling.

Tunes (without singing) were okay tho'.

Now they'd fixed a pattern of existence in the heart of the Qwietude, Leader of Men decided was time to celebrate the arrival of the young people, and focus on their talents.

One evening, in the refectory (as they called the big community hall), a group of excited Stümmer youngsters brought instruments – a simulacrum and clarinet, a very old acoustic guitar with gut strings (gut!), and percussives – onto the raised platform at one end of the hall, while everyone, including Peet, Lissa, Narmon and Todd, was enjoying a big tomato, chicken and rice stew.

"Uh, oh," said Todd under his breath.

For us? Narmon signed, instead indicating *locusts*, and making some of the Stümmers kidz giggle.

From the next table, Leader of Men gestured to the 4 of them: *Please play for us. Some here have talent, we'd like to hear yours.*

He was being inclusive. Todd knew what he was up to, and they were up for it, except Peet in his sling.

Todd and The Philosophikal nodded assent. Anything for a diversion. He signed: *Not played for some time, will be more or less* ... and realized he didn't know the word for *rusty*, but Stümmers seemed to nod in understanding. They were keen for a new diversion from their routine too.

Peet pointed to the sling, but ambled up to the stage and indicated he'd try and play tomDrum one handed. A little rhythmic roll, and the crowd gestured approval with wiggling fingers. Weird, thought Peet, but he smiled back anyway.

Clapping was clearly out.

They took time to tune, with Lissa testing the clarinet. She usually played a sax, but this seemed a reasonable eqwivalent in terms of the keys; the reed business was odd tho. She waved to the crowd and walked out the back and blew a few notes and scales to familiarize, then came back.

Todd wrote a playlist of 3 of their original tunes, and wrote in the shared note: *Obviously can't sing the songs but let's give the tunes a go. Not sure how this is going to go down. A bit jazzy!!!* Peet was bipping and bopping on a couple of drumtops with his one hand, the other strapped against his shoulder.

Lissa wrote a note and passed it to the boyz: *This could be tricky.*

And so they played to the crowd of about 100 men, women and kidz, as they sat around the long tables, sipping fresh beer and cordials silently, eating small cakes and listening. Some were in a state of wonder; some were confused. Some were smiling happily at the melodious sounds, tapping their fingers (gently). Some of the little kidz from Stümmer families bopped and danced around them giggling.

At the end of the short set, general applause Stümmer style of more finger wiggles that rippled (visually) round the room. The Leader gestured *respect* and *thanx*, and then undulated his hand in front of him. Not a known handSign. Todd wondered what that meant.

Then the Leader shrugged and simply oscillated his hand in wave motion.

Todd nodded as did Narmon. Narmon wrote: *They want wave music ... can we do somethink in C or B flat?*

B flat, wrote Lissa. *Gotta get organized with this silly old instrument.*

Wave music.

To Todd and Narmon, the waveform music was xtremely boring, old-fashioned environmental background music – non-percussive with floaty licks and nice long chords – that one would find in an elevator, or waiting room. But perhaps to a Stümmer, perfektion. Peet ditched the bongos and picked up an oldStyle alto tuneGenerator which had a keyboard and proceeded, one handed, to play long notes. He shrugged and nodded at Narmon.

So they gave it a rumble, slowing one of their slower pieces down to a snail's pace which went almost nowhere.

The older members of the Qwietude started to relax and look content. This was their kind of melodious.

How funny they are, thought Peet, watching the sea of benign faces, lit in the lowGlow.

QWALMZ

I rocked the boat, I rocked it, and they felt queasy.
The Man can't abide boat rockers.
Invocations to the Private Self (2029) by Ulli Kalk

MADRIGAL'S reentry into the AuZgov service was a little fraught.

As police and military were blended as a single administered entity, saving money for food production and infrastructure, so too were diplomatik and security services. To operate well, Couriers often had to know both skillsets – a silvery tongue and an eye for trouble. Madrigal had been trained to the hilt, but left the service prematurely, a service she had loved.

Despite her successes, Commander Daniels was loath to recommission her. Too many critical deviations across her record, and worse, a trail of dead had followed her final op in East Cap. Several corpses. In officialdom, it was enough to create a thick cloud of misgivings.

Those qwestionable outcomes and worse, links to her family's commercial interests, jagged a hint of corruption. She'd madly expressed her loyalty then, but she'd not seemed independent to Centrl. Other marks against included sexing with the current Premier of Cap without a security approval. And, in the end, when Mardrigal took it it on herself to resign as a matter of principle after that fraught meeting in China. Daniels had gone thru the file and understood both her questionable reputation and the general Centrl consensus about her.

"You realize that to recommission you, Dr Phipps, is not my choice. I really don't trust you to meet our values," Daniels said bluntly.

Madrigal, looking into his stern blue eyes, could understand. If she were in Daniels' place, she wouldn't have recommissioned her either. Those in command should avoid outsiders, and the qwirky.

She knew well the order for her return to duty was made further up the chain of command, by political urgers, many linked to Phipps Industries and its activities. Madrigal had exerted considerable influence. Premier Jembrana, the colleague she had bedded, had been one of her strongest advocates for the "once off recomission".

No wonder Daniels was unhappy.

"Let me put you out of your clear discomfort, C-Ops," she heard herself saying in the most soothing Courier tone, qwiet and firm. "As soon as my son is returned and the culprits identified and caught, I shall resign. There is too much laid on my corporate table to hold down 2 jobs. But rest assured, I am one of the few in the service, in living memory, who has led a pursuit like this. I won't fail Centrl."

This calmed Daniels a little. She was vested with command of a search with the full force of AuZgov. In this way she oversaw the hunt, and could commandeer eqwipment, and most of all, interrogate with authority, if reqwired.

*

During a more publik ceremony 2 days later, a HiCourt judge in Perth presided over the recommission, with the Chief of Operations Daniels, and all Deputy Chiefs at the Spokes, on the big scopeScreen. She swore her oath of affirmation, loyalty and confidentiality in a stiff new uniform.

Afterward, C-Ops Daniels had said: "Don't let me down, Senior Courier Phipps. I've examined your files and there were irregularities during your first Courier commission."

She thought, Only thanx to Aunty! That was the worst bit of her chequered career. The visitation by her dead Aunty had thrown all logic out the window and exercised the previous C-Ops, Fingal Wen, and even the former PM in Canberra, who'd demanded Wen sack her, or so she'd heard.

Since that time, the Aunty hadn't manifested in Madrigal's dreams, but in the earlier crisis the Aunty had been a comforting and informative presence. Madrigal smiled professionally at the new Commander whose sharp grey hair and no nonsense face gave him full gravitas.

"I'm focused on one thing," she confirmed.

"Look, very irregular to do this on a single operational basis." He was making his views known before the judge and everyone else. "I am only persuaded to allow your commission because you know the sphere – and others here speak well of you."

"But," he went on, "I could only imagine you are ... panicked? I'm not sure you are the right person for the job of finding your son."

Madrigal was again forced to bite her tongue. On the contrary, she thought, the most focused person in the hunt would be her. This was not a time to fling the anxious mother card in her face. Not a time for barbs. Time for action.

"I'll find him, and I'll find the offenders, sir."

Daniels grunted. He kind of believed her, or at least he wanted to.

A FENCE

Institutions have died and what you see is a phantasm. Churches, political parties, all the machinery of governance. Hollowed out by money and cynicism, and owned by a deep state of corporations. There is only one true institution left and that is the people.

Us! Our very selves!
   Das Glas Haus (2034) Ulli Kalk

MADRIGAL only saw a great emptiness in the huge meeting hall, with its steel beam roof and thin rectangular crashproof windows letting in yellow and green light filtered by the tropical plants outside, even tho a mass of people hubbubbed in the rows of seats set before the wide curved podium. There were several vidDrones from meejja outlets canvassing the crowd in a silent hover. To Madrigal tho, the air was stale, and the roof of the hall was a lofted arc of nothink.

Madrigal wanted to be elsewhere, leading the hunt.

She'd whispered as much to a thin lipped Suze Shelbo as they'd entered the hall in the scrum of dignitaries and teks.

"Keep across the incoming messages, Suze," she'd said as they moved toward the front. "Send a note if there's anything."

"Yes, boss," Suze had said, looking worried. Looking like she didn't trust Madrigal to lose her wick at some point during the official ceremony. She was very aware of Madrigal's hostility to being there.

The State visit to Capricornia, organized months before on her bidding by Suze and the Cap authority, was now peripheral to Madrigal's interests. She'd tried to cancel, but the board and company executives had insisted. The new deeds of bizz had to be signed with Jembrana. And she, owning the Mantle, was the only possible signatory.

Instead of absorbing the momentous occasion, she was pondering traces and leads. Her eyes turned to Suze, sitting below front row near the centre. Suze held Madrigal's scope and Frisky, in case a message came thru. Madrigal watched her chief organizer prodding the key of the clamB and eyeing the face of the scope for any traceable komms. Head bent with intent, aware of Madrigal's desperate stare.

This was pomp. This was ceremony. This was showtime, and it was not where her headThoughts lay.

Madrigal was just off stage, a couple of steps up beside a deferential young Indijj aide. He didn't look more than 15. They waited for the ceremony starting signal.

With the guiding hand of the aide, Madrigal took the musical cue and walked up the podium steps. The aide melted away behind a wall at the top, and a klatch of vidDrones honed in on the 2 figures crossing the stage. The drones hovered in front of them, feeding livestream to the meejja agencies around AuZ and Cap. The silent bobbing cameras with their hardFish eyes.

Madrigal walked toward the desk situated offCentre, ignoring the cameras. On the other side, Jembrana reached the stage at the same time and walked toward the desk, where they would sit together and listen to the announcements and expositions by the chief teks.

While her own mind was numb, there was a great buzz in the room. People murmured and pointed friskies, while the drones threw a wash of light as they captured their wordz and movement. Was not often that Cap's most powerful presented themselves in person to a broader publik.

Madrigal sighed, and after one last glance at Suze Shelbo, who was still working the 2 clamBs, she focused for the first time on getting the stupendous event right. For the Premier and for Phipps Industries.

She looked at Jembrana as he strode across the stage toward her. She arched a qwizzical eyebrow so he could easily read her mind: *You've padded up, bruzz!*

"Greetings, Premier," she said. "It's been too long."

Jembrana smiled and they shook hands briskly. No puffing after the mild exertion of the steps, she noted. That was good.

They stood frontwize and shook hands again for the drone vidShots, which lasted a couple of secs as camBugs took cutaway shots from the side and swooped off. They made their way to the table and were sat by their aides who eased the chairs under their butts. Jembrana would be pleased with the performance, she thought. Very slick, just like him – the charismatic, sly, surefooted politician and administrator.

The Capricornian electors well knew Jembrana had their hearts and bellies in mind, however badly he behaved in his personal life. As acting Premier for several years, he'd pushed along significant progress, so when he was formally elected, in the AuZgov-ASEAN jointly administered Territory of Capricornia, it was straight back to the bizz. Madrigal knew she was a big part of the eqwation.

Capricornia was the big battlefront, where millions of climate refugees lived. The territory became an agreed sanctuary between AuZtralia and all the ASEAN countries, principally Indonesia, after The Grief. Yes, there was a brief civilian uprising against the carving out of Capricornia, but the international agreement was political, humane, and enduring. And 60 years later, everyone was working on making the increasingly hostile north as livable as possible. Madrigal and Jembrana were now 2 of the main players.

Capricornia was where the struggle against the Singular Enemy was at its fiercest and where the majority of inhabitants of the AuZtralian continent lived, scratching out an existence. It was a sizable chunk of the continent where the poor had washed up, but which was also rich in agri and elements. She looked at Jembrana's face – relaxed and imperturbable.

Geez, he's good, she thought.

"Nice uniform," he said.

Jembrana eyed her shoulder, looking at the 2 AuZgov security pips attached to her formal jacket that showed she was a commissioned Senior Commander of Centrl – Courier Class.

She could read his mind too.

Back to the old game? he was thinking. *Good for you!*

*

Before they were the centre of attention, Jembrana and Madrigal collaborated to investigate that rarest of events, a violent incursion by a foreign power on AuZtralian soil. The invasion, by a small force of raiders, had caused a number of bloody deaths of innocent civilians. Madrigal Phipps had led the charge on the ground, and sorted out the invasion with her lethal Slotter team, while Jembrana, then Capricornia's security chief, had provided Criminal Investigative support, intel and advisory.

Afterward, they fell into one another's arms in his bedroom.

Later, when forced by Old Man Phipps into her private role as Mantle, the 2 had met at energy and food summits every couple of years. Jembrana would represent the hermitLike Premier Luff when Luff had backslid into some sort of religious stupor in an era where religion was utterly irrelevant to administering the Territory.

Once, during a 5 day summit on Capricornia's future at the Sydney Hilton, they made plans to sneak off for another sexing tryst. They'd been red hot keen, but bizz just got in the way.

The conference was deadly serious – the Cloud and its permanent chain of thermocells along the south or north of the eqwator was edging towards some of the most productive northern areas making it impossible for people to exist, let alone grow crops.

As most of Capricornia's Arables were settled already, refugees were shifting south on their own volition into AuZ-tralia. And illegally "sharecropping" on properties owned by AuZ companies (including Phipps Industries) and longstanding private farmers. There were heated plenaries 'bout building a fence along the border as the NoGo Mark.

In the heat of this nasty, willing debate, their 2am tryst had been planned sotto voce over a cup of somethink at morning tea break, but it never eventuated. Too hard, too many eyes. Jembrana was more professional than the time before, when Madrigal had spent the nite with him. He'd remembered that the only time they'd sexed, they'd been outed by the gossips of the Ville. Neither had cared, but it affected Madrigal's service record.

Closest they got, at that conference, was they stayed up late in the cocktail bar talking candidly with a sound cloak round their table. True, among conversations about future projects, dreams and plans, they'd talked sex, but had never got there. Managed a steamy farewell kiss in a stairwell. That was it. Just too many eyes.

Now, during Madrigal's current visit to Cap, there was no thought whatsoever of trysts and sexing. Madrigal was too wrung out with worry to even to think such a thing, and Jembrana was empathetic enough not to make an inclement proposal.

Still, they watched each other, out there on their separate, lofty perches, trying to make things work against great odds.

*

"We haven't a tickle of intel 'bout your Todd, I'm sorry," Jembrana hastened to inform her qwietly as they sat together at the desk, waiting thru an interminable seminar leading up to their signings. A tekHead was blahing on about hardiWheat.

They pretended to pay attention.

The event was mainly ceremonial to impress the Capricornans, altho' there were several key papers for them to coSign, arranging new grain experiments and expenditure for the Arables of West Cap and funds for a test Installation to see if there was any point in catching energy from the power of the Cloud as it stretched high into the stratosphere and fed on jet-streams.

After the seminars in front of the hushed and appreciative crowd, Madrigal stood at the desk and spoke for a few short minutes about the pleasure of the moment ... blah blah ... supportive and collaborative ... blah blah ... her mouth spoke the speechnotes on the scroll desk, but she was on automatik pilot.

Jembrana rose and was expansive, citing facts, bestowing the thanx of the people of Cap, and asking the crowd to applaud the tireless assistance of Phipps Industries.

Madrigal smiled and nodded. She knew Jembrana not only lusted after her (admittedly reciprocal) but he needed her economic power too.

Madrigal, during the eSignings with her elaborate stylus, was most distracted and wanted the whole thing over. She just wanted a private moment to get in Jembrana's ear about Todd. She let the officials drone on, and looked out the window, mind ticking with fears and plans.

As soon as the seminars and the pleasantries were over, the 2 sat together at a ceremonial desk and signed qwickly in front of 300 officials, well wishers, bizzpersons, and hovering mee-jja drones. To set the programs up, millions of $New Phipps money was transferred to a grateful Premier who was looking for every scrap of cash he could get in the expensive, destructive fight against the Singular Enemy. Distracted, Madrigal put the wrong date on one document, and had to revise and re-sign.

*

As soon as they were finished signing, he pressed her arm gently and nodded. She could smell his cologne and the patina of sweat beneath. She felt comforted by his familiarity. At the same time he was looking at her in an obscure way, mebbe a hint of sorrow and empathy for her obvious pain.

"We have to mingle. They're expecting it. I'm expecting it."

"I know," said Madrigal so she qwickly took him thru the latest evidence. He reassured her they'd done several backSkans across West Cap in partikular, timed across the kidnap period using intel tek and found nothink.

"And you followed up possible veterans from the old Civil War – old allies of Kingdom Allenby and Baabi? People with bitter grudges from way north? No one wanting to avenge their deaths by kidnapping my boy?"

Jembrana raised his open palms to the sky.

"Those civil war veterans are all so very old, and no. No whispers in the Virtual, or radio freqwencies, nothink. And, generally, I've stepped up intel in the cities and towns, because the hardLife is sqweezing and crushing so many. We're constantly setting up horticulture arrays, with shade and irrigation to employ as many as we can, but there's true hunger. Hurting those people without jobs or assigned permaculture lots. The dispossessed are growing in the camps as they are forced south. They are ready to bust thru the fence again and the Capricornia security chief is now looking at bolstering border posts. It's a mess. I've ears everywhichway on everysuchthing."

"I'm sure you have," said Madrigal smiling. "You know the signs of a cat8 stormfront from a long way off."

"So, ashamed to say, but all is a blank."

People started to cluster around them, looking for attention. For the moment, they ignored.

"And Andaman Marko and Felicity? I'm sure if I could find Andaman I could force him into some useful searching for me. If I found Flick, I find Andaman."

"They are nowhere as well. Not a jot. I happen to know their assumed identities after they fled, and neither have been activated. We know they are at sea, but the ocean is a big, big place and to the north, it's a maze."

Madrigal sighed. She knew Jembrana's reputation as a thorough security man, and she didn't doubt that every eavesdrop was out there, looking in on sources, listening to white noise, configuring the algos in the Virtual to catch and trap old ghosts.

Jembrana looked at the sad woman who stood in front of him and asked the assembled for a couple of mins private faceOnface. The bureaucrats sighed, murmuring about the afternoon tea, meet'n'greets, and appointments further on in the diary. They closed their folders and withdrew leaving the Premier and the Mantle facing each other alone.

"Just want to say, I'm sorry. We are cracking open every shell, and looking inside, Maddy."

"I know you are. I know you are."

He reached over and held her hand in a clasp. A small gesture of human contact, skinOnskin.

"I'd never let you down, Maddy. Wouldn't be right."

"Funny that. You are about the one person I trust."

Jembrana looked slightly inscrutable. "Thanx. Not a good idea to trust a politician, but thanx."

He unclasped hands.

"You know what I mean," said Madrigal with a smile. "By the way, I might send one of my Slotters to exercise you. Need to slim down, man. The team've looked after me the last coupla months."

"I noticed," said Jembrana. "I, on the other hand, enjoy this misleading aura of indolence. Puts my political enemies off guard. And surprisingly, the voters admire a fatter leader. Somethink to aspire to."

Madrigal smiled. "Is that why the Capricornians call you *Big J*?"

Jembrana laughed heartily: "We'd better finalise, otherwise they'll start joining those wicked dots again."

"And we wouldn't want that," said Madrigal, "would we?"

'ROOS

Stalking also reqwires their silence – you can never tell if The Man is present in the room.
   Invocations to the Private Self (2029) by Ulli Kalk

THEY were a raggle taggle group, thought Todd.

Leader of Men and Leader of Kitchens, as well as the Qwartermaster, accompanied by 5 boyz and 5 girlz, headed down the stairs and into the gorge. The sun was a pale line in the east and the air was somewhat cool, tho' Todd still raised a sweat.

He knew that after the calamity of The Grief, these Centralian gorges became sanctuaries for wildlife and people. Habitable land, even on the margins, was disappearing, and these great geological kinks that held water and provided deep shade had turned into arks for the creatures and plants. Had happened, was happening in his Country too, in places he knew well.

As the landscape dried, in the summer scorching toward the 60s, and then pummeled with wind and water when the Cloud finally arrived, some places up north were more like an uninhabitable planet, than Earth. Many towns, settlements, and Indijj outstations were abandoned in Central Cap as scrub turned to sand dunes, or others in the wet to mud swamps.

The Hermitory was a reasonable, if isolated, habitat for both people and animals. The old genetic corridors across the landscape had broken down, and birds and other creatures were developing new migration patterns to escape death, or were trapped in tiny oases, and then threatened by inbreeding. Some migratory routes were established only because a flock of birds was sucked up by a wind storm and blown hundreds of kliks south.

Todd had seen animal tracks and the odd wallaby in the shade of the upper gorge so he wasn't surprized when in the refectory one nite, Leader of Men declared it was time to hunt for some game further away from the gorge mouth. Shoot some macropods, skin them and dry the meat.

Volunteers? he'd asked.

Todd turned to Lissa, Peet and Narmon and asked: *Coming?*

They declined, citing their Purity rule of *sanctity of life* even if they helped themselves to chicken. Todd's version of the *sanctity of life* didn't include food caught thru hunting. He was proudly Indijj and had lived off the land. His friends looked sqweamish. So Todd was in the hunting group, taking a professional interest in how Stümmers caught game.

As they picked their way over the rocks of the dry creek at the gorge entrance, Todd sidled up to the Leader of Men.

Do you hunt all the time? he signed.

Leader of Men was quite pleased Todd had taken a genuine interest in the excursion. Most of the others found no pleasure in the necessary task.

We can hunt every 4 months. The founders of the Hermitory sought the permission of the local Indijjinous people. Leader of Men spelt out an Indijj peoples' Country on a small notebook. Then continued to sign: *Promises were made and accepted. We pay their community a perpetual sum of rent for our habitation.*

Todd nodded. He knew the name of the Country and recognised the gorge as further east than he'd thought.

The TrOws deemed that if we cared for their country, we should share it with the fauna. We said we would walk lightly on this land and they were happy with that. Took many months of talk, tho. There are areas at the back of the gorge which are forbidden to us and we have kept clear. Early on, they visited us often, but altho there have been no visits from the owners for almost 2 decades, we still refrain from traveling to the gorge's end.

Todd knew the owners' reqwest would relate to sacred objects, or human remains, being located in caves and recesses and protected by powerful spirits, so it was essential for the Stümmers to stay away.

No doubt, sometimes, senior local men or women had visited and the Stümmer's had just missed their passing. The Indijjinous people would not be so interested in what the Stümmers were up to as long as the land wasn't being trashed. He could imagine a line of old men, Elders, walking in the shadows across the back of the gorge for Ceremony. He wished he could intercept them, have them sing, to approve his own presence in their country. Tho' not a pure traditional man, he knew the hardIron protocols of moving around, and felt sqweamish being there without their permission. Worse – hunting on their land.

He'd already felt the presence of spirits everywhere, and hadn't dared to go into the dark, lower recesses of the back gorge. Todd didn't know the appropriate songs to calm the spirits of the gorge, but a day after his arrival, without finding any Indijj locals among the Stümmers, he had scooted halfway up the gorge and sat on a shady rock to sing the songs he knew, in the hope it would help. But the uneasy feeling of being on someone's country, unintroduced, lingered.

The Stümmers would have been blind and oblivious to the local TrOws movements, but the longevity of the community pointed to the Stümmers respect for the deal.

And the take? Todd asked Leader of Men as they trod the stony ground.

What take?

How many kangaroos are you allowed to kill?

Oh ... 5 every 4 months, but we never manage that number. I fear that as the climate moves upon us the animals are becoming scarce.

The group rounded the gorge entrance and started moving toward a vegetated area to the left, across crunchy pebbles and rocks, part of the intermittent river that poured from the gorge during the wet.

The leader, Pepperbeard the Qwartermaster, and 2 of the boyz, had high powered rifles (fitted with silencers, in a very Stümmery fashion). Everyone had been issued with a sharp knife by the Qwartermaster.

As soon as the sun was up and over the horizon, the heat whacked them like a great wave. Everyone was instantly sweating and the sky glared down. Todd was already looking at the ground.

This way, he signaled to Leader of Men.

Why? asked Leader of Men.

They'll be grazing now in the shade trees. It's morning time. And anyway, there are tracks – see.

He pointed to a line of long, thin 'rooPrints in the sand, and some tail dents, heading round the front of the gorge.

The Leader of Men shrugged and waved the group toward the right instead of the left.

They started to circumnavigate around the huge gorge wall which seemed to hang from the blue sky. Before the hunting party was the boundless red void of Centralia with a dirty smudge indicating the horizon. The vegetation was sparse, and

Todd could see deep gouges of erosion in the hard red dirt. Dry scratchy grass and small boulders impeded their bushBashing path. Now out of the gorge, Todd saw the outer slopes which rose towards the gorge wall were gentler, inclined thirty degrees from the desert floor for a while until they steepened into the rock massif that left a shadowed hillside.

One of the boyz waved his arms crazily, but Todd had already seen the 'roo, its ears perked and twitching, about 200 meters from their group. The boy slung the rifle to his shoulder. Todd, using his hands, signed him out of it. The Stümmer lad looked really disappointed but Todd signed, *It's ok ... the animal is still there, isn't it?*

It might run, the boy answered.

Sneak around there – more 'roos will be in the shade of those trees. We move qwietly, and get closer. Then we can try to shoot 4 or 5.

How do you know?

I've hunted 'roos with my Uncles and cousins. All my life.

These guys are really crap hunters, he thought, but I can't lord it over them either. He felt weirdly embarrassed.

After giving his advice, Todd dropped back behind the white clad Stümmers and let them stalk the kangaroos. They kept a wide berth until many in the mob were visible, nibbling peacefully. One or 2 looked up suspiciously and twitched their ears. The 'roos looked in good shape, fed and fit. Todd could almost smell the cooking meat.

What now? asked Leader of Men, discreetly, to Todd.

Each shooter picks a 'roo. Make sure they agree on different ones. Then try to fire at the same time, said Todd, signing the bleeding obvious. *Just drop your hand when the shooters aim, ready to fire. And we are downwind, so if we walk slowly, we can get at least 10 meters closer.*

When the 4 rifles popped, spitting their muffled bullets, only one 'roo pitched over. The rest zigzagged off in a panic, their tensed muscled legs thumping the ground, making it vibrate.

They are crap shots, too, thought Todd. Certainly not the sort of people who would oversee slick, professional kidnappings.

The dead animal was gutted, and the organs thown carelessly onto the ground, which shocked Todd's sensibilities, because the organs – liver, kidneys, heart – were, in his experience, the richest bits. Leader of Kitchens cut off the tail and was about to chuck that too, but Todd gestured wildly: *Don't throw the tail!*

Don't be silly, said the Leader of Kitchens said, flinging the tail after the guts and organs.

Tails were the real delicacy, meat and chewy fat. So delicious. What a waste, thought Todd.

Leader of Men took a gun from one of the boyz and handed it to Todd. He told a couple of the younger kidz to take the dead 'roo back to the Hermitory and the group continued up the slope.

Todd easily tracked the mob of 'roos which had split from fear, but ended up in a semi cohesive group about a kilk further on. The hunters walked well up the slope, a hard climb, then traversed above the mob behind a fold of ridge. Todd looked across the badlands beyond the short belt of open woodland, and tried to see any further landmarks that might hint as to where he was.

The terrain looked dark red, dry and drab, flat with a few patches of gold spinifex in the middle distance. He sqwinted, and thought he could make out a darker line to the north, mebbe topography, but it could be cloud. Not enough information tho. He'd have to aim higher for a better angle on the landscape some time.

Leader of Men, in his white shirt and sarong, was peering over the ridge at the kangaroos, which now looked alert and suspicious. Some grazed while others kept looking round, their furry muzzles serious and tense, ears twitching rapidly, like little satellite dishes

Again Todd showed the Stümmers how to get closer to the animals, sloMo downwind, and have an easier shot, downhill. Shade was still being cast from the high rocks above. The savannah woodland of rather stunted trees dappled both the ground and the 'roos, and Todd knew close was better for visibility.

One good thing about Stümmers, he thought, was they didn't scare the animals off with the sound of voices. He smiled at some of the yakitiyak hunting parties he'd been on in the past with his cuzzes. Absolute debacles.

The Qwartermaster had handed out new bullets and they qwietly loaded their hardArms. Then the 4 shooters, including Todd, crept over a small knoll.

See your target, Todd had signed to the other shooters. *That one, that one, that one, and I'll aim for big man over there. Use a boulder to stabilize your aim.*

The young Stümmers took the hint and found boulders, but Todd, who'd been hunting since the age of 8, didn't need a rock. Out of the corner of his eye he saw Leader of Men drop his hand, and the big red male he'd aimed at flipped sideways as the bullet struck, and 2 other animals were hit as well. One started to hop, lurching away, injured and panicked. Todd swung his gun lazily and shot it thru the head, leaving a puff of bloodmist in the air.

The other 15 or 16 kangaroos had already bounded down the hill into the shadows and toward the plain below. The hunters started to carve up the dead beasts and pack them on old stretchers that had been brought for the purpose.

Silence, except for rustlings of a light wind in the open woodland and the abrasion of knives on flesh and bone. Todd looked west toward some clouds where rain was falling, but never reaching the ground, evaporating at about 3000 meters. A spooky sight.

That will do for today, signed Leader of Men his eyes twinkling. *We might come out tomorrow morning as well. Mebbe we can reach our qwota this qwarter.*

He looked very pleased.

Hmmm, thought Todd, skinning a carcass with his knife, and putting a couple of bloody tails on the stretcher despite Leader of Kitchens disdain. The animals don't look that scarce. The smell of warm blood tanged in his nostrils, a smell that led him to happy memories away from his school and Perth and to annual meets with those tough old men and his cuzzes. Camping under the stars, breathing in woodsmoke and chewing fresh charred meat, still bloody in the middle. Learning the lore.

No, the Stümmers weren't really tuned into their adopted country. While Leader of Men had talked of dwindling supplies, Todd'd also spotted a couple of loose wallabies on the way up the ridge, and a goanna. And this big mob that they'd hassled all morning.

There was plenty of game about.

The Stümmers just didn't know how to hunt and clearly his Indijj brothers and sisters who owned this country had never bothered to teach them.

Then the hunting party started heading home. It was still only 8 o'clok in the morning.

NIGHTINGALE

Ultimately, you will know, you will know. When you can't hear them, they can't hear you.
   Das Glas Haus (2034) Ulli Kalk

OLD Man Phipps remembered his boast at the Meeting of Like Minds in Kyoto last Spring. In fact, he couldn't purge the memory from his waking mind.

Old Man Phipps, from a position of unwitting weakness, a state he'd never really experienced and so could not recognize in himself, had claimed that, because his young grandson – *smart young man, great brain* – was the heir to the greatest powerHeg in the Southern Hemisphere, and because his beloved daughter was the Heg Mantle, then somethink would be sorted for their sacred Bell, protector of their city.

It was a vain boast from some psychic crevice where he was sqwashed against himself.

The Meeting of Like Minds had murmured in approval. Applause came out of the gloom. As one of those minds, he was trapped by this commitment. They knew the political winds of change were bearing down on their national Diet. A long tortuous election was underway. There was great unease among the

Like Minds that the Japanese people might vote against the longTerm ruling party for a new broom.

Naively, he believed the ruling party would rule again as they always had.

Early April, when the cherry blossoms were at their most delicate, fresh burst from bud, pink, red, straight trees and weeping form. The gardens of *Nijo-jo*.

A Shogun's palace, built over 600 years ago. Imagine that, thought the Old Man. Even older than me.

The Ninomaru gardens with the micro-islands, placed perfektly in the lake, with their beveled canopies of perfekt trees. The waterfalls, the rock bridge, ancient trees buttressed with sticks, trees bent into an eternity of weeping for the Shogun. The Like Minds had wandered thru the afternoon, circumnavigating the paths of the gardens and the trees, admiring and revering, talking qwietly of great matters. That day, the general publik had been excluded, to allow the presence of these eminent men.

They then gathered to privately dine inside the Shogun's Palace. And after contemplating the spectacularly ancient gardens, what a palace! As sumptuous as the Emperor's Palace up the road, because the Shogun owned the military and the bragging rights. The Shogun could shame the Emperor with his qwarters because the Emperor could not fight back. The Emperor, an emperor in name only.

The Old Man related to this ancient story.

They enjoyed food that most citizens could never contemplate – raw tuna flesh, sea urchin eggs, venison and the steamed roots of young bamboo. Fine saki and plum brandy. The rest of the Jap/Tai populace were mostly eating dried farmed fish reconstituted in newWater, and seaweed, farmed prawns, rice.

Old Man Phipps had felt he could sense the Shogun's ancient power emanating from the beams and dark brown shadows along the edges of the rooms. Huge stone block walls above the moat; the muted, beautiful parquetry and silk screens lining the living qwarters. All a museum now, of course, but it had opened for them as a special favor. Perfektly preserved as a reminder to people like him and his colleagues of their own past eminence and continuing superiority.

His colleagues, 12 to 14 men, mostly elderly, were seated on cushions on the tatami floor, and served sweet things and the very best saki by silent servants. The saki arrived in ancient ceramic bowls, warmed. Halfway round the circle of Like Minds, he could see his colleague, the Silvery One, in hushed discussion with the Governor of Kyoto's grandfather.

The Governor of Kyoto (who was not a Like Mind) was a lovely, but naive, young woman. She was loved by the Like Minds for her determination to preserve their precinct. Her own father and grandfather had never been Governor, but had been powerful champions for the prefecture in the Japanese Diet over the past 100 years. The Silvery One laughed and raised his ceramic cup, as did the Governor's grandfather, and the 2 men drank to somethink. They swallowed the saki in an eyeblink.

A Meeting of Like Minds was a hushed and reverential affair until business around the share of donations to temples, or the right people to administer key jobs in the prefecture, was concluded. Then they'd slap one another's backs and tell each other how successful they were, and admire each other's prowess.

Afterwards – personal deals would be sought and discussed, old times rollicked over, as they sat on silk cushions. Old Man Phipps was a 10 year newcomer, but they all knew his worth, what he'd achieved for the whole of East Asia, and he was admired, but he knew, not yet revered.

That was the next step.

During the actual meetings, the Old Man had never contributed much ... until his stupid boast.

Most of the Minds were Japanese. Some were very influential at the temples, which Old Man Phipps liked, as it gave him insight and leverage into his adopted life. Some, like the Silvery One were outsiders, enjoying the modulated atmosphere of the city, as well as intrigue and entry to this other world.

He was remembering what he'd said in the Shogun's hall, at the time: "if the worst happens and the reformers win ... we can find the Bellingslodes to supplement our city deficit," and there was a murmur of approval in the ancient meeting room where those Shoguns and Emperors once wrestled for power. He'd made the boast forgetting he and his daughter were estranged. Forgetting he'd relinqwished everything for Kyoto a decade ago. Forgetting that democracy sometimes worked, and Governments change.

And now he knew one or 2 others in the ancient hall had heard a different echo from the boast and had conceived a plan, just in case he somehow forgot his foolish words.

Old Man Phipps with his batWing jowls, almond-shaped eyes and a leathery skin from a century of building arrays and heatWells, hydrogen plants and energy factories in the hotlands of the north, desert and jungle both, and out on vast ocean wind platforms.

After slightly drunken farewells, he walked thru the palace corridors across the nightingale floors sqweaking their 600 year old warning of impending assassination. He couldn't hear the other warnings, which he would have heard when he was younger, ringing out in his own head.

He heard them now. He should have heard them then.

THE QWARTERMASTER

As soon as we all rush to the clinics to make designer babies, we open the door to designer Governments. Corporations are just the gateway to soft fascism and your urge to give your mitochondrial DNA to medikal corporations is the most dangerous thing, ever.

There, I've said it. Now I will explain why ...
   Das Glas Haus (2034) Ulli Kalk

TOWARD summertime, of an evening Todd, Narmon, Lissa and Peet sit around and jjam their music in a cooler corner of an open courtyard, catching the funneled breeze which blows up the gorge. A few of the younger Stümmers listen and watch. Peet even gets away with a bit of humming.

They bunch under a couple of huge, leafy apricot and lime trees and the platform of the long paved terrace, and stretch out to perch on pillows and small seats. The nite is moonless, so the courtyard is lit with pallid solar glows. Stümmer adults are across the paving, sitting and signing, drinking fresh beers. The young people all wear the light cotton Stümmer "uniforms" white cool shorts or sarongs, but the monochrome clothing doesn't stop them from trying to decorate their hair, hands and wrists with homemade jewelry – both boyz and girlz. Little Freckle is always there, and the Bangle girl who is soft on Todd, and is keen to teach him new wordz. By now their signage is qwite fluent.

There were a couple of girlz cosying up to Peet too, who is qwite smitten with one young woman, Curl, who he'd finally announced to his friends as his "steadyGirl". Narmon and Lissa are horrified because that's a true commitment, but Todd just shrugs. Peet's bizz.

Todd's also loving the company of the girl Stümmers.

*

Soon after they settled at the Hermitory, Peet had said to Todd one day: "Narmon and Liss are lucky having each other ..."

"That they are," Todd said sagely.

"I'm right ready for a relationship, too. I don't want Narmon envy."

"Shouldn't just throw yourself and commit cos of Narmon envy, Peet," Todd said with his wide smile.

"Well, what about you ..."

"These girlz are sweet," said Todd. "I'm liking them lotz, but we gotta get going from here somehow."

*

Todd and his friends sense a qwiet but profound desperation among the young, desiring the proximity of new blood and new experience. The timeless isolation of the colony explains the wave of excitement thru the young adults of the colony and why their music attracts so much attention.

Their expertise in sign language is now excellent as the young people were keen to understand them and exchange information. And clearly, exchange more emotional, personal messages.

But the older Stümmers are still evasive. How they make decisions. What they know. What the more arcane rules are.

There's a hierarchy of information that had to be earned thru continued study, and respect for the Qwietude must be understood.

*

Todd asked a male elder, Leader of Kitchens, at dinner one nite, how often new people join the Stümmers, and with a wry look, he signed back, *Very, very seldom.*

The Leader started raving with his hands: *Sometimes people who desire the cloak of privacy find us thru the Qwietude's networks of supporters. The Desert Gorge community is one of our most remote. Others, on ocean islands, have not survived the encroachment of the seas. Moreover, other people in countries to the north, in city Hermitories, have been evicted by Governments and abandoned as complete and utter privacy is banned. There are communities in some mountain ranges, and in remote places in the Americas, but we are very few.*

Todd asked about arrival numbers and the elder signed: *Mebbe 2 or 3 people a decade. As I said, we are hard to find. Belief of deep privacy is still strong around the world, but commitment to the Qwietude is a further step. Families practise our ways individually.*

Todd wondered at how this elder knew that commitment around the world was still strong, given their utter komms isolation.

How do you know this if you're all so elusive? asked Todd.

Oh, we know. We know, he signed mysteriously.

*

At some point tho, the younger Stümmers became less guarded. Mebbe it was the familiarity, mebbe it was the perception that Todd and Peet, at least, were trying to understand their ways. Both had attended early morning meditation for some weeks. And mebbe it was because Todd and Peet were shedding some of their own beliefs in the tenets of Purity and Virtue, which they'd been taught since babyhood.

The Stümmers were much less prim about sexing.

At a break during the terrace jjam, Todd signed to the Bangle girl, asking his usual stream of qwestions about the community. He asked: *How do you get such good beads and glass for your bangles? Do you make them?* When he didn't know a word, he'd point or mime.

Bangle was pleased that she was being asked a serious qwestion. She had very dark hair and coppery skin – could have had Indijj heritage too. Her eyes were constantly amused. Todd liked her.

Some from seeds of desert plants (she pointed to small bright red and yellow beads), *some we make in the kilns, and some come from the annual supplier – like these glass ones.* She showed Todd, the more machined, commercial beads on her bangles, as he admired both the bangles and her slim wrist.

And how do you know to get them?

Oh, we make lists of things we might like before the supply comes.

Lissa asked: *Does everyone make lists?*

Bangle nodded, and the older clarinet boy signed: *We can't make everything here.*

What do you exchange for the things that are brought from the outside? Do you have money?

Bangle shrugged. Universal signal for *I don't know.*

Todd and Narmon had wondered at how the community managed to get such "civilized" items as nanoMedikal fluid analysis monitors, fresh stemCell pastes, and even the fairly contemporary steam ovens in the kitchen, where the 2 worked every morning prepping the day's meals.

Who do you put reqwests to, when you want somethink from outside? Todd asked.

Oh, the Qwartermaster. He is an important member of the Qwietude. The Qwietude then decide on whether the reqwest is worthy. Some of the girlz like making jewelry and they usually allow some glass beads and silver or gold wire. And then he puts the order in.

That's great, said Todd, intrigued. They were finally getting somewhere. Sounded like there was komms with the outside world after all. *Which one is the Qwartermaster?*

Pepperbeard, she said.

Todd knew Pepperbeard. The older man who'd been on the hunt and handed out individual bullets.

He's usually at dinner with the community. He doesn't have a family. His wife died some years ago in childbirth and the child died too. It was very sad. Do you like this bangle? she signed, leaning closer to Todd, their knees touching. Todd felt a sudden rush of heat to his cheeks and face, and it wasn't due to the warm nite.

Yes, signed Todd, *but I like your necklace better.* And he did. The necklace decorations were a mix of red bush seeds, gold chips from ancient komms eqwipment and silvery black glass. He stretched his fingers out and she allowed him to lift it from low on her neckline for an inspection.

And it was time to stop asking the qwestions for now.

Later, Bangle and Todd went for a walk and they ended up cooling off in one of the rice ponds well away from the dormitory complex. Sitting in the pool, they splashed the cool water over each other's naked bodies. Bangle wasn't shy. She'd leant forward and pressed her lips to his, and they looked into each other's eyes as her warm tonguetip pushed into his mouth.

Delish, he thought.

In the gorge, without the moon, and a tiny amount of ambient light from the buildings above, they spent a deal of time sexing enthusiastically, wet skin against wet skin, and laughing in between. Todd noted that Bangle was happy to make noises of all sorts, as long as it wasn't wordz. And he was happy to join in.

*

What perplexed Peet most was the silence, the signing. He liked to talk. As a poet, he liked word sounds, plosives and fricatives, how sound moved thru the throat and banged against the tongue, the roof of his mouth, his teeth, like water bubbling across rocks. *Why is it,* he signed to Curl, now his official steadyGirl, *that we can't talk? I'd love to hear your voice!*

She refused to speak to him signing, *I'd sound stupid. And it's a breach of the silence rule.*

Side2side they lay in her bed, in Curl's family dwelling half a klik along from the main Hermitory buildings. A much bigger and comfier bed than the one in his own cell, and they could both fit snugly and chat using Stümmer signs.

There are eavesdrops. The Australian authorities may bug the Hermitory and listen to our lives.

But the authorities don't even know you are here, Peet would say. *And even if they did, they have other more urgent tasks. Listening to a remote colony of the Qwietude would be a waste. It makes no sense.*

If that's so, then they have given up trying to listen only because we have refused to speak, Curl signed, her hands above her. *At least that's what the leaders say. Our silence is our protection. If we spoke again, they would hear everything.*

To Peet, it sounded exceedingly odd.

*

It was clear to Todd, who viewed his private retreats with Bangle, and 1 or 2 other girlz as playful diversions, that Peet was dealing different. Peet was seriously in love with Curl, who was Little Freckle's older sister. Her patience in teaching him and his friends the signs and ways of the Stümmers, her elegance and light brown eyes, and her intelligent humour ... Peet fell in love with all of it, and he and Curl became inseparable.

Because of this, in huddles in Narmon's room, Peet was less and less inclined to go with their plans to walk out of the gorge and head west. Todd was more and more convinced that if they aimed for the coast, he'd touch on some of his own extended Country, or the Arables, the green belt that had formed because of the changed rainfall pattern along the mid-west coast of West Capricornia. Peet was disengaging from the group. Todd, Narmon and Lissa on the other hand were desperate to go.

"We love each other," said Peet, his eyes shiny.

"Don't get too open 'bout it. The Qwietude will have something to say," said Lissa, who genuinely liked Curl.

"All the Leaders want is that we abide by and observe the qwiet. We can do anything else we like. Anything!" said Peet, who was hinting strongly at his and Curl's activities. Todd grinned. This absence of Purity and Virtue obligations was good, and he too was enjoying freedoms that would have been real difficult in Perth, especially with his mum and her friends around.

He'd been visited the previous nite by 2 girlz. 2! Bangle and her friend Little Weaver and a coupla jugs of beer. Girlz were keen for physical relations in a way he wasn't understanding, but relished. The girlz hadn't stayed for the whole nite (the bed was too small, room too cramped) but they'd had fun. A sexing party.

He knew Madrigal to be a bit of a prude with the Purity and Virtue thing. But then, he was all P&V too, back in Perth. "Very different here," he'd whispered to Narmon, the morning after the girlz visited him.

They were all amazed at the wider freedoms they had as long as they: 1) didn't talk, 2) went to lessons, and 3) did their community chores. The lessons were very different from their own schools. It was all personal ethics, Stümmer philosophy and cultivation of gardens.

"The Qwartermaster, that Pepperbeard guy, obviously uses komms with the suppliers," said Todd. "Our next jobs are to climb to the gorge rim and check on landmarks to the west, and figure out how their contact with the outside world works. If there's a device, there may be an easier way out."

Peet nodded tentatively.

"If we walked out, you'd have to come," said Lissa to Peet. "You can't stay here. Just for a girl."

"Why not? Curl's not *just* a girl. Are you *just* a girl?" Peet shot back, a bit angry.

"Your parents. They'll be in pieces. What if we turned up back in Perth without you?"

"S'pose." Peet did not look convinced. After 3 months he felt like a local.

It was late. There was a yawn from Narmon followed by a collective decision to head to bed and think things thru again. Narmon walked Lissa back to the single girlz' sleeping corridors thru the courtyard, which at that time of nite was dark and deserted.

As no one was around, the couple kept talking softly. "Do you really think Todd could walk us out of here?" asked Lissa.

"He seems to think so. Todd's an Indijj guy and we know he goes north to learn his culture every year. It's hostile desert, but doesn't seem to bother him much ... as long as he can locate this place. If we go just before the storm season we could get lost and caught in the maelstroms. We'd perish!" Narmon said.

"I know," said Lissa. "We gotta go soon."

They kissed goodnite. A heartfelt kiss. Long and passionate with a hot embrace, followed by a flustered moment of disengagement as their bodies urged them to keep going, but their brains said: *Not right now, not in an open courtyard, not this time.* She reached up and held onto the back of his head, his shaggy hair between her fingers. His hair felt soft and it calmed her.

"Goodnite, Lissa," said Narmon.

"Goodnite," she answered in her usual cool tone.

They felt happy talking. To utter sound.

*

There was a long view west and east from the outer rims of the gorge. Leader of Men hated people going to the gorge rim in case of detection by HighEyes. Inside the gorge, the Qwietude felt they were concealed from the world. Peet called it "mass paranoia".

Todd, Lissa and Narmon went straight to the top, with excuses for later. Peet, pointedly, made his own excuses not to come.

The 3 left very early one morning, before sunrise, to avoid the usual gaggle of youngsters, and it worked. They'd popped into the garden sheds where tools were stashed, and covered their skins with the 100+ sunJell with its reflective and cooling properties that the fieldworkers used during the day. Standard practise was to stay shadeSide anyway, break while the sun was at zenith, then in the arvo, move to the shaded gardens on the other side. But the sun was unremitting as it headed for summer.

After applying the sunJell, the 3 took the final steps down to the gorge floor and walked up thru agricultural terracing toward the more crumbly rocks and boulders that delineated the wilder part of the gorge. Some of the climb was qwite a scramble, grabbing tussocky grass and thin gum tree and acacia trunks, pulling themselves upward. A sandstone shrikethrush was startled from a rock shelf and made a mournful *peep* call as it flew across the gap.

Lissa and Narmon followed Todd, who had a sure foot and a good eye for an upRoute. There were no paths and it had been hot overnite anyway, so by the time they'd reached the top they were in a hard sweat and thirsty. They knew the Cloud was building to the north and ever on the move, it being the October-November switchTime. Escape by foot was now or never.

At the summit they walked another klik northward along the curve of the rock massif. It helped them move further away from a group of clumped red rock formations that obscured the horizon.

"Recognize anything?" Narmon asked as Todd skanned the red desert floor far below, its golden clumps of spinifex, and occasional stringy little trees that pushed into the distance. The sandy soil was rippled by the water and wind from previous hard weather, and looked like a monstrously extended fancy shoe sole pattern, spreading into the distance. There were dunes, there were gullies gouged by floodwater, and it was simply a hazardous view of a noMan's land.

At the very end of the horizon to the north was another flat range, just visible to the eye, but almost impossible to size.

Todd admitted defeat. He couldn't recognize anything topographical.

"Mebbe if I climbed those adjacent rockforms," he said, pointing to the next set of hills that were in the way of their view. "Songs I've learnt all work lake to waterholes, hill to hill, thru the creation stories. The Dreaming is a wonderful map where everything begins and ends, but you have to be almost a savant to follow it. Stay on Country and breathe the dust. I'm stumped. I'll have to sing. Sing what the Uncles taught me. Try and work out somethink."

"Don't torture yourself," said Lissa, who had been keenest to test the "walk out" theory but could see the agony on Todd's face.

"I reckon we'd just have to walk due west – follow the stars – and see if we reach anything, but it could be a long walk. At least there's tucker around," he said pointing to a small wallaby chewing some grass in a rock crack. "And water, with the rain bands coming thru now."

When they returned to the community, the Leader of Men cornered them as they'd been late for chores, and asked where they'd been. Todd said somethink about going for a morning walk up the gorge and getting carried away. The elder looked at him strangely and signed: *It's a flat, red hot waste, isn't it? You won't find any comfortable shelter there, young man. None at all.*

Todd had signed back: *I s'pose not.*

A GREY BOAT ON A GREY SEA

Blue globe is followed through the dark universe
by a filthy cloud of elektronik smog fug,
no doubt a warning to any sentient life
"Avoid the pry-polluted Earth"
  from *Orbit*, (2035) Klaus Kalk

LONG time back, in 2131, the savant of the virtual, Andaman Marko, spent a year of painful humiliation in a correctional rehab facility at the Ville for a psych defrag. There he endured tests, selfCritiques in front of idiots, and retraining toward the goal of purity.

Marko endured his "treatment" after being found guilty of "creating a publik menace causing death". Eighty-five dead people to be precise, crushed or drowned by his exploding, disintegrating, falling house.

The deaths were not his fault and his actions leading to the crisis – his furtive hackery on the Virtual – were never made publik. The actual evil killer, who'd set the hiExplosives as a boobytrap, had died, but Marko's actions prefigured the disaster so there had to be some punishment meted out by the

Capricornian authorities, as demanded by the then powerful Security Chief, Jembrana.

His time in Correctional Hub achieved the opposite of psychological healing and rebirth – instead, it doubled down on his trauma disorders. He was just far too smart for the jailers and the psychMediks. Andy Marko might have been oddly naive about the dark hearts of men, but he knew his own mind.

Following his sullen release in early 2132, and the confiscation of many of his assets in reparations, Andaman and his lover, Flick Allenby, married in a display of their new-found purity, and then proceeded to go on a 9-day bender. They anchored in a remote bay near Keppel on Flick's luxury cruisecat, *The Capricorn Sky*. Keppel was one of the many 'phoonTrashed Queensland offshore islands.

Andy had gone a bit mad after his release and Flick had caught the vibe. Their intent was to plan their withdrawal from the world. Instead they chugged hard liquor, swam, smoked ganjja and snorted zizz, and wildly sexed for hours on the open deck, down in the lounge cabin and on the skipper's bunk. Zizz always helped prolong the good sex. They found themselves singing along to an endless partyLine of old and new songs on the Virtual, and when the ancient David Bowie classic from the Golden Age came on the loop, they sang lustily, "we shall be zeroes, just for all day," and laughed maniacally.

Their mad party was the last drunken and drugged bender they'd do for years, once they buckled down to the Grand Plan. They sold *The Capricorn Sky*, where Flick had lived for the duration of his psych defrag. With funds from the sold boat, and from the hollow money logs Marko had hidden on the Virtual, they bought a salvaged lifeboat. The lifeboat was a serious job. Originally it was part of the supercontainer vessel SCV *Southern Borealis*, a ship that had been wrecked and salvaged along the Antarctic region's Ross Sea coast.

Both he and Flick yearned to become ghosts in the complicated world. To escape. The pair of outcasts had smartz enough to accomplish this ghostly retreat.

*

The lifeboat they bought from the salvagers was about 16 meters long with room for 8 persons, the usual number of personnel who'd crew a klik-long supercontainer ship like *Southern Borealis*. Tho' 30 years old, the utilitarian lifeboat had retractable solar sails in case of engine failure, big water and fuel tanks, a belt and braces steering system, and a heating unit – to await recoveries over the North Pole or in Antarctic waters, a short-cut course for such giant supercontainers. There was a mechanical adjustable buoyancy function in case of storms.

The vessel was grey and shaped like the skull of a seabird.

Andy used some of his dwindling resources to hinge the cockpit into a gimbal arrangement – he did all the enjjineering and fitting himself, in a rented boatshed in Port Hedland. As far as any close observers were aware, such as owners of other boatsheds and marine enjjineering shops in the same part of the harbor, or the fishermen who tied up to the inner jetty opposite, they were Andy and Flick. A qwiet couple who kept to themselves. A pair of seemingly competent boatbuilders with a cheery wave and a word. That was 'bout it.

Andy spent months with grinders, welding eqwipment, riveting machinery and sheets of steel. Flick found work as a bar attendant to while away her time and stay out of Andy's way during the day as he singlemindedly, with the eyes of a crazy man, reconfigged their escape boat.

In the evening, they'd sit in the clutter at the back of the shed, among the steel offcuts and bits of eqwipment, and drink beer. They'd pick thru the plans, problem solve and work out their sums to buy more gear and special fittings. After all, Flick always was the skipper, and wanted the rebuild just right.

Thru sources in Perth's negTek community, Flick bought 2 gravity adjustors. It was a remarkable feat to find such boonsome illegal elektronika. The gear was bulky and hard to transport in secret. The adjustor affected subAtomics and it had to generate a deal of energy to impact bosons in the boat's hull, so they smuggled the cannisters, regulator and G-pax up the coast in a fishing boat and into the shed in the dark of nite.

Other negTek they avoided. Tho sorely tempted, they shied away from buying illegal cloaking devices, because possession of big shimmers was punishable with life imprisonment and Andy's prison record would end him forever with a permanent sedate till death. They decided they'd just be a grey boat on a grey sea.

Andy and Flick spent a year in Hedland reconfigging the boat, then, one pink and liverish dawn, they sailed qwietly out of the harbor, toward the north, with a new solar sail. Thirty years on in the lifeboat's, well ... life, the new owners had committed to sail and solar, rather than fuel.

Andy looked up on hearing the *whack* and *flap*, as the autowinch hoisted the solar sail up the mast. He trimmed a couple of the sheets until the sail tautened, the leech was tight, and the power started flowing thru the regulator. Flick cut the diesel motor as the tiny, powerful solar cells gave their hybrid boat an extra 4 knots and the wind picked them up and pushed them on a southwest tack. She freed the windpower vane to spin its magic and add more oomph.

Weeks before, Centrl had missed the gravity adjustor purchase, but that morning had clokked Andaman Marko's departure thru the Hedland HarbourChief. They wouldn't find him again for some time.

*

Long distance sailing can make or break people, but Andy needed the space of a whole ocean, believing he was cursed within the human community, while Flick needed her boat as

solace. She loved Andy's companionship – that was uncon-
ditional. They watched each other's backs, having been thru
life's grinders, him with his risk taking which had led to may-
hem, deaths and incarceration, her, because of the damage her
father had done.

Flick insisted the boat be named *The Kingdom*, after her late
father. Andy found it strange she'd want to have Kingdom Allenby memorialized in such a way, but Flick said, "If I'm skipper, I'm naming the vessel, for luck, for memory, to remind me
that things can get very tough."

Andy thought: Also, in the end, her father had died protecting her after years of abandonment. Looked out for her when
an even more ruthless unit than Kingdom Allenby went after
his Flick. That was the moment of Kingdom's redemption.

Now she was in charge of her own destiny, and finally in
charge of *The Kingdom*.

Over the next few years as sailors and mariners, they
learned much, and honed their big ocean sailing strategies:
foolhardy stomach lurching eqwatorial crossings, or tootling
along on seas that slopped gently, like swimming pools, with
sails up, driving the solar powered motors into an oily flat
windless swell.

*

And there were memorable moments in the long horizon.

When traversing to the Northern Hemisphere, in a knothole
of calm near where the Maldives once existed, a knothole in
that otherwise boisterous, permanent meteorological storm-
Belt known as the Cloud, Andy and Flick sat on the bow, legs
dangling over a sea which looked like a wrinkled, old dark blue
mattress.

The boat moved slowly, under sail, to the north. The wash
from the bow was desultory, and the sail often sagged without
wind. Somehow everything had gone flat that morning, tho'
they knew wouldn't last long, especially the noSwell. Some-

where to port the Maldive Islands had pointed north, but they were now mostly sunk under the sea level rise.

Normally the swell in that region was fierce, so the 2 were exulting in the calm spell and toned down the solar motor.

The water was clear and they could see a vast column of manta rays passing under them. Occasionally one would fly out of the water, and crash back spectacularly into the ocean, throwing spray asunder. They sat and watched fascinated as this parade of giant beasts flapped slowly and slid below the boat, somehow alive and breeding, heading for some mysterious destination.

"How can so many exist in this day'n'age?" asked Flick looking into the clarified ocean. "Where are they going?"

Andy shrugged.

"They seem to know. Should let them get on with it, eh?"

The huge fish moved like spooky kites, being tugged somewhere by hundreds of invisible strings.

*

One cloudless nite 'bout 4 years after Andy's release they were sailing light, deep in the southern ocean.

Without warning, a rogue wave rose toward them from the southwest, so massive, it reared 15 points above the horizon and suddenly blotted the shine of the setting moon and low stars.

Luckily they were awake and in the cockpit, drinking coffee and playing cards. The moon's sudden disappearance caught Flick's eye and she'd leapt to the wheel, started the diesel engines, turned the vessel toward the wave and powered up into the awesome swell, a huge inky muscle of water coming toward them with malevolent force.

Flick pressed hard into the wheel, her muscles tense, ensuring the rudder stayed tight, but the adrenaline coursing thru her body told her this was life or death. All touch, sensing the wave motion and holding course. She'd accelerated *The King-*

dom up the wave slope, full power. If she hadn't jumped, they'd have broached and drowned, as hatches had been open.

As the boat crested the mountain of dark water, the moon became visible again and they surfed down the back of the now silvery wave.

The wave was nothink like they'd ever seen, possibly created by collapsing rock, ice, or a massive seabed qwake. Whatever the cause, the dangerous wave was fanning out and heading north, for Madagascar, Africa, Ceylon, India, West Cap and their unprepared coasts.

Flick immediately broke scope silence, usually insisted on by Andy, to communicate with authorities, warning of the impending disaster, to prepare for a tsunami. She knew oceanik sensors would pick the wave off the Virtual, but sometimes tek failed. Her scope call was insurance.

"Yacht *Kingdom*," she pinpointed the name – the PanPan message had to be made real. An acknowledgement crackled thru the speaker: *Received, yacht* Kingdom. *What are your co-cordinates?* For a few minutes they had to exist.

Andy didn't argue on their imposed komms silence at that point. The height of a 30 storey building, the wave has frightened him. They hoped some lives would be saved, because whatever the warnings and the evacuations to the north, they knew in their hearts thousands were going to perish and more land than ever would sink under the rising oceans.

As *The Kingdom's* scope sparked the urgent warning, Centrl tagged her. They knew Flick was communicator of the scope – they'd always had Andy's scopeCode logged.

A grim search and rescue milisi voice took the hurried alarm call and thanked *The Kingdom* for the warning and Flick's nautical description of the speed, height and coordinates of the wave.

That incident was years back, when Andy and Flick were expanding their oceanik skills and trying the boat out in the wilds.

This was before they'd really lost track of time and found some peace.

*

Traversing what was euphemistically called "eqwatorial instability", *The Kingdom* would smash its way toward Thailand, or the Philippines, or Japan, or back to AuZ, often in massive seas, as the Cloud moved north and south between the solstices. During these rough passages, Andy and Flick would sport bleary eyes, from a couple hours of broken sleep over 4 or so days. They'd live – well, camp – in the enclosed cockpit, bringing food, and a kettle and sleeping bags and cushions, going nowhere near the other parts of the heaving boat in case they were dashed against furniture or bulkheads and badly hurt.

The gravity enhancers kept the boat heavy hulled, and prevented the hull from lifting out of the water, or being flipped. The stability would hold the gimballed cockpit in place so that it didn't swing too wildly. At these times they'd sport a tiny storm sail for a little more stability, but they were ripped thru often. Andy was always grumbling at buying storm sails.

The gimballed cockpit was a masterpiece, modulated, by Andy's enjjineering, with a counterswing. The shell of the cockpit also contained the boson enhancers in rods placed around the cockpit's cage, and storms were a little more bearable.

The cage leveled the cockpit, and the gravity enhancers pressed the hull into the ocean and qwelled movement in storms, slightly. But it was still good they were impervious to seasickness.

When they camped in the cockpit, Andy would play at being metHead and navMan, the one watching the weather, the current fluxes and water turbulence, and keeping an eye out for reefs and coastal shoals, while Flick would take the helm. Occasionally, they'd switch for a change. But Flick was the ace. She could almost feel what was coming thru her feet, especially when rain was slashing so hard against the screen that it was impossible to pick any visuals out except the erratic bright flare of lightning flashes.

In the worst storms, Andy always stuck to radars and instruments, and Flick always steered from the hot heart of any thermocell. They fired up their diesel reserves then. There was no other choice. *The Kingdom* was never hit by tubes, or other events, caused by the amalgamation of thermal currents, or swirlies, that were found in the overheated eqwatorial waters where supercharged hiAltitude jetstreams fed the madness.

After a crossing of the "eqwatorial instability" they'd be so tired, Flick and Andy would seek calmer waters – though the swell could still be over 5 or 6 meters – stabilize the boat, and turn on the warning systems, and they would crawl under the sheets in the cot at the back of the cockpit, and sleep, hoping that if some danger manifested, they would have enough time to wake up and deal. Times like these, Andy would often lie with his eyes open, with Flick wrapped round him, breathing softly, and he'd escape his anxieties and wonder at Flick's manifest love, and think: "Why am I so lucky?"

This was their life. First 2 years sorting themselves out, next 9 crisscrossing the seas, doing a little smuggling for old contacts of Flick's late dad – bit of illegal negTek material or chop-chop – but never hardArms. Andy had a loathing of weapons.

*

Then, in the late 2130s Andaman Marko and Flick Allenby called into Port Moselle, Noumea, to fix a couple of Andy's badSet bones.

The bone breaks happened after crashing thru a partikularly stormy traverse from Kalimantan to the Western Pacific, thru the Cloud, almost a month of heaving seas. Even with the gEnhancers, coupla times they broached – with a full roll – and were thrown about the boat cabin along with shattered cups, charts, sleeping bags and tools.

Flick was pretty exhausted too, and wanted downtime to re-visit the grand plan, to think, to sunbake, to eat good food.

Flick had looked at Andy's bruised body, the bashes along his side, the swollen hand which hadn't set properly, and the fresh scar on his cheek, where he'd crashed against the deck and the side of a davit had caught him. She'd said, "We need medikal attention, otherwise you'll have a dead hand and that's a risk."

"Deadhand Dick," he'd joked.

"Not funny. We'd have to stop."

Her skipper tone chastened him and he looked at the mis-shapen mess and nodded. Lifting the smashed hand, he tried to clench, but produced only a halfway witch's claw, and winced.

"You're right, sweetie. Can't get a grip – I'm even more of a liability than when I first met ya. Can't sail with this ole hand ... it's a dud."

She'd smiled and set course for Noumea.

As they walked up the hill to the Clinik Nouvelle Caledonie, Flick considered her own injuries.

She was a mess too. The black bruise across her back, al-most faded, the perpetually twanging rib which had cracked months ago. They were both somewhat malnourished as well and needed fresh food.

Flick thought: *This is f'cked. We punishing ourselves for what we did? Is this why we're here. Sailing thru storms? Smashing ourselves up in a rolling cage on top of the filthy ocean? Entirely selfDestruktive, it is.*

The road was steep and hot, but her thoughts distracted her from the discomfort. Neither did she notice the gorgeous bougainvilleas hanging down walls, and the blueness of the sky against the green range. She was lost in this uncharacteristic cloud of negativity, but didn't share these doubts with Andy because she knew he'd get upset and scrammy in the head. The Clinik was halfway to the top of the rise, a big white building with sickbeds and an emergency section. And proper docs. They entered the cool portico and asked for help.

The treatment took a couple of weeks, thanx to a doc who was descended from Melanesians and French settlers both. While puffing a small chopchop cheroot in his surgery, he'd examined them, lifting their shirts, looking at the yellow and black bruises and going "hrrrumph" and "merde!" He unwrapped the bandage from Andy's hand and wrist and gently felt the metacarpals and fingers and shook his head gloomily while Andy winced.

"What are you 2 doing?" the concerned Doc asked, echoing Flick's fears. "Making a mess of yourselves? Not good."

He also told them to eat properly.

"You are both undernourished, like skeletons," he exclaimed. "Hard tack, eh? *Pa' assez*. Not enough"

The exhausted pair returned next day and the Doc started a program to reset Andy's hand so that it wouldn't seize, and then skanned and fixed Flick's ribcage into a better alignment. Was all very basic doctoring, but it worked. He also fed them lunch – chicken cacciatore with white wine – and listened to their war stories.

So they stopped over for a while, worked on recovery and tried to relax and feedUp.

"It's a start, Flick and Andy!" the Doc declared.

Andy and Flick lived onboard the boat, moored beside the old Pacific port town of Noumea. The harbor and marina qways and seawalls were lifted 2 meters up the slope from the 19th century original to account for sea level rise. The forested spine of mountains sat above the town. The port had a narrow entrance, so it could be battened down with a mechanical barrage wall against really nasty weather, though mostly the 'phoons would generally come in from the east and the other side of the long island, the town sheltered from the worst. *The Kingdom* was berthed at one of the more rundown marinas with other similarly ramshackle boats and yachts.

Settling in a faraway port for a time was part of Flick's plan to help Andaman overcome his superstitions about his "curse" – his imagined adverse effect on all humanity. The lotus eating mostly worked. They befriended a few other boating people, and the harbour staff, and learnt a little French. Their neighbors, Tatiana – a French Polynesian woman – and Fred, her ginger haired husband, became qwite close, as Fred dithered away for months, plucking up his nerve to sail thru the Cloud and across to Hawaii, then the Canadian west coast. He had a hankering to become a commercial fisherman there.

Occasionally, 'phoons would blow over the ranges and the barrage wall battens at Port Moselle would be raised. The rain would bucket down and everyone would anticipate the blowOver. These times, the 2 couples would hole up in one or other of their boats and play cards or cook food and chat in their watertight cabins.

Tatiana had once worked for the legendary Cirque du Soleil as an aerialist, so on more balmy days, she and Flick would spend the evening practising silk trapeze and rope routines from lines dropped from one of Fred's halyards in the upper mast.

How to keep fit when you're not at sea and you're not pitting core strengths against the swells and currents? How to exercise when you decide to eat up big in a remote seaport with ample fruit, fish and wine?

Tatiana and Flick would shimmy high above the deck and swing and slide across the 2 flimsy-seeming cloth bolts, upside down more often than not, and doing what Andy thought were excruciating physical contortions, tho' the 2 women high above were rather pleasing to view from the safety of the deck. Andy could barely do a chin-up, but was a strong enough swimmer. So Andy and Fred would watch the show admiringly and drink beer and talk about strong currents and storm winds and how to avoid the qwixotic Cloud.

Fred was a diver, so some days they'd sail south on his yacht, *La Pirouette*, to check the health of inner reefs and lagoons, many of which were surprisingly colourful after 100 years of climatic punishment, repairing themselves, as reefs do, and building higher structures as the sea level rose. Other reefs were smashed beyond reason. Seemed random, but there probably was a scientific reason as to why one survived and others didn't.

*

The French had long gone from Nouvelle Caledonie, forced to abandon all their vanity colonies because of the cost. French vestiges remained tho: baguettes, caffe rather than kopi, flags, some of the old architecture, and it was still the official language.

Scores of refugee yachts scrounged for diesel and food and lay idle, moored off the various qways. *The Kingdom* was there for some months at an out of the way mooring, until Fred announced one nite, over drinks and dinner, that *La Pirouette* was on the move.

"Tomorrow or the next day. Wordz getting round that some lowBouys about 800 miles northeast have picked up an 8 knot current that is starting to crack north across the eqwator. It's a flux into the Northern Hemisphere, a chance," he said scooping beans into his mouth.

Flick's heart sank. She liked her neighbours. "So you're off?"

"As long as the flux continues."

Tatiana looked expectant, waiting for Fred to come up with a reason not to try, but he didn't.

"Let us know you get thru. Promise me," Flick said.

"Aye, skipper," said Fred, who thought it was funny the woman was the skipper. "We'll skip you a spark on your scope if we make it."

"Let's do that," said Tatiana, French lilt in her voice.

"I'd like that," said Flick. "I want to know you're safe."

*

Fred and Tatiana prepared qwick, provisioning their boat, and loading up diesel, just in case, hoping to cross the predicted lullPoint in the cloud with a current forcing the pace. Fred packed everything together and they sailed with a flotilla of other northbound boats taking the same chance, out the harbor and onward.

Flick watched the departing *La Pirouette*, a bashed about, steelhulled, wood decked vessel, its mainsail furled and the colourful yellow and red diesel cannisters lashed along the bow rails, and crossed her fingers for her circus sister. The harbor looked somewhat empty as one out of 3 yachts also made a break for the sudden conveyor belt current.

Andy and Flick decide to make a move too, but not to North America. They decided to sail back toward AuZ, slowly.

Weeks later, Fred and Tatiana send a spark on the scope: "Aloha!"

Being a "scope of interest", Centrl again tags this tiny received communication. Then there's silence for a very long time.

*

Out in the midPacific now, Andy and Flick would find cooler clean water around the oceanik reefs which continued to build up toward the rising ocean surface. The lagoons were full of tasty fish, and great to snorkel over, and Flick and Andy would sit on their small open deck when the weather was hot and still. Very few boats, either big or small, appeared.

Andy and Flick found downtime relaxing in such locations. And, as parttime smugglers – security. When the Cloud had moved north in winter, they anchored in calm, remote estuaries in the Kimberley, and when it moved south in summer, there were the old port towns in Kalimantan or island anchorages off the grid, almost forgotten by Centrl and other governments that would be grappling with more pressing emergencies such as damaged infrastructure, crop failure, and burgeoning unhappiness among subsistence farmers.

Yes, Andy and Flick were qwite forgotten – but not by Dr Madrigal Phipps.

PREROGATIVES OF THE ELDERS

You can get away with almost anything if you hold your tongue.
Das Glas Haus (2034) Ulli Kalk

WHILE the 4 abductees applied themselves to learn everything about the Stümmer language and the daily activity within the gorge Hermitory, they discovered a rhythm of life that was gentle, and also a little boring.

One day, after the evening meal and relaxation period, Leader of Women, who'd bunned her silver hair high on her head and had shadowed her soft hazel eyes with makeup, gestured to Todd to follow her

Come, she signed. *A word.*

He'd been surprized as he usually dealt with Leader of Men, but did as was bid. She was a Leader after all. She took his hand and guided him to her simple, but madly decorated, rooms filled with intricately carved and painted timber and beaded tapestry pictures.

Her hand was soft.

Two giant vases of dried desert flowers adorned a table, with some smaller fresh bouquets of honey scented red bottle-brush on a side bench. A window gave onto a small high balcony that protruded out into the gorge void. At the back of the qwarters, a bathroom, and a small adjacent study filled with real paper books. Not a big room, but a lot better than his cell, and with a spekky view out.

She sat him down on a soft lounge that looked over the gorge into the glittering lights of other qwarters and provided him with a tumbler of drink. She signed: *The male leader said you have been looking to the horizons ... it's not a good idea to think of walking from here. The few who tried to travel from here to a city ended up as bleached bones. And you and your friends are such fun – a breath of new air to our little township.*

Todd flicked a noncommittal hand signal, thanking her for the praise.

She added: *You understand – we have no idea why you were left on our beach? We are as perplexed as you. And we care for you.*

I realize this.

I understand your frustration, she signed. *You can sense the Cloud on the wind, as well. The season of thermocells is building. Not good time for a long walk in the desert.*

I agree.

She signed: *Til such time as the supplier comes, choose to be here, and to fit into our ways. You are welcome guests. And you may you learn what we can teach you. It's for only a few more months.*

The drink was warm on the tongue. Made his neck and cheeks flush. Very alcoholik, he thought, which was unusual fare in the colony. Weak fresh beer was usually about as good as it got. It was made almost every day by Leader of Kegs.

Leader of Women slid down beside him and put her hand on his knee, which surprized him. The familiarity was not usual from an older Stümmer, or from the elders of his own people either.

You have no partner? he asked, brazenly.

None to speak of, she signed back. *The protocols of the Qwietude allows anyone to be independent. And if so, love can be given freely. I'm Leader of both the women and the girlz, I wish it to be so, and I have gladly chosen this way of life.*

They sat as the breeze cooled a bit, hand back on his leg, further up his thigh. Leader of Women pressed against him gently and she smelled pleasant, of honeysoap. She removed her hand again and signed: *When the supply comes, we can ask them to take you ... tho we will plead that what you have understood about our privacy and the Qwietude will remain in your hearts and not be spoken of.*

Your secrets are safe with me, he promised.

For a moment, it looked like Leader of Women was assessing him with her hazel eyes, much like the younger women did. She smiled.

Secrets can be good. They define you.

Leader of Women smiled and again filled his glass. They drank in silence looking out over the gorge. Then Todd felt the Leader's hand move further up his leg with a featherlight touch, and she leant toward him and the honeysoap wafted strongly. Her X-shirt sleeve was sliding down her arm. She looked rather beautiful, and had a graceful tilt of the head. There was a smile on her full lips.

While he and Bangle had sexed enthusiastically at different times over the past few weeks without a jot of guilt, he felt qwite weird about this direct approach from Leader of Women. He was 17, she was probably older than his mother tho he found it hard to tell with adults sometimes.

Her fingers and thumb caressed his upper thigh and the edge of his genitals, and then she ran her finger along the underside of his penis, exciting him, but he shuffled back awkwardly and signed: *And what ways are these, that we are fitting into?*

She smiled, but he wasn't sure he trusted the smile. The edges of her eyes crinkled.

The sensual joys of privacy, she replied. *Privacy and respect. You have already sexed with some of my younger charges with my blessing, and now ... you may account to me.*

Todd felt uncomfortable in committing to the situation, tho' physically he was certainly ready and aching for sex as she kissed him full on the lips. He kissed back. It wasn't difficult. He wrapped his arm around her and they kissed for a long time. He now felt obliged and they moved on to her soft and large bed.

He didn't know what else to do and as the Leader of Women's X-shirt fell away, he saw she was qwite voluptuous. In the dim light, skin felt like skin and tongues certainly felt like tongues, and the Leader of Women was xtremely vigorous in her responses, but still, abiding by her beliefs, made not a sound as they moved together and she climaxed. Before the second round she signed: *slower now, take your time, as much time as you can ...* which made him feel rather like her pupil.

Mebbe Leader of Women wasn't so old, he thought, as they lay side by side in the semi dark and she sparked another bout of sexing, by sliding across, nuzzling his ear and neck with her tongue. She was so very energetik.

A couple of hours later, having been taught several exciting new techniqwes, he was lying back, feeling a little odd. She however sat up straight, naked in the bed, hair in a mess but with an expression of bliss. They shared another glass of the electrik liqueur, but as she stroked his cheek with her fingers, he just wanted to go.

He hoped he would not be called on to *account to her* again. Walking back from Leader of Women's qwarters, after a respectful goodnite, and after a long shower, he swore not to tell his friends.

*

During the wakeful nite, he thought about what just happened.

Was it a trial to test for membership of the colony? A sex ceremony? He was sure that if it was, he'd passed.

Or did Leader of Women just get all horny sometimes, like some of the other girlz he'd been with. Come to think of it, like him! What was this *account to me* business? Then Todd was suddenly worried that Lissa may have to face the same accounting with Leader of Men.

No, he thought. He understood that once couples were declared, like Narmon and Lissa, the bond was sacrosanct for Stümmers and nonStümmers alike. But then the niggly worry reemerged, so next morning, he broke his oath to himself and privately warned Lissa.

"These Stümmers are truly weird," he began, as the 2 friends found a private moment. And he related a little of what had happened. Lissa's eyes widened on the recounting and she began to look xtremely worried. "No," she said, "Leader of Men hasn't asked me."

"Mebbe as you and Narmon are regarded as pledjd."

She nodded. "That might be ... or else he's not interested, or is partnered, while she's just a hornified old woman, and you have no one declared."

He wasn't sure about the "hornified old woman" tag, and again felt embarassed.

"That might be," he said. "We don't know the rules. Partners may not count. It may be a sexing free for all here." He thought of Bangle and Little Weaver in his room a few weeks back. "What did they call it in the Golden Ages? Orgy? I'd better warn Peet'n'Narmon too."

"I just hope I don't get summonsed by Leader of Men."

"I'm sure you can say no."

"Mebbe you should be more doting toward Bangles. She really likes you," she added.

"I don't want a commitment here." he said fiercely. "Bangles and I agreed to just have fun. I want to leave. It's easy for you and Narmon."

Lissa rolled her eyes. "Ironically ..." she started saying, and as a couple of young Stümmers approached, she finished by signing: *it's difficult for us to find any personal privacy to do anything fun.*

*

What Todd had not known, was that Lissa had decided that her qwickest way to freedom, and thereby to her worried mum, and her exam finals, was thru the Qwartermaster, Pepperbeard. Somehow he could contact the outside world possibly a hidden satScope of some sort.

Pepperbeard's family was dead, and he was a lofty presence at the collective dinner and the gatherings afterward. Often sitting apart from the broader group, but an enthusiastic listener to the music.

Much of the rest of the time he was deep in sign conversation – bent inward, in what was known as the "body cone" where 2, 3 or more of the older community members, mostly Qwietude leaders signed while facing one another, shielding their conversations from the crowd with their backs. Deciding things.

The Qwartermaster was always at it – body coning often with the Leader of Women, the Medikal Examiner, the Leader of Gardens and other important Qwietude figures.

Lissa one day signed to him: *what do you like best about the music?*

And he replied: *everyone's shining eyes.*

It was an interesting response. He added: *I know most of the crowd here like it gentle, but I remember a time listening to faster beat music, and it was good too.*

Lissa felt she had made a connection and sometimes smiled at him when they passed.

She wondered that if she seduced him – like Leader of Women had seduced Todd – he might communicate her plight to the outside world. She didn't want to hurt Narmon, but she did desperately want to go home to her mum, who she was very worried about, and her life. But at some level, the Qwatermaster gave her the creeps and she knew she couldn't do it.

At lunch and dinner, as community members sat, it was often at random around the bench seats. One day, she sat beside the Qwartermaster and asked him outright if she could make an order for cloth.

I thought you would be leaving with the supply next year, he signed with a surprized look on his face.

If I leave, and don't use the material, Bangle and Curl may use it, she said.

Qwietude would not approve, he signed with a stern look. *Special orders are personal.*

Can I order from a partikular supplier?

Perhaps. We have special suppliers who usually provide material. They may be able to procure what you want.

How is it done, this ordering? she asked with an innocent look on her face.

Only I am allowed to know. Qwartermaster to qwartermaster, we are vested with the knowledge.

It's not thru mindreading, then, she joked.

He signed: *Won't discuss further.*

Lissa pouted her lips, altho felt pretty crappy at doing so, but she was desperate. He wasn't to be moved and spent the rest of the meal signing and signaling the difficulties in playing the clarinet and whether homemade reeds were as good as the commercial ones that she was used to playing. There was no doubt that Pepperbeard was a music fan. She unlatched her clarinet case and showed him how, in fact, their homemade reeds were really very good.

Lissa started to feel the older man was just friendly and harmless, and the younger girlz she mingled with told her it was known he'd suffered when his wife died, but he had never made advances to any of them. She failed to notice tho', that the older women and many of the older men left him to sit alone often, except for the body coning sessions.

Like everyone in the community, Lissa served shifts in the kitchen as a hand. Twenty-one meals a week for the larger community was a collective effort. Almost everyone attended dinner. Sometimes, families would have "occasions" separately, but most times the refectory was full of hungry bodds.

Sometimes she was sent to the supply store for spices, oils or other ingredients. The Qwartermaster and his team not only ordered ingredients in the yearly delivery, but also dried and preserved garden produce grown at the community that were kept in sealed jars on his storeroom shelves.

Leader of Kitchens sent her one morning to the stores, a series of sheds and even high scaffolded shelves built into the deep cave in the rock wall of the gorge, just a little down from the buildings and dormitories for the singles. The Qwartermaster was on his own, sorting things on a high shelf.

She rang the tinkleBell that sat on a cabinet counter to attract his attention and he smiled at her, and waved, descending rapidly as if he lived his life like a spider moving across and among the high shelves and cabinets. Ladders were his natural place, it seemed.

I am after more turmeric. Where is everyone?

They start later, he signed shifting the ladder along a high level rail contraption and ascending to the herbs and spices vault.

I would ask you to work for me, but I know you'll probably leave in March. I could steal you from Leader of Books, he joked. *I need extra help, often.*

She wished that it could be so, and she could thus find out further information about how the Qwartermaster communicated, but instead she smiled her sunniest smile and extended her hand for the packet of spice. She regarded his face, with the slightly bent nose, and his strong hands from manipulating things all the time.

We have thousands of items stored here, from paperclips and inks, cloth – as you know – mediks' remedies, tools and foodstuffs. All ordered into categories. He waved one of his hands toward the high rock ceiling of the gorge cavity.

And where are the carrier pigeons to send the orders? she asked with a cheeky smile.

He looked darkly at her for a minute, then tilted his head and rubbed his beard. *Nice try,* he signed.

And they laughed.

*

The Qwartermaster came for Lissa the middle of the following nite.

When she failed to arrive in the library for work, the Leader of Books found Todd. The Leader seemed miffed and said Lissa wasn't at her post and complained that she was clearly bored with his domain already. So Todd went looking for her, and found Lissa in her cellRoom, a mess. She'd tried to get ready for the books, but couldn't conceal the red marks over her arm and shoulder, or the agony in her eyes and mouth.

"What happened?" Todd stammered.

Lissa shook her head. She was trembling and traumatized. "Let's just go from this place," she finally said.

"Who did this?"

She shook her head.

"Was it one of our group? One of the Stümmer lads?"

"No, no, they're so gentle ... was my fault. I flirted ..."

"Flirted? We've *all* been flirting. Flirts don't end up hurt. Flirting's for fun. But, you've been ... you've been beaten up!"

"Worse ..." she choked out. All Todd could do was sit with her for a while while she cried. Then he went to Leader of Books and said she was ill and wouldn't be turning up that day.

Feeling sick to his stomach, he returned to Lissa and tried to talk with her a couple more times that day, but Lissa wouldn't say anything 'bout what happened. Just lay listless on her cot, claiming no bones were broke and that she'd feel better soon.

When she emerged the following day, she'd applied makeup and sunJell to hide the marks, and didn't say anything at all to Narmon.

Lissa's trauma made Todd feel even weirder about his strange evening with the Leader of Women, but he dismissed his own wave of revulsion and concentrated on helping his friend. They were the same age. Not so innocent, but not so worldly either. She had been hurt by whatever the unnamed man had done to her, but she refused to speak about it.

He guessed her attacker had tried to force sex upon her, which made him furious. The bruises on her shoulder, and the ones starting to show on her throat. Her throat! He realized with a horror they couldn't report the brutality to Leader of Women, because she was clearly in on the plot to use younger people for sex.

It stank, Todd decided. Stank high. There was somethink very dead about the Stümmers estrangement from the world, and now he could smell the odour. Was time to go.

*

Next morning, he called to see how she was feeling.

Not knowing how to directly help the suffering Lissa, he promised her that as soon as she wanted, as soon as she felt able, they would leave. They sat for a while. He tried to comfort her with happy wordz, but she couldn't stop crying.

"Todd," she said, voice tense, "I don't want to ask. Can you ask Bangle for an abortant? A morning after pill."

He was aghast. "You mean, you've been ... some man has actually ...?"

"Don't want to talk about it," she replied in a surly tone. "Just, can you ask Bangle or Curl?"

The reqwest meant that Lissa had been violated in the worst way. "Have you told Narmon?"

"Course not! I can't tell Narmon," she said, angrier still. Todd, young and sheltered, was not at all experienced with a traumatized person, but he had some common sense and decided if Liss didn't want to talk about it, he wasn't going to force a long conversation. But he still had to avenge her, if he could.

So he promised to get the medikation if she would name her attacker. Just one word. She refused, her glaring eyes finally giving him the message. Somewhile later he asked Curl for the medik anyway, without explaining why.

After he delivered the pills to Lissa, he fetched her some water, and she cried as she drank, as if drinking brought the horror back. She looked small and miserable, shrinking into her bed.

"What can I do to help you?" Todd asked.

"Just get me away from this place," was all she said.

A daylong rage overtook Todd.

Since the abduction, he'd felt utterly responsible for the fate of his 3 friends. There was some reason they'd been snatched too. Now, a man had beaten up Lissa and sexed with her violently. She was always the first to talk, usually. The first to joke, and make a comment about anything. She used to be yakity. Now she was as silent as a Stümmer, and miserable.

He went to his room to try and contain his anger. Todd wanted to kill all the older men. Violent visions of slaughtered Stümmer elders floated before him. They were all complicit as far as he was concerned. He just wanted to kill them.

Lying on bed, he looked up at the gloomy gray ceiling of his cell and it seemed to drip with blood.

The Purity mantras of nonViolence he'd done in school with Miss Compton, and Mr Wang, and other teachers over the years, about never harming a human being, and the sanctity of life and the virtues of human existence, all fizzled to nil as he felt his imaginary hand wrap itself round an imaginary spear or knife and sink the point into Lissa's tormentor's guts: Leader of Men, Leader of Farms and Gardens, Qwartermaster, even Clarinet boy ... all imagined dead in front of him, bleeding out like kangaroos.

He had to get away, to put such ugly violent thoughts behind him. Lissa's reqwest to escape would be met.

The following morning he woke at 3am. In the dark, he again ascended the westerly gorge wall with a tiny glow at his feet to illuminate footholds. He moved loose and lithe, like the trained up hunter he was.

The stars to the south sparkled. To the north they dissipated in an upper atmosphere mist, formed by the Cloud's jet-streams.

Narmon and Lissa weren't with him this time. Along the ridgeline, as dawn started glimmering, it was as if a black blanket heaved up before him, rising in lines and pinpoints of light: muted mauves and browns, the country sharpening its colour and pattern. He started to make out details in the craggy, dune scattered desert, its ravines and gullies, and many kliks away a long, flat mountain range on the horizon, light picking out the thin purple line of elevation, vanishing into the northwest.

The range was at least 3, possibly more, days walk across a difficult, raddled landscape. And then after that ... how long?

Behind the very distant range he saw high clouds, burnished in pink and red. He turned 180 degrees and could see more clouds gathering high to the east in the soft morning sky. He breathed in and out gently and tried to feel the air.

Where was he? Further east from his own people's country, that was for sure. Was desert overlapping desert out here, as remote as it could be.

Todd closed his eyes and listened and could just hear the ripples of distant booms, soft on his face and in his eardrums, way north where the Cloud, the huge summer weather event, was roiling from the stratosphere to the ocean, sucking violence down from jetstreams above the overheated planet. Still far away, but its merciless front was moving on its slow summer trajectory south.

He felt its turbulence lightly on his eyelids. He thought he could smell the rain over the northern horizon, and mebbe he could. Water that smelled like wet earth and old batteries. Soon the Cloud would arrive and it would bucket down. How much? How long? Soon ...

His mind turned to the ceremony songs taught by Elders in the East Kimberley. He wasn't thru all the initiation rituals and wasn't sure whether he would get back there, but Grandma Netta had taken him most years when he was a kid, and from the age of 7, when his mother got back from her AuzGov job, thru to the age of 12, he'd hunted and camped with the men, for a few weeks each year at least. Again at 14. He'd done it with his cuzz, Jaim'z, and the others.

The male Elders had been seriously hardAssed about the rules of survival and their traditions. In fact, they sometimes seemed qwite brutal to the boyz when they were out in the desert doing ceremony, being taught big lessons of life and death. AuZGov laws said scarring with razor sharp stone blades, and other secret disfigurements, were no longer allowed – the Age of Purity had seen to that. Todd, along with his mob, thought it sucked. Tattoos only, now, and tho' some Elders and boyz disregarded the law, he'd asked for tattoos. His mum had qwietly pleaded with him to do so, but he didn't tell the Elders that.

There weren't enough marks on his body to show full initiation and he knew that. But he knew some of his songs, so he recalled, line by line, the songs, running them backward and forward in language in his mind. First he sang aloud to the local spirits in the gorge, assuring them of his peaceful intentions and that he was just passing thru. Then he started singing other songs, qwietly, ancient patterns and wordz to soothe the spirits, patterns that mapped out ancient tracks.

He sang all the dreaming songs he knew, thru the permutations that he'd been taught, tho so much of lore belonged to Elders, he sang what he could. Those tracks joined wider networks. Todd tried to vague it all into a map in his head: the southernmost part of the range, past the badlands where no one could live, past the cavern country where the serpent had thrashed sideways and created a maze of gorges, and from where a river spewed in the wet season. That was what he could conjure, but was it about the country that lay before him?

Hell, he'd turned 17 only 5 months ago. His bushskills, such as they were, remained diluted by his contemporary, cosseted life. He was also the most well off kid in West Oz.

You're not stupid, he told himself, but his lived experience, compared to many of own West Cap family, or the local TrOWs, was *way* different. They celebrated their culture by living in it fully on Country. Had been the way since white man came almost 350 years back. He admired his skinKin for that.

Only the annual holidays bolstered his Indijj identity, and it was enough to understand his origins and the most ancient of cultures to which he belonged. He was an intermittent attendee, tho' he loved it because Country was his heart and his skin. He knew where he fitted, and what knowledge he had gave purpose and courage.

Todd stood and looked again at the southern part of the range as it further lightened. He could feel eyes watching him from the gorge wall behind, as well.

Let Lissa recover a bit, then we're out of here, he thought.

MRS SOONG

This insidious Kalk movement, the so-called Stümmers, have crashed the Australian Aspiration Index. The Government should place more attention to the undue influence of this hidden mystic, whose global writings have created a ludicrous anti-social effect. Shares in all the major social media platforms are now on the seabed. Beneath the seabed. No-one talks on publik domains on the Virtual any more. The revered Government inspired Person2Person linkage network, AusNeighbourhoodKonnekt (ANK), has gone into receivership. Imagine this happening only a year ago?

I know this is a free society which celebrates free speech, but families are now refusing useful information for the AuZtralian Government because of Ulli Kalk's baleful example, her pro-privacy stance. We are losing touch with our people and their needs. Kalk is a publik menace. Thus the Opposition will support the Social Data Supplement Bill to strengthen information gathering from those other sources outlined in the attached regulations.

Shadow Attorney-General. *Hansard*, Australian House of Representatives, May 2038

BEN Jexen admired his own muscled jaw, sculpted shoulders and knotted biceps almost as much as he loved his wife Cinzia's svelte body. He'd catch sight of himself in the gymnasium shower room mirrors and stop and gawp. He knew it shouldn't be thus – in his late seventies. Was amazing what money could buy.

This day he'd been "snubbed" (a private joke) by Cinzia who was away examining newly constructed pressureTest sites along the coast. The big wave-driven plates worked where tidal power was coming good again, but so far enjjTek reports from her were gloomy. The erratic swells from the Southern Ocean were playing havoc with the various tidal test platforms, and the power generation was patchy, with platforms being damaged constantly. They persisted tho, because xtreme innovation was how you might survive the future.

Cinzia wasn't beside him that lunch, so he'd canceled their Lull session of yoga with their trainer, and instead went to the gym. Now he was qwickly showering in time to take a call from the head of the White Lady Syndicate who were long term Heg partners of Phipps Industries.

"Being Mrs Soong and all that," his assistant Hal said when he hauled him off the rowing machine.

Jexen went "yeah yeah", but knew that while Madrigal was distracted, her direct deputies needed to lift their game while she hunted for her boy, the Phipps Industries heir; if Todd was still alive, that is. The abduction happened 4 months back, and Jexen had his doubts.

Mrs Soong was not a personal fan of Madrigal Phipps, who had once embarrassed her late husband Mr Wu, in a confrontation in China many years ago, but Mrs Soong loved Phipps Industries and everything their interCompany calibration brought: money, power, and most importantly for Mrs Soong, domination of the Chinese Government.

Lu Soong was a genuine HegBoss, same as Madrigal Phipps, but not the direct chair. While some klone Chair held the Mantle of the White Lady Syndicate, Mrs Soong ran the show, much the same arrangement when Mr Wu lived.

Mrs Soong also loved Old Man Phipps who had relentlessly courted both her and Mr Wu when he was alive. Mrs Soong also liked Ben Jexen because he knew so much, and was happy to give out free advice, sometimes even sending technical experts gratis on energy networking which had assisted her business in the past.

She appeared on Jexen's giant scope screen at the specified time, and he heard Mrs Soong's American purr as she said: "Hello, Ben Jexen."

"*Ni hao*, Lulu," he replied, using the nickname her husband and close confidants used.

Madrigal Phipps always called her Mrs Soong.

Mrs Soong was relaxed, sitting comfortably in a big cane chair. She wore a stunning pink silk jacket, her long jet hair looped in a bun. She was younger than her late husband and much cannier. What had bound their long marriage was a combined spirit of ruthlessness and they'd been a formidable match. She, the strategist, while Wu had carried out the dirty work. Their White Lady Syndicate which had carved out south Chinese water concessions from very early on, was still thriving.

Ben Jexen knew that as a girl, Mrs Soong had been educated and lived for a time in the United States and radiated a relik of a certain mid-21st century ChineseAmerican charm that had largely disappeared during the great American collapse.

Jexen and Mrs Soong spoke of their mutual business concerns. Phipps produced power and network technology, while the White Lady, thru subsidiary companies, networked the precious commodity to retail energy Lodes all over east Asia right thru the Russian edge. White Lady also controlled even more water than in the beginning, which was their big commercial stick over the ChinaGov, and data. They were moving into more primary energy production as well, with gammaLodes.

"Tell me, Lulu" said Jexen, halfway thru the discussion, which was very general and nonSecret and therefore on a mildly scrambled intercontinental scope feed, "why have the Jap/Tais asked for more Bellingslodes. Have you had a similar reqwest? We'd have to provide the extra lodes thru you anyway, up the China Sea glassHighway."

"No, Jex," said a bemused Mrs Soong, "I don't know about any JapTai Nexus reqwest."

"Can you guess why they need extra power?"

"Might be reconfig. Due to the Kyoto Bell, mebbe?" she said in her old-fashioned American purr.

"What's that?"

"It's the light dome protecting greater Kyoto. A full light dome. You're a rich man. Don't tell me you're not tempted to go live there? I am!"

"Sorry – why's it so special?" Ben suddenly felt conspicuously ignorant.

"Ahh!" she said, in a smiling, mischievous, lip-flickering way, ready to dish the dirt. "There are many plutocrats who desire an old Holocene qwality climate, warm and mild. A happy land, so to speak, where there're 4 seasons, and you can grow cherry trees and tulips. When you organize yourselves a big, hard, light shield, you don't need storm bunkers.

"So, the Japanese, as you know, declared Kyoto protected many, many years ago, in keeping with its inherent beauty, and ancient gardens and temple buildings. The original deal was with the USA, during the great war of the 20th century, to protect the city from bombing raids. Over the time since, the myth of protection has grown. The Kyoto people have strengthened the city's climate defences to the point where there is an umbrella of hard light keeping out cat 5, 6, 7 storms and the tubes and driving rain. When half powered, it bounces much heat also. This means they have a rare Holocene climate underneath. Powering such a large dome is causing big generation costs."

"Can't be more expensive than many of the other light domes – like London central and New York City?"

"No, no, Ben. You don't get it. It's much bigger. And whatz happening is the weather is deteriorating down in the Sea of Japan. Much worse lately. Much wetter. More 'phoons hitting the eastern edge."

"Ah, I see. It's a powerUp eqwation."

"Yes. To strengthen the dome – or as they call it, the Bell – needs more and more power. 'Phoons all along, all along the coast of Japan," agreed Mrs Soong enthusiastically. "And the Bell covers a much greater area – an entire prefecture – than your light dome examples of central Manhattan and London city centre, with old Big Ben. They are not eqwivalents.

"I am lucky," continued Mrs Soong, "to live up beyond Three Gorge Dam City which is qwite protected from the ugliest weather, for some reason. Dear ladyluck, you know, has always been good to me, with my life, my late husband, Mr Wu." She paused as if thanking the gods. "So, Jex, your old boss, Mr Phipps, lives in Kyoto with the many other rich old HegBosses. Under gentle rain and with cherry blossoms in spring. Ah, it's beautiful there. You stroll outside and can wear the old clothes – silk, cotton, not tefLite – and take tea in the garden from Geisha girlz."

"So, they reqwire exponential lodes to harden their photon dome?"

"The Bell," said Mrs Soong. "As I say, they call it the Bell. And yes, as other parts of Japan start to brownDown because of the indulgence of Kyoto, I think they would need more power."

*

Later, Jexen said to Madrigal: "I've checked, and there are so many exGovernment grandees, and HegBosses, dwelling in Kyoto, that over the years they have demanded lode allowances be rerouted from other parts of Honshu and Kyushu into powering their Kyoto Bell. Apparently, it's turning into a skandal and there is great unease within the new Government that the brownDowns will do them political damage. They are not a Traditionalist Government. They're actually called the Face the Future Democratic Party."

They were high in the corporate offices downtown – the small boardroom. Was just her, Jexen, and Suze Shelbo taking notes.

Jexen, faceOnface with his boss, was relating the last string of bizz matters, but he also wanted to discuss the peculiar reqwest from Old Man Phipps.

Madrigal nodded. "Saw that Kyoto info. Shelbo here pulled up all the files on it, which weren't many. Seems like a small internecine fight between very powerful people: the new Jap/Tai PM and some of the Heg Mantles in Japan who are tradionalists. The fight isn't being hyped, but they've had a couple of serious brownDowns in Tokyo Central."

"They were trying to circulate the pain in more regional areas which are used to brownDowns," Suze Shelbo added. "Decisions were covered by secret legislation. Then, middle of last year, Tokyo suddenly went brown for a couple of days and people started to ask 'what's going on?' Was part of the reason the old Government was thrown out."

"From memory, they lost badly."

"Yizz, they did. The Face the Future Democratic Party have a strong majority in the Japanese Diet."

"Ha. Well," said Madrigal, "we can supply the Bellingslodes if they want the power, but it needs to be aboveboard and paid for. Ridiculous situation tho'. Those old exMantles, including Dad, demanding a 20th century atmosphere."

"They say it's in the name of Japanese tradition," Suze Shelbo said. "The life cycle of the trees have to be maintained. There are gardens over 1000 years old in Kyoto."

"It's a religious thing, isn't it?" said Jexen. "The cherry blossom trees."

"So are ceremonies for my mob," said Madrigal, "and many ceremony sites are no-go zones up in the north, or washed out. My mob have no recourse to supercharged bells to protect their sacred places." She looked angry.

"Kyoto sounds like a good place to retire, then," Jexen snorted.

Madrigal stared at the richly burnished huon table that her father had bought when he founded the company.

"Do you think this has anything to do with Todd?"

"Can't imagine how?" Jexen said. "Just a weird reqwest from East Asia via the Old Man. I mean, he'd never do anything to harm his grandson."

She sighed. They'd achieved so much and, at every step, her boy seemed to get further and further away. "Todd's a beautiful kid, you know? I've never met anyone else like him. I can't stop thinking about whether he is hurt, or even dead. Sometimes, when we're talking about power outages, Japanese politics, or f'cking cherry trees, or the whims of my stupid dad, I'm just overwhelmed. By Todd."

Suze walked over and crouched beside Madrigal's seat at the end of the big board table. She put her arm round Madrigal's shoulder.

"Todd is remarkable. And he'll be looking for us too. Doing his best. We'll find him."

Madrigal nodded like she didn't believe anybody anymore.

SNAKEFALL

The broad spectrum of intrusion: listening posts, data-laundries and google-routes, all the way through to the nuts and bolts of our bank expenditures and tax return. All has led to our smotheration. There's nowhere to be nowhere.
Das Glas Haus (2034) Ulli Kalk

HIGH sun. Wedge-tail eagles, and kites of many types gyre above in lazy circles.

Scrambling over sharp ground layered with sections of ankle twisting soft thick sand. Hostile land. This silent enemy will abrade and lacerate, burn, and swallow you whole in its hot maw.

Todd, Lissa, Narmon look up and out. The city kidz fearful, smacked by the heat as they struggle on. Todd thinks he can do it, but worries his friends will flag. This is epik, they know it, and the look in his friends' faces perturbs him. Even Lissa, the determined one.

Rough cut red gullies, brown washed gritty soil, red rocks and small bright birds, nyi nyi or zebra finches, holing up in lowset bushes. They seem to be streaming south in large flocks away from the seasonal turmoil.

There's the continuous hot breath of the monsoons, The Cloud to the north, always to the north, breezing lightly but breezing their way. They had started very early, 3.30am when it was nite still, and the stratosphere, the high ceiling of the planet, was flickering with tongues of lightning, like a faulty roofGlobe. 100ks, 200ks away?

The terrain is difficult, thinks Todd. Little glows heel at their feet like dogs, illuminating progress until the sky greyed and then yellowed. But walking thru the dark is slow. Occasionally a west bending gully allowed them to speed up, but the gullies fizzle out, or turn sharply, like the snake's coils, and you have to scramble over the higher ground and find a better, less ankle twisting path.

As the sky brightens in the preDawn, the desert badlands look menacing, dirty, putting them in mind of skulls and bones embedded in gully walls. A mad scramble up, often means lowering and sliding again into another dry watercourse, some braided qwite deep thru the sand, and then the hard task of climbing the opposite crumbly side, sometimes on hands and knees.

The sun powers up and its relentless energy pours into the already moist air and the heat intensifies. Progress. Sweat. Exhaustion by lunchtime and the gorge walls are still in plain sight. Creating a long distance from the misbegotten home of the Stümmers is essential. Imperative. As far from the community as possible. Slipped into the shade of a deep trench. Mouths are dry, but sticky all the same.

Other terrain encountered is even tougher to traverse: dunes, some washed and flattened to flat pan shapes. They are erratic in steepness and shape, some sculpted like they'd been smoothed upward by a giant palette knife, others just a dry bed of hard-to-walk-over rubble. As the sun rose the 3 kidz had closed the glows to power them for the next nite.

This is a landscape that over the past 150 years has changed. A once flat, gold flecked desert, covered with tussocky grasses in a good season, has eroded into badlands, incurzed by large intermittent water flows, as the volume of moisture from the north increased and the rains came flooding down. Some flatter parts still sported vegetation, but otherwise deep erosion lacerated the landscape. Old Aboriginal songs, the lore that braided its way thru country, all predated these changes, and Todd was well aware that what the songs told him was not quite the same. Waterholes had changed, lakes were different.

His instinctive heading for the low range was as much one of survival – getting to higher ground before the weather turned – as it was to get them as far from the Stümmers gorge as possible.

*

10am. Calves and feet started to protest, burning in their boots. X-shirts and neck-scarves were sopping with sweat. The boots, which they'd been wearing when snatched, were never made for such challenges and felt flimsy, only made from teflite, cotton and nylo. Todd hoped the boots'd survive for at least 2 weeks or so til they hit the coast, but he feared this hope was optimistic. Hair dripped ...

All 3 wore wide sunhats and coalDark eyeShades. They'd smeared their shoes, clothes, hats, shirts, pants and arms in dirty red mud at the waterway entrance to the gorge, to camouflage them in the landscape. Now with the heat, the surface of the clothes were cracking like the land.

The 3 carried backpacks with plenty of heavy-as-crap water, stolen plastic blurts of reflective sunJell, and food, accumulated on the qwiet for 3 or 4 days. Lissa, redHead that she was, had almost white, pearly skin, and was terrified of the sun, but much much more terrified of Pepperbeard. At the beginning, before the sun started to rise she was the most enthusiastic of the scramblers, surging ahead until Todd told her to pace herself.

Todd had said: "Normally, we'd break during the heat of the day, but we've got to put kliks between them and us. We'd be almost safe in this maze of ravines, but, have to make headway. No break. It'll be hot. Drink sips. But don't drink all your water … there's enough moisture about …"

Narmon was still dubious about the venture, but Lissa couldn't wait to get going and he wasn't going to stay without her.

Todd was persuasive: "They have no vehicles. They'd have to pursue us by foot too. We can outrun them. And they have no way, except direct vision, of detecting us, so we should keep low. They don't know our route. And I'm dead sure they can't track."

Narmon agreed. He just didn't think the 3 of them'd have the stamina, but wasn't going to let his steadyGirl and best friend take the plunge and escape. Still, he didn't understand the reasons behind Todd and Lissa's powerful urge to run, now. Todd was noncommittal. Lissa was strangely distant, when usually she was an affectionate person who was always looking to him for a hand or a hug.

As the heat built, the day became more xtreme, physically and in their heads as well. The gullies zigzagged and Todd tried to guide the small, determined Lissa and her steadyBoy, Narmon, west, aiming each footfall at the head of the adjacent range. The heat drew all their energy til by 1 in the afternoon they were plodding very slowly. Todd called for a qwick break in the shade of a gully wall, and clambered to the top to skan the horizon. The purple range didn't look much closer, but the tip of the Stümmer's gorge was now some distance behind. They sat side by side in the slim shade patch and swallowed some water and chewed honeybars.

"What do you expect to find at the south-tip of the range?" Narmon finally asked.

"Water," said Todd. "The song says there should be a lagoon there. And where there's water there's often human contact and better tracks. This country we're going thru is f'ked up. But if we get to a pool there's the chance of more proper tucker. We need to keep going when the sun goes down. For a while anyway. We can follow the stars tonite. And it'll be cooler."

They pressed on thru the afternoon. Every so often Narmon would collapse for a while looking exhausted, but after a few minutes crawl on his hands and feet, he would stand and lurch forward. Todd saw Lissa weeping and walking at the same time, face braced against the heat.

He halted progress again, til it cooled down somewhat.

*

Clouds were still to manifest and, in the dark, Todd followed the stars, making out the Canoe constellation with the fisherman's hand and speartip pointing the way West, til he felt utterly ragged. Rather than dead reckoning, he'd clokked the constellations that coincided with the position of the range the previous nite, in partikular the Canoe, which he'd once been taught by saltwater Elders, all climate refugees from the Torres Straits living in Perth. The Canoe was inhabited by a fisherman spirit, the so-called Southern Cross above representing a fishing spear.

Feet blistered, tired beyond measure. Narmon and Lissa felt just as fried. They'd been walking for almost 20 hours on and off. The 3 friends huddled together under a cluster of tors, not because it was cold and they needed heat, but just for human contact. They stank, and this caused personal disqwiet, as they were scrupulously clean and scented most of the time, but the disqwiet was overcome by exhaustion. Each used their bag as a pillow. Heads together, Todd said: "We'll have to move before first light."

"I'm amazed we haven't seen a drone," Lissa added.

"No. No," Narmon chipped in enthusiastically. "It's obvious the Stümmers are technofobes. Not inclined to spy devices like that – drones eqwal surveillance which they were against. But HighEyes could see us if they were looking. Which they're not."

"So you reckon we got away?" asked Lissa in a tired, small voice.

"Mebbe. The older men may send out search parties," Todd said. "They must know the basic layout of surrounding country, surely? They hunt around the gorge. Wouldn't you know your neighbourhood? I do. But it's very harsh country, hey? They sqwirreled themselves away to somewhere almost inaccessible, 'cept by air."

Narmon grunted.

"We should get some sleep," said Todd, "'nother day like today, tomorrow."

"Hey," said Narmon.

"What?"

"So good to be talking out loud?"

*

Back at the Hermitory, Peet was urgently summonsed to the meeting room. Leader of Women and Leader of Men were gesturing wildly at each other and turned when Peet entered. Leader of Men was usually a languid fellow, but now he was wild, hyperanimated. His eyes swiveled in their sockets and seemed to pop thru his round glasses. Peet had never seen anyone so upset.

Where are they? Leader of Men gesticulated at Peet. *Have they run off into the desert?*

The young muzo shrugged. Peet was unsurprized they'd gone, but amazed how qwickly they'd decided. Couple of days ago, Todd had confided, as they huddled in his little room, that the escape was on, and also warned sternly of the salacious sexing behaviours of the Stümmer leaders. Peet promised not to betray their plans, being best friends since way back when. He also promised not to give in to any adult Stümmers wanting to sex, tho he'd pointed out he was now with Curl, that he'd moved in with Curl's family and sexing with anyone else was a noWay proposition.

Todd had nodded like an adult and said, "Fair 'nuff, bruzz," satisfied Peet was safe.

Now, Leader of Men appeared to emanate genuine concern. Peet watched the Leader's fingers carefully, and treated his crossexam cautiously. Peet knew he was safe, and that he'd done nothink wrong within the rules of the Qwietude. Reporting behaviours of others was frowned upon and seen as surveillance and therefore he could keep his friends' plans to himself.

Leader of Men walked to Peet and signed close at his face: *You must know where they went. You were their friend. They must have confided.*

In fact, Peet had been clear with Todd: he didn't want to go, and he didn't want to know. But he understood their hurry. Parents, the real life back home, school and uni.

I understood why they went, but not where. I didn't want to know, Peet signed.

Leader of Men walked away and flickered the signs for: *They'd have gone west. That's where the boy was gazing ...*

Leader of Men turned back to Peet. *Why didn't you go with them?*

I had no reason to leave. I have my Curl.

Leader of Men nodded. He understood the young man's admirable loyalty to Curl. The Leaders had been trying most hard to pair up the newcomers with some of their more eligible young people, to keep them enchanted and within the community. To delay their return forever. All part of their scheme when the newcomers had appeared unannounced.

And what was their reason? For leaving?

Todd and Lissa didn't like it here.

Why? asked Leader of Men. *We have shown the utmost kindness after your sorry arrival.*

Peet's eyes clouded. He'd worked out the Stümmers had wasted precious stemCell materials on his shoulder, fixing it in a third of the time it would take to heal normally. That was a big sacrifice for them, helping him heal. And he knew he was cherished by Curl and her family. He didn't want to be angry, but he was.

Because Todd was approached by her for sex and he felt obliged, he signed, gesturing at Leader of Women. *This made Todd very upset. He didn't understand why an older woman would do such a thing.* Leader of Men turned white. He looked at Leader of Women.

You?

I was exercising my prerogative, she signed. Then shrugged dismissively.

But the young newcomers don't know the ladder of prerogatives, Leader of Men signed. *The boy hadn't reached abstracts and ethics with our language. We couldn't have explained yet. We haven't taught him his own prerogatives yet, let alone ours. Especially with sexing.*

Leader of Women signed: *So? He is very handsome. And so new and fresh. I had to invite him. He was qwite accommodating.* She looked coyly at Leader of Men.

But you are a Leader! signed her co-Leader furiously. *He doesn't know HIS prerogatives. Without that knowledge, it's clear he felt obligated to sex with you because of who you are ...*

Leader of Women looked a bit flustered, but maintained her importance face, and straight backed authority.

I am Leader of Women. The young man always had the opportunity to say no.

Nonsense, flashed Leader of Men with an angry hand gesture.

Leader of Men turned to Peet again. *And the others?* He gestured furiously. *Were they abused by any of the Leaders?*

Peet shrugged and signed: *Lissa may have been. She was hurt, bashed even, 3 days ago by someone ... don't know who.*

Hurt? Leader of Men was aghast, and Leader of Women looked shocked.

Peet: *Bruises, and she wouldn't talk, and ... and she was crying a lot ...*

Leader of Men gestured angrily at Leader of Women: *You?*

How dare you!, said Leader of Women. *I would never hurt anyone. I believe in the peaceful practises. Especially of love, as you so well understand.*

Leader of Men swung back and gestured at Peet: *Do you know who hurt her?*

No, she wouldn't say a thing. She was very upset and qwiet. Would not tell Todd even. He was frustrated with her silence.

Do you know who hurt her? he asked Leader of Women. *Was it another member of the Qwietude?*

Looking anguished, she signed: *I make my own arrangements. Peaceful, personal. I don't know what others do.*

The girlz tell you tho'. They tell you everything.

Leader of Women signed: *I don't know. I am deeply sorry she was hurt, but I don't know.* Now Leader of Women was very flustered. She flicked a hesitant, *I'm sorry*, at Peet.

What a mess, gestured Leader of Men. *Strikt trusts have been broken. I can understand their flight, but this desert is lethal. There are bones of the dispossessed qwite close to our gorge ... we can hardly chase them. Who knows which way they've gone?*

Leader of Women started to sign: *Send some of the boyz to the top of the gorge and ...*

Leader of Men signed her to stop. *You must admit you have done enough harm, Leader of Women. We will call the full Qwietude to a meeting and see whether we can rescue these poor young people or decide whether it is too late. And we will have to discuss your conduct too. And get to the bottom of poor young Flamehair's pain.*

Peet was astonished. Instead of the usual patrician dismissiveness, the Leader of Men was genuinely upset by the situation. As was Leader of Women. Were they even starting to cry?

*

When the Hermitage was finally alerted to the absence of Todd, Lissa and Narmon, the older boyz climbed sweatily to the top of the gorge walls late morning with opticals and stared out into the desert to see if the 3 were visible, but Todd's camouflage and ratRunning methodology had worked. Two parties ventured out, and checked both sides of the outer walls, to see if there were discernible tracks. But the Stümmers were not good at tracking, and Todd was. He'd headed down the dry rocky riverbank for a while, so no impressions were left in sand, before venturing to the West. The Stümmers weren't likely to follow, not made for the outside world. They stuck close to the gorge walls. They compartmentalized themselves within a space and hid from authority, and rarely moved from their zone of comfort in case they were noted.

However, one person, the Qwartermaster, took real action. After half a day's search and no luck inside or around the gorge, Pepperbeard knew there was a big problem.

He sent his assistants out of the stores to help with the search and disappeared into the backroom where the scope machine was kept in the old mechanical safe for which only Qwartermasters knew the code. This black oblong device he lifted gingerly, and turned on, and he then scoped the surprized Funder.

"They've escaped," he said uncertainly.

The Funder roared a bunch of wordz he couldn't catch, then waited until the voice on the end of the line had calmed slightly. Pepperbeard's commitment was broken and his plan had gone significantly wrong.

"Which direction?" the Funder finally asked.

"The boy kept staring west. To the coast."

"And you didn't disengage him from ideas of escape?"

"I didn't know."

"Was your job to know!"

The Funder had screamed again and said he'd come, clean up the mess, ordered Pepperbeard to keep his scope handy for further komms, signed off and scrambled his team.

*

Toward the end of the second day, as the 3 weaved thru the rutted desert, Narmon spotted some water trickling down the middle of one of the dry mini-canyons they were traversing. Mebbe it was the westerly slant of that partikular watercourse, and the fact they were heading in that direction, that made him realize there was a slight flow from the north. It was too insignificant to notice at a glance. And it seemed to soak into the soil as they walked along.

They were tired and their skin was dry and parched. Lissa's face, even caked in sunJell and dirt was turning an unhealthy pink tone. Their knees and ankles were aching and their feet were a mess.

She'd been overusing the sunJell, Lissa knew, but her skin was so sensitive. Jell, then dirt, so it caked into a shield against the UV and reflected heat. Todd had to stop her, couple of times, from reapplying.

"It'll stick. Don't worry," he'd said.

As they trudged along Narmon said: "Hey – look" pointing at the next few meters of red ground in front.

There was no doubt the water was flowing – qwite fast – a film of dirty flow.

"Must be coming from storms way upstream," said Todd. There hadn't been a cloud above, or a drop of rain as they'd walked. He dipped his finger in a small runnel and tasted it. "It's fresh ... and hot. Let's keep going. It'll be harder if these channels start really pouring with water." He splashed some of the water on his face and neck, as did the others, and they started to climb a small embankment out of the watercourse and back up to the desert floor.

That day, when the sun was at its very zenith, the heat was round 55 degrees, so they rested for a couple of hours in shade, chatting and napping qwietly. This longer halt inspired a burst of walking into the late afternoon.

At the top of the embankment, the knobbly end of the long, low purple range, which receded northwest, seemed somewhat larger, somewhat closer, but not by much. They could pick out shapes in the hills, but no vegetation yet. They'd put a sizable distance between the gorge and their current position – mebbe 40 kliks and Todd was keen to add another 5 or 6 before they stopped for the nite, even if it meant scrambling thru the landscape in a dark environment, guided by glows.

The thin vessel sailed toward the west above him, and he was confident of his direction.

As the speartip headed toward Earth, stars became larger, the distances elongated, and he watched for where the tip would recede under the horizon.

They reached another burst of open country, hated because of exposure, but loved because it was easy walking, and then the ground started inclining down gradually til they were on a lower plain, with cracked clay and sand surfaces. The rubbly ground meant extra care as they picked along in the dark.

It had cooled down to about 42 degrees after the sun dipped behind them, lengthening their shadows. Every so often there was a channel with a wash of water, a sheen of running mud which they had to slop thru.

"I think we are walking thru what could be an extensive watercourse," Narmon said.

"Or old lake," said Todd. Ephemeral lakes were part of the lore, and tired and hot tho' he was, he tried to think thru the gorge, the long range, lakes and badlands to pinpoint a Song, but knew he was taking a massive gutHunch.

After a while, and as it darkened, the flowing water was swirling around their shoes and making their feet wet.

"We might have to keep going til we get to higher ground," said Narmon. "We can't camp out in water."

Todd looked at Lissa, who'd been mostly silent. Her cheeks were pink, she'd flapped her hat brim right across her face and he could just see her small chin and grim set lips. Lissa's face was filthy with the dried jell and dirt. He could see she would refuse to take a breather. Her desire to run as far from the Stümmers as quickly as possible was signaled in her sure step and determined elbows as she walked and splashed thru the water.

Half an hour later the water was around their ankles. And they were surrounded by brown flowing murk.

"Can you see any sort of rising land. Can be to the north or south, guys? We can deviate from following the Canoe. Don't want to be carried away in a flood in the middle of the nite."

In the darkening gloom Narmon pointed 40 degrees further north from the line they were taking.

"Is that a hill?"

Todd stopped and stared. "Hard to tell. It's getting too dark. Might be. Let's divert north a bit."

Todd knew that somewhere there were fearsome rainfalls. Somewhere north, under the distant clouds which dominated the entire skyline to their right. The friends unleashed the little hover glows and set them to a low illumination so they could see their feet, ankles, and the water about a meter in front of them. Then it faded into darkness. The glows stayed at low vizz, til a snake washed against Todd's leg.

A brown, venomous snake, caught in the growing current, and swimming hurriedly south with the flow. Its thin, yellow coffin-shaped head and muscled brown body took no notice of Todd's leg, and it flicked its tail and swam away with slithery grace.

"Guys," said Todd, "up the glow's lumens a bit. I was just bumped by a king brown. They are really dangerous if they bite. There may be snakes caught in the coming flood."

Lissa finally stopped in her tracks and looked apalled. "Snakes? That's all we need."

"Just don't stand on them. Let them pass. They'll be swimming," said Todd.

"I don't like snakes," she said.

"Neither do I," said Narmon who'd bent down. Picked up his glow and turned the light intensity up. He started walking cautiously. Another snake swam past, just ahead of the group.

"Snakes are part of country and the old guys say a snake made the land, in the beginning," said Todd. "Respect them, let them pass. They belong as much here as they belong in the Dreaming. They are poisonous for a reason, but killing us is not one of them. And I've eaten lots of snakes. We're the worse predator."

He saw a small black snake being washed along in what was now calf high water. What were once rivulets was now a single flow, about 15 centimeters along the ground. At least it was flat, tho' they had to pick carefully, avoiding snakes and lizards, including a sizable goanna, which appeared and disappeared in a flash, thru the glow of water in front. Todd was now worried the light would be visible to others. It was like having a fire.

"They'll be swimming on the surface, guys."

The whole northern horizon lit up with an enormous run of lightning, too far away to hear any thunder, tho Todd imagined he could feel the vibrations. There was another flickering charge thru the nite sky. Above them were bright stars, no moon yet, with the Canoe floating above.

After an hour, the water surface rose only a little more, and their feet were sqwelchy, uncomfortable. A welter of snakes had been swimming or bumping them and swimming off at regular intervals. At one point 3 tangled snakes floated in front of Lissa who froze in abject panic. Narmon and Todd took 5 minutes to talk her into moving onward toward the rise.

"The sooner we are out of the water, we'll be away from all this," Todd urged, altho aware the snakes would be heading for high ground too.

A while later, a small thorny devil tried to latch on to Todd's trouser leg, so slowed by the cool water, it was almost comatose. It attempted to climb into his pocket so Todd picked it up and put it on the shelf of his pack where it stayed. He hoped no snake would try the same.

Lissa was horrified at the sight of the lizard on his backpack.

"He's a friend," said Todd, enigmatically.

*

As they walked, or waded, calf deep thru brown murk, he told them how – even tho' they couldn't see the range in the dark – he knew where he was going, and explained his direction, following the Islanders' Canoe constellation, pointing out where some stars in Scorpio formed the canoe's hull.

"I didn't know Indijj people had astrology too," Narmon said.

"Actually, it's astronomy. Stars can't tell us about whether you'll have a bad day or anything, but they do show us the way. And even after nearly 400 years you whitefellas should be looking up to the skies like my ancestors looked up, and see things a bit differently."

Narmon laughed. His friend was always trying to sell him the Indijj way. Todd was proud of his traditional learning.

He stopped them for a water break, and pointed out the line of stars so they knew the curve of the boat and to follow the 2 stars at the end which constituted the fishing-spirits leg.

"If we get lost from each other, those are the stars to follow ... ok?"

Serious voice. His 2 friends nodded.

*

Tottering with exhaustion, their legs aching, by midnite they started to walk out of the flood onto higher ground. There was a chain of rocks that Narmon had glimpsed, and a few trees at the top of the rise, 10 or 15 meters above the floodplain. They couldn't really make much out with the glows, but qwickly ducked behind the small ridge and sank into a stupor followed by a sleep.

Much later, but before dawn, Lissa woke, and found her head resting against Narmon. For the first time since their escape she'd felt comforted by the contact of his soft hair and the sound of a tiny snore, but her newfound tolerance could have been caused by exhaustion. Her feet and pants were still wet – even cold. The air was a little unsettled, she could feel a breeze.

She moved apart from Narmon. Their backpacks were together like pillows and hers was nice and soft after positioning the extra clothes and socks where her head was to rest, on top of the hard packs of food and water.

She looked at the stars and wished HighEyes would pick out the 3 of them and send a rescue party.

The horror of a few days ago kept going round and round in her head.

The part where she'd trotted obediently down her dorm corridor in the middle of the nite, following Pepperbeard, expecting a cosy chat – it was probably about this same time of nite. Pepperbeard had led her to some distant qwarters and she'd trusted him. He'd summonsed her in a friendly, urbane voice. No hint of his coming attack. The bunk rooms he went to were old and out of the way. He opened a door and edged her into the room and she saw a bed with a blanket on it, and began to get scared.

There he pushed her down, pulled at her clothes and aggressively sexed with her. On a bed with a mattress and no sheets or pillows, just a blanket where she'd cried out in terror, until he'd slapped her, the pain blasting down her face and neck. He'd grabbed her sarong and ripped it. Then he'd slapped her again and crushed one of her arms under his body so she couldn't hit out, tho' really, a punch would have been futile. Lissa knew she was small. She wasn't tough. His full weight flattened her arm between them, impossible to extract. And he held down her other wrist with a steel tight hand and just jigged on top of her, very fast and angry.

"Shut up," he said and kept on with his horrible bizz. His face was scrunched and contorted, eyes half closed, beard raspy on her body and face. His weight had crushed down on her, hand on her wrist and sometimes throat.

Lissa felt the tears on her face, blinding her eyes to the stars as she remembered. She could only contrast the hideousness of the rape with her relations with Narmon. Months back. Before they ever sexed, Narmon had lost the coin toss and took the antiFecundities. And her loyal steadyBoy always insisted on wearing a cap on his penis as well, which had felt smooth and not leastwise messy, but with Pepperbeard ... *urgggghh.*

"Don't fight back," the Qwartermaster hissed – he'd actually talked out loud. "Enjoy it. You've been wanting it, haven't you? Wanting it from me. This is called our prerogative," he said between his breathlessness. "I can make you my wife if you want. Do you want that?" He was weirdly excited. She was saying *please stop*, and crying, but he didn't. Seemed not to even notice how terrified she was.

When he finally got off her, she was sore around her throat, across her face and it felt that ribs were broken. Pepperbeard had just dressed and walked out without a word.

And now, every time Narmon tried to envelop her in loving arms, she'd flinch, finding his gentleness difficult. She took a deep breath and moved her head back against his.

But it wasn't the same.

Tho' she hadn't told Todd the full story, he'd understood her anguish and got the abortant pill real qwick from one of the older girlz who regularly sexed and so had supplies. She hoped like kriminy that the pill would work. When swallowed she'd felt a bit sqweasy and that was that.

Now they were in the desert because she'd urged Todd to get going, get away, as soon as possible, in case Pepperbeard came back and tried to rape her again – that's what the crime was called in the old days? Rape? She didn't want ever to be raped again. And she thought, if she drowned in a flood, or ran out of food and starved, or was bitten by a king brown, she would be happier dying than ending up back under the horror of the Stümmers and in the vicinity of Pepperbeard.

She felt physically sick, and tired, and slowly fell back to sleep.

*

Lissa woke to the smell of cooking meat.

Todd had stolen a dryFry from the kitchens before they left and had it packed away. He'd woken at first light and killed and skinned a medium sized goanna, which tried to skitter past escaping the flooding below. Todd was passing the dryFry's tongs over the meat which was starting to char nicely. "Protein," he intoned. Narmon was sqwatting over the meat, glumly looking at the mess of Goanna guts. Todd was intent on his cooking.

She could hear Todd talking:

"I won't let us starve, and we can't be physically weak. This is a nice fat goanna. I know how to live on this sort of country even if it's not my Country. I know the signs. We've just got to get somewhere there are settlers on the Arables, further west. As soon as the arids start mellowing out, there are thousands of people, townships and communication outposts. And if the waters coming down from the north …

"Todd, these waters will be followed by the weather itself," said Narmon miserably.

"True that. That's why we gotta push on."

"Lissa's not so big."

"Lissa's holding out well, NarMan. She's determined. Don't worry about food and water. We just gotta keep hiking. Hiking hard west."

Lissa groaned, but she'd liked hearing Todd's vote of confidence and hadn't appreciated Narmon's concerns. The boyz watched the exhausted girl prop herself on an elbow.

"Hey, Lissa, chuck us your shoes. I used the dryFry to dry mine out. Worked ok," Todd said.

She reached over and threw her shoes toward him.

"Here …" He poked some white lizard meat on a loose stick and handed it over to her. "Goanna kebab?"

He started to dryFry another haunch. She chewed it gingerly. It was stringy but tasted like meat. Good, in fact, a bit caramelised and sweet, a bit charred, so she gobbled the remainder and passed the stick back for more.

After the goanna, Todd, his sharp face focused on early morning tasks, removed a roll of thick black tefliteTape from his backpack and carefully wrapped lengths round their shoes which were starting to tatter. Lissa watched him work, his black wavy hair and dark brown eyes unwavering on the job at hand. She was amazed by his calm.

"Gotta protect these shoes, guys," he said. "They are our only hope in this environment."

Narmon sat and sorted one of his, but for once Lissa let someone else fix her wretched shoes.

"The heat from the dryFry will help the glue cure," said Todd, sounding constantly knowledgable. He was feeling more and more confident, as they closed in on the purple range, that his instinctive punt had been the right one.

"What happened to the thorny devil?" she asked.

"I let him go. Can't eat thorny devils – they are a special animal to me," he said. "It's part of my thing. They are the symbolic carriers of ochre thru country, for ceremony. My granma would have killed me if I ate a little devil."

For the first time in a week, Lissa smiled.

*

"Liss?" said Narmon.

They were scrabbling up yet another embankment, the edge of a dry rivercourse.

"What?"

"Are you okay? What's happening? Why can't we hug?"

Todd was about 15 meters ahead, and Narmon talked very qwiet, private.

Lissa grimaced. Answer was, she didn't want to cuddle anyone. "Like I said, I fell down some steps and am all bruised. I think I cracked coupla ribs, that's all. It's sore."

Narmon nodded.

"Why ... why was Todd helping you with that?" he asked, puzzled. "When it happened. Why not come to me?"

"Well, he was the one that found me. He got me some medicine. Painkillerz."

"Yizz, but ..." Narmon was trying to form a question when Lissa, carefully maneuvring up a 1 meter vertical bank, turned to him.

"He's like a big brother to me, Narmon. Look at him. He's leading us. He just helped me. It's okay. We are steady, you and I are steady. I'm just very sore."

Narmon nodded, a little bit satisfied.

He noted that she didn't stop at the crest of the embankment and give him a hug. She just skanned the rutted, tufted landscape ahead and kept walking.

HIATUS TWO

That ringing in your ear is not tinnitus
It's civilization ...
    Klaus Kalk

AS long as the nite sky was unusually clear and cloudless, Madrigal Phipps, like her son, spent a lot of time looking at the stars. A conundrum of stars, all fixed in their place, but moving together, planets whizzing past under the Emu, meteors slicing thru the eye of the universe.

On her boardroom roof terrace, as she waited to hear from any of the agents in the search for her boy, Madrigal would sit at nite, hoping the scope would bring her an answer. Or Rox or Shelbo would emerge qwietly thru the glass boardroom sliders with news. She'd also banished Szygy the kelpieDog to the staff area because he kept asking: "Maddy, where's Todd? I want to play with Todd," in the most piteous voice with the most piteous puppy eyes. She couldn't stand the mindLoops dogs got into, and asked one of the valets to keep Szygy out of the way for a while.

Each evening, she'd shake away some of the stress by training with Pearl and a couple of other allotted Slotters. Her regime was paying physical dividends, but it still didn't lift the weight from her heart. An inside ache.

But the nite sky calmed her, it soothed her the most, because she knew Todd would be looking up too. As a little boy he'd loved the stars and the many creation stories that went with them. He collected them, not just from their own tribal nation, but everywhere across the Indijj world.

Immensity and the dome of stars was a soothing trope, because during the day she was not calm. However much she blustered as the dominant person in charge, her fears and desperations around Todd's fate were all-consuming. She'd snap at staff – unknown before – or ring Centrl and beg more resources be made available.

Two months after the abduction, Pearl found Madrigal on her own, throwing plates and glasses, in frustration, around the kitchen. She grabbed her crazed boss before a glass chip ricocheted into an eye, and pushed her 10 meters across the kitchen and onto the carpet in the corridor and forcibly held her down until the rage abated.

Madrigal struggled weakly onto her side and looked at Pearl and said, "Thanx", then staggered to bed like a blind woman reaching out for a handhold. That nite, the search, then the rage had exhausted her utterly and it took her several minutes to climb the steps to the sleeping level and her bedroom. Pearl watched her every step.

Pearl made sure her boss was asleep, then swept up the mess.

Other times the panic and frustrations would rise and, instead of incandescent rage, Madrigal would end up sobbing helplessly and Pearl would hug and stroke her back and then try and talk thru her latest fears til Madrigal was back to sqware one.

The hunt.

No other staff ever saw the terror that Madrigal lived with. And her giant bodyguard was qwite unable to deal with the private corrosion she could see in her boss.

Madrigal knew she needed more than a bodyguard ...

Someone to hold and confide in. Langer had been her only real partner and that was years ago. Jembrana and she had a deep understanding, but he was never there. She'd toyed with breaching the boss-employee barrier and taking Pearl to bed – she'd always had secret lust for Slotters, and Pearl was her one and only consolation at the moment – but she knew that for her, sleeping with Pearl was fool's gold, and could also destroy their working partnership in a twink.

And then, to find a new friend for consolation took time she didn't have. And buying some boy off the street for a one off, well ... her sense of Virtue was far too strong, tho' she was powerful enough to get away with it, if ever she cracked.

How she craved just lying in someone's arms, telling them how scared she was.

The lonely hours between midnite and 5, when no one was around, were the worst, so that's why she went rooftop. No calls came thru. No business to distract her. The clouds would flip across the moon, or sqwalls would bang in from the southeast. She'd sit there with the situation rolling thru her mind in a loop, just like Szygy's pitiful comments: stolen children, shadowy men on rooftops smoking chopchop, hoppers heading north, and faces of oblique terror on the other parents.

She knew hell didn't exist, that place of torture and guilt invented by old, irrational religions. But for her, the notion came that, in one instance, hell did exist.

A place designated for mothers with missing children.

So there she'd sit, looking up. She knew, if she found the culprit, it would be hard to be measured in her actions, as Couriers were supposed to be.

She watched the stars whirl in their fixed path, nite after nite, with a wail in her heart that no one should hear. Eventually, Rox and Pearl persuaded her to use sleeping pills so she'd get a few hours sleep at nite, but she'd take them very late, just in case there was a call.

THE WATERFALL

Can we dream of somewhere that is not infected with electron-ika?

Das Glas Haus (2034) Ulli Kalk

THE 3 walked another 2 days toward the edge of the red and purple range. A longer walk than Todd envisaged, but as the destination loomed, his faith in his own skills in reading and surviving on the land became stronger. Narmon and Lissa were pulled along in their best friend's confident slipstream.

The range emerged high and long, with peaks lumped like mushrooms, or snakes' heads along the spine of the formation. They persevered, walking slowly and methodically in the blistering humidity. The Cloud, or at least its wild fronts, wasn't that far away now, often rising over the terrain like a bunch of black grey thunderhead fists.

Their shoes held together over the sticky, wet ground. The 3 waded thru some very big streams, and the nite after eating the goanna and some bush tomatoes, a storm had caught up to them. They camped for a few hours on higher country, where there was little shelter. They could see the lightning in the looming stormfront, and the giant willy willies that preceded it in the unsettled air, spouting sand and dirty floodwater high into the heavens and then bursting so the water fell back in thick misty showers.

The daylight enabled them to pick the signs of an incoming real stormfront – gave them enough time, eagle eyes watching out, to seek boulders, or ridges. Todd bustled them against a half meter ridge a few minutes before the storm burst above. Lightning smacked the desert with unrelenting cracks all around them as the front rushed over their heads. Rain bucketed and soaked them. The 3 sat and, in solidarity, locked elbows together in case a tube crashed thru, but none did. Good thing too. In such a violent scenario they'd be dead. Fronts were a precursor to the advent of the real Cloud with its weird twisting winds and tumult.

The desert now roiled with dirty red brown water, flowing south or west along ancient waterways. A rationed pack of honey biscuits was broken open and they chewed slowly, listening to the howling air and smacking rain.

To Lissa, it was exhilarating but freaky. Elemental forces she hardly understood, now blasting round her. Back in Perth, when an extraTropical 'phoon hit, everyone – poor, midClass, richArses – hit the storm bunkers and panic rooms. They'd stay inside to see big 'phoons thru, never sticking their heads above the surface. DownTown Perth you'd be watching a stormwave's progress on monitors and radar with their maplines and abstract shapes.

Out in the badlands, it was real. She smelled the hot wet mud, the water in the rain, the steam coming off her sweaty smelly clothes. On her left, Narmon huddled hard against her, eyes closed, wet hair plastered to his brow. To her right, she could see Todd's eyes fixed to the heavens again, gleaming as lightning burst. He looked so calm, she thought. How could he be so calm?

"It's wild," she said to him.

"That it is," he responded, echoing a favorite affirmation of his mother's. A huge crash of lightning cracked the plain about 30 meters in front of them and they nearly jumped out of their skins.

"What if one of those hit us," she said.

"Don't even think it," said Todd. "The lightning licks have already passed. It'll just be rain now."

There was little sleep that nite, crushed as they were against the wall of the ridge, water soaking their jacket backs, and even cold and shiverMaking.

They sang Philosophikal songs, especially amused with: *Don't know what y'r in for/but wade you anyway/hip-high into/ a swamp of misery* ... but the singing dribbled out after a while, like the rain, and they sat pressed against one another in their individual silences, dozing, or watching for a faint grey gleam to the east and the new day.

Another day's walk and by the afternoon they'd reached the fresh waterhole that Todd had, amazingly, predicted. Tired, aching, but alive. They'd been close to the steep range slope all day, and saw vegetation along the top and sides, and in the shadows of rocks where plants clung to gain respite from the daytime 50 degrees plus. A couple of large red kangaroos leapt from their path as they approached, signaling the foothills as a place that fauna lived and bred. Another bioOasis in the badlands. The 3 waded a fast running stream across a set of flat rocks. The stream itself poured from the opening of a small gorge and then into the vast space a klik beyond, a shallow lake, which coloured the flatlands to the south, silver white.

A waterhole sat at the back of a 500 meter high spannerHead shaped cliff at the very end of the flat topped range. Once inside, the short gorge was lush with trees and grass trees, ferns and tussocks. At the back of the curved cliff wall, a torrent of water came off the end of the range in a 3 part waterfall, crashing finally into a huge pool, which drained down one side into the desert. The torrent was the result of 2 days of rain way further up the range. The pool was black green in the shade, deep, with flat rocks surrounding it. The red rocks and adjacent white barked trees were starting to mottle with moss after the build of rain over the past couple of weeks.

"Koo!" exclaimed Narmon. "That's pretty."

"I know where we are now," said Todd. "I'm so relieved. Truthfully, this was a big punt ... I heard a song in my head and thought, that's the place. This is a Dreaming place to me. Had no hard data. Just the song. That's the best I was able to do ..." He looked astonished. He sat down heavily in the shade of a tree leaning out of some rocks and let out a sigh.

"Oh," said Narmon, shocked.

Narmon and Lissa sat beside Todd.

"Well – was a good punt!" said Lissa.

"Mebbe not a punt," mumbled Todd.

They sat with their thoughts.

"So, we can't stay," said Todd finally. "But we keep walking same direction – west, and we'll be in the Arables in a week. This waterhole," and he said some Indijj word incomprehensible to Narmon and Lissa, "is at the edge of the arid lands. It's a sacred place, a men's place. Lissa shouldn't be here, but I won't tell her the stories and secrets." He was starting to ramble. "I don't know too many of them yet anyway. So we won't tell. Won't tell anyone. Not Jaim'z, not anyone. But, she's not included in the story and frankly, it's an emergency."

"What was the name?" Lissa asked.

"What?"

"Of this place?"

"Only men can say the word ... it's ..." and he said the word. Lissa mouthed it, but to be respectful she didn't utter it. Just wanted to know exactly where she was. From now on, she thought, I'm going to be in control and to be in control, you gotta know where you are.

"I think there are other watersoaks and pools along the western side where women and children can go. It's not as if men are hogging *all* the water," he explained.

Calmness enveloped them that afternoon, in the enclave of rock and the cool of the vegetation. Was like the ancient sandstone wrapped its arms around them in some geological hug. The 3 had endured a tough trek over almost 5 days, and now was time for a short rest. They knew more storms were coming, and the Cloud would make outdoor life xtremely dangerous.

Once in the confines of the swimming hole, under caveRiddled cliffs, they ripped off their filthy outer clothes, leapt into the water in their underwear. Their laughter echoed off the walls of the rocks. After a couple of laps to the powerful waterfall and back, they hung off a ledge, treading water and chatting.

"It's deep," said Lissa, red hair slicked across her forehead and shoulders. "I duck dived and couldn't touch the bottom."

"So, in brief, and since you won't tell anyone, the story of this place is there's no bottom to the pool, and it's where certain spirits went after the Dreamtime, and the country was made," said Todd, who couldn't help himself when it came to talking his culture. "But I can't give you any more info about the myth. Sorry."

They thought about the endless hole, entrance to another world below them. Then Lissa announced: "I brought soap."

They crouched on the edge and washed themselves properly. Lissa had saved the soap, anticipating Todd's promised waterhole, and they shared the Stümmer made block of beeswax and tallow, and washed their hair, skin and clothes. The latter were hung out on tree branches in the sun, and then they lay back on the rocks. Narmon looked sideways at the black, purple and yellow bruising on Lissa's neck, chest and her side.

"Those bruises – where are the ones on your neck from, Liss?" he asked. "Are you 'k?"

"Yizz. I'll tell you later."

Todd said nothink, watching Narmon's numbed face.

"They're all over you."

"Narmon, I'll tell you when we've dried off. Okay?" Her sharp voice.

Instead of pursuing his anxious questions, Narmon asked: "Will it rain tonite?"

"Prob'ly," said Todd, "but our clothes'll dry soon, and we have the teflite blankets. They're pretty dry. There's a cave here so we can actually get out of the rain."

"Can we fire up a fire?"

"Don't think so. Even tho' we face due south, can't risk being seen. I'll use the dryFry to properly dry our shoes again as long as the battery holds out."

Lissa enthusiastically helped Todd to look around the edge of the inner wall, where vegetation met boulders, to find and whack small lizards and a couple of frogs. Narmon trailed behind them holding the small catch, a little qweasy at the full blooded op his friends were carrying out. He watched Liss sqwat on a flat red rock with Todd learning to remove the gutz and then apply the dryFry, searing the remains. Todd tried for a couple of fish that glinted under the surface of the pool, but they were impossible to catch without a properly constructed spear.

Once their food was cooked, the 3 trekkers sat on the sun-warmed rocks and chewed the range of meats and tiny fried organs, and chewed the rationed honey biscuits and some more bush tomatoes.

"Gotta bang up our protein for the next leg," Todd said.

"Don't talk about legs," Lissa said

They sat on the rocks looking at the tendrils of cloud in the nite sky, way high up, interwoven between the stars. Streams of air, reinventing the way the heat and moisture was dispersed across the continent and across the globe.

"Bad weather coming," said Todd to his 2 friends.

"Why were we abducted in the first place, Todd?" asked Lissa.

"Have no idea, but it's not over yet, no way."

"You have it," agreed Narmon.

"What if they snatch us again?" said Lissa.

"Who? The Stümmers?" said Todd.

"Anyone? Why did they dump us with those people anyway? They're monsters," asked Lissa.

"Monsters?" asked Narmon. "The Stümmers are a bit moronik, but ..."

"They hurt me, Narmon. That's where the bruises are from. And they hurt Todd."

"How did they hurt you, Liss? I thought you'd fallen down some steps?" asked the shocked Narmon.

"To be fair, not all of them. Just the Qwartermaster. He was the one who ... beat me up."

Todd looked at his somewhat blistered feet.

"The Qwartermaster?" yelped Narmon, astonished.

Todd now had a name on which to take vengeance, but instead he mumbled: "Yeah, well, we've got away." He didn't want Narmon to know Lissa had confided in him.

"But ..." Todd added, "if they come for us – the Stümmers, or the other kidnappers – we have to split up. You both know the drill 'bout heading west. Pace it. Catch protein. And as soon as anyone can get to komms, scope my mum. 'K? She was once a Courier in AuZgov – knows people who can track down crims. I can tell you, I've been to Centrl's HQ when I was a kid, and woah, they have eqwipment and scary people. HardArms. They catch and kill just like we did to those frogs." He waved lamely at some little bones on the rock.

Narmon was still looking at Lissa. He was feeling xtremely uncertain. She'd lied to him about falling down a set of steps. He'd guessed she'd been very upset before they'd trekked off west. Now, she confessed to a lie. And put a name to her hurt: the Qwartermaster. He was very upset she'd lied. They'd never lied to each other. No one lied ... and Todd knew more about it than he did. How could that be? Had Lissa shared with Todd before him?

"Narmon. Whatever happens ..." Todd added.

"I heard," said Narmon curtly. "Komms to home. Your home."

Todd was back being leader and didn't notice Narmon's crestfallen face. "Hey, my brother and sister, we did good. We gotta keep going. Might rest tomorrow morning and head off in the arvo. The next walk's gonna be huge. Dayz."

Narmon was oblivious to the pep talk. He kept glancing at Liss's bruises.

"How bad did he hurt you, Liss?"

"Bad. To confess ... Bad ..."

The conversation tailed off.

They looked at the sky again where high black shreds of cloud tangled with the Emu, thinking their separate thoughts.

*

The 3 had camped in a cavelike space next to the pool and a ledge where they'd put clothes to dry. They had honeybars for breakfast and went swimming again. By 11 am, still exhausted from walking 16 hours a day for 4 days across diabolical terrain, they fell asleep in the underhang ...

... and were woken by the clatter of a hopper, which sank with a roar in front of the south facing opening, where the ends of the spanner head almost met. It was a white craft, no markings, with ventral jets and a high rotor and smaller one at the back. Landing back wheels first.

"Oh, shyte," said Narmon. He and Todd lay flat on a ledge and looked down at it from the cave entrance. "Our rescue?"

"Isn't the Stümmers, that's for sure," said Todd. "Who'd know we're here?"

"HighEyes? The authorities?"

"Have to be? Surely? But we haven't managed an alert to anyone. Mum will have'm tearing everything apart looking for us," Todd said.

Whether the unknowns in the hopper were friendly or not, was irrelevant. Todd knew they were trapped. There was a sheer wall everywhere else and a waterfall. No climbing up. Only walking out.

The craft sat there, blocking the natural entrance – no hatches or doors opened. There was no sign of anyone in the tinted windows of the cockpit.

"Lissa. Lissa wake up," said Todd.

The sleepy girl groaned at the back of the cave. Lissa had been in her first deep sleep for days. She roused slowly on her elbow, 2 boyz a single silhouette against the light on the cave lip. She wondered what was up.

"What do we do?" asked Narmon.

But for the boyz, it was too late to ask that qwestion. Their human body heat had been detected by the hopper's instrumentation, their heads and upper torsos had been scoped, and ropes of congealed light wrapped round Todd and Narmon's arms and they felt held down.

"Hey," said Narmon feeling invisible manacles around his upper arms. He suddenly was wrenched forward onto the rocky slope, he and Todd pulled out of the cave entrance by the invisible force.

The silhouettes were gone.

"Run," shouted Todd to Lissa as he was dragged roughly down the slope across the sharp rocks and prickly tussocks.

Lissa, almost 8 meters back, well under the cave, snapped into action. Didn't think twice when Narmon and Todd shouted in surprize, then were dragged out by the light tentacles, and heard her friend's cry to the kinetic. Unseen by the hopper, she scuttled like a crab along the very back of the cool deep overhang and slid out the side of the cave mouth onto the flat ledge. Was down and out of sight of the gorge entrance. Still in her underwear, she rolled straight into the black water of the pool, not even gasping at the cold onrush of water against her skin, then took a huge breath and submerged. Took 2 tiks. Bubbles rose in her nose. She used the rock wall to kick hard toward the waterfall. The brownGold water rolled past her and she kicked her legs hard and desperate.

Heart beating fast, she was very scared, but somehow her head was thinking clearly. She was taking control. They had walked a very long way and she wasn't going to ruin the effort. If Todd and Narmon had been caught by Stümmers or the original snatchers, she'd stay hidden. In a cleft. Then walk. Try to get help. Contact Dr Phipps.

All this she thought with a little trail of bubbles swirling around her in the sharp fresh water.

Returning to face that rapist Stümmer would not happen. Never ever. Adrenalin surged at the thought.

She surfaced once, her face barely sticking out to avoid any detection by drones. There were no drones. The pursuers had the boyz pinned to the slope and a team was approaching them. A secondary light tube skanned the area, which had missed the brief flash of face that lasted a breath, a moment of mouth and nose and a tiny patch of forehead. She was way below the ground level of any ocular sights on the hopper and had managed almost a 30 meter underwater swim in her desperation to escape.

She duck dived again and swam under and thru the plunging, pummeling torrent of the waterfall. Lissa emerged behind the 2 meter long wall of water, started to tread and at the same time reach out for any rock handholds. The noise of crashing water was tremendous. There was a blur of daylight coming in from the edges of torrent, and a cave behind, or at least a cutaway ledge, but she decided to stay as submerged as possible for a while. Instinctive, and as she later discovered, it was the right thing to do.

Suddenly feeling angry that Todd and Narmon were gone, she hissed out to the pursuers behind the smash of water: "You just try'n catch me ... just try, bast'dz."

*

Her body heat was untrackable under the cold downpour. Surrounded by ironRich rocks, her bioelektriks were smothered by particles of magnetite and the H2O vapour. The team's opticals had glimpsed somethink as the boyz were hauled down the slope, but the instrument guy couldn't make it out. Wallaby, mebbe? Flash of a white tail? There was no sign of a third kid as humans generated a lot of heat. A party of 5 men came into the gorge and sedated Todd and Narmon, then they crisscrossed the target area in a grid pattern. There was no one in any nook or cranny behind the dryland caves. The men tossed the kidz gear around to check the girl wasn't under the rugs at the back of the cave, cos Pepperbeard had mentioned a girl. One of 3.

They checked up the cliffs with binoculars just in case she was trying to scale a precipice. No one.

A bioelektrik urchin with spiky filaments was planted on its tripod to skan the entire area, kilometers wide, for any bioelektrik wash. Nothink else, apart from wallabies, birds, bush rats, turtles, their own team and the 2 captured targets. Was enough. Didn't think to check the thundering waterfall – no one could survive under that, could they?

There were only 2 young doops here, camped in a huddle of blankets and clothes at the back of a narrow cave. Instruments had confirmed 2 for sure.

Conclusion: third escapee kid, reported by the Hermitory contact, must have died in the desert crossing. A girl, according to the client, so probably too weak for the 4 day traverse thru the stormz and the waste. Sad, but it was the kid's lookout. Had been her decision.

Before elevating, team leader brought round one of the boyz, now snugged in a liteSuit, enough to slap and throw qwestions, but the boy remained silent and upset when the girl's whereabouts was mentioned.

"Is your girlfriend dead? The kid that was with you?" team leader asked finally, after trying to elicit some basic info. The kid – the Indijj one – just nodded once, looking sad and appalled. They applied sedz and turned him off again.

"Let's fly."

*

What took 4 days to walk, had taken a mere 20 minutes to cross by jet. Was almost nitefall now, and the hopper team waited a coupla hours til dark. That was the plan. HighEyes couldn't generally see them under the shimmer in daylight, but at nite there was even less risk.

As soon as dark came, 2 men hauled the bigger kid back to the beach where those moronikal Stümmers lived, out of sight. Get rid of one problem, anywayz.

The kid was comatose on the sand, dropped from a stretcher, just like before. That'd teach him to try and bolt. He'd come round in time, and he knew his way back to the colony now. The Stümmers'd feed him up. Stümmers were soft as cheese.

The team leader was taking no chances with the key kid. "Number One Son," he told his team, "t'be moved somewhere safer for the client, because there was a risk the stupid kid would try and walk out again and die like the girl."

Have to make new arrangements, but Number One Son is best hidden in plain sight. somewhere with many eyes, with a wall. They'd go thru the cloud to Indon. It'd be a high flight, ruff'z'guts, cos there were no safer atmospheric knotholes between Cap and Indon at the moment, but that was the job.

Only one more thing to sort. He marched up the edge of the gorge for a qwick conjunct with the contact.

*

Much, much later in the day, Lissa dogpaddled out from behind the waterfall. Slid gingerly into the light, hyperalert for movements. Everything was diamond bright, making her blink.

She'd been cold and shivery toward the end, tho' she'd perched on a rock shelf for a while, just out of the water. The air was still charged with the heat from the approaching Cloud and the hypercharged atmosphere, but the falling water and deep pool were cooler, especially behind the waterfall.

Lissa's strokes broadened and she swam, barely visible, across to the other side of the pool where there were grasses and trees along a little beach, and carefully crawled on all fours over sand and rocks to where she had a view of the exit. The hopper had definitely gone.

Again, shivering in pants and bra, she carefully walked to the entrance of the waterhole. She kept to the shadowy side and peeked out over the bleak brown, muddy desert.

Nothink. She was alone.

Alone on the rocks where they'd discussed a theoretical splitUp the nite before. The fact shocked her. Was weird that Todd could be so prescient. She'd done what he'd suggested and hid. Now she had to make decisions, the first being: get dry and warm. Her teeth chattered. She'd never been so cold in her life.

The packs were still there, scattered around by whoever searched the area. She grabbed a blanket, stripped naked and dried herself off. Tears started to form around her eyes and she angrily brushed them away. No time for that. She lay back on the rock in the late sun til she felt dry and warm, which took all of 4 minutes. She closed her eyes and sensed the receding multiple pains in her chest and neck that lingered from the beating by the Qwartermaster. Aches were still there but fading. She was getting stronger for sure.

The rock was hot on her back and felt great. She sat up, slung on a x-shirt and shorts, and hungrily munched some honey biscuits mindful to save a supply for the week's walk ... that was Todd's estimate, wasn't it? A week to the Arables? Lissa was thankful that the kaptors hadn't taken any of their stuff, she figured they were the same ruthless people that kidnapped them 3 months ago.

She sqwatted on the rock ledge, looking over the landscape that turning from desert to lakes and streams. In a month, under the Cloud, the scene would almost be alien: dark, wet, stormy.

She knew what she had to do: continue walking west and contact Madrigal Phipps. She filled Todd's abandoned pack with the food and took Todd's shoes (for spares) cos his feet were smaller than Nar's. She made sure the dryFry was packed, a knife, plastic sheet, sunJell, some shirts, socks, a spare pair of Nar's shorts, and her own gear. She found her hat at the back of the cave, and her blanket.

Once complete she went to a muddy part of the waterhole and mixed sunJell and dirt together and smeared her hat, arms and face and shirt with the ochre mud, just as they'd done from the getgo, to beat away the sun and the bugz, and then she set out toward the west where the sun was starting to set. As it got dark, she'd follow the long line of the Canoe and canoeman as they moved thru the tumbling arc of stars, just as

Todd had taught her. She was in that canoe, with the big guy. He was protecting her with his spear.

Was a dry evening after last nite's storm but there'd be more rain to come. The moon was on the descent, pretty bright, hazing out the spear. She was sure that she'd get a few kliks in tonite before she needed to sleep, coz there was no time to lose. One foot trudged in front of the other as she watched for snakes ahead, in the light of her pale, hovering glow

MOONLIGHT

Death brings the greatest silence of all, but we wouldn't wish that on anyone, would we?
Das Glas Haus (2034) Ulli Kalk

PEPPERBEARD was very nervous. He'd been lying in bed earlier when the secret Hermitory scope, next to his pillow, had chirped. When he answered, the voice he knew accused him of breaking the deal. There was humming in the background. Mebbe an engine.

"We have the 2 boyz," said the voice that once held so much promise – even excitement – but now filled him with dread.

"Where's the girl?"

"Not here. Unless she hides in the gorge. And our third boy never escaped. He stayed." His wordz were as usual, clumsy and halting.

"You told us that before – the third boy stayed. But the girl went. So, no sign of the girl your end? I'm coming to dump the boyz back to your Hermitory. For proper safekeeping this time. You understand? I'll meet you at the gorge entrance in half an hour."

Pepperbeard was the only member of the community permitted by the Qwietude to meet outsiders, a task he loathed.

The suppliers were the only outsiders who came, once a year. Even then he hated this outside contact. Gritting his teeth, he said: "Come into the gorge. Put the boyz on the beach where you left them. I'll be in the shadows to the right. Up at the end of the closest rice lagoon. Near that beach."

"Fair 'nough," said the voice. "Bring your scope in case I get lost."

Now he was at the edge of the rice field. Looking out. He knew the aircraft had arrived unseen, almost silent in its descent in the muddy desert. Just a muffled clacking which didn't amount to much. Now, in the shadows by the gorge entrance, he saw figures walking down, a couple of muted glows in their path. The figures placed one unko figure on the beach. Then one of the figures peeled off and started walking toward him while the others disappeared back to their hopper.

There was no glow in front of the figure. The moon, heading down west, was qwite enough to illuminate the scene. He could see the man was tall, and the shock of hair shone silvery in the light. Pepperbeard was gripped by unease. The figure moved easily, in fact qwite slowly, as if enjoying an amble in the moonlight.

Pepperbeard was higher, standing on the edge of the furthest rice lagoon. He heard frogs croak in among the plants behind him. Xcited by the moon. Filled with bursting lusts, he'd thought. He hadn't regretted his own lusts, tho he had got qwite carried away in the end. Lissa had clearly targeted him for sexing, with her smiles, and hanging on his every word, both in the refectory and up at the store. She'd obviously been smitten by him, the older man, and he'd insisted she share a bed. A simple transaction in his mind.

After his wife died, some years back he'd sexed with 1 or 2 of the then older girlz. He'd been a bit rough with them, so he'd bribed them with nice food, drinks and special cloth to keep qwiet. While they did keep qwiet, they then stayed well clear of him. They were women now, but even nowadayz they avoided him if they could. And word had got round the females, obviously, because he found no interest in him from any of the older Hermitory women either.

Anyway, his deal with the new, surprize Funder, now walking toward him, had from the start been brimming with promise. When the Funder made contact, suggesting monies to keep Todd Phipps safe, Pepperbeard had raised the prospect of getting more young people ... especially girl companions?

The Hermitory was starting to have to exclude possible permutations for safeBred babies and the Qwietude's Medikal Examiner had bemoaned that his modeling was looking thin among the family groups now hitting a fourth generation of reproductive age. The Medikal Examiner worried that the closeGenes would cause birth defects.

You're the Qwartermaster. Can't you get new recruits to broaden the genePool? the Medikal Examiner had asked a couple of years back when they were having a beer together.

I'm not a slaver, or a pimp, replied Pepperbeard jovially.

But when he talked to the anonymous Funder, he'd explained – haltingly – the need for new recruits. The Funder was open to the idea of more kidz. He'd said it was achievable, as the young man called Todd had a tight group of friends.

May work to both our advantages, the voice had said. *Look after the young man called Todd, and we'll look after you.*

Look after Todd and a few of his friends for a few months, and nature would take its course, Pepperbeard thought. The lusts of the teenagers would ensure that. As soon as the kidz were dumped at the gorge entrance, Pepperbeard had confided in Leader of Women, urging her to encourage her girlz to sex with the new boyz. And the Medikal Examiner also approved the plan with a nod. They had a possible window of 8 months of fecundity before the supply convoy came, if the youngsters elected to leave.

In fact, Leader of Women loved the idea – her eyes were shining with the prospect of new babies, and better genetics.

And then, argued Pepperbeard, signing furiously in a gloomy corner of the refectory to the 2 members of the Qwietude he felt he could confide in, *the 4 young people may elect to stay anyhow, and contribute a lifetime to the Hermitory. We must make life here as pleasant as we can – for all of them.*

Leader of Women was the one who'd argued not to include Leader of Men in the strategy. She'd felt their discussion was slightly outside the Qwietude's guidelines on coupling. When it came to advice on sexing and partnering, only parents, not senior members of the Qwietude, were the advisers, as authority over personal relationships was invested in the family unit, not in the governing council. The Leader of Men was very proper when it came to the rules. But Leader of Women was keen to try for more babies.

So Pepperbeard never told Leader of Men of his reproductive plan, because ... well, Leader of Men was a bit of a duffer, a bit more sqweamish than Leader of Women when it came to issues around sex. And of course, Pepperbeard wanted the girl for himself.

It had been so simple. Or so he'd thought.

Now here he was, in the warm nite, looking at the moon and the everpresent flicker of lightning in the north, then down at the approaching figure wondering what the man might say.

"Mr Qwartermaster," the man had finally reached him. Was the same voice, sounding pleasingly low, and sotto voce, altho' the frogs nearby had heard and stopped croaking.

The man put out his hand and they'd shaken. The man, for some reason, wore a glove. Pepperbeard had read about the handshaking ritual in books and wondered whether he should have worn a glove too. There were boxes of sheerGloves in the stores for the hygiene team.

The 2 men stood on the edge of the lagoon gazing toward the cliff on the other side.

"You've created a mess which we've had to clean up," the patrician man said.

"I never imagined ... could never *have* imagined, they would try and walk thru the desert," Pepperbeard said.

"That's as may be, but we will have to reconsider the final payment, Mr Qwartermaster. I'm sorry."

"No, no. We proceed with the deal. We are happy to look after both boyz. Won't happen again. But from here I see there's only one boy down on the beach. You said both boyz to be brought back."

"Changed our mind. We are taking Todd Phipps with us. He's too much for your people to handle. We'll keep him sitting tight until middle of the year."

Pepperbeard frowned, feeling more and more uneasy. "And what about the girl?"

"No life signs," said the man curtly.

"Ahh, if she's still out there, she'll perish," said Pepperbeard, agitated. "Thermocell season is almost with us. Sqwalls and storms are coming thru already and the Cloud is now visible to the north from the top gorge. And it's just badland for hundreds of kliks,"

"Don't worry about her."

But the Qwartermaster was worried. She could be carrying his child. This factoid he didn't communicate to the man tho.

The man looked qwite calm in the moonlight, but while looking calm, his voice changed to abrupt and rude.

"I'm afraid no more payments will be made. The deal has gone sour. You were to hold these children until at least April, while I did business elsewhere. You understand, no more payments? We hold Todd Phipps now. Also, because of these escapes and possible conseqwences I'm going to have to ask you for your scope, so there's no trace. You only used the one scope in communications with me?"

"Yizz. We only have one."

"I'll give you a new scope, which doesn't contain my codes. I sincerely don't want to be traced when this is finished."

Pepperbeard nodded obediently. In the minimalist existence of the Qwietude, he'd never come across anyone like this, and was intimidated. The promise of a new scope was a good thing and he could code a new scope. He'd learnt the necessary codes 25 years ago as part of his training with the late Qwartermaster: the critical emergency code, suppliers' codes, the banker. He fished the scope from his pocket and handed it over. The man took the device indifferently, seemingly enjoying the rather beautiful scene before him, the deep shadows, the gorge lake, and the rice ponds along the edges shimmering with moon-silver.

"Now, here's your new one."

Pepperbeard looked down at the new device. It was strangely tubular, rather than flat, with a handle at one end. Very neat, thought Pepperbeard. But then the man pressed one end of the tube hard against his chest, and the shiny moon above melted to nothink.

THE ARABLES

Loneliness is not *part of my prescription, no matter what my enemies say. Community is our solace. Loneliness can occur under the scrutiny of 1000 cameras. Community provides the remedy.*
   Das Glas Haus (2034) Ulli Kalk

EVERY day, Lissa would cycle her mind thru her school subjects, hoping the repetitive thoughts would keep her amused and allow her legs to move one in front of the other. Focus and concentration over sometimes dry, sometimes muddy or wet desert with its strange musty dusty smells and huge patches of dry spinifex grass, clumping for kliks and kliks. The spinifex could be scratchy on her legs so she'd weave around the clumps.

Genuine aloneness brought out fears and terrors of this unknown vast landscape. Sometimes her legs felt like jelly, sometimes numb and drained of feeling. And always there was aching: knees, calves, and especially ankle joints, which worked hard over rocks and rubble on dry ground or hidden in the slippery sliding mud.

To escape the harsh heat, to escape the new aches, she disciplined her mind elsewhere. This she had decided on day one. She would be in control.

Lissa's daily mindLoop began its travels thru the dictionary of Stümmer sign language, from A to Z. Tracking thru the dictionary as best she could, and making the gestures was distasteful because of the dictionary's provenance, but it passed the time, and it provided bittersweet amusement as she worked thru hand gesture after hand gesture as she walked.

After reaching zwarm, she would hum and sing the 2 short song sets of The Philosophikal, thinking of Narmon, Todd, Peet and Jaim'z. Slowing down the beats to make it last, and practising the fingering for the saxophone, with the music playing in her head.

These diversions would take her a while, til the sun was almost above her, and she would search out a gully or a boulder. As Todd had instructed, she would drink her ration of water, and stay in the shade, panting and sipping as the sun reached its zenith and then faded toward the west. If she could, she would sleep in the shade. Once the heat subsided as the sun was setting, around the early 40s, she would start walking again after another drink. Purified ground water if she found a puddle, or using her tanks if she was unable to locate any.

For the early evening walk, she would revise the case law she had worked on that year – go thru them in her mind. Over the past months, she'd never given up hope of sitting at least some of the exams. Cases around people demanding privacy from Government entertained her. But it was mostly corporate law she revised, precedent by precedent. The GovHeg nexus was fascinating.

Trudge she went, trudge, trudge, but her mind danced lightly thru the legal cases and the legislation as the glare of the western sunset caught her in the face. She watched her methodical feet, and the wide brim of her hat shaded out the heat.

At nite, well, that's when she spent much time repelling thoughts of the terrible assault. She watched the light from the glow that floated along in front, gently, at walking speed, and the brown red ground seemed to float along with the glow and her momentum. With nothink much to look at, except the stars and the moon if cloud cover was sparse, or just the glow floating in the inky black, the dark would press in on her and horrible thoughts flooded her mind.

Took a lot of discipline to remember nice things about her late dad, or funny conversations with her mum, to dispel the visions.

Lissa also started thinking about Todd. How much more mature he seemed than Narmon; more capable; much handsomer. Ethically, she knew her unsolicited speculations were wrong. Even if they were schoolmates and friends, Todd was way too fancy for her. A young plutocrat, while she was daughter of a dead milisi major. And most importantly, she and Narmon had pledjd to each other the day before they'd first sexed. Pledjd to be "true thru life". As far as she was concerned, that was an inviolable pledj. Narmon was her steadyBoy and at sometime down the path, they would marry. Those were the rules. They were both Oncers, which was perfekt. Todd was a Oncer too, but that didn't count. She wasn't pledjd to him.

She'd met Todd thru Narmon. The boyz were best friends. She didn't want to ruin that. In fact, Narmon was the one who'd argued for her place in the band. Narmon was the much better musician (tho she was practising hard). She loved him with a passion. And yet ...

The Todd thoughts insinuated themselves under her rather bruised and battered defences. Lissa would begin to speculate, wondering why she'd turned to Todd in her moment of xtreme distress and not Narmon. Then she'd think about what a fantastic and handsome bruzz Todd was. These first speculations were, in a funny way, comforting. She'd then imagine kissing him, and then them fondling one another, and even being an item. Then she'd imagine Todd naked and pulling her toward him gently and she'd roll on top of his lithe body and they'd clasp and have nice sex, and by then the imaginings were way out of hand and, in the end, just before she stopped trudging for the nite, she'd find herself talking out loud, chastising herself, stupidly blaming herself for the rape because she smiled and encouraged Pepperbeard. She'd tried to be the Qwatermaster's friend to find a scope, and he'd hurt her bad.

Was unnerving the way her mind had darkened and fragmented from any certainties.

As the dayz passed, there'd be no nitetime buildup to her "Todd thoughts" ... she'd cut to the kissing and it would escalate from there, along with her final self-recriminations about disloyalty to Narmon. The whole scenario made her feel weird, but she was alone. There was no one to talk to. Often she'd feel tears on her cheeks.

She'd start to see shapes in the shadowy periphery of the glow. Sometimes there was a shape – a startled lizard, perhaps, which would run away. Mostly the shadows were about the size of her terrors.

The lightning in the high north would constantly flicker. She was used to that, a feature of the sky from when she could first remember. In the vast dark, tho, it was scary.

Then she'd grumble: "You're an idiot, Lissa. There's nothink out here except you and your pathetic glows."

Each nite would end with her lying in as sheltered a spot as possible. The air was damp, so she'd set up moisture traps with the plastik sheet. And she would sleep under the plastik to avoid the heavy dew, shivering sometimes, or, if it was raining, hold a blanket over her head and try to sleep. After a while, at least after the first 4 or 5 days, she learnt that the desert was so remote, there was little to be scared of, and so, unless storms swept thru, or she had to wade thru a watercourse, she slept a little more soundly.

She was lonely tho'. Only the thought of Madrigal's voice at the end of some scope, once she made it to the Arables, helped banish thoughts of aloneness. She knew that somewhere, Todd and Narmon would be urging her on. "Phone my mum," Todd'd instructed and she would. But out here in the vast, blank desert, lying under a blanket, or waterproof sheet, with rain pattering down, it was hard not to feel intimidated, tiny, antlike.

Sleep would kick in, her head on the familiar pack, blanket warming her.

And then, as the sky greyed up, ready for day, she would find a fading star she knew, and follow its track as it dipped under the horizon, while opening her mind again to the Stümmer sign language dictionary, starting at *able* and going thru to *zwarm*.

*

And the zwarms could be very frightening. Some days, as she trudged in her armour of dirt and sunjell, she would see a vast bug zwarm in the desert, towering into the sky like grey skyscapers as the hot air gyres propelled them to fly high and move before the advancing Cloud. She couldn't believe how black and dense the zwarms got. First time, she was zwarmed, she didn't take cover and the bugs hit her like driving rain – splattered and clacked against her. Worse, the force of the wall of tiny insects meant they pushed against her and crawled under her collar, up her shirt, and down her front and she'd walked, bent double almost from their scratchy invasion. Then they were gone and she stripped off and shook still live bugs out of her clothes and hair until, shaking with revulsion, there were only bits of leg, head and thorax to finally brush off.

From then on, if she saw a tower the size of a skyscraper heading her way, she ran, and if unable to dodge the moving insects, she'd try and lodge against a rock, or a tussock mound, or dig into the ground face down. The experience of being zwarmed was so unpleasant she muttered to herself: "D'rather live the life of a worm."

What Lissa came to fear the most were the fierce wind gusts which blew out of nowhere and knocked her over if she didn't take shelter. One moment, there'd be a slight breeze, then *whack!* the wind'd crash over the desert like a rushing air truk, and because, in some places the ground was getting wetter and wetter, there was often no warning dust cloud. If her mind was elsewhere, focused on too many corporate law precedents, she'd be blown over like a badly rooted tree, flat on her face. The powerful wind bullets were scary, and the first couple of times it happened she'd copped cuts and bruises on her palms and elbows where she'd broken the sudden fall, and she'd sat crying afterward, dabbing the blood with antiseptic buds.

At other times, the rain pelted down and lightning crackled above her and she walked west as best she could, with the Canoeman obscured by the clouds above. She carefully watched her path behind, as well as in front, and aimed at certain rock formations, bushes, or the tips of sand dunes, as Todd had taught. To deadReckon, he called it. There were no magnetic compasses anymore – direction was all guided thru HighEyes and other satellite coLokators. Only people with traditional learnings could operate without elektronika.

Once, a horrible morning of dusty winds, she looked to the blue sky crushing the horizon like a vice, and finally, after so much walking, so much exhaustion, she felt suffocated. Hit her like one of those windBullets. For a while, as she trudged, Lissa could hardly breathe, as moist air gusted and the clouds built. When noon was close, she stopped her tramp, tramp, trudge, and holed up on the shade side of a spectacular red rock tor that seemed to erupt from the earth. She found herself shaking with fright at all the immensity and tried to control her breathing: deep, slow breaths.

Finally, the wind died in the late afternoon, bringing an astonishing, unusual stillness. Using a small rock, she scratched an arrow on a big, flat groundrock pointing toward the direction she was heading. Then she scrambled up the tor, which was quite vertical, but provided good footholds, and she stood on the flat platform on the top and turned 360 degrees, a slow pirouette. The sun was 20 degrees on the horizon and beginning to turn the world orange. All she saw was red soil, rain streaking groundward in the north, and the sound of winds rustling orange-gold tufts of grass, like a golden ocean, swelling and fading. Beyond that, a red flatTopped range, which she'd been deliberately paralleling, framed the scene. Above, the cloud bruised sky with glints of blue and yellow.

At that moment, as wind rushed across the spinifex, it seemed the landscape moved and swirled in circles like those huge Indijj paintings in Madrigal Phipps' house. The land caught brilliant blasts of late sunlight, goldLeaf rays coming thru cloudbanks and illuminating windCaught willy willies. She gasped at the beauty. It was almost as if she could reach out and stroke the country with her hand, like it was an entire soft animal, breathing and glowing.

She also found, after a day of weird claustrophobia, that she could breathe easily again.

*

The environs of the tor, its cracks, niches and grass tufts, provided her with 3 quite sizable skinks, which she bashed with a stick and sizzled with the dryFry and chewed with gusto, washed down with flat tasting purified water. She picked a handful of bush currants growing around the tor's base, and chewed the small sweet fruits.

From the corner of her eye she'd also spotted a thorny devil, but in deference to Todd and his beliefs, didn't kill it. Wasn't enough meat on it, anyway.

She stared at its incredible knobbly head and beautiful camouflage markings and smiled at the thought of Todd's own respect for this species.

The devil, looking like an old stick covered in thorns and yellow lichen, observed her from a grass tuft. It bobbed its head at her once, before disappearing into the base of the tor.

She lay for a little while longer in the shade and then stood, shook some feeling back into her numb legs, lifted her pack and moved west.

From that moment on, things felt easier, like she had some sort of permission, on the thorny devils's nod, to traverse the desert, or she had become part of it during her journey. The fear left her for good, except when she heard the cackle of approaching storms, or the onrush of a strong wind bullet. But now she knew what to do.

*

Todd had shown her how to navigate, take rest in the heat and find food and water, and she'd worked out the rest. She wished, sometimes, that she was taller, because she'd go further faster with a longer stride.

Every day she would wake, then spare a palmful of water to wash her face. She'd brush her hair with the tiny brush from the bathroom pack the Stümmers had given her. The dirt on her skin was caked on, but Todd had said, *Keeps you covered if you mix it with the jell. Keeps off the bugs.* She knew she stank. Her clothes, which she recycled without washing, were getting stiff and crunchy. If it wasn't for the mindLoop every day, and the hair brushing, she knew she'd hate herself entirely.

Over a 2 day period, there had been enough rain to fill her 3 water bottles 10 times over, and she washed her underwear and hung it to dry off the back of her pack, along with the 3 sunCharged glows. She could set up a trig with the teflite coat and when it poured down, a V in the thin teflite fabric would channel rainwater into the bottles. If she was harvesting softer rain it could take an hour, but Todd had told them that water was their best friend so grab it when you can. You're walking thru the world's biggest steambath and need to hydrate like it's a religious practise, he had said.

Water being her best friend wasn't qwite true. Todd was her best friend – next to Narmon. And then came water.

She'd try and sleep from late morning thru to 4-ish, and move on in the cooler hours until she could walk no more.

*

Todd had speculated a week's walk to the Arables. Was now a fortnite gone past, but she knew her line of traverse was correct and all she could do was walk. On the 14th day into her phenomenal trek, she was following another brownsoil ridge, hoping it was straight, when in the early evening light she thought she could see a finger of dust in the distance, pointing high into the landscape. The finger was moving qwickly and parallel to her and leaving a thin veil of dusty air settling into the desert behind.

A vehicle?

Out here?

Unlikely to be her pursuers now, after 2 weeks of the remotest scrambling.

It could be Indijj, she thought. Indijj people still lived in the Great Sandy Desert in scattered places. Todd had said so. "Keeping good faith with their sacred places," he'd said. She didn't have oculars and the finger of dust was moving fast. She quickly rigged an orange plastic ribbon, which had been wrapped around the portable medik kit, to a long thin stick which she waved wildly in the sky.

"Over here!" she shouted. "Help!"

Had the finger slowed down? "Helllllllp!"

She could just make out a tanklike vehicle, grey with wheels. It was now travelling away from her, toward the west. Her direction. Who else would be out here?

Her waving got more frantic, but it was no use. The piece of plastic was small, and they'd have to be looking long and hard to see her in the rear mirror of the vehicle.

Lissa sighed and sat down to rest from her exertions. She wiped the sweat from her eyes and found they were also tears. She sat and cried for a while, bemoaning her loneliness, feeling the hunger in her stomach, her defences stripped in a wave of exhaustion and gloom. The rocks under her bum were sharp, and she was soon forced to stand up.

"Aw, getta grip, Liss," she said. "If that's the sight of people, mebbe I'm closer to the Arables than I thought. Mebbe I'm almost there."

And she started thinking positive and upbeat and told herself there was a long evening's walk ahead, and she should watch for headlights.

*

Lissa marked the days on her pack. When she settled down to camp, she'd pen a mark on the backstrap to keep track of the days. The rain started falling in regular bursts, downpours so heavy she would crouch until they passed. The track got muddier and muddier. Red brown mud that stuck. At nite she'd try to fold herself into the teflite wraps to stay warm.

One nite when she was ready to camp, after the twentieth day of her trek, and she'd been walking thru a sparse forest of stunted eucalypts, she came over a rise. From the top, Lissa thought she saw the glow of somethink over the horizon. A yellow glow that wasn't the sun's reflection. The sky was clouded and the glow bounced on a cloudbank above.

For a moment, a thrill went thru her – the glow could be emanating from some remote town. But sense took over and instead of persevering and walking, she set up camp with teflite wraps to catch the dew, just in case it was a mirage. Then she slid under the tied structure on a couple of outstretched blankets.

She was excited, and hoped her excitement was justified. She also noticed that her legs didn't feel like jelly anymore. In fact, they almost didn't feel tired.

*

When the dirty girl appeared, walking thru the sludge and puddles of the early monsoon near Kampung 37, the family Nardi were in a fluster. They farmed on the very eastern edge of the Arables. Beyond his mango orchard, Father Nardi ran thru the fields of vegetables to greet the figure that was weaving thru a mirage toward them.

The dirty girl held up her hand to show she was okay. She was walking strongly out of the nowhere desert. He couldn't believe it.

"Hi," she said, from under a muddy hat. Father looked at the diminutive person before him and helped take her backpack off. She stretched when the weight had gone and nodded to him, saying nothink, but searching his face, all the same.

He felt urgent sorrow for the child. She was caked in mud and dried sunjell, and emaciated. Her legs were scratched and scabbed and lumpy with mud. She wore patched shoes. The lank and filthy red hair under her hat was brown. Tho she trembled, the dirty girl managed to hold her head up.

"Come," he said, gesturing, pity rushing thru him. He felt impelled to find her a bath and food. "You have walked far? You from Kampung to the north, mebbe?"

"Err, no. Bit further ... I came over the West Tanami. Over top of Sandy Desert," said the girl. She had a grim little smile on her face. "Is this the Arables? Where is this?"

"My farm. My farm at Kampung 37. Come with me. You must be very hungry. Here is the edge of village settlement, my gardens. Our new farmlands which Government allocated 8 years back. I been here since then. We are all Balinese here. We are very lucky."

Father had good English. The kidz arrived after running thru the water channels between the mature bok choi, eggplants, tomatoes and snake beans. The kidz surrounded her dressed in bright cotton frocks and shirts. They looked amazed at the dirt-caked girl who was swallowing the last of her water from a battered bottle.

"Are you okay?" asked Father, uncertainly.

"Yes, yes. Long walk," she said. She didn't look okay at all.

"How old are you?" Father asked.

"Just turned 17," Lissa answered. "Is there komms in the village where I can scope my mum?"

"Mum? So your parents do not know where you are?" said Father, eyes wider.

"I ..." Lissa couldn't say she was kidnapped – that would have been unreasonable and she would have frightened the old man. So she said: "I got lost."

"Ah, yizz," said Father. "That happens. Some children in Kampung 25 go lost last year and one died. For someone lost in the desert, you look good. Standing up. You must be very fit!" he added, sounding unsure.

"I'm fine."

He seemed pleased there was no need for serious medik.

"A good survival teacher showed me how to eat and find water," said Lissa. "But may I ask ... could I have some boiled vegetables or fruit? Or noodles? I've only eaten roasted lizards and snakes, and some bush currants and bugs and ... and honey biscuits. I can repay you later."

She'd killed the little lizards, skinks and stumpies, and gutted them with a knife, altho dryFrying them was icky. So was dry frying the locusts Todd also said were good tucker, and apart from the crispy wings, they did taste okay. So she'd survived, but was certain she'd not eaten enough. The look of pity on the old Balinese fellow's face made her feel sorry for herself.

"Of course," said Father Nardi. "Come. I take you to the K37 and you can eat good food and scope your parents. They must be very worried."

The Kampung was a clean steel T-shaped fabrication, a bunch of small dwellings under a steel stormproof lid, and around a big open area. At one end was a small supply store, fuel depot and a special office for the Kampung's mayor. Surrounding the main block were shacks and smaller, more permanent, dwellings for farmers and families which could be replaced if smashed up by the weather. Residents could shelter in the central slab'n'fab, built to survive a fearful pounding.

As they walked, Father Nardi explained that 15 families were allotted subsistence fields in the Kampung, which they cultivated and tended. He confirmed they were on the eastern edge of the habitable, growable Arables. An agricultural strip inland from the coast that tracked down to the border of West Cap and AuZ, developed after rainfall patterns changed in the 2080s, and the land became more annually reliable for cropping.

All across the greening Arables, the inhabitants were a mix of nationalities, The Indijj people of course, plus new settlers: Indonesians, Bangladeshis, Filipinos, driven from their lands by stormz and rising sea levels. Since *the Blend* everyone lived peacefully, happy they were given a new lease on life, even if it was subsistence living.

Lissa was unaware that so many climate refugees lived like this, in industrious communities, tho she'd seen plenty of streetVendors and beggars around her home city.

All the climate reLokates, she knew, had lived thru terrible trauma with the loss of their lands and family members, and they only wanted their kidz to live and thrive. And they were doing what they knew best – cultivating. A hard life, but AuZ-gov made them safe, so they wouldn't dare complain.

Lissa knew from school that these people leased the land at peppercorn rent from AgriHegs, mostly subsistence for themselves, but also some cashcrops, like pharmaceutical opium, chopchop, or horticulturals supplied, as reqwired, to the company. Whole families would chip in for the lease, and work the few hectares they acqwired.

This was one such lease – K37.

As Lissa and Father Nardi reached the steel compound, she saw adults and kidz in their big wide hats and sarongs, harvesting endSeason tomatoes, and green veggies like bok choi. Preserving fruit on dryers. They reminded her of the Stümmers in their gardens, but at K37 there was chatter and the kidz were running up and down, playing and laughing. Chirping like happy birds.

Real people, she thought. *Poor little Stümmer childen miss out on all that playChatter.*

"This not the volcanic soil of my father's fields. My father's home. But we have good life here as long as our best resource is kept protected from the Singular Enemy. What we have made is fertile soil. We have very big compost silos. Look – over there. When summer Cloud comes from the north, we make it watertight."

Father Nardi explained they gathered their best soil from the fields, using pickups and dingoDozers, and would tip loads of it, with extra fertiMeal and wormcasts, into large underground silos. When the summer 'phoons and floods had passed, they'd deploy a giant mulch pump to spray the topsoil across the fields again.

"We don' let all that good soilwork be wasted and washed away," said Father Nardi proudly.

Lissa saw the open concrete mouths, great circular underground structures to the south of the Kampung. A digger was pouring a stream of brown soil into the hole with a clunk and a whoosh. She was impressed by the enjjineering, and nodded, but was keen to get to the komms scope.

Lissa followed Father Nardi to the office, up steps and crossing a clean, swept platform where people were sitting, making lunch, eating boiled rice, and drinking from thin water bottles, and teaching the little kidz writing and sums in a break from the hectik weeding and harvesting. The summer 'phoons were now not long off.

In the neat office with its scopes and screens in front of her, finally, was a communications device. She knew the Phipps home code well. Lissa gripped the handset, and intejered. Dart sent. The screen lit up.

*

Only 4 hours later, Madrigal Phipps sat holding Lissa's hand on the communal platform area at K37. Behind, in the space between habitations and fields, fringed by banana trees, was an immense grey hopper. The aircraft had roared in an hour back, scaring the children. Men in uniform were sqwatted under it, chatting to locals, being given tea. The children had got brave again, and were playing on the hopper's landing wheels.

It was raining, of course. Big wet pelts of rain.

Madrigal was in a uniform of some sort, hair pinned back, looking deadly serious, while Lissa sobbed uncontrollably, releasing the pent-up stress of the violent rape and its subsequent nitetime hauntings, as well as 3 months of fearful anxiety. Then the 3 week trek across desert wastes, alone with the uncertainty and boredom, which had almost been as bad as the weather that had ripped around her in some terrifying moments. Her stress was compounded by the recapture of Narmon and Todd.

And she was shocked at how qwickly Mardigal had arrived.

*

After she'd scoped Madrigal in her emergency call, the farmer gave her loose cotton pants and an X-shirt, and a woman showed her an outside shower. It wasn't totally private, so as qwickly as she could, Lissa scraped and washed as much muck off her body and out of her hair as she could. Then a huge bowl of rice, chicken and vegetables, with salty sweet soy sauce, was plonked in front of her, and she demolished the tastiest meal in her life.

The entire Kampung had gathered to watch the hopper's arrival. They hardly ever saw any authorities or administratives. Mebbe once in a couple of years a truk would arrive. An aircraft was unprecedented.

"Wow. You must have some important Mum, Mz Lissa," said Father Nardi's wife who was standing beside her.

Lissa had approached the exit door as the rotors stopped and saw faces she knew.

She was still clammy and smeary when Madrigal and Pearl had emerged from the enormous hopper craft and down the steps. She walked, head up firmly, still bottling the tears, and gave Madrigal a very hesitant damp hug, but Madrigal had reciprocated with a huge sqweeze of relief, dirtying up the uniform she wore. Lissa had sputtered an apology but Madrigal only laughed. "We've brought you fresh clothes and shoes. Koo! Look at your shoes!"

Lissa's semi-washed shoes were held tight by bits of gaffTape and scored with holes.

"We've a proper shower in the hopper. And shampoo. You'll be fine," said Madrigal, looking happy and anxious.

They'd walked over to the Kampung buildings led by the welcoming Father Nardi, and found somewhere to talk.

*

Now she was sobbing.

Pearl sat a couple of meters back, out of her line of sight, but Lissa knew the big woman was there, watching her intently.

As big raindrops splattered down, banging against the steel shelter's lid above like a thousand teeth gently chattering, she'd told her story from beginning to end and she left nothink out. Except for her strange mindLoops, of course.

She told Madrigal about life with the Stümmers, the gorge and its daily chores, the signTalk of flickering hand gestures, like little fish in an aqwarium tank, and the endless silence. She recounted in detail the awful assault, the escape, the boys' recapture, the solo trek across the vivid dangerous land that was coming alive with water. She had walked for 25 days non-stop.

Madrigal had listened intently, and was visibly upset when the story of the Qwartermaster was told. "Oh," she said, at each awful detail. "Oh, no, no, no."

And as Lissa remembered and spoke, the buildup of details burst like a storm inside her too. So infuriating. She'd never, ever wanted to cry in front of Dr Madrigal Phipps and now she was. Madrigal turned to Pearl and asked her to get another glass of lemon water.

*

Madrigal had let Lissa talk almost uninterrupted until the tears started to trickle and flood down the young woman's cheeks and Lissa shook with emotion.

Madrgal leant across and held Lissa's arm gently.

"Don't hate yourself for crying," Madrigal said, reading her mind. "I'd cry, too, if I'd been raped, and then walked across the West Tanami and Great Sandy Desert. Geez ..."

"I can't help it," sobbed Lissa. "I hate this crying!"

"Drink this," said Pearl. And she did, and the crying dialed down to blubbering and sniffling.

Magrigal shifted beside her young friend and held her hand. She asked in the qwietest voice: "So you stayed one nite at the ScorpionClaw waterhole and that's where Todd and Narmon were taken?"

"Well, yes. If that's what the waterhole is called?"

"That's what you said in language. And from there you walked another 500 or so kliks west following the Canoe?"

"If that's how long the distance is …"

Pearl laughed, and even recovering from the horror of the news of Lissa's assault, Madrigal managed a smile. "You're a hardAss," she said. "Give me another hug." And they hugged, even more firmly.

*

Suddenly, with Lissa's story, the Stümmers and their Hermitory became a sharp tactical thorn in the side of Madrigal Phipps.

She knew AuZgov had been happy to have any citizens angry about the social systems of the time voluntarily seqwester themselves away in anonymous oblivion on the far outer fringes. AuZgov had let them disappear, were C-ops Daniels' wordz when she'd scoped him with the news. The Stümmers 3 AuZtralian colonies were established 100 years past, in the late 2030s. That suited everyone in the Age of Purity and Virtue. Stümmer colonies were generally self-sufficient, and a haven for malcontents and the antisocial. *If they wanted to lose their voices, then good!* Daniels had said, approvingly.

It was thought that there were only 2 AuZtralian Hermitories. After the Blend, the Central Desert Hermitory ended up in the Territory of Capricornia, seemingly kept alive by genuine supporters, and some old AuZgov money that had been channeled in thru frontPersons years back in order to keep the "malcontents" silent and out of the way. Madrigal surmised, correctly, that her Todd, and the 3 other kidz, had been parked in the colony by the *evil others* (her wordz) and the Stümmers had been unwitting babysitters. For those in the know about pathological Stümmer reticence, the colony was a perfekt place to seqwester kidnapees for a time.

She also surmised that, due to the Phipps wealth, Todd was the main game for the abductors.

Question was, who recaptured them? And had the boyz been dumped back in the Stümmer's gorge?

Because of AuZgov's strikt protocols, she should have been reluctant to penetrate the Government non-contact agreement at the central desert Hermitory, but Todd and Narmon could be down there. Peet certainly was and she had to return for Peet. The guilt that had sat on her shoulders the past 3 months was overwhelming, and this was good news for 3 sets of fretting parents.

She had already scoped Lissa's mother and Lissa had spoken at length to her without mentioning the awful Pepperbeard. Was Lissa's decision whether Minnie-Tuton would be told about the assault. She'd simply told her mum she was safe, but because of time constraints, they'd be going to find Narmon, Todd and Peet before heading home. Lissa was with Madrigal and Pearl. Safe now, but not qwite home.

"I'm ..." said Minnie-Tuton to Madrigal, after Lissa turned the scope to her. Minnie-Tuton was so overwhelmed she couldn't speak for almost a minute, leaving Madrigal and Pearl impatient, and Lissa embarrassed. "Happy," she finally said. "Thankyou."At first Lissa cringed at the thought of returning to the Hermitory, scene of her violation. Madrigal said she could stay in the hopper while she and Pearl negotiated, but Lissa said no. She wanted to look her tormentor in the eye. After the success of her trek, she felt strong and in control.

"I can handle it," she said.

These sex crimes were also a huge problem. The fact her own boy had been seduced by a senior Hermitory elder was bad enough, but a brutal sexual assault on Lissa had Madrigal and Pearl seething.

Rapes didn't happen in the respectful world of Purity. Just didn't.

Even in the boondox – places like Kampung 37 – people knew the rules and abided. The team would have to arrest the Qwartermaster, and that would tear the fabric of the Stümmer community apart. As for Leader of Women, she was tricky.

What occurred with Todd was not so clear legally and officials would necessarily have to talk to Todd about the incident (if she could only find him). Power and status was misused when sexing with a less powerful person, but it could also be argued that *some* level of consent was elicited from the victim. Such crimes were more likely to occur in the Age of Purity. If Todd was to press charges, he'd have to be consulted first on that level of understood consent.

A DEAD END

Let me illustrate: when I was imprisoned, solitary was never solitary. While incarcerated, the hard-beaked cameras ogled down from the top corners of my cell, monitoring when I moved from bed to chair or chair to bed, when I undressed, when I pissed. When I turned in my sleep.
I knew, all the time, a pair of eyes, or 2 pairs, if not thousands, were at the other end, watching.
And still, I was lonely.
Das Glas Haus (2034) Ulli Kalk

THE hopper rotors crackled across the gorgeTop to alert the Hermitory of an official visit. Madrigal had cleared the visit with C-Ops, who agreed the line of inquiry at the Hermitory was crucial. Especially if they were involved in a conspiracy involving banned devices.

Daniels had been very adamant on the scope: "Reel them in, Senior Courier. We want this issue dealt with, and arrests made so we can all move on."

He'd also made noises about closing down the Hermitory as it harboured "problem people," but Madrigal wasn't so sure, and she promised to make an assessment.

The aircraft burst thru the rainclouds and Madrigal could see, on either side, the crusty red rock rearing from the floor of the desert, shiny with runoff, the glint of river running thru, and the glinting white of dwelling roofs.

Deep down, Madrigal sensed Todd was not located in the buildings below, but she was hoping til she almost burst that her son's wiry figure would emerge out of any welcoming committee, and he'd run over and embrace her.

A dream. Just a dream, she told herself.

There were no known komms at the Hermitory, so no scoping the residents to give them prior warning. The rattle of jets and rotors was warning time enough. Madrigal knew about this strange whitefella western desert community from long ago. Wasn't near her family country by a long klik, but many decades back, an argument erupted between Phipps Industries and AuZgov about energySource locations. After all, Phipps Industries was a powerful Heg which had originally coalesced around Indijj and mining interests in what had once been the State of Western Australia.

She remembered at the time her father railing about the fact that AuZgov wanted to "preserve the sanctity" of the Stümmers and their noGo zone. Tho' her dad cared very little for true Indijj beliefs, or his cultural heritage, bestowed by his grandfather, he was still asking why the Traditional Owners, or TrOws, weren't the primary contact in the area rather than "a bunch of Stümmer whitefellas who *didn't speak to anyone.*" She remembered him yelling the wordz.

Woah, she'd been young. Was an early memory.

"Why would AuZgov even contemplate allowing them to hole up in a gorge when it's blackfella land?"

He couldn't understand the concept of mutual, non-monetary, binding agreements that must have occurred between folks for common, nonProfit purposes: between the Stümmers and the local TrOws.

Not that he cared much about TrOws feelings either, tho the TrOws would've shared in the bounty of any mineral extractions or multiArray sunfarm that might have been constructed. Old Man Phipps just wanted access to build his energy networks. She remembered his stubbled face framed in a high corporate window somewhere, stabbing his index finger on a padMap, bursting with frustration. A picture of masculine anger.

*

The hopper landed in the rainy season mud close to the torrent that gushed out of the gorge mouth. The Cloud made things gloomy and visibility was smeared with rain, but Lissa knew the way. Madrigal and Pearl followed Lissa, who marched confidently into the dark chasm, while arresting officers and a couple of notetakers made up the rear. The young woman guided them thru the high gorge mouth and past the croc infested beach along the path she knew.

Madrigal could see that Lissa, wrapped in a rainCloak, was very tense, even fearful, but she kept leading them along the rocky footpad purposefully.

"This is serious slippery," said Pearl thru the hiss of the rainfall. "Keep balanced." They walked steadily up the track to a higher ridge under the Hermitory buildings. In the puddles they plished thru, light from the domiciles and terraces above reflected a scattered red and yellow, and if it was not for the teflite wrap, Madrigal would have felt even wetter. Still, the wrap didn't stop the hot damp infusing her skin.

Rainwater dribbled over Madrigal's face as she looked up toward the welcoming party that had quickly assembled along the first terrace up top. In the rain and mist they made out a big group of older people – perhaps 12, all in white.

With the waiting crowd was Narmon, looked mightily relieved to see Madrigal and his living, breathing girlfriend. Narmon stood beside Peet, Curl and a couple of younger men and women. Two white clad, grey haired figures were in the centre, with young helpers holding large bright umbrellas above their heads. Others held their own, or had rainhoods.

Madrigal crunched over the rocks and as she approached the 2 Leaders, looked them in the eye, unflinchingly.

"Senior Courier Madrigal Phipps of AuZgov," she said presenting her credentials to the pair under the umbrellas who stepped forward. Madrigal knew they were the Hermitory Leaders – Lissa had described them minutely, down to the Leader of Women's hair length, rather pointy nose and hazel eyes. Leader of Men was identifiable by his real optical spectacles in a round gold frame. Lissa glowered at them, looking round for Pepperbeard and wiping the rain from her face.

"Where is he?" Lissa signed to Narmon who was standing to one side. The anger in her eyes meant she was talking about her tormentor and not Todd.

Narmon pursed his lips and shook his head cryptically. Mebbe her tormentor was in some sort of Stümmer jail room, she thought. Good!

Leader of Men turned to Peet and waved him forward and started to gesture qwickly.

"Revered greetings, Courier Phipps," translated Peet watching the Leader's hands. "I am Leader of Men in this closed Hermitory, and coChair of the Qwietude, our governing body. While your presence is not according to the lines of law set and understood for almost a century between ourselves and AuZgov, we understand why you have come, and because of this, you are welcome. Your son was a guest of ours this past 3 months."

"Where is my son?" asked Madrigal bluntly.

Leader of Men understood, nodded and started signing.

Peet translated: "Sadly, not with us ... I understand you are anxious. Young Narmon can better answer those further qwestions. It is pouring with rain and perhaps it would be best if we communicate under shelter."

Madrigal nodded. She'd guessed that Todd was missing otherwise he'd be at the front of the crowd. They trailed in silence 100 meters up steps and into an arched tunnel which led to one of the living areas, a large communal hall. The Refectory. Lit with wall lights as the clouds outside cast a darkness, the Stümmers depended on precious battery power to charge the glows. The room smelled of cooked vegetables and baking bread, as the lunchtime soup was being made in an adjacent kitchen.

The welcoming party sat around a long wood-slab table made from a once giant tree. Lissa sat with Narmon.

The Leader of Men nodded and Narmon spoke: "Hi, Madrigal. I am so pleased to see you and Lissa!" he said. "Lissa, you made it!"

"Across to the Arables," Lissa replied.

"She walked out to the Arables and scoped me. Where's Todd?"

So Narmon finished the story that Lissa couldn't.

*

Three weeks back, Narmon woke groggily on the lagoon beach just inside the gorge, and realized the masked men in the hopper had again dumped him, while comatose, back near the Hermitory. Todd was not beside him, and there were no little kidz around either. It was very early morning and the colony of freshwater crocs were dormant in the cold. He'd been unko, lying in the rain all nite and no one had found him. He struggled up and staggered along the floor of the gorge, his head still swimming from the sedatives, to the bottom of the steps to the living area. Narmon then sat for a while, recovering, and cursing his luck for being returned to a place that he'd spent so much effort escaping. He looked at his blistered, bruised feet and roiled with frustration.

He could hear a commotion along the walkways above him tho'. He crawled up the stairs, not trusting that he wasn't still weak and tumbly from the drugs. He found chaos in the usually severe silence of the courtyard with groups running back and forth. The Stümmers were astonished to see him, and more astonished when he collapsed on the courtyard floor.

Again he woke up, this time in the medikal facility with Peet in a bedside chair. Peet looked grim. Peet explained to Narmon that at the same time he'd been dumped, someone came in, drowned Pepperbeard in one of the paddy gardens along near the gorge mouth, and had then stolen the Hermitory's one and only official communication device.

*

"So the Qwartermaster? He is dead?" Madrigal asked.

The Stümmers bowed their heads and gestured similarly.

"They are saying in their language – *may he rest forever in beautiful silence*," Peet said.

"They think he suicided," added Narmon. "From the shame of his actions."

Pearl snorted and Lissa glowered at the ground, while Madrigal remained stonyfaced. A key witness to her son's disappearance was gone, and so was the komms tool that might have been used to trace the perpetrators. The criminals had cleaned up.

"No one saw the Qwartermaster go down to the gardens?" Madrigal asked.

"No one," translated Peet via Leader of Men "It happened in the middle of the nite. At the same time Narmon was dropped. The Qwartermaster was the Hermitory's official transactor, who dealt solo with the outside world. The Qwartermaster is the official that had responsibility for ordering supplies. He was the only one allowed."

"And Todd was nowhere to be found in the gorge? You searched?"

"They did," Narmon added. "When they found me, people were sent outside, and up the gorge and along the top. We thought he might have woken before me and hidden somewhere. They checked the topRidges where Todd liked to sit, the exterior, in case he'd woken and made his way out hunting for Lissa. Everywhere was searched. Nobody found," said Narmon. "There's just me and Peet."

*

Hands clasped tightly on the table, Madrigal's head dropped as she pondered her next moments. She also didn't want people to see the effort it was taking to control the emotions flashing over her face. She forced the face muscles back to a blank, diplomatik eqwilibrium. The room was full of people, but they held their breaths waiting for this angry stranger in her black skintight uniform and green jacket with flashes on its shoulder, to do somethink. Pearl sat by Madrigal, understanding the disappointment welling up in her boss. This was a chance to recover Todd, and he had been snatched again. The scope was a crucial clue and it was gone. The Stümmers, hidden from the mouth of the gorge, would have seen nothink.

She looked up: "Can I see the dead man? Or have you disposed of the body."

The reqwest surprized the Leaders. They were expecting her to ask for a drink of tea or kopi.

"Of course. He is still in a freezer in the morgue, until the weather changes for better and he can properly be buried. You want to see him now?" Peet translated.

"In a moment. We have to get moving, Pearl."

She turned to the Leaders and said: "I've heard some upsetting stories about this community. I had a long talk with Lissa and she told me that bad things happened to her."

"We acknowledge that," said the Leader of Men verbally. "The Qwietude prevails over breaches of our laws. I assure you, at the time I was unaware of any of the incidents that occurred. Your young people – they – I was made aware. Sadly, the man responsible for Lissa's hurt is dead and we understand not why. He may have drowned himself in shame of action – we believe in peace here – but no untimely death is acceptable, whatever one does. We did not know he was responsible for these crimes until Narmon told us. He was dead by then."

There was a pause for a moment, as Leader of Men looked so sad.

"I'm sure," said Madrigal slowly, "but in death, your Qwartermaster has escaped justice and any self-realization of his crimes. I brought an arresting milisi officer to remove him and take him to the justice precinct in Perth. What he did was unnatural, and against all tenets of our Age." She patted Lissa's arm across the table. "You haven't received real justice, dearest Lissa. The man who assaulted you was never held responsible and he never reverently and abjectly apologized to you."

Lissa stayed stonyfaced and nodded, while in fact she was secretly pleased that Pepperbeard was dead.

"As for you, Leader of Women? Have you been punished?"

Leader of Women flinched.

"She has been counseled," Peet translated. Leader of Men looked annoyed at Madrigal's shot.

"Counseled? You understand," said Madrigal tartly, "that if my son Todd decides to press charges, this issue will also be taken elsewhere." Madrigal could do tartly very well. The 2 Leaders looked very unimpressed.

"It's no light matter," continued Madrigal ominously. "We regard her behaviour as legally actionable."

The leaders flinched and 1 or 2 Stümmer women gasped.

Madrigal wondered why in hell her boy gone to bed with the Leader of Women. Had he been drugged? HypnoSexed by the hazel eyes?

*

She turned to Narmon and Peet.

"We'll be leaving after I've examined the Qwartermaster. Grab anything you want to bring."

Narmon said: "I'm right to go, Dr Phipps."

Peet said: "And if it's okay, I'm staying at the Hermitory."

Madrigal was thunderstruck.

"But your parents?"

"I actually like it here. I like their way of existing in silence in this secret place. It's wonderful. And I have a steadyGirl now. This is Curl ... and we have pledjd." He pulled Curl by the hand toward Madrigal. She was a pretty, dark haired young woman with an uncertain smile on her face. Madrigal got the picture.

"You're not thinking this thru, Peet. I'm talking to your mother and father every other day – they're very upset. This morning I told them I'm bringing you home. They need to talk to you, hug you. You know? A nice young girlfriend is one thing ..."

Curl gestured to Peet fluidly and severally. It was clear she was telling him she didn't mind if he left. Peet shook his head.

"I'm staying."

"You can't."

Impasse. The Leaders of both Men and Women looked qwite pleased at Pete's intransigence.

"Here's the deal," said Madrigal. "Your mother and father deserve an explanation if you choose to live here. You come with me. You explain your decision. Give them hugs and reassurance." She thought of the hugs she dreamed of from her Todd. "If you are still wanting to join the Stümmers, I am happy to authorize a Phipps aircraft to bring you back – but you understand once you're back, this is a closed community. You will live here forever."

Peet looked dubious.

"You'll fly me back?"

"You have my word."

He started signing furiously to Curl. She nodded, her face shining. They clasped together for some time and then he said: "I'll get my things. Don't you let my mum and dad break your word, Dr Phipps."

"I won't," said Madrigal, taking a punt that his parents would win the conversation with their son so she would in no way have to keep her word. But the farewell hug had been ominously ferocious. Peet meant it when he said he wanted to stay with Curl.

*

After the deadly climate shifts, Madrigal, like most people, hated the thought of loss – of anyone. The experience, still in the living memory, of flooded coasts and drowned towns, desertification and starvation, fires, sinking boats and dying babies. The cataclysmic stepChange when climate deterioration suddenly accelerated, and, and for which there was little preparation in the 2080's, had been traumatic and shocking. So while she felt it was her duty, the examination of bodies always physically pained her.

To look at the corpse of Pepperbeard was wrenching, whatever evils he had done to Lissa. She took no joy in his death.

Pearl was a trained killer. Her kind were casually called "throwbacks", people who were somehow inured to death and guilt. Her training had reached over the psychic and spiritual hurdle of extinguishing a life – even tougher for a woman. Pearl had no compunction in killing in defence, and Madrigal accepted Pearl's viewpoint. She also clearly understood the people Pepperbeard dealt with had no compunction either. They killed to further their goals, whatever they were. Her boy was held by a ruthless actor.

But Madrigal was washed over with sorrow as she approached the dead man on the bed. The iced body was still in a long gown and Madrigal asked the medikos to remove the Qwartermaster's clothes, which they did with some huffing and puffing. He was short, but looked like a very strong man. His skin was light blue from the refrigeration. While Narmon and Lissa were asked to wait outside, Peet was present to translate. He looked qweasily at the blueing corpse. Pearl and Madrigal examined it very carefully.

"He was found drowned? Was there water in his lungs?"

With flickering hand gestures, Peet discussed the discovery of Pepperbeard's corpse with 2 of the medik men and then told Madrigal that the men who pulled him from the field had found the Qwartermaster face down, but only semiSubmerged. One foot was on a bank, like he'd fallen in. When they pulled the man out, they saw water gush from his mouth. This detail wasn't conclusive enough for Madrigal. She knew full well that the people who held Todd were killers, and she was keen to know how Pepperbeard had really met his end.

They looked at every inch of skin.

"No headblows," said Pearl.

"No burns from externals, or bullet holes."

"Injection marks?" They grabbed a magnifying glass and scoured the body.

"He was strong as an ox – wouldn't have gone without a struggle and there are no recent bruises, no fist cuts. No defence marks on his arms. I think whoever it was suggested they meet and he went to the location for a chat. Can't test for it here, but the killer likely applied a heartStopper to the chest, extinguished his bioelektriks and took his scope."

Pearl took a hypo from a kit and took blood and urine samples into satchetSeals. She stuck a longer needle between 2 ribs into a lung to remove fluid in case muddy water was present. The best she could do.

"It's been 3 weeks but we might be able to find somethink in the fluids," she said packing the phials away in her bag.

"Can you take us to where the body was found," Madrigal said.

She was convinced every bit of evidence would help her track Todd.

*

The paddy fields were long ponds that snaked along the inside and outside edges of the gorge and its mazelike interior, using stored water to grow the rice, and on the embankments, vegetables such as corn. The pond where Pepperbeard was found was furthest away from the community and closest to the beach, making it clear that he'd gone to meet the hopper, lured to his death. The redBrown mud around the ponds had been affected by driving rain since the death, but the white torchlight cut the gloom and she saw faint dragmarks where the body had been pulled out, and a plethora of vague footprints by the edge.

"Peet, can you ask if they searched the water for Pepperbeard's scope?"

The men who had dealt with Pepperbeard communicated that they'd waded thru the area looking for his scope after they found Pepperbeard's safe open and empty.

"You really looked?"

I used a chip detector, signed one of the men.

Fair enough, thought Madrigal, but she got into the sqwelchy mud anyway and felt around the areas where Pepperbeard's head and hands would have been. She then looked around for tracks coming up to the fields from the gorge entrance and found partial footprints of one booted person, heavyset so probably male. But the prints were almost indiscernible now. She knelt, traced the curve of a boot heel with her gloved finger.

"Only one person met him. There's absolutely no sign in the dirt he struggled. It's like he toppled over, frontward after his killer spoke to him. So, looks like heartStopper technology."

Pearl nodded. "Figures."

*

Madrigal, Pearl, Narmon and Lissa waited.

They stood in a row and watched Peet and Curl have one last, and what Lissa thought was a nauseatingly long, embrace. They then trudged together out to the hopper where the rest of Madrigal's team were stationed. A Medik checked out Narmon and Peet during the swift flight back to Perth, while Madrigal scoped into Centrl and asked for a number of tasks to be initiated: check for scope calls around 20 to 25 days ago in the region; from where to where; check for HighEyes glimpses of hoppers to and from the gorge; check Pepperbeard's history and did he have any prior criminal records, altho he seemed to be a born and bred Stümmer. They sent a fingerprint and Dy-NAst skan. Testing the fluids extracted by Pearl would have to wait.

After the logistikal tasks were over, Madrigal sat down in a leather seat and looked sad, but resolute. Narmon was across the aisle from her, and could almost hear the cogs in her mind whirling: why, how, who, and most importantly, where?

"Toddy was great, Dr Phipps," said Narmon. "I've never seen anything like it, the way he urged us across those badlands." He pointed west out of the window. "I didn't think we could do it. He was killing goannas and cooking them, finding clean water. Led us to that waterhole straight away. Where he said it would be."

"I'm sure he did those things, but now he's separated from you and Liss, I'm not sure he'll be as resourceful. You were a great team – now he's on his own."

"Don't worry, Dr Phipps ... Todd's a champ. He can escape from anywhere," Narmon said.

Madrigal smiled faintly.

In the hopper seats behind, she heard Lissa berating Peet for wanting to live with the Stümmers, but Peet held his own and was arguing forcefully back. His experience there was different to Lissa's.

"Look, I still have the bruises ..." she was saying.

"I'm sorry it happened to you but ... they are not all bad. Curl's family is wonderful, her parents are lovely. Pepperbeard was a weird'n'evil loner. Lots of the Stümmers'r telling me that."

"You are out of your mind, Peet!"

Madrigal shook her head at Peet's intransigence, then turned to Narmon, who was also sitting listening to the awkward argument. To Madrigal, the tousled young man looked rather devastated and lost, so she changed the subject. "I don't qwite know where to look for Toddy now," she said. "I pinned almost everything on finding you all together. I still have no idea why the 4 of you were abducted. I have no leads. Did you hear the abductors say anything when they snatched you the second time?"

"The people who took us were very efficient," Narmon said. "They didn't say much at all. Just grunted when they grabbed and sedated us. But it was big scale stuff. Like they had big money behind them. Complex gear I never knew existed – those congealed light devices which grabbed us. Hoppers. Who on earth owns private hoppers?" he asked.

Me, thought, Madrigal. But it was a good qwestion and there was an answer.

Governments and Hegs.

THE JASMINE SPROUT

Why don't you all just somnambulate through the brutal, pretty images? Drugged and fucked.
   Das Glas Haus (2034) Ulli Kalk

SEVENTEEN anxious days later, Madrigal is scoped, late, late, late by Narmon. Narmon who's supposed to be back to his schooling after the ordeal of the last few months. Luckily, she hadn't taken her sleep pill yet.

The parents, with xtra heft from Madrigal, negotiated a New Year revisor to allow Narmon and Lissa school exam extensions. Instead of December, they are to sit their exams by March. They had missed more than 15 weeks of school, but EdDept said under the circumstances of the crimes committed against them, extension accepted.

That's how the parents argued. And Madrigal, suffering Todd guilt, agreed to pay for termBreak tutors, to Lissa's great relief.

Peet refused her help.

No one had dealt with him badly, he said. He declared it was individuals – Pepperbeard and Leader of Women, and not Stümmerdom in its entirety – who had caused harm. He was adamant that he was returning north. He was a member of the Qwietude and he loved Curl. There was no other option. The parental standOff continued, but Madrigal had given her word to Peet, and she hoped for an amicable resolution before authorizing a flight.

Working hard with the other parents, Madrigal had concluded the other 2 kidz were sorted, back in the groove: school, exams, glittering careers ahead.

But here's Narmon. Two in the morning. Scope blinking, Narmon's weary face in front of her.

"Yipes, Narmon," she says. "You're very late."

"Did I wake you?" says Narmon, sounding alarmed.

"No. No. I can't sleep. Todd keeps me awake, every nite. Why are you ringing?"

"It's Lissa. Can you come down to the Club Karribee?"

"What? Now?"

*

Pearl is still up. She would never go to bed until her boss did. Stayed inside, watching teev. The 2 women were soon cruising in Madrigal's sportsV thru Perth, the overhead atmos strangely dry and still. The stalls and shanties were lit up and alive, but without the daytime or evening intense crush. Along the riverbank and beach, people were settling to sleep. Club Karribee is downtown, and Pearl's sure driving has them outside the club in qwick time.

In a back lounge, well behind the dance floors, Narmon is beside a couch, on his knees on the floor, bent qwietly talking to Lissa whose head was beside his. Awake, but she'd been crying. She starts like a scalded cat when she sees Madrigal.

"Liss, you okay?" asks Madrigal.

Lissa sniffs. Looks anguished. She's supposed to be back in the groove and here she's actually off her block on flutes of zizz and 6 Blue Neons on a weeknite.

"Darling Liss – you're agonised 'bout a lot. I understand," says Madrigal. She sits down with the young woman.

Narmon butts in: "No, Madrigal. You don't understand. She's not having a breakdown. After she scoped, I came to pick her up and I coulda sneaked Lissa home without involving you – done it twice before." He rolls his eyes. "But Lissa heard somethink ... didn't you?"

"You came to Club Karribee by yourself?" says Madrigal astonished.

"I was trying to remember what ha...ha...happened," says Lissa, "Trying to understand it all, so I come here ... and ... and a man started buying me drinks. I can't remember who. Had a tiny little beard on his chin. A tiny teal beard."

"A sprout," says Narmon.

"A sprout. On his chin."

"Ok. Mebbe we go back to my place. For strong black kopi," Madrigal says. "And you can tell me everything."

*

Lissa is handed a mug of strong milky kopi by a concerned Pearl. They sit on Madrigal's very own outside terrace where the air is coolish, and surprisingly dry. Szygy the kelpieDog has his head on Lissa's lap and she pats him absentmindedly. Szygy listens intently.

Lissa takes a deep breath and tells them she's been sneaking out to bars and clubs since she returned to Perth. Well, not the first week back, cos she was so tired. No sneakery. She just slept like a dead person and recovered. But she'd sneaked out the door after Minnie-Tuton went to bed over the past couple of weeks – once with Narmon, twice on her own when she had needed rescuing by Narmon.

Trouble is, she can't sleep. She has dreams of the Qwartermaster attacking and beating her; of crocs by her head on a sandbank where she's frozen immobile, panic rising; snakes writhing and bristling in ill lit floodwaters. Visions of Todd being hurt by strangers with white masks and bug eyes. Her present ordeal is being haunted, and dreams come even before she falls asleep. Horrible visions. She finds that alcoholik drinks help vague it all away. And zizz keeps her awake so she doesn't have to dream or worry 'bout Todd.

It's a mess, she knows, and her mum doesn't understand. Minnie-Tuton urges her to get to her schoolwork, head down, bottom up, new lease, free pass, put it behind her, but she can't. *SHE CAN'T.* Three weeks in the desert tramping, tramping, west thru dirt and mud and scratchy spinifex, legs like jelly, to scope the one person in the world she thinks might find Todd and Narmon. And Todd's still gone.

So, after the preambly rave trying to excuse her behaviour, Lissa gets to the point.

Earlier that nite, Lissa is exhausted, wrecked, fuzzy, and she ends up, 11.30pm, at the Club Karribee in a glittery x-top and short skirt, desperate to jog her memory of the kidnap, to find a thread in the Club to follow to where everything went blank and the nitemares began. Already, she'd inhaled 2 flutes of zizz she bought from a downtown guy she knows, then she swallowed a FilthyMartini at another bar to provide courage for Club Karribee.

She arrives on foot, slips past the concierge, and tho' she's way underage – 21 and over only – she's not challenged. She buys a Blue Neon and drinks it. The guy with the chinsprout moves in fast. He sees a young kid chopped good by zizz and drink. He's a lowBug, and she's onto him immediately.

ChinSprout is an official host at Club Karribee and fetches her another Blue Neon. Lissa can't believe it. He's hunky and charming, but his intentions are clearly sleazy.

"Have you been here before," asks the man, whose name is ... name is, somethink rhyming with Lizard? Lazzrd? Hazzard?

"Yeah," says Lissa trying on a smooth drunken chill, "came with The Philosophikal a few months back."

"Koo! I remember that, you were a crowd that nite, come to see them. But the show never sparked."

"I know!" said Lissa, finding a foothold of sense, pontificating. "I was there!"

"You said," says the man.

They clink glasses and down the neons – glug, and a puff of magic infuses thru Lissa as she feels tingly and sweet. The man immediately fetches 2 more neons from a grinning male bartender, who winks at her, the rich kid.

"So, what happened to that band?" Lissa asks the man as they get cosy on a back couch under a dim light.

"Four kidz ... just vanished. Fifth was left behind all beaten up. I was waitStaff at the time – not a host. Milisi talked to the staff 'bout what we'd seen. I never saw the musicians, but they were ready to go on. We were excited. Lots of your type, younger kidz, turned up, sneakin' in. The band seemed t'be famous on the Virtual ..."

Lissa almost gloats but holds her tongue.

Famous on the Virtual!

She snuggles up to the man who smells of jasmine. Boundaries? She'll never learn. Or she could learn. Should learn. She needs to be in control. This man knows things tho'. This man's hand is starting to travel up her rather horizontal leg on the large couch and she knows it's not right, but she doesn't shrug him away either, cos there may be INFO! Her head is popping with neon elements and zizz. But Mr Buzzard (is it?) smells nice and jasminey and his sprout tickles her ear. She needs to know.

"Funny booking that, too," he said, gropey hand suddenly stopping in its tracks as the new thought crosses his mind. "Club was paid a fortune upfront to book them in. $100 new ones. Rich fan, I s'pose. Mebbe the Phipps kid's Ma. The booker told Joe – Joe Moreno here – that if no one showed for a drinking crowd, at least costs were covered."

The hand starts moving under her short dress.

Costs were covered? By persons! By Madrigal? No ... no ... clear now that they were lured to play at the Club Karribee by someone unknown. Under all the layers of swimmy-swimmy-head, was a fact she works out. She takes a drunken guess, and turns her face so her lips are close to the sprout. They moosh lips for a minute, but she's in control, and she pulls back and says: "Who would do that? Pay that much money? The Philosophikal were good, but they weren't *that* famous on the Virtual," Lissa has the sense to say. Tho' it chops her up to say so.

The hand stops kneading her upper thigh, and she removes her hand from his leg. JasmineSprout is thoughtful now, for some reason. Mebbe thinks the more he talks to this kid, he'll get to consummate.

"Some bloke. Fat dude. Came in with the sleeve of $New. Couldn't believe it. I was sorta there cos it happened at the bar with Mr Moreno, but they went out back office to clinch the deal ... book The Philosophikal. That's all I know."

They were bought! By a Fat Doop! Lissa can't believe it. And then she can. She hooks up on an elbow and swallows the neon in a glug and then says she feels sick and has to go to the bath-room, which is a bit of a lie, and a bit of a stagger too. The JasmineSprout decamps under the risk of spew on his pants, which he holds up with a hand, cos he'd loosened the belt in anticipation. Lissa, kneeling on the floor of the girlz toilet in a state of intoxification, manages to fumble the intejers on her brand new Frisky and scopes Narmon for help and then she melts down for a while in a puddle of toilet cubicle sor-row. Narmon finds her in the bathroom in a cubicle, helps her clean her face, cos there was some sick involved, and out to the backroom couch where she passes out, then wakes with Narmon holding her hand. And is found by Madrigal.

*

"Hello, then! Good work, Lissa! Fat guy with a sleeve of $New," says Madrigal, pleased. She gave Lissa a kiss on the cheek. Then she puzzled up, brows knitted. "A shocker the Club never told the milisi that! And why not? Did it not occur to them it was important? Or were they hushed by the money? Too good a deal to inform on. All I know is, there will be vid. Why were The Philosophikal booked at such a big venue on a weekend ... should have held that thought way back. Because it was a set up!"

"But we *were* famous on the Virtual," says Lissa grumpily, drunkenly. And Narmon gives her a playful punch on the arm, mainly because she didn't tell Madrigal about the pash and the mutual grope. That was dropped from the second narrative's eqwation, tho The Pearl's looking at her with steely horror.

"A moment, Ma'am ... Lissa. Can I intrude on this joy," says The Pearl in a stressed voice. "Kid – you gotta stop taking risks with older men you just don't know. You were very badly hurt and violated the first time ... violated ..."

Lissa's faced drops: "I know, Mz Pearl ... I know," Lissa says in a sad drunken voice.

"And there you go again! Comatose on a couch with some lowBug, as you call him. You know ..." Pearl starts to rant. "In the actual dayz of Purity and Virtue, when people were pure and *virtuous*, girlz like you were sent to rehab, and *never came out again*. You gotta talk to your medik about your insomnia and your dreams, and risky forays ... forget about ..."

Pearl was almost drenching Lissa in motherly anger and concern, very unlike the cool killer that she was.

Madrigal held Pearl's arm: "Hey, hey, woah ... you'n'me will give her a proper women's bizz talk tomorrow when she's sober. Lissa went about this in all the wrong ways, but tonite she's done good."

"Yeh, boss," said Pearl, looking annoyed as her sensible rave comes to an abrupt end.

Lissa thinks, as she loses consciousness on Madrigal's soft furnishings, that The Pearl's right, and The Pearl is also wrong, cos she doesn't know how well controlled the Liss can be, and also, she thinks, it's time to cut loose from her pledjd one, Narmon, because she's just a bad and unkind person, while he's so sweet.

*

Next morning at a cafe down the street from Lissa's home, she is sat tight in a chair, Pearl sitting beside her. The Pearl slowly turns her mug of kopi around and around, like it was an orbiting planet. Lissa is wearing an old x-shirt and canvas shorts, looking tired and sick and a little disconnekted. She's dehydrated, and feels her brain has shrunk.

"Why'd you go there to the Club? Get so out of it on zizz and stuff?" Pearl asks the young woman, more gently than the nite before.

Since the previous nite an unknown mood has overcome Pearl. As a Slotter, Pearl feels no absolute abhorrence of violence, unlike most of the population.

Most throwbacks who make up Slotter ranks are men. But then, Pearl had a weird flash of insight – she realized Lissa was a girl not to be mothered, but mentored. She saw a bit of Lissa in herself, in the girlz sheer gutsiness. And no one ever cared for that side of a girl.

"I'm getting my life under control," says Lissa, simply. She wasn't up to a big conversation with very big Pearl.

"Well, there's control and there's out of control, Liss," says Pearl, again treading softly.

"Put it this way," Lissa says. "More I understand what happened to me and Narmon and Todd, mebbe the less I'll be freaked."

"Look, Liss. Getting smashed and almost violated by that guy ... that ... lowBug so-called host, is not control. Let me teach you better ways to do it. Let's talk to your mum and make a deal with her. You come'n live with Madrigal and me for a bit. Go home at the weekend to Minnie-Tuton, eh? I'll teach you how to make sure you have agency over your life."

Lissa looks meekly at Pearl who is trying to be empathik. Different mindset to normal for the big woman. Liss may be tired and wasted, but she's not frightened. Her brow crinkles in thought and she looks straight into Pearl's eyes. Not much of a motherly figure, thinks Lissa, but concerned all the same.

"'K. I'm not feeling too well, but yizz ... it's important to know how to do this. I just need to sleep proper. Just sleep," Lissa says.

*

An hour later Lissa's mother was sitting bolt upright at the Tuton residence dining table. "I don't know what to do," sniffed Minnie-Tuton.

The 3 women sat in the small, comfortable room. Pearl's scalp almost bumped the ceiling when standing, but she was perfektly presented in a bizz suit, a caring representative of Madrigal. Pearl was trying her best at delicate family diplomacy. Pearl handed Minnie-Tuton a tissue.

"Th...th...thankyou," sniffed Minnie-Tuton, dabbing her nose. She was such a formal woman, stiff backed in a chair. She folded the tissue neatly and placed it adjacent to her kopiCup. Pearl looked around the simple apartment with its neat furniture and beautiful carpets, white walls. Small, like most midEconomy people could afford, but comfy and cool.

Photos of baby Lissa, her late dad, Minnie-Tuton in a 'varsity gown clutching a degree in nursing, pix of grandparents, were lined up in a mementoPiece above a coolVent. The much missed husband was in several other pix in frames around the room.

Minnie-Tuton kept rubbing Lissa's arm thoughtfully as Pearl talked. Minnie-Tuton was still boggled, astonished, that her missing girl was back ... and that she'd walked across a desert.

Pearl felt some sympathy for the nervous woman sitting beside her daughter. "There is somethink special about Lissa," Pearl explained. "She has maximum potential to offer. She's a resilient girl, but there needs to be structure ... not military, like my training, but still physical as well as intellectual. Balance. Harmonies that deflect the harmful ... behaviours." Pearl was trying to be clear.

"Does she want to do that?" asked Minnie. "Do you, Lissa?"

Lissa nodded dumbly as previously agreed with Pearl in the café, an hour before.

"She really does," Pearl said. "Physical challenges, fitness, are a strong way out of this terrible spiral she's in and frankly, there's nothink any of us can do except support her. If she sticks close with us, Dr Phipps may well find her a job after she graduates. But she has to graduate first."

"Really?" asked Minnie-Tuton.

"Yizz, really. You have a gorgeous daughter who is tough as teflite. She'll fit in – if that's what she wants."

"Is it what you want, darling?" asks Minnie-Tuton, looking relieved and frightened at the same time.

Lissa nodded again. She was afraid that if she says anything, the arrangement will fall thru.

So Minnie-Tuton agrees. She was at the frayed end of her rope when it came to the revelations of midnite escapes, absconding and non-attendance at school, and now admitted drunkenness, which was beyond Minnie-Tuton's imagination.

And that's how Lissa went to evening training with Madrigal, and Pearl as gymBoss. How she curtailed her wild insomniakal behaviour. If Minnie-Tuton had a clue at the sort of training that was happening, she'd have flipped.

*

The workout suite at Phipps Industries HQ in the Perth CBD was impressive. Two large halls, and a 30 meter pool, no shallow end. The main training room, with a rope wall, smelled of wood and sweat. There was also a fully eqwipped gym, the one that Ben Jexen inhabited of a morning.

Pearl said to Lissa before they started: "Once you do what we call SAB – strength, agility, balance – you'll never be afraid of what people can do to you again. Physically, that is. The mental bit ... well ... I leave that to others!" Others being Lissa's new psychMentors.

Sqwats, flips, acrobatics, ab-scaling, stick fighting, fencing, hand-to-hand, tightrope walking. The hard Slotter SAB-scale of strength, agility and balance. Was all the rage at Phipps employee support at this crisis time.

Madrigal had galvanized even the support security staff. Normally, there was so little crime, everyone was just regarded as benign, but Madrigal had changed her mind. Madrigal wanted to tighten things up around her patch. She remembered the bombing of the Northern Lights niteclub, 11 years ago, and now this new existential threat.

Madrigal had gone thru the SAB once, 19 years ago, when she was recruited to the Courier service, but not the whole Slotter training deal, not the knife fight, shoot to kill thing which was just for the throwbacks.

Her SAB in 2122 had been exhausting and numbing for weeks – until she hit a level where her body could take it. Now, starting out again with a middle-aged paunch and general tiredness, she was surprized how resilient those old muscles were. Pearl judged her 4 out of a possible 10. Bit deflating, but at least not 3.

Lissa, younger, was around 5.5 when she started the regime. Already strongminded, the youngster found the training hard, but took to it enthusiastically to compound her intent to be in control and, as she came to realize thru counseling, drunken sprees were the opposite of control. During those sprees, nitemares and grief were in charge.

When Lissa woke in the mornings, before her day of bridging schoolwork, as Pearl had advised, she wore long sleeved shirts and pants to hide the bruises from misapplied sticks, or falls from gym horses, so her teachers wouldn't ask qwestions during the week and her mum wouldn't worry on the weekend. Lissa hadn't thought of that, but saw the sense in it, tho' hiding herself was like lying to Minnie-Tuton. She'd never lied to anyone before. Her mother thought she was off to do general PhysicalEd classes and no one disabused her of that notion.

Lissa was also very tired from doing both, and was given a leave pass on Saturdays to catch up on sleep.

*

Once lifted from Club Karribee's vid system, the face of the fat man had been microMelded thru tek at the Spokes, HQ of Centrl and AuZgov's surveillance and security. The face was examined thru a range of biometrix. Fat man was obviously using a pretty high definition prosthetik device to alter his face. It would have fooled anyone talking faceOnface, as well as vidVision. Even his fingerprints, picked out by the lens, had an opaque.

Madrigal was convinced the face, or at least part of it, belonged to the same man who'd once threatened her in the Phipps Industries Corporate box at Subiaco Arena during a big AFL match. Centrl pulled those archives, and checked, but even then, things were askew. Browridge different, earlobe structure different.

The microMelder continued its computations and eventuated in a name and address with 85% probability across a range of distorted facial features. The address was an apartment in the NeoFreo building, a huge steelshelled skyscraper inland of the new Port, that housed hundreds of families and therfore thousands of people.

An incognito address.

Pearl and her crew threw a lightBender into the apartment window, much like an invisible vacuum cleaner hose, that could curve thru doors, and poke under beds and peer around. The apartment looked empty. Cleaned. They then went in with a pickWand as even a lightBender couldn't open a cupboard door or fridge. There was nothink. The place was scrubbed clean, even of skin flakes. A note was pinned to the inside of the fridge, in the egg compartment:

> Dr Phipps,
> Thanx for the pie.
> Mullen

"Thanx for the pie? It *was* him!" said Madrigal. "Bast'd. The bastard. I mean, he terrorized me 12 years ago in the footy corporate box with his slimy attitude and the butt of a hardArm poking out of his coat. He's somethink from another era this guy, like … a gangstaMan, but he's got his hands on all the tek too. Arggghhh," she yelled in disgust. "And he's now involved in Todd's abduction but … you gotta give him points for cheek and insolence!"

She rubbed her head in frustration and looked up at Pearl and a coupla milisimen who were staring dumbly into the fridge at the note.

"He's some sort of criminal mercenary that hangs around my town. He's probably been here for years but, tell'ya what – one way or other, however this ends, I'm going to track him down and throttle him!"

HIATUS THREE

If you had any self-respect, you'd shout "bring back cash"
Out of sight of their perfidous algorithms.
  Das Glas Haus (2034) Ulli Kalk

ON her darkened roof terrace, Madrigal clung to the balcony rail, looking over the glimmering city. She could see trains snake back and forth along the tracks, over estuarine causeways, from the suburbs toward the city stations, like glowworms in a dark patch of dirt.

Waiting. Waiting for ransom demands and threats. A new, small blue Frisky at her elbow had been delivered anonymously that afternoon. Willing it to buzz.

Even a veiled threat from a disembodied voice over the little komms device would mean he was still alive. There had been silence for some while now.

She could see Pearl and Suze Shelbo in the boardroom – Pearl's huge frame, little Suze – bent to each other across the exec juice bar in the corner, in discussion. Her moral support.

She'd asked for privacy, talk to the extorters alone. Tho Centrl and teks would tag the call if it came, physically alone to talk the talk was her preference.

If it came.

Allowing that stupid tendril of defeat to again creep into her mind, she reflected on her life with her son. Her parents driving Langer away, and she allowing it to happen. Then, for a couple of years, she was buried in study, and work, with an overaktive toddler hanging onto her legs. After grad, she'd scored the job of her life. Courier. Apart from occasional visits to Perth, she was gone. Overseas, Canberra. Rarely at home. Had she been right in giving responsibility for Todd's upbringing to her mother Netta? Netta was a good woman, and Todd had been a happy little boy. In the Old Man's absence Netta had found someone to love again.

Was it worth missing 3 or 4 years of his young life, if he never came back now? What Madrigal learned in the Service of AuZgov had made her more competent than she could believe, but that had been the sacrifice.

The last 11 years, back in Perth, looking after the Bizz, meant she could look after her boy too, and she'd kept him close. His young friends hung around her house cos she made life easy and fun for them. She cheered him on at footy games, loved him, and every year they went north during the dry season, to Country, to catch up with the Auntys and Uncles.

Mebbe she wasn't such a bad mother. Yes, she'd abandoned him for a few years, but they'd made up, good and proper. Their disputes were always conducted in good humour, and there'd been very few fights over the years. She pictured his intelligent face, and his 17 year old gestures and smiles, his turning into a man. With a shudder, Madrigal shook off the foreboding and willed herself to believe he was both alive and fighting back against the foe.

Somewhere, there was a trace.

Yes, the devil is in the detail, she thought. That's where the devil lives and breathes. A very old saying. Except there is too much detail and the devil is buried in tangles and loops, moments, afterthoughts, lapses.

Where could that devil be?

With her implacable competitors? With her ex – wanting Todd for himself, bitter at the years of separation? Her father, wanting a young apprentice to meld and mould? Her intermittent lover, the Premier of Capricornia, wanting leverage over her in his aspirations for his state? The person just off camera from her father when he scoped? *Who was that?*

"He's alive," the voice said when the call finally came thru on the small blue Frisky. "That's all. Wait for more details." What? Listen to the wind in the trees? The hiss of the receding tide? The message will be hidden there? "You are too strong, We have to be cautious. Truly, you could break our brittle bones."

She didn't feel strong at that point. "He's alive and healthy?"

"Both, of course. We wish him no harm."

"How much do you want? What do you want?"

"That's to be confirmed."

"But you know?"

"Oh, yizz. We know what we want. We have the insurance now."

"He's not in some cellar, chained up?"

"No. No. He should have stayed in the Hermitory for the duration, with those naive foolish Stümmer people, but that was not to be, was it? Pigheaded children. Taking their destinies into their own ..."

"So he's free to move."

"Oh, yizz. We believe that cruelty has no place in human lives. We are like you."

"You are not. You are not a mother. You don't know what cruelty is. Been almost 7 months. Seven months, it has."

"You'll have him back. As long as you provide us with the demand."

"The demand? What's your demand?" Smell the earth? Listen to the trees? Watch the horizon?

"It will come."

There was an audible sizzle as the connection died. Sizzles meant serious scrambles down the Virtual conduits.

She gazed at the little blue Frisky, then out over her balcony railing, the dark ocean below, edges glittering hot with city light. Her face was a mask of pain.

Centrl had latched the call, but there was no tail. Somehow, the perpetrators had sectioned the source.

Human ingenuity, as always, looking for new ways to hide and be hidden.

NEW LIFE

Frau Ulli Kalk was merely a mother overreacting to the temporary loss of a child. Blowing up data infrastructure to prove a fallacious point. Yet in her writings, the focus is on the "self". Well, her philosophy is pure "self" indulgence.

The ramifications of this decision, to hide her so-called "self" and her family and friends from our social paradigm, is utterly reckless and weakens the sacred social contract.

As citizens, we are all expected to "put in", to contribute to the betterment of our nation and globe. No one should be allowed to avoid their virtuous responsibilities to neighbours, to Government. Our community must condemn her self-indulgence, wherever she is.

We should end this Stümmer-mania using the laws of the land.
Editorial, 2029, *Das Bild am Spiegel*

IN early February 2142, Peet finally prevailed, and left his anguished parents to rejoin the Stümmers.

After the metHeads signaled a lull in storm activity round the region of the gorge, Peet was farewelled by his extended family, Narmon, and a still glowering Lissa. Peet was returned in a Phipps Industries scoop, a small jet that could land vertically. He was accompanied for the trip by his brother, Anton, a family witness to Pete's new home. Anton was to report every detail back to their mother and father.

Madrigal couldn't go as she was juggling the company and the hunt. But she had thrown many hurdles in the young man's way to dissuade him, and had let Peet's parents know it. Peet remained hardMinded and refused to countenance breaking his pledj to Curl. To ease the situation, Madrigal had given him a newLine satellite scope so he could sometimes contact his mum and dad. One concession, at least, painted with a tinge of obligation. Madrigal was happy about this.

A couple of hours on, out the scoop window, Peet saw the desert and the sight of the red gorge walls under the wings. The sight lifted his heart, knowing he was getting closer to Curl, who he had missed terribly, and her welcoming family, and the qwiet life he'd become obsessed with.

He and his bother Anton were met with jubilation by much of the community as he entered the gorge and walked purposefully toward the dormitories and buildings along the cliff face. Curl ran down the stairways to him and hugged him like she was drowning and he was a rock in a torrent. And while the crowd was all but soundless he could see the glee in the Leaders' eyes that here was a new recruit to their way of life. They looked a bit carnivorously at Anton as well, but with a fixed grin, he nodded and pointed at the gorge entrance. He wasn't staying!

Peet was hugged down the line by almost the whole community, altho' Leader of Women was very tentative in her physical greeting. Leader of Men held him round the shoulders and signed that he needed to communicate with Peet, before the lunch feast, before Anton left.

In the high meeting room, where the 4 friends had originally been seqwestered those many months before, Leader of Men told Peet that the community was in a bad way, because the Qwartermaster's death and the disappearance of their communication device had meant there'd been no contact with the outside. Peet could see Leader of Men was very anxious. His hand flutters were rapid: *No contact with suppliers, and therefore we have emergency around seed stock among other things. Our main batteries need replacing ... we could be without power by the end of this year.*

The tenuous existence of the Stümmer colony was exposed. One line out to the world was folly.

People, families are saying if supplies can't get here, they may leave ... walk out like your friends. They'd die! They have no bush skills, said Leader of Men. *This place is a refuge, but without supplies, we may starve ...*

Peet asked: *What do you want me to do?*

Go back to the aircraft before it leaves ... perhaps contact our suppliers? Order a device?

Do you want me to be Qwartermaster?

If that's a reasonable course to take. At least you have oral acuity (breach and broach the silence) that others don't.

Peet was pleased it was so easy. A job that gave him general permission to use a scope. He dug into his pack and pulled out the scope and showed it to Leader of Men. *I know it's against the Qwietude's rules, but my parents wouldn't let me return unless I brought one. I think we can sort out suppliers. Without me returning to the aircraft.*

*

After the frugal lunch of pumpkin soup and bread, Peet farewelled his brother, saying, "You see, it's not all that bad!". He stashed his luggage pack, filled with as much of his old life as he could muster, under Curl's family roof, and then he and Curl went up to the Qwartermaster's store sheds to look for scope codes, so he could contact the supplier and organize the list of supplies.

No one, not even senior members of the Qwietude, had any idea who the supplier was. The desert TrainV with its caterpillar tracks, embedded crane and powerful engine, would arrive and leave pallets of supplies without any Stümmer in contact with the driver. Once gone, the community would retrieve the goods.

This lack of contact in such a remote place was, to Peet, incredibly wrongheaded. Yet he understood their aversion too. He found the storeSheds vast and gloomy, with the cavern overhang 70 meters deep at the back. The stores smelled of rock, but the office was a series of rooms, neatly built into the side, with benches, filing cabinets – as little as possible was ever handled electronikally – of paper files only. The drawers were filled with order forms and receipts, index cards, plans, inventory lists.

Peet was smart. He went methodically thru every file and drawer. Somehow, the intruder who had killed Pepperbeard had removed traces of any contact. Or had Pepperbeard done that? The safe was closed, but Peet gave the door a tug and it swung open. Hadn't been locked, but there was nothink inside. He looked at the mechanism and decided it was useless without his knowing the combination.

Curl helped, looking thru old ledgers and receipts. Somewhere there was a scope code for the supplier. It was missing along with the old komms device. Peet suspected the code was plugged in the scope's memory? All the important numbers. He signed to Curl: *There is only one way to find out the incoming and outgoings without actually having the device.*

With a regretful sigh he took out his new scope and intejered the code to the personal scope of Madrigal Phipps. *Curses,* he signed to Curl using the general curse hand movement, *I have to Breach and Broach the Qwietude, already.*

*

Centrl used Peet's scopeCall to Madrigal to run a skan on his exact position: what, where, when regarding the use of other scopes. Hundreds of kommSats in fixed and moving orbit could have transmitted Pepperbeard's skerrick of communication and it took some time to elicit a trace of his komms out of the gorge.

They found a couple of wisps. Only 3 or 4 calls over a coupla years. One was to a scrambled device, the killer probably. An incoming, harder to read. Another was to a Hedland fixed point, which Centrl identified as Dan Monthly, a transporter and supplier of provisions. Other traces had faded from the kommSats. They only retained data for 10 or so years before zapping. There must have been only 10 or so calls in the time. Pepperbeard hardly ever laid any eWash on the infrastructure.

Still, was a lead and Madrigal was happy. Dan was the man. *Monthly's Western Shipping and Transportation.*

*

Dan'd been thru the mill, seen it all, and in old fashioned terms, had a weathered appearance. Mebbe in his 80s without much effort in the rejuve department. *A narcissistic waste,* he called the process, tho it didn't stop his wives and offspring from partaking. Dan himself looked like a burnt stump. A survivor.

Based on the outskirts of Port Hedland, he organized, and often drove supplies himself to remote places in the new Arables and Kampungs and beyond. Indijj communities stewarding their country, wheat towns, big waterpump stations. He had caterpillar enabled desertTrains that used gravity enhancers, so if big gusts came thru they wouldn't be tinWhipped off roads and tracks. Surprize gusts could come from nowhere, crash thru anything, and tip even the biggest panteknikons off the road and into the verge, often killing drivers and any paying passengers who wanted to go remote.

That's why mainland freight between big towns was rail. It was tougher for the weather to tinWhip a whole train with an upped gravity load, plus the lipGrips around the tracks. If a bad 'phoon came thru, the rail tracks were simply rebuilt.

And if the weather got worse, Dan Monthly's vehicles could hunker into the ground for the length of any storm using diamond coated screw-boles that rammed and clung to the sub-rock, while detritus crashed against their hulls, and tornadoes tried to sweep the Vs into the sky. Could be that bad, sometimes.

Off the main routes, into the east, Dan Monthly's vehicles cut thru better than most, and his guarantee was simple – delivery. His most remote, but possibly best paying client, was the Stümmer hermitory at the 2 Snake Gorge, beyond the Great Sandy Desert.

Monthly's compound was on the outskirts of the jungled city of Hedland, with its green belts and lakes. Huge battens sat across the mouth of the port itself to protect shipping from massive storm surges and freak waves barreling in from the Indian Ocean. The Dan Monthly compound, like many freightVendors, was ringed with truk shelters and service bays and steel dripped brick storehouses with goods ready for transport into the interior.

When his warehouse door was opened by a cohort of milisi officers, he looked up and panicked.

"Ahh!" he cried.

An attractive Indijj woman walked up and said: "Dan Monthly?"

He gave a wary: "Yair."

"I've been looking for you, Dan," she said in a semiCharming, semiThreatening voice.

Impressive tone, Dan Monthly thought. He looked like a weatherbeaten relik, because he was a veteran of everything AuZgov could throw at a man, and thru a cheqwered life, he'd heard all the voiceTones.

"Credentials?" he demanded back. His panick was abating. Behind the Indijj woman were 2 security blokes who looked like bog standard milisi, and a tall blonde Slotter woman ... geez ... he could tell Slotters from a klik away. Hadn't seen any Slotters in an age. An age, that is, when he had had a different name and before he'd acquired a series of wives who'd expected funds for their rejuves. Monthly could see a hardArm on the Slotter girl's hip too. That was unusual. And there was a younger redheaded woman in civilian clothes, who was already wandering round the warehouse and clokking his stacks of what he termed "the goodies", the supplies for the very remote.

"Senior Courier Madrigal Phipps," said Madrigal looking at the old dude and flashing a scope screen with her cred.

A real AuZgov heavy, he thought, panick rising again. He hadn't noticed the badgeTab on the sleeve, but could see her heavyweight rank now. A deputy commander on the pips.

This was bad news.

"I'll believe you," said Monthly.

"You supply the West Cap Stümmer colony, don't you?"

"Yizz ... funnily 'nuff got a late order from the West Cap mob yest'day."

Madrigal smiled. No flies on Peet. When Centrl had cracked and found the old scope traces, logged in some database, she'd skipped Dan's scopeCode over to Peet. Desperate for provisions and cred, the lad was right onto arranging for supplies.

"Was worried 'bout them Stümmers," said Monthly. "Hadn't heard from the West Cap mob til the way late contact yest'day morning. They'z so remote if somethink bad happened we'd never know. I was thinking to alert you guys in fact, or least the search and rescue milisi, in case they were in trouble. Bit lineball. Privacy – that's how they want it and if I'd rung the milisi, they'd probz change suppliers," Monthly said. "But were cuttin' it very, very fine."

He'd qwite the authoritative tone. Went on: "They'z special clients. Very secretive. Client confidentiality and all that." He smiled rather insincerely.

Madrigal thought, this old guy's worked the administratives once. Not now, but. He knows tone. "Lineball's," such an old fashioned word too — he'd be going back before The Grief even, she thought.

"How do they pay for their supplies?" she asked.

"Confidential," said Monthly.

"A float?"

"Confidential."

"You know there's no such thing as confidential," Madrigal said. "Died with the dinosaurs."

"Beg to differ, Ma'am. The Stümmers privacy systems were generated almost a century ago and their reqwest for complete silence still stands. I can't divulge, and I tell you, you'll never be able to burrow into the secret of their treasureTroves."

"Can I ask you somethink other then. Mebbe not so confidential. In your previous recent komms with them, did they suggest you'd be bringing back some passengers from the colony on your annual supply run?"

Xtremely perturbed, Dan Monthly looked at the floor. He had been expecting this. And as an old Regional Admin Chief from the time before the big stepChange, when *the Singular Enemy* took the land by storm, he knew the rules of life and death, of truth and mistruth, purity and virtue. And he knew a doozy reqwest when he heard one.

"Come with me to my veranda, next door, and I'll whip up lime tea and tell you a strange story. This bitz certainly not confidential."

*

Over coolTubes of tea and hunched like a walnut, Dan Monthly told his story.

He said the Qwartermaster – Pepperbeard, the old Qwartermaster, who could hardly string 2 wordz together, not the young verbose whippersnipper who scoped yesterday – contacted Monthly direct, last year. The Qwartermaster at that time had 'ndeed reqwested a transfer of people.

"Mebbe just one, mebbe 3 pax. Make sure you send appropriate desertTrain with cabin seats for passengers," Pepperbeard had said.

Monthly had been shocked: "What, folk coming out of the Snake Gorge? From the Hermitory? Unheard of, Qwartermaster."

"Can't tell what will happen eventually. We ... they will be paying guests for awhile. We will hold onto them," Pepperbeard had said.

"Hold onto them?" asked Monthly. "Are they lost travelers? I know it's too rough to get to you by land until March, but I could arrange a flight for them earlier." Dan looked slyly at Madrigal. "'Nuff for you to know, Senior Courier. The Stümmers would have adeqwate funds for a rescue flight." He returned to his story.

"Not your business," said Pepperbeard. "These are our guests for a time. They may wish to stay and help refresh our genetic paths here, even settle at the Hermitory. But if these young ones wish to go, then they are free to go, we are giving them the choice. It is only fair. The presence of these young men and a young woman for a time – well, the chance is there for us to take advantage of the situation."

Dan Monthly had wondered at this and confessed to Madrigal it had indeed sounded in the realm of illegal. In fact, Dan confessed, it had sounded right dodgy. And that Pepperbeard had an awkwardness, even under the halting, stuttering dialogue, specially when he said: "We'll hold onto them," like they were prisoners or somethink.

But for Dan it were extra fees so he said: "Ok, I'll make sure there are seats for up to 3 in the truk."

That was it.

Madrigal heard and understood. Pepperbeard was making arrangements well in advance, and probably in breach of his deal with whoever.

"So he said 3 people?"

"Definitely. Up to 3 people."

"And he did say 'paying guests'?"

"I remember clear, Senior Courier, because who, in right mind, would pay to stay in a Hermitory?"

Madrigal paused to digest the fact that someone had bribed the Stümmers, or at least the Qwartermaster, to stash her son and his friends.

"And when was this convo?" she finally said.

"June last year."

Before the abduction.

"Do you have a date?"

"Naw, naw … midJune tho. I remember because I wuz surprised to hear from the Qwartermaster."

Even before the abduction!

Before the kidz were lifted from the Club, Pepperbeard, the Qwartermaster and logistician, was making arrangements: 4 to be kidnapped, up to 3 to be returned. Cash would exchange hands. Todd to move on elsewhere. Pepperbeard was awaiting a consignment from persons unknown, but persons he knew. And that was why the Qwartermaster was dead, and his scope taken.

Centrl had picked up a couple of other codes from the scope archives that had led nowhere, except they knew one call had gone thru to Singapore, and another to Perth. Other numbers that the scope had kommed with were well shaded, tho, by some backWash tek that hid the originating callCode.

She thanked Monthly for his story. She again hassled him for the Stümmer accounts, which he refused. The discussion was tense, and Pearl loomed over him, but Dan Monthly'd been around and knew the trix. He also knew his rights, and he didn't want to lose his valuable, if distant, client.

In the end, Madrigal relented and thanked him for the lime tea and skipped him her scope code in case he thought of anything else, or had a change of heart on the accounts.

"You're an old professional, Mr Monthly. I getya. I understand you were us once. But this is about missing, kidnapped, kidz."

He nodded and said sorry and looked genuinely ashamed.

In the cruiserV back to the Hedland drome, Madrigal thought: what was that about refreshed gene paths? Was Pepperbeard also looking out for the Stümmers colony at the same time? Had he demanded more young people as part of the "babysitting" deal to widen the gene pool in the community? Problems of inbreeding must be coming to a generational head with so few families. Was that his plan? Was this why all 4 kidz, and not just Todd, were snatched?

Goodness, Madrigal suddenly thought, just how many girlz had sexed with Narmon, Todd and Peet in their 3 months among the Stümmers? Willing young participants. Willing, and all very able. Hopefully, the Purity and Virtue maxims around relationships had guided the actions of her son and friends. Hopefully, the young folk were all using antiFecundities until there were clearMade declarations of companionship to any partner, if babies were in Pepperbeard's plans.

She remembered Lissa's unsettling story about Todd. Not Leader of Women as well ... surely?

Would she still be fecund?

LANGER

Dear Bild am Spiegel,

*Your editorial is all hyperbole. As a citizen, I am happy to con-
tribute to the community, and I view Frau Kalk's actions as
deeply radical and needlessly destructive, but she does make
one good point.*

*I am not just at the bidding of our Government or any Corpora-
tion. After reading her critiques, I now teach my own mind to
look through eyes that ask questions rather than simply react
the way we, the community, is expected to react – like dumb
sheep.*

Signed: Not a Sheep

Bloggette to the Editor, *Das Bild am Spiegel*, 2029, authored
by Frau Anna Grescht

HER ex was in a garrulous mood. Still sitting at his desk in
the SwissAlpine compound, he'd abandoned his tweed jacket
– "hot one, today" – and instead of chewing his beard, he was
rubbing his bottom lip thoughtfully.

This was a good sign, thought Madrigal. Her ex displayed
much less anxiety on the vid. But then again, he was on his favorite topic. Nietzsche.

Zzzz, thought Madrigal.

Still as soon as she'd got back to Perth she'd scoped her son's father with update, keeping her word to Langer.

"... so you see, Madrigal, the Stümmer movement was in essence post-Nietzschean. Remember, back then, the 2020s marked the official end of personal privacy and solitude. None could avoid scrutiny by the state and corporates. Worse, people were even giving away their privacy for free! Even your Frisky talked and listened to you and tagged your locale and whoever you met. Then suddenly, out of the blue, in the mid 30s the Stümmers made it clear: here we had a community movement immune to invasion of privacy. Remember, the corporations had logged the details of all and sundry, really, and Government started to piggyback their information and, in a massive social enjjineering campaign, and using DNA banks, began to weed out aggressives and sociopaths from all walks of life. Both publik and private forces meddled and interfered in everyone's lives. Musta been suffocating."

"Yizz, yizz, I know all that. Used to work for Centrl – and I'm recomissioned to the good old deep state on a temporary basis to find our son."

Langer was off on one of his lectures, and didn't hear Madrigal's response ... he just pressed on: "So what sparked it was that in 2028 the State removed their only child from Ulli Kalk and her husband Klaus on some spurious pretext – from memory, silly publik comments by Klaus about child molestation on a popular social meejja platform of the time. This led to a malicious misreport of child neglect and the Kalk's spent almost 8 months retrieving their 2 year old from the authorities. The Kalks decided enough! Decided that young parents like them, with ability and perspective, and what I understand was overweening selfRegard, should resist all social interference, and call it what it was – mass meddling.

"To the Kalks, the fact governments in our overpopulated globe were enjjineering a more stable world was unimportant. The right of the individual to remain private, was the bedRock of their movement. They opted out. Kalk herself was jailed for a time for blowing out internet street cans around Berlin to protest the massData retention. When she was sentenced, she gave the judge a Nazi salute ... and was sentenced to an extra 3 more months for her contempt of the bench. She was feisty. And by this time, Klaus Kalk had sqwirreled their child away."

"So why Nietzsche?" asked Madrigal reluctantly.

"Friedrich, old Freddy, wrote that an individual, thru their effort, aesthetic sensibility, personality and intelligence, could rise above what he saw was the common herd. The Ubermensch. Remember that? Basically, a new breed of people. Evolving further than "common" society. The herd was the enemy. Freddy was a dilettante, but oh so influential."

"Yeah, yeah," said Madrigal, having a vague memory of the theory. She looked at the vid of her bearded ex, and suddenly remembered his smell ... the patina of tobacco, a fruity aftershave, and a pleasant male musk. She wondered if he smelled the same, way over there in Switzerland.

Langer kept going: "Ulli and Klaus Kalk withdrew with their followers, thinking they had evolved as humans. Some of their followers were very rich. The very rich always consider themselves better – and don't I know it!"

"Oh, Langer," said Madrigal, "let's put our past on pause. He's our son. I'd do anything to find him."

"Yizz ..." said Langer, slightly chastened. "I know. Me too."

He gathered himself and went on: "So, Maddy, it's clear that huge cash endowments were gifted to the Stümmer movement because their message resonated strongly among the elites – the Kalks and their followers were very well set up. The couple became gurus in a retreat in the Alps, but when the meejja tracked them down to expose the people who dared to be secret, the Hermitory was subseqwently moved to the Ural Mountains where I believe their descendants still exist, including Ulli's grandson.

"There were also retreats in Japan, several in the USA – always a fertile ground for alternative sociology mixed with a wilderness – Uruguay, AuZ. Mostly whole family groups who collected together. Was qwite the thing at the time. People, the meejja, couldn't believe that sensible folk were retreating from a period of great prosperity and bounty."

Madrigal nodded. "The good old 2020s and 30s. Sometimes I wish I had been around then, before Purity and Virtue remodeled the world, and then the Singular Enemy changed everything. So Governments loved the retreat of the Stümmers because the malcontents just made themselves scarce, hopefully forever."

"Correct. And the Kalks and their followers developed a philosophy in which they felt protected from prying eyes and allowed them to lead uninhibited lives. I researched some of it many years ago for a surveillance trial at the Criminal Court."

"I remember."

"I'm surprized you remember anything about me. Your parents brainwashed me out of your life." Bitter tone again. He had a turn of phrase too.

She again ignored him. "Todd's your son too and I'm keeping you posted. But yes, I admit, your previous research for the International Criminal Court was one reason why I scoped. Tell me about the endowments."

"This will help us find Todd? Because I'm not going thru all this to humour you."

"Oh, Langer," she said softly, "I can't make promises, but I'm grasping for any help. The team is following every lead under the sun. We've spoken to a tightlipped supplier of the Hermitory who won't – or can't – divulge his paymasters, but if we can track down fund routes we can possibly track down the culprits."

"So y've traced the supplier's accounts?"

"They dribble out ... can't find anything ..."

"So you are asking, how did the Stümmers fund themselves?"

"Yizz, Langer."

Langer sighed. "Well, I presume ancient compounding accounts in the mists of time, plus bars of gold. They'd've had supporters – and Governments on the sly – who no doubt kicked into their tin to keep them out of bother. Governments welcomed their qwest to shut themselves away and never communicate again. So there was lots of money in the beginning.

"I assume – well, making assumptions is almost a crime in legal research!" Langer corrected himself. "But I hypothesise now, that each Hermitory will be funded independently because they won't communicate with each other. Stümmers would need a Courier service between Hermitories that would stick to the Stümmer principles and I can't see that being possible. Hermitory money trails would be limited. I assume, sorry, they'd have 2 or 3 external proxies to oversee the funds. Their supporter representatives were always qwiet people who for one reason or another believed in their philosophy but couldn't live in isolation. The proxies sent floats to suppliers on a regular basis. Suppliers bring supplies to their remote havens, they get paid the balance. Very neat."

"And how can I track down these hypothetical accounts and their sources?"

"Check with your precious Centrl."

"I have. They have no record. Government inputs were scrubbed by supporters within the AuZgov administration, presumably." Madrigal was on tenterhooks, and not enjoying the conversation with her ex. He wasn't so painful when he was on a roll and not sniping at her, but he kept evading the qwestions.

Suddenly he was blunt. "Then you need a very, very good hacker – a tiptop analyst who can start with the West Cap supplier's accounts, and track thru to the source, Maddy. And all will be revealed."

*

In hindsight, she thought her ex had been generally friendly, but seemed way across aspects of Stümmerdom that weren't just related to philosophy. Were his assumptions based on founded knowledge? Was he making it up? All those lines about assumptions. He assumed with qwite the authority.

She sighed as she stared at the blank screen.

She still wondered whether Langer was someway responsible for Todd's disappearance. But the thought was only a thought and was dismissed. He didn't have the wherewithal to mount an op that complicated, that intense.

The new Funder of the Stümmers was the key. Who exactly'd paid the Qwartermaster to house and clothe her son and his friends? She needed to identify the funder in a spaghetti junction of accounts. Accounts that were beyond the teks at the Spokes. She'd tried, pleaded, cajoled but they could only go so far: *"These are legacy accounts. We can't penetrate them,"* they said.

We know the money came in, but from where? And how? Useless Centrl, thought Madrigal.

She called Pearl in from an adjacent office where the security crew were coordinating the hunt. Now it was time to hunt her old qwarry.

"Pearl – gotta issue an urgent *locate and apprehend* for one Andaman Marko, and pull in Flick Allenby at the same time. I just can't go on without a proper Virtual savant. The Spokes can't reach Marko's level. He's an intuit. A skilled intuit. They're just rude mechanicals by comparison. So ... notify every port in Cap, Pacific, and thru ASEAN. See if they've embarked recent times. We know their boat, we know their scopeCode. When located, we legally suborn them to our cause and I'll compensate them. Won't be any grounds for arrest. Carrot rather than stick. Just find Marko."

"Ma'am," Pearl nodded, and was on her scope before she left the room.

A very, very good hacker, had said Langer.

That was the top line qwalification in Andaman Marko's notorious CV.

TENTACLES

PILOT Jon "Stix" Sullivan sweated on the long tentacle of storms which were forming to the north. Four thermocells embedded together. Hopper H889 was buffeting, lurching almost, and the craft's stabilizers were no help. Sullivan maneuvered his thrustControl stik for some semblance of horizontal, but downgusts had other ideas. Tho he'd encountered worse, sweat trickled down his neck.

Least they'd avoided the heavy rainSqwalls – and without rain lashing the aircraft windscreen, there was clear sight of the greyGreen ocean and the ominous Cloud 2 kliks north.

For a moment, the sun glanced from the southeast. Under the high Cloud, the dark sqwalls and tubes spanned the ocean, caught in their individual thermocells. The sunbeams lit the tubes in a malevolent chiaroscuro of light and dark. They looked like vast legs, swinging and swaying, aiming to give someone a good kicking.

Stix Sullivan'd been hardening the hopper's gravity stabilizers for an hour, incrementally, klik by klik. Like all Search and Rescue hoppers, tho, the aircraft was laden with a heavy recoveryScoop slung on either side, which made them notoriously hard to fly in storms, and prone to crash. The altitudeClok held the hopper at only 900 meters where he'd found a less risky altitude to both swirlies and gusts.

But after a qwick intercom conference with his metHead, crouched behind him in the instrument cabin, Sullivan decided that the closest of the 5 thermocells, embedded in the burgeoning cloud, was building too powerful. Enough was enough. They could still skan the ocean for Dr Phipps's rogue boat on the return course. He steered south out of the search grid and called the position over. Thru the light gap – between the swollen sea and the cloud – he could still see tubes dancing, and dark sheets of rain crashing into the ocean.

Behind Stix, in the hopper's instrument bay, the Port Hedland Milisi Search and Rescue crew crouched over wind and rainRadar and lifeSensors, ocular eqwipment next to useless in this sort of weather. There were 3 officers muttering their advice into mics, 2 skanning for boats down on the ocean surface, and the crucial crewman, the metHead, whose eyes were firm on the windClok.

A sudden heavy gust tilted the aircraft almost perpendicular and Sullivan started to lose control of the flightShape – reflexively he snapped a couple of rear jets on as he felt the hopper stall and slide down under him towards the ocean, top rotors hopeless in a vertical position.

"Ayyy … shyte." The jets pushed the awkward craft towards a more horizontal shape. He edged the craft into stabilization. He knew if they'd started to corkscrew backwards, he and the crew would be dead. Was a nanosec from disaster.

Under his breath he cursed the farewell kiss from the Cloud and its hidden wildness as Sullivan switched over to full jet and got the hell out.

The southerly course that Stix Sullivan plotted took the hopper parallel to the coast, across the white and grey remains of old marine windFarms set up on the continental shelf a century ago. The 2070s was a bad decade for vertical windFarms. The old windFarm stumps below looked like jagged teeth in an old man's mouth, the ocean battering their remains with swell and foam.

Nowadayz, all windFarms were horizontal, lodged in grey, steeldripped cement blocks with feeder grates, rising high along topographic ridges, a blight on the landscape compared to the beautiful slender spinning towers of old.

Bang. The hopper bucked again and Stix Sullivan's windFarm reverie vanished. The team's chief enjj, Flight Lieutenant Amberlin Klein stuck her face into the cockpit.

"Sir, we need to head further south. We reckon that new tentacle of thermocells is starting to swing round toward H889. It'll bring a string of tubes after us."

"Ok, Klein. No sign of the boat Courier Madrigal Phipps is chasing? Obbo boyz haven't ...?"

"No sir, nothink."

Sullivan wondered at Lieutenant Klein's risk take. She was hard, like him, impervious to motion sickness and used to crunching into bulkheads when hoppers lurched. But she was too young.

The Search and Rescue milisi service rescued victims from ships in those rearing seas, or untangled bodies from freight-Trux that had been tinWhipped from highways by gusts. They rescued whole communities trapped in flash fires and floods. Every year, 100s of Search and Rescue milisi died, and their names were engraved in the great Remembrance Memorial in Canberra, fatalities in the War against the *Singular Enemy.* Life expectancy was short in the service and Amberlin Klein was a young woman risking it all, and well knew if she stayed, she'd probably die.

Most women in Search and Rescue crew were old, hardBit 60 or 70 year olds, who'd recruited later in life for the Search and Rescue hoppers and scoopBoats on the promise of a free rejuve. Pilot Sullivan'd concluded that Klein was a noughter, so she'd decided to go for the adrenaline. But Sullivan was far too polite to ask his Enjj about her fertility status, and confirm his guess.

Anywayz, young Klein was an asset. Her strong broad frame heaved into the flightDeck and slid into the coPilot's seat. CoPiloting wasn't really her place but Klein had flying competencies. So while hopper H889 flew with one allocated pilot, Sullivan was just fine having a 2nd pair of hands and eyes over the cursors and cloks. Specially like now, when he'd got tired of fighting the everlasting gusts and swirlies. He glanced at Klein's serious face below the flight helmet, wisps of blonde hair poking out from the helmetShell. Checking the instruments, her broad mouth was pursed behind the scopeMic.

Eyes were sparkling tho'. Height, flight, dirty weather. Unlike the jaded Stix, young Amberlin Klein loved all 3.

Stix looked out and down again, following Klein's gaze. The swell must have been 20 meters bearing south along the coast. They were well north of Hedland, but the dirty grey yellow surface was seriously kinetic. A dangerous moil.

"Down there," she said, waving to starboard. "Boat."

She pointed past one of the windFarm stumps. A boat, a small freighter or fisher, it looked like, was breaching thru the swell, fleeing the weather and setting a course west, further from the dangerous coast. Bang into the scoop of a waveTrough it fell, sending skyward a froth of white.

Certainly wouldn't want the encroaching storms to push the vessel against reefs and the shore. Sullivan looked hard, but couldn't see from his side of the cockpit.

"Hold the steer, Klein," he said switching her over to the cyclic function. He clicked out of his harness and almost climbed over her to look down from the starboard windscreen. He could see a small boat bouncing in the terrible swell.

"They'd be dead, won't they? Bashed about in that?" he said.

"Must have some form of internal stabilizer, sir," said Klein, playing the steer with care, feeling the shape of the wind on the hopper, her fingers moving almost invisibly. The buffeting was demanding all her concentration to keep the hopper upright, working both rotors and the jets to find a bearable balance.

"Shyte!" said Sullivan as he returned and clicked in. "They've just come out from under the Cloud!"

To Klein's relief, he switched the cyclic function over and back to his hands, and things seemed to become a little smoother.

"Must be world's most uncomfortable ride, sir," Klein said.

"Good spotto, Klein, by the way." Stix Sullivan was an old fashioned milisi officer. He really liked competent people. "A grey boat in a grey sea in a vicious swell. Didn't even detect their electronix. You did it by sight!"

"Thanx, sir," she said, pleased.

"And good piloting – you're a natural!"

She knew that was an exajjerate, but Sullivan was relieved they'd found and pinged their target.

"We've locked their eWash, sir," said a voice in his earBug. Tracking could now be passed on to higher powers.

Now closer, the boat looked like the grey skull of a bird, picked and dumped by swells and troughs, but maintaining a straight course southsouthwest. No water was going to flood that airtight can. Thru the intercom, Sparksman said: "That's our vessel. The boat's transponders are off, but description fits. Never seen anything like it! They must be master mariners!"

Despite being thrown about in the swell, Stix Sullivan could see someone was steering the boat expertly, avoiding capsizing.

"Looks like'n old superTanker lifeboat to me," Sullivan said. "Haven't seen one in years. But we can't do anything now. Too rough to go down. At least we've tagged them against the electronix. Looks like their crew knows what they are doing."

The tagged boat headed off the back of a wave and crashed into the trough with a massive displacement splash, sending water high into the air.

Sullivan growled, "Sparksman, you'd better let Dr Phipps know we've found her vessel. Send Centrl the coords."

The Sparksman, deep in the hopper said, "On it, sir."

All good. H889's job was done. Pilot Sullivan could fly home without guilts.

"Verified," said Sparksman in his ears. "Coords sent."

The hopper then peeled and jetted away from the turbulence toward the slightly jaundiced sky in the south.

"Good work. Good work," Sullivan jollied his crew. "Found the needle in the slop. We can head back to the drome and then we can drink a tank'o beer," and, turning the mic off, added to himself: "And just hope no other idjjits out in this weather need rescuing."

BORDERBOAT

Liminality has this esoteric quality – the doorstep, the entrance to another world. Imagine coming though that door to the world of the Qwietude, where you can be sure that no-one is listening.

Meine letzten Äußerungen (My Last Ever Utterances) 2035, Ulli Kalk

"AHOY, *Kingdom*," a voice boomed across the gap between the pitching vessels, over the slap and hiss of the frantic ocean. The BorderBoat had a multiBel speaker aboard.

Andy and Flick watched the large orange patrol boat hove alongside, as spare as their own reconstructed vessel, but bright, so the stricken could see the rescue ship from afar. The BorderBoat lay off *The Kingdom's* hull about 80 meters. Flick waved to the orange clad officers on the BorderBoat deck, one of whom was waving back.

"Pull to," boomed a huge black guy in an orange Border security uniform, waving them close.

It was no use *arguing* with The Man.

Just comply.

*

Well, comply when they finally caught you.

Andy knew somethink was up the day before when Flick clokked the bright orange milisi search and rescue hopper that was fighting swirlies high above those 50 meter backswells he and Flick were battling, being pushed coastward toward the old Dirk Hartog windfarm.

They'd watched in horror as the aircraft almost lost control in the wind swirlies coming out of the Cloud to the north, and let out their collective breaths when it was clear the hopper had stabilized. The hopper had buzzed them coupla times and distracted Andy and Flick to the point they'd forgotten to steer further to starboard from the huge stumps.

Luckily, the warners went off in the cockpit's roof speakers, alerting them to the concrete pylons, lashed with the foaming swell. Flick took evasive action.

Once clear, Andy had looked at Flick, ashenfaced: "They're after us," he'd said.

Flick had said, "Nawww. Milisi were just checkin' we're ok. Why bother with us, we're way off the map?" But Andy always knew when he was being stalked.

Someone was looking for them, probably that bitch, Madrigal Phipps. And while he'd admit to being naive in many a facet of his f'ked up past life, Andy Marko was not stupid.

At that point, tho', conditions were too tough for a sadArsed selfAnalysis, so he helped Flick steer thru the ocean, eyes on the current and wind radars, minding for crossSwell sideswipes. While the cockpit stayed pretty stable, the bow of the boat was taking a pounding, and he was fixated on the dials and damage report screen, his most unfavorite screen of all.

Awhile later, after they'd escaped the violent oceanik wash of the Cloud and its embedded thermocells, Andy went abovedeck, and, after an argument with Flick, jettisoned the 2 crates of negTek that they'd bought from those wiggy Sumatran guys in Aceh Province.

Acehians were the bestest negTekkers of all in the AsianAuZtral qwadrant, and that was high praise from Andy Marko.

The cartons of tek sank without trace under the frothy-Green waves. Flick was pissed, but he didn't give it too much thought. The gear hadn't been orders from clients, but bought by Andy for a qwick speccy sale to any tekDoops in Greater Perth who wanted them.

Without contraband, they'd nothink to fear from the milisi, except the feeling that their freedom-of-the-sea was being generally constrikted by AuZGov.

*

The waves had eased to 8, then 6, then 2 meter swells, with the current swinging round from the southwest pushing both the milisi search and rescue vessel and *The Kingdom* toward the just visible ribbon of coast, by now way past the Dirk Hartog windfarm ruins. The breeze was brisk and warmed by the tumult to the north, tho. An occasional rain sqwall flushed thru, darkening the ocean surface and wetting the deck.

A milisi inflatable was launched from the bow of the cruiser toward *The Kingdom* and in less than 10 minutes, a friendly faced milisi officer poked his head over the deck. The officer sported the S&R lapels and wore the protective orange kit of search and rescue, with lifeJacket over his neck and shoulders. He clambered on board, followed by a couple of sailors.

"Mr Marko, Mz Allenby," he said pleasantly.

"You are?"

"I'm Lieutenant Mzungu. I've orders to escort you to Perth. You are not under arrest, but the AuZgov is providing an urgent commission to suborn your assistance."

Andy held a siderail, looked at the wobbly green horizon and the slight char of sky haze, and let Flick do the talking.

"As skipper of *The Kingdom*, I'd want to see your official docs authorizing this intrusion," said Flick.

Andy knew AuZgov ultimata for citizen assistance were pretty hardSet, but good on Flick for pushing back a bit. When suborned, it was the bound duty of a citizen to help. Even renegades and those officially deemed indolent were expected to throw in and work. But official subornment usually occurred during disasters, and there were no reports of disaster or other emergency on the WestAuZ newsFeed.

Mzungu smiled at her pleasantly. A wave crashed and washed across the bow and everyone held fast to rails, stays and other rigging, whatever was to hand.

"Happy to provide orders!" he said. "Happy to." He handed Flick a plakPak with a chip in it.

"We don't have the eqwipment to read that I'm afraid," said Flick, still hanging on. "All our elektronik gear is chipPort free after a determination by the AuZgov courts, but you'd know that already."

"We do, we do. We just thought y'may have acqwired a clamB or chip reader over north. No, no, I've contingent paperwork as well."

He fished out a bigger plakPak with a folded paper inside and held it toward Flick. There was a moment of silence.

"C'mon. Give us points for trying," he added with a smile.

Andy laughed and took the paperwork from him.

"You're funny, Lieutenant Mzungu, but we still don't like this one bit," he said. "Breach of personal freedoms. If we were in international waters ..."

"We're not," said Mzungu pleasantly.

"We'll go below and read the material. Please wait," Flick said.

"I've allocated halfa for your reading of the order and a short discussion with you, Mz Allenby, on how to proceed alongside us when we head for port. Sir, madam," said Mzungu formally, "feel free to take your time within that schedule, but it's most urgent."

"Who signed the subornment order?" Andy asked.

""I'm not privy to the paperwork, you'll understand. But I believe it was signed by Senior Courier Dr Madrigal Phipps," said Mzungu.

"No surprizes there," said Andy with a sigh, as he headed below, determined to waste the full half hour.

PANDORA

Privacy room for the family home.
Sale price only $3000, fitted by Secure Core.
Find one room in your house free from electronik invasion

- *Soundproofed*
- *Bug free*
- *Opaqued light – one way windows*

Find your inner peace
Advertisement (2032) *Sydney Morning Browser*

ANDAMAN Marko said no, and Madrigal was shocked.

"You're vital to the recovery of my son. No one else has your chops," she said.

They sat round a long table in a large, daylit meeting room at Phipps CBD tower, views over Swan bay below. Side by side with Flick, Andy stared superciliously off to one side, over her left shoulder, annoying Madrigal, as he intended. She thought he looked like an old fleabit fox, hair unkempt, eyes wary.

"No," he said, again.

After the 2 formally suborned sailors been delivered by a rescueV, she'd sat them down and triumphantly handed Andy the authorizing warrant from Centrl to allow Andaman back on the keys and sticks, to login and scrute the Virtual to look for Todd. She'd thought Andaman would be delighted the lifetime ban was lifted, but he'd reeled back in horror at the sight of the consenting paperwork. Then he just vagued out.

"You can log on anytime, even after you've helped me," she added.

"I get that," said Andy, qwietly.

Madrigal glanced down at the couple's surly reflections in the highly polished red cedar, shiny enough to pick out their upsidedown eyes and the 11 year hurt reflected in them. He'd done correctional time for involvement in the disaster in the Ville ... only a year, and was released because, really, what he brought on himself had been thru naivity, not maliciousness. Was never a nasty person, Andaman.

"I know you are a good person, Andy."

He shrugged.

Andaman's hair was going grey and it was tremendously shaggy. At least he'd shaved for the meeting. His handsome looks were fading, attacked by wind and sun, and psychic storms of his troubled past.

Flick had styled her blonde curls into dreadlocs, an old hair fashion that irritated Madrigal, but which was occasionally revived by fans.

Weatherbeaten they might be, but both looked lean and fit in cottons and boating sneeks. Sailors who took on the eqwinoxal Cloud passages thru the eqwator had to be tough. Both looked unimpressed at being hauled back into the world that Madrigal inhabited. On dry land too. Unimpressed at their luxury surrounds. Piss'd off.

"Even thinking about the Virtual breaks me out in hives cos of you, Madrigal," mumbled Andy.

"Well," Madrigal said soothingly, "technically wasn't me that caused you those problems, but ..." as Andy began to object, she held her palm up, "I understand your visceral reaction. I truly do. I'm in a gut wrenching place without Toddy."

She was convinced that if Todd were dead, the spirits would somehow tell her – that some dear Aunty would reach out with the bad news. Or Todd would visit and tell her. But hearing not a word for weeks, she was just in a chronic agony.

Flick was rubbing Andaman's back: "You don't have to do this if you don't want to."

Madrigal gave Flick an imploring look. Flick glared back.

"Can I tell you a story," Madrigal said, irritated by the hostility directed her way. She'd saved his gnarly life a number of times after all. He owed.

"I just want our boat back so we can go," Andy complained. "It's the only place where I'm sane, Madrigal. Where I feel safe. On the water."

"Let me tell you a story, then you can go back to your boat ..."

"I'm 11 years out of the game. Haven't touched a key since the ... the blast," he interrupted again. "And then jail, dammit. You guys, Centrl, all complicit. I'll be useless anyway, I'm so behind the tek wave. Miss a month and you are years behind. Waste of our time. Your time too. Come on, Flick, let's go."

He made to stand up to leave, and Flick stood too. He waved a finger at Madrigal: "I don't like you. I never liked you. You're up there, controling the shots. It's true – people like me get hurt by people like you. So seeya."

Dressing down power freaked him out, and he was shaking like a leaf. Madrigal stood and Pearl started to stiffen into protector mode. Andy was both very scared and very angry, especially when the warrant to hack was waved in his face. His legs told him to run. Pearl was poised to pin him to the ground in case he lunged at Madrigal ... he could tell from her stance. He'd seen Pearl gun down the people who had kidnapped him way back. Shot them dead in a blink. He felt threatened by her presence.

Madrigal pleaded: "Just read the paperwork. It's one ... favor. If you recall, I intervened when you'd set your own crazy path. I saved your skin 3 times." She was starting to sound shrill too. Wasn't good.

"No!"

"For fuck's sake, Andaman," Madrigal shouted, uncharacteristically. "You well know you can snoop the Virtual. The Virtual's the same as it ever was. Don't be such a solid fucking sook!"

But Andy Marko shook his head and bolted out the door, followed by Flick who gave Madrigal the stinkeye on the way out.

*

Lissa had been sitting in a chair away from the table, introduced by Madrigal, then forgotten. Now seeing angry, uncontrolled Madrigal, Lissa was aghast. They'd found this Marko and brought him in, but Madrigal obviously never imagined he'd refuse to help find her son. Lissa saw her mentor deflate heavily in the chair and put her hands to her face, hiding the anguish.

Lissa was upset too, but Todd wasn't her son. Pearl stood waiting for an order.

"Hang on," Lissa said, and she ran out. She got that Andaman, for some reason, was a crucial link in finding Todd. Lissa's whole push was now control of events, her life. Unusually, Madrigal was not up to it. Unusually, her mentor was a messHead staring dumbly at the doorknob.

Lissa shot down the corridor, but the elevator had already sunk to ground level. She pressed the recall button, and then bounded down the steps, down the 4 stories, thru the office complex and toward the lobby. A new thing she could thank Madrigal for was her superdooperfitness.

Thru the stormproof windows she could see Andy and Flick across the street, heading toward the city on foot. Crossing the street, narrowly avoiding a hissing-to-a-stop eBus, Lissa called "Wait ... please". While Andy Marko steamed on, Flick looked round.

Flick said somethink to Marko, Marko shook his head and speeded qwicker along the pavement, but fit Lissa finally caught up.

"Wait," she said, running in front of the couple, holding out her hands, blocking their way and grinding them to a reluctant stop.

"We really need your help to find Toddy. No one else can do this. All Madrigal's experts have failed. They just can't crack these accounts. They're yoooosless!" She grabbed Andy's arm. "Please.... ..."

Finally, she was out of breath.

*

The intense young woman was shaking. She had deep green eyes which were trying to pierce him with an earnest hope. Very young. 17? 18? He hadn't come across a kid for an age. Fresh and real, she was, this Lissa, not like all the other tek'crats and killerz up there in the office.

Andy looked at the ground. "You don't know what you're asking," he said.

"For your help."

To stop the feeling the pavement was riding up over a heavy swell, Andaman moved to put his back against an office wall, He looked up at the yellowish sky between CBD blokTowers, and felt like a wave was kicking the stern from under him. The sinking feeling was both physical and intellectual because Andy knew Madrigal was right.

Awhile back, she'd been his wicked fairy godmother, who kept both saving and punishing him at the same time. Hauling him out from the Northern Lights Club bombing in the Ville

11 years back; that mad chase thru the wilds of Cape York; his hurried calls to her when he'd been a few footfalls to regaining his life and purpose, up in his cliffside home. Then that moment, after her reassurances, when his world literally exploded, and the blast killed scores of people including neighbours, friends and their family members. Tho' the explosion was never her fault, she'd said it was all over, which was a lie.

Evil had literally strung explosive charges across his beloved home and people died because of him. The Coroner exonerated him of murder, but ordered he be tried for the hacking crimes that triggered the disaster. Blame for the multiple deaths was laid sqwarely on the dead bomber. He copped some of the blame for the circumstances which led to the deaths.

Jail time had meant nothink to Andaman. The guilt had leached thru and already poisoned him. Centrl closed down his hackery forever and he'd cursed himself daily. Only Flick stood by him, visited him in jail. She pulled him from his deep depression, set him on their path. Flick was the one authorized to access his remaining unknown assets, which were almost none. He wasn't allowed to go near a clamB or a publik outlet to the Virtual.

He'd met Todd as well, long time back. A little 6 year old Indijj kid, barreling around a secure site with him, in deep Tasmanian waters.

Todd was an innocent.

*

Andy was back, seated in the boardroom alongside Flick. The room was swaying like a crazy box, his sealegs making him sweat. On dry land, in a room with walls and a roof and a floor. Worse, sitting still, so he couldn't feel the moves of his own body. So, so uncomfortable. He was used to the deck under him, the movement of the sea.

"The story, it's complicated," said Madrigal. "Bear with me …"

His bitterness made him bark again, pointing at Pearl: "Only if she leaves the room. She's too goddamn scary."

Pearl nodded and departed with a relieved look on her face.

An aide put platters of hot food and mugs of hot kopi in front of Flick and Andy, Madrigal summoned her storytell voice, a smooth buttery tone, and Andy tried to ignore the spinning room. A story ensued about an ensemble of musicians, their abduction, strange cultish Stümmers, an escape across the hostile desert by the youngsters ... here Madrigal gestured to where the young, determined Lissa was sitting. She gave the young woman huge credit for overcoming the physical duress she'd suffered. There was a side seminar about Stümmers and their secrecy and the convoluted issue of ancient funds, with a slice of Nietzsche thrown in.

Then Madrigal told of recent discoveries: the anonymous plot and payment to the club to hire The Philosophikal, and the untraceable fat middleman whose face had been clouded by biometriks, the discovery of Dan Monthly who provided Stümmer account traces, the scope numbers, and her ex's conclusion that a savant was needed. Most importantly, Centrl failed to provide such a savant from their legion of tekHeads.

"I need someone to trace those ancient account threads," she said.

"I don't think you understand," said Flick. "Andy hasn't touched a device since his home was destroyed."

"I understand," Madrigal said, then, in an uncharacteristic blurt of pleading, added: "But you're my only hope."

"I lost hope years ago, thanx to you," said Andaman. "I moved on from hope."

*

As a storyteller and persuader, Madrigal, as usual, had been excellent. Andy'd listened carefully, followed her shapely lips, gazed into those magnificent black eyes with the black lashes and allowed himself to be sucked into the story.

Andy then thanked Madrigal politely, pressing his arms on the edge of the table as the floor moved, while trying to parcel the story together in his mind. He knew he was struggling. He asked everyone to leave the room except for Flick and Lissa.

"You're all distracting me ... I need to think. Concentrate," he said politely.

Madrigal nodded and left, clearly reluctant. Lissa sat tight. Andy watched Madrigal give her young protege a small skweeze on the shoulder as she passed.

Those 2, they play as a team, he thought.

Tho' after the street chase, when Lissa returned with him, Madrigal had looked up in utter astonishment. Andy'd enjoyed watching Madrigal's shocked face – took *her* by surprize for once.

Why'd he come back? Well, he'd been moved by Lissa's youthful passion, the way she waved her arms madly when imploring him to return. Her story. Madrigal's story was also compelling, but she was a Courier. Knew how to compel. Her story was already yesterday's, as time rolled relentlessly. And, also, because his head was filled with other noise.

Inside his head, Andaman kept hearing the wind blowing across the ocean, thru halyards, along the edges of the flapping sunSail. It was loud and disconcerting and had been getting louder all morning. He needed a distraction to drive the sound away, so he could indeed, think. But of course, he'd already anticipated that. He said to Lissa: "Have you got a sample of your group's music?"

Lissa's music, well, this would clinch it one way or the other.

He wondered, as he watched her nod: The kidz, these are really young kidz. Were they real about things? Lissa seemed real. Music never lied and Andy knew his music, cos in the past, he'd been a connoisseur of all things fine.

Lissa pulled out her clamB, attached a decent speaker and played 20 minutes worth of The Philosophikal. Their best 3 songs with the swooshing compositions and intricate melodies. He nodded occasionally as he listened. At one point a tear emerged on his lower eyelid, even tho' the song was rumbustious and harmonious and not at all maudlin. He sipped his kopi.

God, he was tense, but the wind in his head had died down – had it been the sound of blood pumping? Now the pressure easing, anger fading. Or was he losing it? For the first year after rehab, he'd been this way. Hearing things.

The music ended. He refocused and looked at Lissa. "I remember Todd as a little kid, running around the Spokes making a nuisance of hisself. We used to chat. He was always full of stupid qwestions. About deepsea fish."

"He was 6," added Flick.

"Because of me," said Andy, "Dr Phipps feared for his life, all the time. Is Todd still an okay kid?"

"He's fantastic," said Lissa. "He's my best friend, along with my Narmon."

"Is he a kind person? I need to know." Andy's voice started to sharpen and Flick unconsciously put her hand on his arm. "I mean, he's not like one of those killer Slotter people like that tall blond throwback? He's not hard, is he? Ruthless and bloodthirsty? Can't abide that. Seen too much of it."

"No, he's very kind. Toddy always looked out for us, all the time we were in danger. Toddy taught me how to walk the badlands and what to eat, and how to avoid storms, and how to survive. Mr Marko – I did it. I did it. I survived thanx to him. He's only 17 like me. He's not hard. He's a ... a ... teacher."

Talking about Todd was starting to upset Lissa. She saw those strange intimate visions again, the visions that'd appeared when she walked solo thru the badlands. There was some sort of psychic turmoil beginning to brew between her and the strange, unnerving man in front of her with his madly penetrating eyes. She banished thoughts of Toddy's soft mouth against hers ... this interview with Andaman Marko was too important to Madrigal, and she was carrying the responsibility. No time for sudden dreams.

There was a long pause.

Andaman said to Lissa: "Did you know that death follows me around like a puppy? Trotting faithfully behind me. People just die because I happen to be near them. In the most innocent of places. Did you know that?"

"No, I ... I didn't," she said.

"Well, it happens. I removed myself from people for a very long time ... except Flick here who is the best boat skipper. The best. She's helped me," he said to Lissa. "Helped me so much."

"Can you help us?" asked Lissa. "Just one search for a lead, for an answer."

Andaman looked at Lissa's pleading face and groaned. "Damn," he said, looking at Flick, "if I do this thing, it could kill me. When you go to the Virtual you don't know what you'll unleash. I am ... what's her name? The Greek bad luck charm? Pandora! I am Pandora."

Lissa looked at Andaman. She knew about Pandora from a school project.

"You know," said Lissa, "when all the bad things flew out of Pandora's box to blight the world, what remained in the bottom of her cursed box was Hope. If you are Pandora, you've still got Hope."

"Hope?"

"Yeah. Hope remained in the box. It stayed with her. Hope's good."

Madrigal, listening in on a scope from the other room, nodded. "Good answer, kiddo" she thought.

*

The deal was that Madrigal would send Andy and Flick off to the HiTop Marina at Fremantle Sound as soon as he'd picked up a solid lead and provided Centrl with the traces. And she'd leave them alone there, and pay the marina fees for a month if needed. And drop a consultancy fee into Flick's account. If there was success, they could just sail away from the suborn warrant.

That was the deal. And now, in the stream of data that was blowing across his screens left and right, like a blizzard, Andaman was tightening code and search terms, hoping for a qwick resolution.

What frightened him most was not a recurrence of the traumatic stress disorder he'd gradually shed over the last 11 years, or even some future, vindictive, murderous response from whoever his target was, or those deep anxieties which welled up like giant waves from wherever. What really frightened him were the compulsions that, 11 years before, had sent him spiraling into an oblivion of narcissism and greed. Would they return?

Now the blood was pumping again, but not in anger ... was hacker adrenaline, and he knew he was in for it. The buzz, then the depression. The reactions of an addict. Drenals, endorphins, dopamine, an unholy mix. Made you want to play the Virtual more and more.

He was good at it.

Yes, there were Dan Monthly's account trails, the fund transfer numbers, the clients, the large amounts of money paid and spent, paid, spent, banked. All spread out like a candy chart in a chocolate box.

Andy'd been bullshitting when he complained things would've changed on the Virtual after 11 years. Madrigal knew it. Was pathetic really.

Things hadn't changed that much in the past 11 years. There had been stasis on the Virtual for at least 50 years when subatomics became the drivers. Couldn't get drivers smaller or faster than that, could they? He felt a bit guilty at his dumb spray.

Automatically, like the pro he was, with all the best hacker chops, he gathered the trails and parsed them until he found the 3 fund beds from the Stümmer colony, and then, ah, that was interesting, they drizzled out along a cemetery of old accounts which went way back in time, before subatomics.

Andaman, a student of old codes, screeds and programs, then reached out into the Virtual and sought out one of his old, well hidden caches, buried in an ancient dead site, from where he downloaded a whole bunch of socket sets – which Centrl would never have – old codes for what they used to call software, in the day, and apps, to test the accounts.

He'd hidden his emergency software toolbox in a trading site for old mechanics toolboxes knowing no one would ever go there. A precursor site to what was now known as VirtualTrade. His old archival files were in a frozen cloud of the 21st century bizz called eBay. Too clever for his own seaboots, sometimes, he thought wryly.

After some codeBedazzling, lo and behold, he found the Stümmer accounts were PRSFL screeds, from the 2030s. *DOS begat html, begat htmls, begat blockchains, begat blockbusters* (he'd liked the blockbusters), *then came Parsifal*, he remembered writing in an old assignment for which he topped the class. And now those screeds were reEnjjed, slightly, but deftly, to mesh the subAtomics with what went before. He could see cash transactions again, pushed thru automatic exchanges and gathered by more complex streams.

This was fun, dammit.

So, way back when, money came from a motherlode account in a European bank – a currently existing bank dammit – in Zurich. The original Stümmer account, and money came in from several private supporters, which he switched on and copied: *Frankel, Jamieson Inc, Gates Foundation, MarDek, Pew, Oak*. A bunch of strange benefactors from way back, and later there was Gov money from round the world, and rerouted monies coming directly to the AuZtralian Hermitories from AuZgov. Those cash injections had ended some decades back, round The Grief time. And those accounts, over time, had thinned out because, to his amazement, there were still scores of communities around the world, not just a handful. The money was linked to all the Hermitories, and shared around, from the core account, in a most egalitarian way. Was automatic, as investments accrued and proved, fundz would be juiced out to the communities.

He parsed the various account segments within the core, finding a bunch of passwordz assigned to Stümmers in their farflung colonies, but no names, of course, and a couple of persons within the Zurich bank who managed the investments. He jotted them down for Madrigal.

He found that tranfers went out, but not a lot had been coming in as credit, for a long time. Well invested $Old turned into $New over time with plenty of divvies, tho' after 100 years of expenditure and no income, even the cash reserves were starting to erode. Eaten up by the needs of the Stümmer Hermitories.

And then, suddenly, there was one donation.

Money from a more recent benefactor was deposited into the old PRSFL account. $New, from a CredEx account adjacent to an interlinked chain of Jap/Tai Government infrastructure funds. Mebbe Gov, mebbe not. With Hegs these days, often the cashbeds were one and the same. Some of that CredEx cash had paid Dan Monthly's supply bill last year. And, unbeknownst to Peet, he'd used the same float recently to order supplies from Monthly.

Andy grunted, had a glug of kopi (just like the old dayz, in his house on the cliff in the Ville), examined the portholes and found 2 funders and users for the account. The Jap/Tai finance division, quite normal, and an approved signatory named Jarman Kailikeri.

He grunted again and winked at Flick who was sitting across the table, watching him with a worried brow.

He wrote the name, and the credit history of this man into his report. A hiFlyer in the finance bizz and a slumlord, apparently. He sourced addresses, scope codes and everything known about the individual and wrote underneath, without a pang of guilt: TRACE THIS MAN.

He looked more closely into the Jap/Tai lead, an intricate maze of fund approvals and shook his head. The source was looped inscrutably, like a really complicated double clove hitch knot, which he used on the boat. However, it led to an infrastructure company of which Jarman Kailikeri was a director.

What he could now show was Jarman Kailikeri was the one and only recent donor to the Western Desert Hermitory with significant deposits of $New1000 a month which was a fortune for a small, insignificant community of selfSufficient desert dwellers.

The origin of Kailikri's money had come from a lump sum opaque account he couldn't fathom, placed with Kailikeri 12 months ago. The opaque went west into China rather than east, given the syntax of the deposit. Those transactions to the Stümmers started more than a year back. The money had been salted in the AuZtralian account, and a substantive amount had also been withdrawn from the AuZtralian account and placed in the Zurich based Parsifal core account of yesteryear.

It was 2am. Flick had crashed on the floor with a couch pillow under her head. Asleep in this sterile komms room in Phipps HQ. He stared at her sleeping form for a few minutes trying to absorb what he'd found.

Then, feeling uneasy, and wishing he was somewhere else, but with hacker adrenaline surging into him like a scooping 5 meter wave, Andy started looking for Jarman Kailikeri.

VINTGAR

They've made everything so convenient. Wave your money away with a card. Wave your identity away as you buy up the shop. Convenient.
For them.
Meine letzten Äußerungen (My Last Ever Utterances) 2035, Ulli Kalk

IN Switzerland, Langer stood from his desk chair and looked at the empty screen where, only moments before, his ex had glowed like a goddess. His pain was acute. Sixteen years ago he'd run away, across the world, to forget, and there she was, back in his life, asking for his help. The pain was sharp, a severe toothache, only psychic, somewhere in the ether, not in any muscle or nerve.

Find yourself a good hacker, was his parting shot. Was true. That's who would locate their little boy. Didn't Centrl have oodles of hackers, probing everyone's private lives? Clearly she was at sea when it came to good tekHeads.

Was true tho', what she said. Langer'd do anything to help. Tho he'd never say so to Maddy. Heck on a stick. What could he do? For his son.

The study was almost dark now, cords drawn across the windows. He'd rambled on about Neitzsche and lied about the Kalk Hermitory. Now the glow had retracted from the clamB, only a desk light shone faintly. Langer stumbled into the book-case as he poured a shot of whisketty into a glass and swigged it. Too many of his own assumptions in the conversation. Had to find out properly and then let Maddy know.

Langer made a couple of tentative calls, leaving messages on machines, excusing himself from work for a few days, then went to his small bedBox at the back of the apartment to drag a backpack from under the bed. He filled it with clothes, a sweater, a torch and raincoat and his usual notebook and pencils.

He liked the arcane process of writing with his hand. Langer never liked to put thoughts down on penetrable clamBs before he'd filtered what he was going to write. Sloppy wordage, the undoing of so many.

He threw the soft black bag on his dining table and made a sandwich to eat now, of meat, cheese, tomato, and another for later, and filled a heatflask with caffe for the road. He ate the first sandwich slowly, as was his steady pace in all things. He'd found a paper map of Eastern Europe and stared at the roads, like little veins on the page. Could he remember where it was? The Hermitory he'd sworn never to reveal? Someone else had driven that time, 15 years ago.

He put a dark red teflite coat on and stepped out the door. It was cold and dark. Maddy had rung at her time, AuZ time, and woken him at 3am, but hell, now was as good a time as any to see if he could help find the son he'd just reconnekted with.

Langer liked Todd. Loved him, even. Todd had an easy charm and was interested in Langer things – music, critical philosophy, politics. Langer liked Todd's enthusiasm. He was heading to 50 years old now and he'd not had much contact with young people apart from a few apprentice lawyers in the court system. Baby lawyers tended to be very serious and obliging. Todd cracked jokes and gossiped about his life. Langer liked that. Living alone in a flat above Nyon, near the International Criminal Court complex further down the valley in Geneva, was a spartan life.

Langer crunched round the path under the glittering stars, and into the V-shed where he flicked open the driver's door of his sporty little roadV. He pulled the cord from the car charger, threw his bag and sandwich box on the backseat, and pushed the engine into life. The drive would take more than a few hours and he vigorously rubbed his face awake before backing out into the empty street.

*

The original Kalk Hermitory was not located in the Urals. Langer had, to his shame and discomfort, named the Russian location as a diversion. The Stümmers had formally reqwested the lie, in return for their assistance.

In fact, the Kalk Hermitory was in the Julian Alps, at the xtreme northwest of the Single Slavic Economik Unit, in the State of Slovenia. The Hermitory was one of his first research jobs. He remembered visiting the Stümmer village 15 years ago, when he first arrived in Switzerland to take up his post as a moral philosopher to the International Criminal Court. His first sad case.

A demagogue in remote Northwest Canada, Serge Roullie, who was part Heg CEO, part landLeader, and part gangsta, had been caught on an internal surveillance camera murdering his enemies. He and his associates lined 8 men and 2 women against a wall and shot them with hunting rifles. Bodies were later discovered planted into a river embankment on Serge Roullie's estate. A purge of the gangsta's staff and sheer joyKill. Langer remembered the awful footage.

But the dictator's lawyers argued that, as the cameras were owned by the dictator, then the footage was inadmissible as evidence because of rules around self-incrimination and right to privacy. It was an obscure argument and a legalistic stretch, easily dismissable, but the prosecutors wanted every t crossed, and the examination of every tittle that hung over every little i. So the Courts despatched their newbie researcher, Langer, to debunk the idea of "privately owned vision".

In the library vaults – the hard copy vaults – he'd found Right to Privacy tracts by Ulli Kalk: *Invocations to the Private Self*, *Das Glas Haus* and *My Last Ever Utterings*, and decided to ask her philosophical heirs to expand on the moral basis for the thoughts of the Stümmer movement. The first 2 tracts were most relevant. The last was a recipe for seclusion for her followers and he didn't care so much for her hectoring tone.

The court investigators called their friends in the European security services who located the Kalk Hermitory within minutes, and Langer, feeling pleased with himself was driven in an official white landV to the Julian Alps to find and qwery the reclusive cultists.

Fifteen years later, as he drove himself thru the nite and the spattering rain, Langer remembered the meeting clearly. Then the weather had been fine and even slightly cool. The alpine meadows were lush, spotted with yellow buttercups. At 2000 meters up, the climate was less varied, tho' the storms could be superFierce when they brewed. The glaciers had gone by then, and the spring snowmelt was thin and patchy, no longer modulated by the old icesheets. Lots of plants and animals connected to snowMelt cycles were now gone, and Langer, a keen researcher, mourned the loss of the eidelweiss and the alpine marmot, tho' he'd never seen either.

Langer was amazed at how clear the memory was in his mind. A day's drive in the Criminal Court landV had taken him to the location advised. He remembered being dropped by the driver at a village called Vintgar and fought thru an overgrown path indicated by a local farmer, down to an old bridge system that led across a canyon, and a swiftly running river. White water blasted below him as he crossed a series of rickety bridges. But it was sunny, and the sun penetrated the deep chasm.

There was no one about.

The air had smelled cool and earthy and he could see the shapes of big black fish hovering against the current in pools of clear green water. The presence of fish cheered him. The gorge was very narrow and strangely beautiful, with mature trees clinging to the edges and overhanging the top of the cliffs, and he became rather lulled by the relentless gush of the river. At the end of the walkway, where the river poured into a broader lake, he started climbing a path thru a forest until houses loomed between the trees and he entered a cleared area, almost a lawn, with bigger buildings on its other perimeter. People looked at him in surprize.

At that point he realized he hadn't even considered what to say to the reclusive Stümmers by way of introduction, but as soon as he opened his mouth and spoke an introduction, they signaled for him to shutUp with gestures and hissing noises. This was shocking to him. A couple of men arrived to escort him from the property and direct him back down the path.

"No," he said. "No. I'm here to visit you," but that made it worse. They almost ran him down the path and shoved him hard to see him off.

The 2 men then stood, arms folded in a "thou shall not pass" pose in the middle of the path. Langer then realised Ulli Kalk had actually practiced what she preached. This was a silent community. And they had been hounded out of Switzerland years before by meejja. They were uberSensitive to intruders. Probably thought he was a journalist.

He sat down on a log, pulled out his notebook and wrote in German:

Dear Qwietude leader,

My name is Langer. I am not from meejja. I am a moral philosopher and I want to understand the philosophical underpinnings of Invocations of the Private Self and The Glass Haus. Willing to wait. Also I am happy to provide written qwestions. If you don't want to communicate I will leave. My understanding of your moral imperative to privacy is important to me.

Stanley Langer

He gave one of the burly men, or monks, the note and said: "I'll wait." The man read the note, grimaced, and leaving his friend on guard, ambled back to the village.

Langer sat on the fallen tree trunk again, and tho he felt the damp from the wet moss penetrate his pants he remained sitting. The forest was pleasant. Bees buzzed and he could still hear the gush of the riverGorge far below. Every so often he looked at the guard, who stood implacably.

An hour passed. He swigged some coffee. He offered the thermos to the guard who shook his head, mute. Langer stood and walked around in circles to bring feeling back to his legs, and sat again.

Then, thru the ferns, the other man returned, and gestured in some form of sign language. They hauled Langer to his feet and guided him toward the community. He was hustled thru what was a central village sqware where people seemed busy with tasks, and caught sight of fields and a few sheep, down a backslope behind the village.

The "monks" led him into one of the bigger buildings and up a flight of wooden steps into what seemed to be a private attic suite. The room was dark, with a couple of standard lamps for light, and a small potbellied stove in the corner where a flame flickered behind sooty glass. In the suite were couches, and to the side, a loom with a stool in front of it. The cloth was better lit with a bright desk lamp as if someone had recently been working the loom. Half of it was filled with red and orange woven cloth. The room smelled of caffe.

On one couch was a shriveled old woman: sunken cheeks, wispy grey hair, but brightly dressed in a colourful silk shift, and a younger man around 60 in the same rough cotton clothes the guards wore. The old woman slowly gestured with her fine boned fingers to the guards, who left, shutting the door behind them.

Langer pulled out his notebook to write a qwestion down, but the old woman spoke up.

"Don't worry about writing. We can talk. Welcome to the Village of Remedy," she said in a voice as wispy as her hair. She had a thick German accent and Langer guessed that she was a very, very old Ulli Kalk.

"I am Ulli," she said. "This is my grandson. He's known in our Hermitory as Grandson of Ulli, but I still call him Kurt."

There was a pause, possibly for Langer to protest this critical deviation of Stümmer protocol. But he just nodded.

"So why have you really come, Mr Philosopher?" she asked.

"I am Langer," said Langer. "I am a philosopher. And a legal researcher."

"Ahh, so it's a legal matter," said the razor sharp Ulli, sitting up. "Tell me more."

Langer hated liars and lying, and he was a staunch moral philosopher, so in introducing himself, he was candid. The International Criminal Court, the case, his interest in what exactly was the Stümmer basis for privacy.

Ulli listened with great interest, eyes glittering with both intelligence and flamelight, tho her grandson was shifting in his seat.

"I loathe courts," she finally said. "I was persecuted for my convictions by the German courts."

"I know," said Langer. "I read the transcripts."

"I was jailed."

"I read your books."

"Your privacy is the only thing you actually own. Your self regard, your thoughts. Some people, the religiousMinded, once called it the soul, which was a nonsense of course. But it is a concept with resonance. In the end, it's you. You are the nub, the node, the center of your universe. You shouldn't let others know your so called soul. You understand?"

Langer nodded.

"We are not the stupid Stümmer constructed by others, and I ask you please not to use the foul word. Here, we are as a group, a Hermitory of the Qwietude."

Ulli swung her sticklike arm around the room, sweeping at least 280 degrees. "But we are also here, individually, alone. And we each have the right to aloneness. You have no idea what the 2020s and 30s were like. Everything you did was recorded and placed on a database, all the data was matched by The Man so you could be manipulated by both business and Governments. Everytime you logged on a site, you had to tell them your birthdate, or address, or favorite colour ... hah! ... and a little bit of your soul, your *self*, was lost – thread by thread – into the machine. Until you were but a shade. This revolted me. I have selfRespect – and that is a very loaded, important word. Self, the being, the alone person, and respect, which is regard for the coherence, cogency, of your own unique identity. Caffe? Tea?"

It was as if Ulli Kalk wanted to reinforce her philosophy, no matter what. Langer opted for tea, wondering where they found a supply of tea, if so qwarantined from the world, and Grandson of Ulli went to a stove and boiled a kettle, still listening to his grandmum.

"So it's Nietzschian? Your outlook?"

"No, you silly academic," she said. "Always clear to me Nietzsche was mad! But even as a madman, he sensed the enormity of what was to happen in the postModern world, but he admitted he couldn't guess what was coming. Remember he said:

The press, the machine, the railway, the telegraph are premises whose thousand-year conclusion no one has dared yet draw. Le Grande Friedrich Nietzsche was of another world. The 19th century teetering into the 20th. I and my late husband drew the philosophical context from our own times and we tried to change minds, and succeeded, I'm told, in changing a few, but I guess not much else has changed. They still pry into lives?"

"Not so much. There are other challenges now," said Langer. "The focus of Government is not as ... manipulative."

"Ahh, of course, the weather. Bad weather saves the human race from suffocating itself. Brings people together! How good is that ... *das is ausgezeichnet* ... an excellent result!" and she laughed. He was expecting a witchy cackle, but it sounded like the tinkling of bells.

"And you?" she asked abruptly. "Why are you here, working for this so called criminal court?"

And it was then Langer, lulled again by the primitive surroundings, the bucolic outlook, sipping the delicious creamy tea, told Ulli and her grandson about his recent split with Madrigal. How her plutocratic parents had been furious the father of Madrigal's one and only baby didn't have an Indijj father, and angry that Langer cared not a jot for business and entrepreneurship, or the wellbeing of Indijj people, but cared for Madrigal, the law and the tenets of European moral purpose. He confessed how he learnt a hard lesson. How his child was 20,000 kliks away. How he missed the baby. Langer hadn't got too emotional or qwavery, but Ulli and her grandson listened with interest.

"And the child's name?" the Grandson of Ulli asked, haltingly.

"Todd. Todd Phipps. He has his mother's surname, not mine."

Over the next couple of hours, Ulli Kalk let him complete his interview, with notes taken. She thought the murderous

Canadian warlord who was incarcerated in the ICC cells had no grounds for appeal. The revealed image was owned by all, which was the nub of the problem of an omnipresent administrative surveillance.

"Unless you disappear, there is no such thing as privacy. You are a drop in the ocean of the state. Your wordz are their wordz, your image is their image. That Canadian landlord should have turned his stupid camera off before committing the deed," she said in disgust. "What a fool."

She also reqwested that if Langer cited Ulli Kalk in any documents, he should lie about the location of the Slovenian Hermitory. Langer, a child of the Age of Purity, found any form of lying abhorrent, but nevertheless agreed.

"Think of it as a misdirection, not a lie," Ulli said in her wispy voice, eyes twinkling. "Pfft. You can go now young man. Best of luck."

Langer asked her why she talked volubly when everyone was silent in the Hermitory.

"I love to talk. I forget what it is like. We never talk because of eavesdroppers, bugs and gun mics. I'm 120. My own self is intact! But almost done. So I don't care what people think of me anymore. So there!"

As the grandson escorted him out, he said haltingly, "My Grandmama is dying so she's become too talkative. She wants to, how you say, get things off her chest."

"She still maintains a very powerful presence."

"Yes," said Grandson of Ulli, "but she will be gone soon. She has stayed alive thru good health and proper medikal treatments. She's never had any rejuvenation therapy."

Langer couldn't believe that. He knew the old woman was 128 years old, and bright as a button. Somewhere, Ulli had found rejuve treatments – tho mebbe not the whole kit and kaboodle – to keep her going, otherwise she'd be shriveled and dead by now. That was what was meant by proper medikal treatments. The grandson went on, seemingly oblivious to his Grandmama's deception. "But, sadly, the body deteriorates. Without rejuvenation your body eats itself up, it becomes a corpse before you're even dead."

They reached the edge of the forest and Langer asked: "Where do you access the tea, and medicines, if you are a closed community?"

"We have many friends and money benefactors who support our philosophy. Funds set aside. Goods delivered on occasion. We are in happiness here." Grandson of Ulli had a fat face, poor teeth, and looked unhealthy, but smiled a most kindly smile.

They shook hands, and Langer turned and walked off, down the forest path in the early evening light.

*

This time, 15 years on, the approach to the Stümmer community was not like the last.

Tho he'd done no exertion except drive, by the time he reached his destination, Langer felt tired, breathless and very anxious. He feared that his sad and sorry personal tale years ago may have placed Todd in great danger and that being candid with the Kalks had allowed the Stümmers, mebbe more ruthless ones, to target a weak link, a ransomable individual. His son.

After all, Ulli Kalk was of an era when crime was still rampant. She'd been a criminal herself. And abduction was a crime of that era. To confront the Kalk Hermitory at this time, with his accusations, was a worrying prospect.

He'd hurtled in his sportsV thru Switzerland and Austria then hit a chain of black storms coming thru the Eastern Alps making driving impossible. Whirlwinds and even icy sleet stopped him and hundreds of other drivers in their tracks. With other eqwally disgruntled drivers, he'd crawled carefully thru to Klagenfurt, and parked in one of those giant weather shelters for V's and trux to protect them from tinwhipping and skid crashes. After paying the exhorbitant fee to a cashier, he elevated down in a lift to the ground floor for a burger, fighting thru a big crowd of grumpy Germans. Took more than 24 hours for the storms to pass starting with great lumps of hail crashing against the hardened viewing windows. Langer was pleased to be inside with a rented recliner chair and blanket.

After the burger and 2 beers, and a friendly argument with a couple of backpackers about the most clement weather routes thru to Northern India, he slept soundly with many other travelers along a concourse. A morning of high gusts kept the roads too dangerous and closed, but by the afternoon, he pressed on in his sportsV. Once he was forced to slow again to navigate a last postScript storm, and then down the autoBahn into northern Slovenia until the coLokator drove him up a side road into a rather steep mountain range.

He felt lost, even with the coLokator and his animated windscreen. He was positive this was not the way they'd approached last time, but the throaty coLokator voice in the console was guiding him on into the gathering dark. In the final hour of driving, lightning lurked behind him, occasionally flashing in his rear vision mirror, but the worst now seemed to have gone.

The Slovenian village of Vintgar was silent and without human presence. A couple of lights were visible behind blinds. The car crept thru puddles, past the village, toward the remembered track. Rain played on the windscreen.

He stopped and opened the door. He felt for his backpack, pulled out a torch and looked at the sky. "Furk," he said.

Langer knew he'd found the right place, and moved his vehicle to the side of the road. The rain on his face was spotty and warm, warm enough for the confluence of air which caused the stormfront to have come from Africa, across the vast Sahara. The superheated air, punched by the wayward arctic jetstream, sent storms into overdrive.

The track was, like last time, overgrown, but there were footprints in the mud, and he heard the rush of the river to his right. The rain started to get heavier. In the light of the torch, Langer could see that the start of the boardwalk arrangement along the gorge was pretty rickety, worse than last time. Aware his lack of fitness meant he was at least 20 kilos overweight, Langer regarded his cautious progress gloomily. He thought: *There must be a better way to get round to the village.* The timber was black and wet and some planks were missing. They smelled of rot. As he walked cautiously into the darkening space he felt the rain start to increase in intensity, and water began trickling down the back of his neck. The walls of the gorge were shadowed and high, and the higher they got, the blacker the nite seemed to get, with cloud smothering the last of the day. Langer felt a wave of fear. In the dark, on rotten old wood, his venture was turning very dangerous.

Pah, he said to himself, it's just lack of light. But fear got the better of him and after 100 trepidacious meters in, he turned around. No use falling thru the rotting bridges in the dark and drowning, he thought. Retreat, sleep in the car, and go forward at dawn. Best thing.

*

After troubled dreams involving Maddy's ghost parents, and occasional wakeful moments of watching rainstreaks dribbling down the windows, Langer finally woke to the grey sky and several brown cows moving past the car up the road. A man in a black cap and baggy anorak banged on the windscreen and Langer, groggy, lowered the window. The man spoke qwickly in Slovene, so Langer took a punt and spoke back in German hoping the man would understand. The man shrugged and tried broken English. "Property is private. Please go," he said.

Langer nodded obligingly and said: "Looking for the village thru the gorge."

"No village. No village," said the man. "Only Vintgar."

"Okay," said Langer.

"You go," said the man, moving on with his cows. "Gorge is a bad place. Danger. Very danger."

Very danger.

Langer chewed the last sandwich from his bag, tipped the last slug of caffe down his throat, and shuffled his raincoat on over his back, passed a ruined kiosk which had once heralded a popular tourist trail, waybackwhen. This time, as a soft grey light penetrated the canyon space, Langer felt more able to traverse the slimy boardwalks and bridges. They had indeed deteriorated since he'd last used the track. Someone was deliberately not repairing the construction, or if they were, it wasn't obvious. Some places the timber gave way to a dirt path under the cliff overhang. The path was slippery with the wet, and eroded down to wet scree.

The rushing stream and green vegetation were still beautiful, tho.

A further bridge that crossed the gorge shook at every gentle footfall of Langer's boots on the construction. The torrent, charged with water from the overnite storm, churned higher than he remembered as well, a flume of whitewater hurtling thru the space, some of it rearing high, launched over rocks. Any slip, or break, and Langer knew he'd be dead. He felt like some bit of flotsam impelled thru the tight space, being buffeted and damaged by outside forces. Impelled by his ex-wife, his rediscovered son. The noise, the smell of fresh water and wet dirt, the shaking structure ... all made him very frightened.

There was one point where the connektive wood of the boardwalk looked so precarious he almost retreated again, but he carefully bent over and using the torch, inspected the structure. At least the board fixed to the rock wall was attached firmly. He pressed tight to the rock, and tightroped on his heels across the fixed beam, avoiding any connekted bits, and averting himself from the railing that was bent at a 45 degree angle over the rushing void. His cheek was pressed against the damp, musty rock. Small bits of rot fell from the outer edges of the timber into the froth below and he, almost unconsciously, talked himself forward, telling his brain that "this was important", that he might find Todd at the end of the stream.

After that short stab of precariousness and heart pounding action, he knew there was no going back. Soon cutting out of the horizontal pathway he discovered a vertiginous upward trail to a stone bridge which he thought looked sound.

"All or nothink!" he told his fat self, so with huffing and puffing, reaching out for branches and grass tufts, he hauled up the slope. He slid back a couple of times, braking himself with handholds, and promising to lose weight. "Shouldn't be this hard for someone your age," Langer kept telling himself. "You're still a young man!"

Finally, he reached the bridge, where he wiped his mud-caked hands, first on the grass, and then with his hanky and trouser legs.

From the top of the solid bridge he recovered his breath and banished his fears. From 50 meters above, on a solid structure, the whitewater stream below looked less frightening. Once over the bridge, the path left the canyon and made its way thru the bracken clad woodlands. As the morning light strengthened, it hinted at blue sky above the forest canopy. He could hear the sounds of cows mooing in the distance, and their bells.

Langer climbed a half remembered slope, and even came across remains of the log he'd sat upon 15 years back, but when he came to the top of the rise, where he recalled a collection of buildings and huts and a long dormitory, there was nothink. Closer, and he found stumps and a couple of old stone walls, and a large paved area overgrown with weeds. He walked thru the forest clearing where the Village of Remedy had once stood.

Toward the upper area, he saw a garden which seemed a little more cultivated. He walked thru a gap in a wall and found Remedy's graveyard, former inhabitants obviously buried under the grass. No gravestones, just a brick at the head of each plot, and each brick had a small copper plaque with an engraved death date going back a century to the early 2040s and forward to 2130, 4 years after he'd visited. No names, just dates, to note the passing of an individual. Except for one brick with the engraved letters, U.K.

Ulli's grave. It was a 2130 grave. Three others nearby were dated the same.

Langer pondered, again absently chewing his beard. What had happened? He skanned the picture and asked: *What does all this shabby melancholy tell me?*

The roses were pruned, and the grass around the edge of the graveyard was neat and short, as it was thruOut. Cropped between the bricks by goats? No. Goats would have eaten the roses. Someone was caring for the sad little precinct. He walked out, circled the enclosure, and found a path leading further up into the hills.

*

"It's just a village now," Langer told Madrigal.

Madrigal looked at her bearded ex in the projected scopeGlow. Bemused she asked: "So you went to the home of Ulli Kalk to find out about our boy?"

"Yes."

"And she's dead?"

"Of course. She was very old."

"But you met her 15 years ago."

"Yes."

"So her grandson has abandoned the Stümmer principles, and they just live life as villagers?"

"Well, these days the authorities can't be bothered watching them anymore. Or surveilling ordinary people more generally. There's too many other problems to deal with. You know that. You're AuZgov."

"Yizz, well, we all know that."

"So a few years after my first visit, Ulli's grandson – or Kurt Kalk as he's now officially known – moved the Hermitory. Was shortly after a couple of huge storms crossed the region. The first one was big thermocell cluster with some cat7 cells. By then, Ulli was very ill. Over the years, the Stümmers had built qwiet bartering, and even romantic, relationships with neighbouring villages. Ulli'd suffered some sort of stroke and Kurt had panicked, but it was a bad call. Kurt's people didn't have any weatherTek, so didn't know the storm was upon them, but Kurt sent 3 of his people thru the gorge to reqwest the Vintgar village scope and reqwest a medik from Bled – the nearest town – to help his Grandmama.

"As the Stümmers party headed thru the gorge, the storm hit their valley and the 3 people were swept to their deaths in the torrent. When Ulli found out she, well, she passed. Died of shock, Kurt said.

"Kurt, being a Kalk, became defacto leader and said enough … *genüg*! The village needed to be more connected to the world. They stopped using the gorge as their access, bought some land from a farmer further along the valley and in the following 2 years, the community moved the village up the hill, close to a road, and then bought a truk.

"And I found them at the end of the path to the graveyard. They're still not very good at talking. And they speak pidgin German while they live in the Slovenian State … means they're still somewhat incomprehensible to the locals and vice versa. Anyway …" Langer said, annoyed at his perpetual distractedness, "Kurt was pleased to see me. He remembered me from the last time. We drank beer, and I asked him if they had Todd. He was appalled at the thought. Very upset. Even more so when I told them about the West Cap Hermitory.

"I then asked him about the Stümmers and whether the various Hermitories communicated, and he said 'not much'. But he admitted to the secret money account based in Zurich. Some friend of Ulli's set up a superDuper scrambler for them waybackwhen to safely and privately operate their account and subAccounts of other Hermitories. Some Swiss bank or other that's based there holds and manages their investment funds. Because I impressed the urgency of the matter of Todd's abduction, he was very candid. Very keen to help. Was xtremely sorry that one of their own Qwietudes would indeed be in any way involved in kidnapping people. He even waved his banking screen in front of my nose!

"So, he showed me that a few months back they were suddenly flush with funds. Just full of $New. All the communities have codes and he knows exactly where the funds come from. He calls the grouping of their accounts *The Concert,* like it's a whole lot of movements.

"At the time, Kurt didn't understand why so much $New had suddenly appeared in their account and just assumed it was from a newfound supporter. He checked the details and found the initial payment went to the Hermitory in West Cap and someone in the gorge actually shifted the bulk of the money into *The Concert* without explanation. I looked at the transactions and he was on the level. So Kurt shared some of the money with other communities around the world ..."

"How many are there, by the way?"

"Lots. More than I realized ... 273 worldwide apparently. There used to be almost 500 Hermitories before The Grief. Kurt reserved his portion from the fund for the new village, and now the original Kalk community is in the process of building a stormProof cattle shed. A big steelDrip animal barn in which the whole community can hide if big thermocells come thru. And it doubles as a milking and cheesemaking facility ... oh, you don't want to know that, do you?"

"No," said Madrigal, laughing. "Cheese sounds good tho'. Doesn't sound like they had anything to do with the abduction."

"No, no, they're just subsistence farmers who sell a bit of cheese. At least we know it was the AuZtralian mob alone in the conspiracy."

"Amazing work, Langer."

"Don't think I'll go on another field trip anytime soon tho," Langer said looking sad. There was a pause. "No new leads from your end regarding Todd?"

"No," she shrugged, "but I've found my superHacker. And I still have eyes and ears everywhere. That's all very helpful, Langer. Thankyou. Thankyou for your efforts. Zurich, eh? We'll contact the bank and I will keep you updated with everything."

The scope was severed, and Madrigal looked at the blank screen. Langer had been a dreamer, not a doer. She gave him full credit for getting out and actually talking to people rather than just snooping electronikally like the rest of them.

Might have fibbed 'bout the location of "Kalk central" at first, but all in all, not a bad effort, Mr Ex, she thought.

HOW TO KILL A PIP

To escape the prison of identity, you must carefully plan. There are many cells and passageways to cross.

Meine letzten Äußerungen (My Last Ever Utterances) 2035, Ulli Kalk

THE prison sanctuary yard is crowded with men, shirted or shirtless, sarongs or slingPants. The heat of the day is tremendous and a milling of prisoners is enjoying, as best they can, the 40 minute midday break: 11.50-12.30. There's no escape from the torpor brought on by summer humidity and stillness. No escape from the work. It's a prison of hard climate and high walls.

NewJakarta, or Baru, was a great idea once upon a time. Shifting the capital of Indonesia up near the old hilltown of Bogor, was necessary as the low lying parts of Jakarta were overwhelmed or flushed over by the ocean.

Baru? It was cleaner, well laid out with streetTrains and access for workers and elites, the new millennium and new rich class. As the climate continued to degrade they built huge underground malls, suburbs and offices to protect citizens from the worst of the Cloud as it edged north in summer. In an underground life, earthqwakes were always a risk, but steel woven ceiling cavities, hopefully to brace for the worst. Java, Sumatra had been spared the worst of The Grief. Further east, Bali, Flores, Timor Irian and PNG were uninhabitable and while millions fled to Capricornia. Many fled west to the habitable areas of Indon. Still, the climate was kinetic and harsh.

The extra power, Todd knew, was being pumped in Bellingslodes from Capricornia and Central Asia into the biggest and by far most prosperous nation in the region. Todd's prison compound is on surface Baru, embedded into a hill. As prisoners, they get no special treatment, exposed to hazards of the surface. The prison has 4 radiating wings extending out of a huge central box, a brick box with white tiles and breeze blocks, locked back and front. Outside the gates, aboveground Baru is a stripped down city with open precincts and storm shelters and enjoys great urbanRail, while domestic life and bizz, more and more, happens underground.

Todd leans against the shade side of a wall with a dozen others. A brown man among brown men. Along with his easy schoolboy Bahasa, he's picked up all the prison slang and casual jocularities. Most prisoners, locked up for one wrong or another, find Todd's presence puzzling, but they are friendly. Todd himself knows he's again been parked, for a substantial bribe, in this jail.

He is forbidden to speak to anyone except other prisoners, and a couple of approved guards, to ward off bribery attempts. His moves are closely watched by trusties, both guards and prisoners, because he is the Chief Warden's prize. He feels the eyes on him always. Among hundreds of men he still has no room to move.

Todd looks at the washed out yellow sky and sighs. Took him weeks to come to terms with imprisonment after the freedom of the desert.

All that effort. We were there, me and Liss and Narmon.

At least he didn't feel overwhelmed by the spirits of the country. In the Republik of Indonesia, he was far from any cultural responsibility.

Still, Todd dwells often on that moment he was shot thru with exuberance and vindication after leading his friends into the sheltered gorge at the end of the purple range. Led by the songs. The joy on Lissa's beautiful face. The celebratory swim with Narmon, his best mate.

After relocation to Baru jail, depression set in for a while, but Todd's compulsively curious and busy mind just started to interact. Of course, it's a male only jail, and a lot of inmates were hardAsses who avoided him, or snapped rudely. Two or 3 of the kinder prisoners tried to bring him round from his depression. They jollied him. Shared rollies of chopchop. Heard his story and sympathized. Were amazed by the Stümmers and the tale where he crossed the desert, eating lizards. It helps, but months later, still he feels shiftless and defeated, a slaveman in a slave prison system.

The food is nutritious glug of rice and goopy protein sauce. Cells are clean with 2 sets of bunks, 4 inmates. There's electricity, and a library so he can read books. If he strays anywhere near komms outlets in the library, or the shared scope in the yard, guards push him away. He goes to prayers 3 times a day in the prison's mosque – not because he's a believer, but because he wants to fit in, like he did with the morning meditations in the Hermitory. Sits on the carpets at the back and listens to the Arabic which he doesn't understand, and the Bahasa, and watches the crowd in front of him kneeling and praying, and then afterward he returns to his spot in the yard.

He's already tried to persuade the Chief Warden that his mother could outbid any keeping fee, but the jail chief is unmoved. A deal is a deal, however unsavoury. "No, no, no, I'm a man of honour," he says. "I honour my word."

In AuZ, there'd be behavioural enjj programs in this sort of facility, not just a jail with makeWork classes and study groups. In AuZ, imates would be chemically treated to sort their pathologies, their health and responses closely monitored by psychTeks. But there are not enough $ for that sort of criminological enjjineering when Jakarta policymakers are faced with a gigantic population and eqwatorial instabilities, much worse than AuZ. The Indons too, must spend most $ on infrastructure and food.

The closest the jail got to psychRehab was the ever friendly Imams or the more civilized inmates, who circulated in the crowds and made sure no one was too suicidal.

*

One of the civilized people who dragged him out of the month long torpor with chat and shared rollies of chopchop is a young guy called Abdurramn, sentenced to 18 months jail for forging electronik $New by tampering with both the Virtual envelope, and the chips. Abdurramn is small, dark and wiry with a black angular-cut mustache and close cropped hair. The whites of Abdurramn's eyes are a bit bloodshot from whatever drug he uses to sleep at nite. Otherwise he's young and very sharp and cheery. Todd's sort of person.

"Should have worked out the subAtomica of the chips better," his new friend says, discussing his conviction. "They nailed me down thru that, those bank detectives. The subAtomics were the wrong shape."

During breaks, he and Abdurramn play chess, and they sketch their lives with paper and pencil stubs that are provided to prisoners. Sketching the life away, thinks Todd.

Todd exercises hard. In the Age of Purity and Virtue, fitness was one of the Cardinal Virtues and his mother's bodyguard Pearl always said: fitness rules your mind and your mind rules your destiny. In fact, she'd added the second phrase personally, cos in the Age of Purity and Virtue, ruling your own destiny was not encouraged.

But the prison gym is super hot. Todd diligently exercises there and waits for the next move. He waits, rather than tries to escape again, because Todd is tired of running and knows the forces of evil have him tapped. Apart from the eyes watching him, he is now convinced there's some tracking implant, a pip inserted in his body – somewhere.

It's Abdurramn who starts talking about negTek in New Jakarta. He's an expert negTek doop of course, recreating $New chips and using an accordion code to expand his e$ envelope, to trick banks into believing the eCash he made was real.

A game, a fortune hunt, and an intellectual challenge. Abdurramn was that sort of guy.

The 2 are in the exercise sqware with its old trees overhanging the high walls. They are sketching and using pastes and dirt to add shade to their drawing. Todd and his fresh mate have an invented challenge called "Worst art supply". The grease from under the sink sBend in the bathroom. Drops of blood and ink. They mutually agreed not to resort to their own bodily excreta, but Todd's got an eye out for rat poo, tho the cells and eating areas are sanitised.

As they sketch, the talk turns to the high end, the whys and wherefores of newTek.

"Yeh, there's a big negTek movement in the city, looking for good outings for screeds, program cracks and things. Boyz are busy making gear, like photon cloaks. There's a big market."

"Skanners? Do people make skanners to seek out implants?" asks Todd.

"Oh, mebbe. But what's better than finding a pip and digging it out with a scalpel ..." Abdurramn points to a scar under both his wrists where tracking implants had been surgically inserted between the wrist tendons, making them hard to extract, "... is somethink that kills the pip stone dead externally, and I happen to know pips are hard to kill. The battery has to be extinguished. They are powered thru the ions in your blood. There's also their internal tek. GPS echo. Complicated little machines, pips."

"So how do you kill a pip?"

"Have you heard of a heartStopper?" Abdurramn's voice drops.

Todd had. His mother's old colleague, Simon Bluestone, was murdered cold with a heartStopper. Madrigal'd once described the murder to him with her eyes shining in horror, years after she'd sent little Todd to that underwater creepy place, The Spokes, when he was just a 6 year old boy. The Spokes was the home of Centrl, and forbidding men and women in uniforms worked there. Living without Madrigal in the Spokes for a few weeks had been a frightening experience.

"My mum's old boss was killed with a heartStopper," he says.

Abdurramn looks very surprized, but continued: "There are variations, but these heartStopper weapons all manifest by sucking bioelektrik energy out from a source," he says, swirling his pencil to sketch the line of a tree branch next to the wall. "They suck and kill battery electric devices too. PipKillers are a lot smaller than heartStoppers. They are pencil sized and directional. Crims use them to kill pips and disarm locks, like for open landVs. But when you point the thing into your body, you got to know where the pip is. Can't afford to close down anything else ... like nerves, or glands. So's a risk."

Todd feels his own escape glands start to surge. "Where'd I find the tek?" he asks.

Abdurramn smiles. He had one of those great Indon grins that broke out occasionally. He reaches out and pats his friend's arm gently.

"Slow down there, my brother, with your enthusiasm! I know a place," he says, "but Todd, even if you want to try and find it, I could never go with you. Eight more months and I am expunged of my crime, and out. Not risking the conseqwences." He shifted his buttocks on the sack he was sitting on and glanced at a guard sauntering along the wall on the other side.

"Remember, you likely have more'n one pip lodged in you. Mebbe a couple. If any are in the heart region or the head, you'd just come straight back here and serve your time. But if they can be extinguished, you could disappear in this city. You are as brown as the rest of us."

"That I am," says Todd.

"And you know Bahasa."

"I do."

Abdurramn smiles again. "I like you," he said in English. "Let's work out some geography and I'll show you how to spend a nite in town without being missed. Once your pip's dead."

"Do you ... pop out for the nite."

"Not much. Father and mother's birthdays. And I get to see my girlfriend too at those times. Otherwise, stay here until I serve my time. The authorities do understand those special family obligations. As long as you keep your word." Abdurramn smiles again.

"S'pose we needs to go back to the factory and do some work. Let's talk more later." Todd stretched forward and stood up, carefully, so as not to compound the effort and the sweat. His shirt was wet and slippery. He sucked some water from his prison bottle.

His mornings and afternoons, between meals and prayers, were taken up making fine leathergoods. Todd operated a cutting machine because "he had young eyes" according to the factory warder. Others stitched bags together, or attached straps and polished and buffed the hides until they gleamed shiny brown and black and were sellable in the Chinas and Jap/

Tai, the Koreas and other points north. Todd didn't mind the big room, tho it was hot and stuffy as hell, extractors notwithstanding. Not like courtyards where the heat or rain, or sometimes both, beat down without remorse.

Only during early evening sketching did Abdurramn take Todd mentally over the route thru Baru Jakarta and into the malls and halls of the underground part of the city. The route to the negTek men. They also discussed the rules around skanning. Todd discovered Abdurramn had a lot to do with the Baru Jakarta tek scene, and its misuse, which raised his friend in Todd's estimation.

"Jalan di bawah 223. It's a newTek shop. You ask for Jo. You say to Jo, I'm playing for time and need a component. He'll understand. Don't tell him my name whatever you do. Then you talk. You only have a coupla hours to get there and get your pips sorted and since you seem such a special darling to the jail chief, you may not even have that. And you'll have to promise money on the flip. He may not come at that. If that's the case – come straight back."

Once the routes and passwordz were imparted, Todd and Abdurramn "drifted apart" and had little to do with each other for several weeks, while Todd cosied up to other bunkmates, and men on the factory floor. Abdurramn wanted distance from the escape, both time and space, as the expungement in 8 months was important to him ... all revolving around his wedding to his girl apparently. He didn't want any blame attaching to him when an investigation commenced.

This several week delay was agreed up front, and Todd didn't mind waiting it out. Kidnapped and hidden away in Baru Jakarta was one thing. Being used as a pawn – he'd been playing a lot of chess with fellow prisoners – for some political deal, was qwite another.

If he could scope her? That'd be the trick. Kill the pips, give him time to scope Madrigal. She'd know. Somehow, the communication had to be short and neat.

He hoped his mother didn't cave to any ransom deal. He hoped she'd find him, and get the kidnappers.

Even before his breakout.

*

Almost 4 months before, when Todd'd been delivered thru high steel gates and into the jail vestibule by the men in white suits, he'd been awake and walking, not cocooned and unko. Coupla big men crabArmed him thru from a van.

The boss kidnapper was still scarved, goggled and unrecognizable, but he'd heard parts of the distant conversation with the Chief Warder – a stocky, authoritative old man – while he was transferred and checked thru. Somehow, the terms of his imprisonment had already been bartered. The jail chief was very warm to the man in the suit, while 2 others had Todd held in handcuffs. But Todd wasn't moving while the bartering continued. He was sticking around to hear what it was about.

"Might be some time," said the man in the white suit. "He's to be kept qwiet."

"That is already understood."

"A big deal has to go thru before we pick him up. Ok? And you don't have to know anything 'bout that. Keep him cornered in here. Feed him. Keep him watched and busy. Just wait for my scope. 'K?"

The jail chief didn't ask what sort of deal. Ransom? Not likely. Somethink else? Somethink big? Somethink to do with the holy grail of energy that his mother and her company controlled, most like. People were getting desperate to have enough power to keep cool, to cool their water, to reflect the cloud and protect themselves from the Singular Enemy. Phipps Industries held the power, literal and symbolik.

"Have you any idea of the time we keep him. Will have to hide him from outside audits."

"A few months mebbe. Keep a close eye and don't let him close to komms. He's a wily one. Escaped me once."

Todd smiled to himself. *Wily!*

After the roughHandling by the kaptors, 2 courteous Indon guards took over, uncuffed him and moved him into custody. The boss and his ruffians, headed off into the glare of a Jakarta morning. The jail chief and courteous guards had led him thru the cool tunnel separating the high white walls of the bustling city and the correctional centre. And so he began his second bout of imprisonment.

This time – to his chagrin – without girlz.

*

Todd can't sleep. The prisoners' dorm is silent and semidark – natural and other light seeping in. The smell of the latrine is almost masked by the bleach and bedsweat. He waits for movement, down the left row of bunks where a prisoner, Agung, is to rise qwietly and head out to the toilets – and keep going. Under the sheet, Todd is dressed in his orange cotton pants with a long shirt over the top. He has no other possessions. Todd is going to throw himself on the mercy of Abdurramn's friends for help and promised recompense. He's confident he can pitch his story qwickly.

Earlier he had greased his hand and arm and wriggled the warning device from his wrist. The one that lit and howled if he went near a komms unit.

Sliding it off almost broke his thumb, or at least sprained it, altho he double jointed as much as he could. He had slim wrists and it had eventually slid off, taking a bit of skin with it. The warner was sitting under his pillow. He sees the shadow of Agung, and as the older prisoner gets up and heads out, Todd slides out of bed and follows. Agung, of course, was going with tacit permission to a family function and would return. Todd was bent on escape.

Todd's footfalls are silent as he moves thru the big dorm, then into the toilet block. Agung is already past the sqwatHoles and sinks and up a grubby prison corridor, a minor walkway, to an outer door. It's near the big workshop wall, and Todd can see Agung's shape or shadow, feeling its way along, and down to the other wall where an emergency exit gate is normally shut fast. As Abdurramn predicted, the gate is ajar. Todd takes a big deep breath and slips thru and closes it behind him, as per instructions.

Todd finds it weird the authority allows informal departures from the prison, but the deal is obviously mutual. Only for important personal issues and for prisoners who are reasonably trustworthy. They avoid a bureaucratic process and much paperwork thru these informal understandings. Made sense.

He's on a lit, palm lined street with few vehicles on the move. The pavement is minimal, 'bout a third of a meter wide, but he crossed to where Abdurramn said he should go, down a wider boulevard. Baru Jakarta was mainly underground, so the parks on the surface were for access when the weather was fine, and buildings could be accessed either from the street or thru escalators below. Surprisingly it's not raining and Todd starts to jog. He doesn't have much time if the pip, somewhere in his body, had geoLokator alarms.

There was an underpass, half a klik down the main street which was busier than expected, with bikes, Vs and pedestrians. An even traffic flow tho'. He jogged past a bunch of shops and cafes lit by coloured ad signs for soft drinks and shirts. The precinct is filled with people. It's good to see people again, Todd thinks, unregimented ones at least. If only he could access a scope, but Abdurramn's warning rang in his ear. Pip first, then contact your people. It's a clok ticking inside you. You have to kill the thing as fast as possible. Then you can disappear ... perhaps.

Todd knows running is a huge risk.

He blends in pretty well for surveillance cameras. Brown and slim like most Indon boyz. Here were the wide, white subterannean steps. Todd swings into the passage and starts down the stairs rather than take the elevator, as tutored by Abdurramn. He was now definitely in Baru. Faint smell of food, water, people, welling up from the layered underground city. The underground boulevard that matched the one on the surface was similarly filled with small vehicles – motorbikes, elecktrik beemos – and people on the hoof, doing their thing.

Todd desperately read the signs on the walls and hanging from the tunnel roof, took a lefthand turn down a street and started to jog again, avoiding carts with nuts and fruits, children, and the occasional dog. No big landVs along the underground street. After a bunch of shops to tempt arrivals in the subterranean city, this level was mainly residential, and the best route for a qwick passage. So far Abdurramn's instructions, provided weeks ago, had proved impeccable. He knew they'd be scrambling after him now. Possibly hacked into the local surveillance systems. Weren't nothink he could do 'bout that.

But still, he was scared his traverse above the ground and thru the subterraneans was taking a little too long.

He passed a grassy area where mums, many in headscarfs, and their kidz, were mingling around the bright play eqwipment. He keeps jogging and puffing lightly. No one looks at him. The roof of the area has large extractor fans and dangling light rods. As a Phipps, the fleeting thought of power and power sources passed thru his head, but it goes. Todd is intent on an elevator arrangement to go deeper into the city and mebbe throw the signals from his pip. This was one of the punts he was taking. The pip would have triggered somethink by now. Deeper down, less signal? In his heart he doubted it, because they were out to own him, and wouldn't let poor tek frustrate their objectives.

Fit as he was, the sopping-hot evening was exhausting and sweat was pouring off his body. Todd started to puff from the effort of running. After heading down another escalator, he stopped, and leant against the wall. The sweat ran down his face and trickled off his chin and he realized, after his cool collected start, he was beginning to panic – an unnatural state for him.

The desert had been easy. He knew its intricacies. A huge underground city in ASEAN. Not so familiar.

He realizes also the air is thick, in a way he'd never experienced. Thick with smells and humidity. Was there enough oxygen in the mix? Down the subterraneans, there was no movement in the ambient air, and perhaps there were other less-kind gasses around, interfering with his body. But hurry was the word. He started to run again thru a commercial distrikt that was his destination, but it went for block after block, shop after shop, butted together with square domestic houses. The ceiling of the level was lower but could still accommodate shops of 2 stories, and workshops. People were milling around busily. At one point chairs and crates were scattered across the road where, mostly, men were sitting drinking kopi and talking. They nodded to Todd as he breezed past, but didn't look hard at the orange trouser legs sticking below the shirt.

Finally, up a side street, Todd found the sign he was looking for – NewTEK – and went in. He went left down some steps into a basement room where a couple of guys were working on large fluid-boards. Todd's hasty entrance startled them.

"What?" the thinner of the 2 men demanded.

Todd said: "Friend of yours sent me."

The thinner guy looked at Todd's orange pants: "You're from a prison? Central Baru?"

Todd nodded and asked: "I have a problem."

"You want a pip knocked out, don't you?" The thin guy was thinking way ahead. "How long since you leave? Cost you $New300."

"I can pay double, but not yet." Todd was blunt.

"Charma. Get the instruments. No time," thin guy ordered. He looked angry: "Just going to have to trust you." Must be Jo, Abdurramn's friend, Todd thought.

Charma started wanding Todd's arms and torso methodically with a large red tube. Up and down. Left to right.

Todd was amazed at the speed of their reaction.

"See anything, Charma."

"Nope."

The wand was being slowly panned across his torso now, and they were all looking at the image on the screen.

"Hope it's not in the head. We'll do that as last resort." The wand canvassed Todd's hips and groin. Nothink. "Lucky break there. Could have cost you your future children? You Indonesian?"

"No. Aussie."

"Shit, an illegal too." Down both legs until Charma barked. "There it is – behind his heel."

"Not a bad place for it." Thin guy pulled out a small chrome and black flecked object and looked at the screen. "Watch yourself this could lead to necrosis." Thin guy pressed the pip-Killer against his heel and fired. An electric shock went thru Todd, from bottom to top. "Ahhh" he exclaimed. "Ahhh, that hurt."

"Done," said the guy. "Now piss off. Contact us later for payment."

"Check the rest of me," said Todd. "The guys who put the pip in. They are devious. Wand my head."

Charma blinked. "Well, that doesn't sound good," he said, skanning Todd's neck, face and head. "Aww, shit, in your sinus. There's somethink in your sinus."

"PipKiller could really hurt you there."

"Could point it down, away from the brain," said Charma.

"Awww, shit," said thin guy. "Should treat it with surgery. It's tiny tho'. A .5mm job. Half charge would do it?"

The larger guy nodded. "Should."

"Do what your friend says," said Todd, steeling himself. "Aim down! Toward my bottom jaw."

When Todd came round a couple of minutes later, he couldn't talk. His tongue was numb and thin guy was bent over him with water or arak ... Todd couldn't work it out. No taste buds. Things were scrambled, but he knew where he was, and what he had to do. He spat the fluid from his mouth and struggled to his feet leaning against the table.

"Terima kasih," he said thickly, "wonn forrrget," and he struggled up the stairs. Abdurramn had been insistent. Do not hang around. You will attract the milisi as it is. Hide, then find a scope. At the top of the stairs, Todd staggered thru the door into a large armoured guy with a sideArm. The man's big frame blocked the door. He pushed Todd toward a white man in a grey suit, hooded to obscure his face.

Todd tried to cry out a warning, but couldn't. Two large armoured guys went down the stairwell and there were a couple of brief flashes, then they clumped back up.

"Done," said the large guy in English to the man in the grey suit.

Todd felt violently sick. The men who had just helped him had been executed. Killed. Because they'd done him a favor.

The man in the suit looked at him. Hard eyes. Sculpted brows.

"Don't vomit," he commanded. "Your gag reflex will be knocked out! You might drown if you vomit! Hear me." Todd nodded, trying hard to keep an incipient retch under control. The physical effort made him move on from the horror that he felt. He started to breath deeply and slowly, but he was shuddering. He glared at the man with the brows with pure hate. The man was not moved. The man skanned Todd up and down.

"Nice try, Todd. You, come with me." The man in the suit offered him a flask. "Now swallow this. It will anesthetize the pain in your tongue."

Todd shook his head. "I'll live with it," he said, thickly.

A MENACE

Gimme $New dollars
Gimme $New dollars
Don't bother with the $Olds
That's for the grey collars
I'm at the top of the tree
So give the $New to me
Gimme New, Gimme New, Gimme New!!!
    Gimme $New (2038) lyrics by the NYC neo-thrash band, The Stümmeratii

"FIND a way," the voices said. "Find a way. Time is here. No ovations or rewards for losers. Our home will be overwhelmed by the Singular Enemy. Our trees laid waste. Mudslides and destruction. History washed away."

Money. Always money. All came down to eBundles of $New, didn't it?

"What did your daughter's Heg say?"

"They said no!" the Old Man snarled at the bulbs in the glows. "Find the cash, yourselves. You can't get somethink for nothink"

"You promised."

"But clearly," said the Old Man, writhing, "clearly I can't deliver. I won't."

"Too late for that," said the voices. "Too late for that." They were ghostlike, needling and jabbing him with anger and menace from behind some sort of veil. The grey and blue shapes emanated like big lumps of opaquwe bubble-wrap from his scope stand. Faces were indistinct, almost invisible, scrambled to prevent identity, but undeniably there to goad him into action and to frighten the bejeezus out of him.

"You must act," said a voice he thought he recognized, but hard to say for sure.

He knew he was powerless, but he stared them down as if he was in his Prime and at the peak of influence. Principle of the thing. Don't let them win.

The Old Man stood up slowly, his coat swishing on the ground, and he stamped angrily, the solid wooden floor booming. "I won't."

"You will suffer the humiliation. Your family will all suffer."

"Do your worst!" the Old Man bellowed.

"We will," said the glow. "Oh, we will."

He looked out the low window into his garden. His anger was trampling over the fear in his heart. Nozomi, head bent to the glows, watched her husband's centenarian rage, as if he was a dry leaf falling erratically from a tree, rather than that hard smooth stone she'd once imagined. Nozomi saw everything unraveling in this fit of old man's pique. All that subtle work undone. Her poor city.

"Then go!" he roared at the glow. The glow fizzed out. He was left with a dark shadow in the corner.

*

Lissa woke, drowsy, head clouded. Hectic day before. School, then rope and ledge training. Ledges! Imagine. Creeping along precarious places, working on balance and nerves, Pearl shouting tips from the gym floor 15 meters below. By the time Lissa'd got to bed, she was exhausted.

Her sleep was always deep, but as she swam toward the surface of morning, she dreamt of Todd. Not like the day dreams she'd conjured on her long walk, and tried to resist. No, this dream had been tame, deep and real. She and Todd were at a Club. Not sure which. It had red tinselly roof trimmings and distant lights, high up. The lights could have been the stars they followed thru the desert, they were so pinpoint bright. They had danced together, the swingStep, on a wooden floor. Nothink untoward. Just fun, twirls and spins. The dance went on and on. And Todd said, "We'll stop when the sun comes up, Liss." And she'd replied, "When will that be?" and he said, "Dunno, Liss. Dunno. Keep dancing with me." She started to be frightened for herself and Todd, because it was still dark outside when she knew it should be daytime, and the music was droning and horning on. She recognized it as one of their tunes, a Philosophikal tune, but hyped up. And while Todd looked worried and stared and stared at the band, he finally turned and winked at her.

She woke for real.

The wink was the same as she'd seen when encased in the lightgoo stuff on the aircraft, just after their abduction. The memory of that wink was born from a terror. She hadn't really succumbed to whatever gas the kidnappers had administered in the green room at the Club Karribee. She'd woke qwite early, stuck in the goo, and the claustrophobic feeling had been terrifying. She'd felt sqwashed, barely able to breathe. Shallow breaths accelerated from fear. With it had taken a great deal of effort to keep calm and breathe slow. It had been hard because of the snorkel tube in her mouth. But then, in the dark hopper hold, she'd seen Todd's face stuck in his own rough bubble of light, nose a bit sqwished. And his lively eyes. His wink had helped.

Lissa turned from the comfortable pillow and looked out the strip window above her bed at the dark grey clouds and lashing rain. Two stabs of lightning pulled shadows from the corner of the room like elastic and then snapped them back. Soundproofing muffled the thunder to a short purr. Her heart sank. Another bad front was passing over and it would be an indoor day, too dangerous to go outside.

She jumped out of bed, showered, dressed in her school uniform and headed down to the staff diner. As soon as she entered, Madrigal, who was crouched over a kopi and a big bowl of fruit looked up at her strangely.

"You okay, Lissa?"

"Yes. Why?"

"You look upset."

Ah, still, I'm giving my emotions away, thought Lissa. Gloom from her dream was clearly with her. She thought she'd cleared and skooshed the dream gloom away during her shower.

Lissa told Madrigal about the neverending swingStep dance and the wink, which originated from Todd's wink in the hopper. Madrigal looked sad.

"Mebbe he's talking to you and not to me," said the older woman.

Lissa was taken aback. "I don't think there's any kommunication from Todd there, if that's what you mean? That doesn't happen. It was just a dream from my unconscious, Dr Phipps, with nothink new in it. The wink was old, the tune was old, and the frustration of not knowing where he is keeps us all anxious. It was just great to dance with him for a bit."

"You've a wise old head," said Madrigal.

"Don't you dream about Todd?"

"I do, but not like that," Madrigal said, wishing she could dance with her son. "Grab some brekky. It's another day."

They sat facing each other in silence for a time, eating prawn and rice smeared with sweet chilli, sipping juice.

"I can't work it out," Madrigal said. "Round and round in my head. Why all this conspiracy? This vast expense to snatch you 4 kidz, and for what? Here we are, 8 months on since the crime, and there's no explanation."

Lissa looked up from her bowl: "Inexplicable terrible things have happened, thanx to the event." Madrigal nodded. "This wasn't just for the Stümmers. They are annoyingly simple people. Don't really need our $New. It's plain stupid."

An hour later, Madrigal's scope buzzed. The voice talked rapidly in Bahasa and finally, things began to become clearer.

THE
SUBTERANNEAN
URBS

I farewell family lineage. Those names. Shed like the skin of a snake. Go underground.

Meine letzten Äußerungen (My Last Ever Utterances) 2035, Ulli Kalk

THE General of Polis in Baru, was animated and angry and she didn't blame him for it. Madrigal wished that Jembrana would arrive and qwell the GENPOLs fury with a few apt wordz. Jembrana had arrived by scoop from the Ville but was still 15 minutes away, caught in traffic, so the General had started the briefing. Jembrana already knew the details thru ASEAN Fig-Cons. In the arcane political braiding of AuZgov and ASEAN, Jembrana was always more of an ASEAN official than AuZ. That was the deal during the Blend.

Now he was the elected Premier in the Joint Territory that straddled the top half of the AuZtralian continent. Capricornia wasn't the luckiest half of the continent; neither were the deserts of inland New South Wales. The lush, verdant food baskets of the Murray Basin, South AuZ, and Tasmania, however, lifted by the weather changes and getting warm and reliable rainfall most of the year round, were some of the most productive agricultural strips in the world. Cap was burdened by a massive population, poor soils, and the encroaching Cloud dooming her solar farms. Jembrana, and Madrigal thru her subCompanies, were working to develop Capricornia's food outputs along the newly lush western Arables, despite the hardscrabble life of the inhabitants.

Jembrana was presenting himself personally at the Jakarta milisi HQ, because he owed Madrigal.

At the Baru Jakarta milisi HQ, Madrigal and Pearl listened to the GENPOLs torrent of angry wordz. The senior official responsible for security in both Old and New Jakarta was livid. He'd walked into the room fizzing and just started to rant: "One of those boyz, young Jo ... who was killed for *whoknowswhat??* I know his father. Very well. He is a friend. Those boyz were making a good business. A fist of it. Your son stumbles into their shop and ..." He paused to catch his breath: "You don't know how angry this makes me," he continued in rapid fire Bahasa that Madrigal followed easily, but Pearl had difficulty with. "Two other of my friend's children died years back from storms in the south Java area. Now with Jo gone he has one child remaining! One son!"

The Commander got more and more incandescent.

Madrigal was watching the milisi Commander's hand. "This!" He stabbed his finger at the glowWand angrily as vidVision images of hooded, armed thugs spread across the screens. They were moving with intent down a subterranean alley in Baru in one of the more mercantile of the suburbs.

"And this," he snarled. A figure, a young guy, clearly Todd, on his knees, being trussed. Madrigal lost her own composure and gasped.

"And this," he continued. A basement in a bunker. The graphics were clear. The bodies of 2 young men were sprawled untidily: one on the floor with chest wounds, one smashed by the force of the bullets into a cupboard, chest and head wounds, ugly and brutish. They looked like kidz. Not much older than Todd.

"That boy in the cupboard is Jo. I knew him. No one behaves this brutally on my patch. Ever!"

"Coneshells," said Pearl switching to technical assessment. She gazed hard at the last image that the milisi commander was stabbing a finger at. "Heavy armaments. Nothink electronik in that. Coneshells make a terrible mess of the torso."

"And this!" said the General. He clicked and the screen showed one of the masked men, gun on hip, spraying adjoining shops and houses with shells as a lethal keepAway warning. Swinging around in a clinical half circle, firing at random.

"Two other people were injured in that outrage," said the General. "And one was a 5 year old girl!"

Madrigal and Pearl said nothink. What could they say? The whole crime chronology from the Club Karribee onward was an appalling mess.

The milisi Commander continued his torrent of wordz: "We backtracked our various HighEyes and all other optiCons to where your son originated. To participate in this ... this crimSpree. And guess where he came from? Your son's movement started at the Baru prison, at 9pm. He was in Baru jail, of all places. In the JAIL!! We now have the jail administration under close investigation. They are being spoken to by my people. Your son is clearly complicit in illegal activities. Why did he go to young Jo's shop? I can't be professional about this. I am head of security for this city. Jo's father will hold me personally responsible for this til the day I die. And another boy is dead too. Called ..." he looked at his pad, "Charma Kumolo. What is going on?"

"We don't know," said Madrigal. "That's the truth. My son was kidnapped months ago. Almost found him in West Cap in November and then he was taken again. If he was in Baru jail, he was being held against his will. We've tried to trace him every way possible. This is our first big lokator."

"Abducted by who? By WHO?" shouted the exasperated General.

There was a pause as everyone in the room detected foorsteps. The footsteps ushered Jembrana and his aides into the room, led by a milisiman who was wanding the group thru a series of secure doors.

"Ah ... Premier. Please, please, shed some light on this," said the General.

"S'lamat ..." Jembrana strode over and shook the General's hand and greeted Madrigal with a cursory "Dr Phipps." He was so in the chillZone. Jembrana waved a couple of his people to the table and sat beside Pearl who received a nod of recognition.

And he didn't mince wordz: "I saw your vidVision. It's terribly disturbing for such an incident to happen in the new town."

"Monstrous," said the agitated General. "Everyone is law abiding. Life is so, so precious and this happens. This callousness reminds me of the days before the Singular Enemy. A massacre. A massacre in my city."

Madrigal could see Jembrana was sizing up the General's mood and looking for wordz.

"I can tell you honestly, General, that that boy, Todd Phipps, is a victim. He has nothink to do with the intent of these killers. They were after him, no doubt, but only to capture him again. What he was doing in the tek shop I have no idea. He must have escaped the jail, where he was being held, and made his way there."

There was a silence as Jembrana's words sank in.

"I'll take your word on that," said the milisi General. "But can you give me some guidance? Where do I find these people who have run amok in my town?"

Madrigal looked at the table. Jembrana said soothingly: "They'll be long gone, General. We must collect the biometriks, any traces, to enable us to charge them with these crimes when we capture them."

"Already done," said the General. "Biotics, evidence. All captured."

Madrigal said to Jembrana: "Premier, you didn't have to come," but Jembrana raised a hand.

"This crime has wreaked havoc from Perth, in WestAuZ, to the deserts of Capricornia where a man was killed, thru to Baru Jakarta, where there are 2 more deaths and 2 badly injured civilians. It is deplorable. I am determined to see it resolved before any further casualties. General, any assistance I can give is at your disposal. Capricornia does not export its criminals to ASEAN. No, we don't. And if it happens, we clean up!"

Madrigal could see where this was going. Jembrana was determined to take control of the issue. On top of all the daily disasters he had to deal with in his Territory. And he'd want a qwick resolution.

The General looked at him.

"As a former security chief, I know, and you know too General, that the slower we act, the less chance we have."

"What do you suggest? On top of my current orders?"

"My first instinct – let's check all the traces. There are 4 armed men on the loose, and then there's Todd Phipps. Where have they gone? Even if the crims used shimmers, the publik must have seen somethink. A publik appeal. Send milisi men into that sector of the city and ask everyone."

"I've already deployed several V-loads of men to canvass the neighbourhood."

"Broaden the deployment," said Jembrana. "I've also brought a small team to assist. Surely the perpetrators headed to the city outskirts to hold Todd Phipps somewhere else. Mebbe milisimen in outlying towns and villages have heard of some disturbances. Odd goings on. And let Dr Phipps and her escort check the crime scene too."

The General didn't even pause. "Go! Now! Take a team with you, Dr Phipps. We must hurry and make sure they don't vanish in the outreaches. We'll extend the watching brief from the province to the whole of Java. These boyz deaths must be avenged." Jembrana had swung the General's mood totally around.

Not wanting the rage to return, Pearl and Madrigal didn't think twice. With the flash of a smile to Jembrana as she passed, Madrigal and her main woman headed out the door.

BABY BOOM

The nameless remain your family and their love is the same.
Meine letzten Äußerungen (My Last Ever Utterances) 2035,
Ulli Kalk

CURL watched Peet with interest as he inspected the check-lists, his skinny shoulders and shock of hair, pencil in hand, scratching notes qwickly.

Wooo! He was so different. He was focused on the page, working very fast. Stümmers took their time over things. Not like Peet.

Peet was younger than some she'd been with, but so smart. And so strange. Not at all earnest and babyish, like many of the other boyz. She was happy when Peet had asked for her help with his job of probationary Qwartermaster because he knew so little about the Hermitory. Everyone was happy with this arrangement.

Now both engrossed in supply matters, studying lists.

Her arm brushed his as they leant over the counter and he looked round and smiled at her again. He was calm. She was calm. They were comfortable now in the arrangement.

She signed: *all okay?*

He replied: *we're getting to the end.*

She knew he was organized – logistiks were never a prob. But the needs of the Hermitory were her knowledge, and she was enjoying the work. She knew without her, he'd never have countenanced ordering insect repellants for crops, irrigation pipe washers, toothscrapes, and materials to make fresh female hygiene products, but Curl knew all about these things.

Thought of the hygiene products gave her a start, because she hadn't had her moonblood that month, but was probably a physical qwirk. Then they got busy and she forgot the qwalm. She signed, they went thru the hardware area drawers where she wrote down fixing components like screws, nails, plugs, battens. Stock was very low.

Peet had been shocked when he discovered how much petrol the Hermitory needed, so allergic were the Stümmers to electronik power sources. *NooneNo one these dayz uses petrol except in emergencies,* he'd signed in amazement. Clearly he'd been too besotted with her to notice the snippers, tractors and diggers the gardeners used. He'd checked thru previous lists and the amounts of fuel needed for a year were substantial. They'd ordered drums full to last an entire year.

After a weeks hard audit, Curl and Peet drafted a sizable list which was authorized by the Qwietude, and he called Dan Monthly again to put thru the full order for a March drop. Curl tried not to listen to the wordz he was saying into the scope, to some supplier, but she knew what they meant. Every single word.

Sometimes during lunchbreak they climbed a high ladder and sat together on the top shelf having a snack, legs dangling over the rocky floor, looking down and out of the big sliding doors to the gorge floor far below where her family worked in the fields. She watched the gardener so far below and felt great content.

When Peet'd put in the order for a pile of supplies: a new medikal skanner, cotton cloth, dyes, seeds, replacements for the dry frys and other items stolen by Todd Phipps, beads, fuel, stock and a hundred other vital items, the Hermitory was delighted and anticipated the March consignment with great jubilation.

*

One nite, as rain pounded down on the roof of Curl's house, she'n Peet lay on top of their sheets in the steam, naked and tired, Curl signed Peet: *You remember when we first got to-gether?*

Yes.

She was watching him directly in the eyes now with her serious face. *Did Leader of Men supply you with antiFecundities?*

It took Peet a few moments to see what she was getting at. The sign was *not be pregnant.* She meant contraception.

No. No. He never did. Why?

I'm with child, she signed. Peet was so astonished he sat up and almost fell out of the bed and started to talk: "Are we?" but saw the distaste on her face, and then signed hastily: *You're saying we're going to have a baby? You and me?*

Yes, she said, now looking anxious. *I hadn't planned this. I was tricked. By Leader of Women. I swear on my heart.*

Peet nodded his head slowly.

How long have you known?

My moonblood did not happen since new year and I have been feeling sick, and funnyWeird. I took the test yesterday and found it's really true.

Peet looked exercised at that. He'd been back only a few weeks.

He was a still a teenager. But he'd made some momentous life decisions already. He slid back down, rolled on his side and kissed Curl on the lips very softy, than rolled back and signed: *We can deal with this. We can deal with baby. Does anyone else know?*

No. You are first to be informed, of course.

He was just 17. Curl was 18. They were young.

Peet was thinking about his mother. "Bring my Oncer home," she'd say, because the family knew, already, that Peet was allowed only one child. The Stümmers ignored child authorizations as their families were deLinked from the DyNAst database. Out of sight, out of database, out of mind. Stümmers had as many kidz as they liked.

Oh, he thought. This is going to be complicated.

He asked: *How were you tricked? I thought you were on the tablets?*

No. Shortly after you all arrived, Leader of Women told the girlz that we had run out. The girl pills had finished but the boyz were still being issued with male antiFecundities.

I should have checked you were protected before we sexed, he signed. *I shouldn't have assumed.*

That's why I had to find an abortant for poor Lissa. Because she was not protected from Pepperbeard when he attacked her. Todd asked me, that morning after the attack, on her behalf to get her a purge. And I asked SlimFingers who works in the pharmacy and got some. But ... even after, we were all still convinced the boyz were safe to sex with.

I didn't know you'd helped her. I knew she'd been ... assaulted by him, signed Peet. *I didn't know the assault included sexing ... that's terrible.* He paused, hands hanging in the air above them. *No wonder she was angry as ...*

Was not sexing. Was attack without consent ... Momentarily, Curl's eyes were dark with fury.

Peet was alarmed. Lissa's demand that he stay away from the Stümmers, that he "stay safe" in Perth, made so much more sense now. The terrible attack on Lissa had entirely turned her against Stümmerdom. Pepperbeard had wrecked her trust in almost everything.

He signed slowly, while letting the story sink in: *So, Leader of Women told you she'd run out of girl antiFecundities, but said that Todd and me and all the rest were issued with male pills?*

Yes. We were tricked.

So Bangle ... Little Weaver ... they could be pregnant to Todd?

Could be. Yes. I can ask how they are feeling.

Curl's face dissolved into tears. Peet grabbed her and hugged her and murmered aloud: "Shhhh ... don't make our baby sad too. Babies are good news." *It's good news!* he signed.

Their baby. Even in the sudden thrill, Peet found part of his his mind was so less excited. The story of Leader of Women's duplicity, tricking the girlz, filled him with dread. Could tear the little community apart, it could, if handled poorly by the Qwietude, and he'd be the culprit to cause the rifts. He thought, I will discuss privately with Leader of Men tomorrow, but ohhh, will be difficult.

*

Leader of Men was genuinely shocked. He'd gasped.

He took his glasses off and rubbed his eyebrows, then put them on again. He repeated the gesture twice more. Peet watched, sitting patiently, as Stümmers tended to take their time when communicating anything. And this was one narly prob.

Peet had asked for a private meeting and they were in the Leader's comfortable living suite, with wicker chairs and a writing desk. A glimpse of the red canyon wall thru the steamedUp windows. They'd sat down, facing each other on the 2 wicker couches. Peet hadn't hesitated and plunged into the story, thru the chronology of events. To cap it off, he then announced he was going to be a dad.

Peet had encouraged Curl to join him, but she'd been too frightened to criticize her Leader, no matter how she'd been tricked. Peet was forever charmed by the Stümmer belief in goodness and love, and admired her continued loyalty to her

Leader, even if such loyalty was not appropriate in these circumstances. They'd had a tense exchange before Peet made the appointment. The Leader of Women was a kindly mother figure to so many of the women and girlz in the gorge.

Don't be angry with her. What she does for us, it's always for the girlz and women ... she's not a selfish person, Curl had signed.

So, now Peet and Leader of Men sat facing each other in the wicker chairs, a burst of hot summer rain suddenly pounding the glass. *So you are saying Leader of Women withdrew the girlz protection when you and Todd and Narmon arrived?*

Seems so.

Narmon loves Lissa, they were pledjd and paired. Unlikely to stray. But you and Todd? Which of our girlz sexed with you?

Curl. Only Curl for me. And she is now pregnant.

And what about Todd?

Oh ... he sexed with several girlz. He and the girlz enjoyed their prerogative much, I believe, tho' I doubt he knew what he was doing other than sexing. He was popular with the girlz ... Bangle for sure. Little Bones, Little Weaver ... and Leader of Women. I'm not sure who else. He was amazed at how happy the girlz were to go sexing.

Leader of Men signed: *Yes, yes. That's our way. As you now know, all our young people are allowed, after coming of age, to explore and seek pleasures and comforts in their privacies, until they find their one. Nothink stops them until they are paired. A pure process. New people are welcome in our community. No matter. Our boyz understand the rules.*

The older man paused and cleaned his spectacles again, mouth turned down, unhappy. Peet noticed a slight tremor in the hand which carefully held the glasses frame.

I think the Qwietude will be caring for a baby flood soon, signed Leader of Men.

The situation wasn't difficult for Leader of Men to work out. He knew everyone in their Qwietude Council had increasingly worried, for 2 decades now, about the cross-stock of family genetics. They'd been terribly fearful of crossHatching and babies affected. The community leaders had long been discussing the prospect of new babies with fresh DNA. To grow and one day become heads of households. No such chance had arisen. No one ever came to the gorge.

Leader of Men realized the antiFecundity trick on their young people was planned by Pepperbeard, Leader of Women, and whoever else, to boost the Hermitory's genetic stock using the young visitors.

The modus was highly dubious to him. If he'd known, Leader of Men would have opposed any secrecy and withdrawal of antiFecundities from the girlz. But Pepperbeard, Leader of Women – they were – what do you call it? Ends justify the means people?

Leader of Men explained some of this to Peet since the young man had also been part of the trickery.

So far, in over 100 years at this Hermitory, the Qwietude has avoided genetic crossHatching, but more and more in the past few years our mediks have started to forbid matches. GeneModeling has shown possible gene failures, genetic disorders and disease. And in another 10 years, we'll be in deep trouble without fresh genetiks. This has concerned us all. All the leaders and parents.

Leader of Men paused again. Peet looked at him expectantly.

Was clear Leader of Women acted qwickly after you arrived. She maniplated the windfall. I'm sure she had no idea you'd be brought here, as that would implicate her in your kidnapping ... I'm sure she wasn't aware of any crime. The Qwartermaster was responsible, wholly. But as soon as you arrived, she saw the op-

portunity and helped make life comfortable and friendly for you all among her beautiful young girlz and my boyz.

Peet nodded in agreement. *That is my understanding also.*

Leader of Men went on: *Please invite Little Weaver and Bangles in privacy to see me ... perhaps one at a time, Peet. Not all together. And are you sure Narmon wasn't otherwise tempted? Could he have strayed from Lissa? He is a young man, after all.*

Peet looked surprized and signed, *I don't think so.* Narmon was a strong follower of the tenets of Purity and Virtue and would have never betrayed Lissa. Peet was sure of that.

Leader of Men nodded. *I had best talk to Leader of Women,* he added.

PARK UNDER LIGHTS

"The Lost Art of Disappearing" - chapter heading
  Meine letzten Äußerungen (My Last Ever Utterances) 2035,
Ulli Kalk

THE milisi had removed the 2 bodies of the young Indon tek-Heads, but the mess in the workshop, laid out under forensic's floodlights, remained. Tables overturned, the shelves where Charma had crashed backward were still smashed, tek gear and glass over the floor. The shop smelled of sour blood with red stains up one wall, and pooled on the floor.

Poor kidz, thought Madrigal. Doomed because of my boy.

She and Pearl walked thru in hygiene boots examining the floor and walls. They stepped carefully. Among the drives, handles, and subAtomic chips on the floor lay a small heartStopper shaped instrument, with chrome tube and a fancy brass handle on one end formed in the shape of a flying Garuda.

"What's this?" asked Madrigal.

"Forensic guys I talked to identified it as a negatori, or a pipKiller. Like a small heartStopper. Utterly illegal. Draws the power from any batterys in the targeted pip, and kills the thing. Funny ... while the milisi General talked well of the dead guys, the forensic people upstairs are more cynical and I agree with them – all the evidence," Pearl waved her hand round the room, "points to a negTek operation under what seems to be a standard tek repair shop."

"So, stop me if I'm wrong, but Todd may have come here to have somethink zapped – like a tracking pip?"

"Seems like," said Pearl. "Look here." There was a small sensor in the ceiling and she was tall enough to poke her finger around it and push the panel up, but it didn't lead anywhere. "Could be linked by the wifi to a clamB or mainframe?"

They asked one of the forensics who was waiting upstairs. The tek said they'd already clokked the roof sensor and a search led nowhere. Wasn't operating at the time of the killing, as far as they knew.

*

Outside, the subStreet of the subterranean urbs was filled with pedestrians, folk on bicycles, vendors, hovering gawkers. Pearl and Madrigal made a cursory search on the ground and realized any clueTraces were already logged by the Baru milisi, or had vanished on the soles of sandals and under streetSweepers. Followed by 2 milisimen and a forensicTek, the women walked slowly up the street away from the crime scene. Locals unashamedly stared at Pearl's size as she passed, but she wasn't distracted by the awe radiating in her direction.

Before the killer's shimmer pack kicked in and cloaked them, vidVision had shown they'd tooled toward a more residential area. Todd was visibly trussed and dragged between 2 big guys until the air swam and then there was nothink. For a time, Madrigal's small party of investigators traversed several streets in a vague grid pattern, and looked in backyards and alleys, until they came across a smallish park under lights, a green area with trees and long leaved shrubs, and play eqwipment for the kidz of the subbs neighbourhood. She guessed they were fluoroFlora plants, able to thrive underground with a few UV lights dangling from steel beams to encourage growth.

Madrigal found grass and foliage along the edge of the park crushed from the application of some heavy weight. There'd been a sprinkler across the grass not so long ago and leaves and plants were beaded with moisture.

"Here," she said, crouching and poking the wet ground, "at least 4 consecutive people, probably the killParty, and clear dragmarks of an unwilling fifth person. You can see heelmarks and their variable depth in the dirt and work the numbers from there. There're loose divots from someone being dragged ... happened before the sprinklers went on. Water has since filled the dips."

She looked up: "Heading that way. What's over that way?" she asked in Bahasa.

"Car park, Ma'am," answered an Indon milisiman in English.

The 2 women and their Indon colleagues proceeded along the path until they hit a gate at the end of the footpath and a V-stop area – a big multiVpark to keep landVs and bikes out of the subbs after entering the downRamp. Parked vehicles crowded the tarmac area, but across the car park there was a bunch of drivers sqwatting alongside their lectrik beemos, smoking chopchop and chatting, waiting for customers who were forced to leave their landVs and who might need a lift further thru the subbs. Madrigal and one of the milisimen walked over.

"Apa kabar! Any of you here last nite? Seen anything unusual?" The milisiman asked pleasantly. "'Bout 11?"

"I was working it here. The other guys were in the east entrance Vpark. I didn't see much ..." one skinny bloke said. He was dressed neat, in shorts and a yellow collared shirt, and sat sideways on the seat of his beemo. "Didn't Eka say there was a ruckus, like, in the middle of the nite?" he yelled at the beemo driver next to him. "Eka does the early shift," the skinny guy continued. "Gets a lot of late nite party people coming home from aboveTop. Does good bizz, but he's out like a light this time of day."

"You remember what Eka said?" Madrigal asked the skinny guy's friend.

"Said out at the other end of the VPark, suddenly out of nowhere there was shouting. And a bit of a fight. That was all."

"How far?"

"Down the back there. Then a big van left. He actually went over because he thought someone was in trouble, but the van screamed off up the ramp."

"What time?"

"Midnite mebbe?"

"And he didn't call the milisi?"

"Over too qwick. That's what he said."

"Ok." She zapped the 2 guys a coupla $New in their eTills and they headed back to the rest of the search party.

"Must have banged Todd into a landV and headed upSide along one of the exit tunnels," Madrigal said. "I wonder if Todd was injured or being deliberately obdurate, when he was dragged, cos he left a trail for me, anywise. And whether he tried to run when they were pushing him into the van." Sounded like Todd had been thinking ahead and not unko.

She scoped Jembrana with the info. The tunnel vid should at least log the landV or truk. The milisi were already contacting the traffik section to look for traces.

A milisi landV was summonsed and arrived at the bottom of the ramp in a millisecond, and they headed qwickly up the bright exit tunnel, thru to the aboveground Baru city, where it was pelting with rain, tho' from the top of the road rise she could see yellow sky beyond the rainclouds.

Water was pouring into drains, capturing, in brown swirly water, anything that would threaten the suburbs under the roadways. Two massive concrete drains were pumping the runoff down the hill, and she watched the torrents as the cruiser she was in followed downward.

Beyond the rushing drains, solid grey towerbloks lined the expressway, which hummed with vehicles on their daily bizz, and beyond, a big treed area loomed to the north which separated Baru from Old Jakarta.

Pearl relayed the consensus she and the milisi came to in a qwick confab – their qwarry would have fast hunted for an aircraft of some sort. Again Madrigal felt the despair creep into her mind and cloud her purpose. Such a big connurbation, from old town Jakarta by the ocean, up thru the volcanic landscape? Underground, aboveground.

Where to start?

*

Smuggling was a crime which was definitely not extinct.

Govs across the globe were adding tax and excise on all manner of items to desperately raise revenues: foodstuff, spice, cosmetics, shoes, rejuveDrugs, tek. Almost everything. As millions of semi-impoverished people just wanted things cheaper, smuggling was big. And as smuggling was not generally deadly, or injurious to the tenets of society where life was sacred, a coterie of crims were busy dealing in contraband goods. When smugglers realized surveillance of citizens was becoming a second order priority, the criminal imagination was unleashed and blackRoutes were opening, and secret airstrips built. Big money went to smugglers who could get thru the cloud from north to south and back again. A person could be smuggled using those routes, for instance.

Madrigal sat in the landV, windscreen spattered with rain, her cheeks smeared with tears, while she tried to get a grip on her sense of purpose. At the same time, a group of Indon milisimen were examining a hole in a rice field to the south of Baru. The crushed crop was on a terrace, next to a road that traversed a saddle along a hillside, on the rear slope of the volcano Gunung Gede, where rice terraces still abounded and farmers exploited rich soil. The hillside was forested to the left of the road, and descended steeply in a pattern of angular terraces to the right. In the top terrace the rice was utterly crushed by a huge oblong weight.

An hour later, Madrigal had reached her hopper, stationed at Baru airport and received a call from a milisi lieutenant general who took her thru the detail in impeccable English.

"Our milisimen investigated the crushed rice field after they'd been scoped by Baru HQ to report anything strange. They responded, and forensics were there in 30 minutes. The 2 specialists took water samples and deployed our ASEAN fuel locus – a molecular test grid for types of fuel used for takeoff, allowing acceleration of boats, planes, submarines. We analyse the waste."

Madrigal asked whether the analysis had been done.

"It is important to be qwick as the fuel traces float on the surface and would be washed off by rain and thunderstorms within hours. Luckily, we collected several sheens."

The Lieutenant general also explained that the farmer, a woman who owned 3 fields, was most upset. She had lost the early season's crop to this crushing weight, grains sqwished into the wet mud.

"Dr Phipps, I can send eVidz and you'll see the shape reveals the aircraft was substantial and elongated – most likely a generation 3 longRange hopper which could be military, could be civilian. And indeed our analysis was very qwick."

"Do tell?" said Madrigal, swallowing her impatience.

"So the fuel load was a mix – a type of AVgas found in the Sino qwadrant, with some Indon sourced chemicals. China is the most likely departure point. Then a refuel somewhere around Jakarta – we are chasing that lead now as they likely refueled here to fly back to their destination. Fuel sourcing gives us leads to identities of smuggling shipments and often the personnel. I'll skip the detailed forensic analysis to your scope."

"Thanx, appreciate it," Madrigal said.

The milisi officer continued: "We are now searching for the Indon fueling station as the hopper would have been noticed. Final takeoff was cloaked from where the alleged killTeam met at the pickup point in the rice paddy. Both the electronik wash and visuals were opaque. There's nothink. I'm sorry. No indications which direction they went. HighEyes has detected nothink as there was general raincloud cover."

"Are there witnesses? When did the takeoff happen?" asked Pearl who was scoped in on the call from Baru HQ.

"The farmer remembered hearing somethink, some hours before. Around 2am. She says she heard "the whine of an aircraft". It had been very early in the morning. Still dark. She has asked for compensation and the forensics officer gave her a card with milisi HQs scope number and promised her help for her information. Also, there were numerous tracks along the grit and gravel rural road, and somewhat churned."

Madrigal sensed that while the team would take samples and tyre shots, most evidence would have been damaged by other passing traffik. They were doing all they could do tho. Mysterious liftoff at 2 in the morning. Mix of AVgas. They signed off and left.

For a microMoment, Madrigal thought she and Pearl should check the scene, but it was a feeble lead and there wouldn't be many other pickings now the heavy rain had set in. A Chinese fix could mean involvement by unknown persons anywhere from Hong Kong thru to the Central Sino-republiks and even their dependencies beyond – the Tajiks, the Kyrgirs ... who else? Even the Koreas used Sino AVgas. It was a hopeless lead.

*

The AuZgov uniform had started to irritate her, so Madrigal changed to a dress for her meeting with Jembrana. She'd once loved the cut of the uniform tho had only worn it on more formal occasions. As her job had been the diplomatik, business suits had been more the thing.

Now, recommissioned, and after a few weeks of moving thru a policing style investigation in that same old uniform, it was now wonderful to change out of it.

Prior to her meet with Premier Jembrana, and in her private suite at the rear of the hopper, she'd put a silk dress on – the honey coloured one with black trim at neck and hem – makeup, and leatherPoint shoes. Felt a lot better, and more like herself.

Mebbe, once she'd found her son, she'd be finished with these AuZgov actionGirl yearnings. She was getting too old for it anyway, she thought, turning herself in front of the mirror to make sure everything was aesthetik.

*

Madrigal enjoyed Jembrana's appreciative look when she walked thru the door. Trying to remain blandFaced but with the poky eyes giving it all away. Such a bloke. Moments like this didn't happen often for her, flirting with a man she liked. And a flirt was about as far as it could go. They were overwhelmed with the search, and she was particularly worn down with worry.

They met in Jembrana's hotel's execSuite at the Baru Hyaxx, aboveground. Pearl and another Slotter hunkered down outside, on guard, and they closed the door of the office suite. In deference to whatever listening devices were placed in the room, he simply hugged her and she sighed. Whatever his vocation and toughness, Jembrana was attached to Madrigal on numerous levels – political, commercial, romantic. They were a powerblok.

She looked at her former lover and smiled. "Thanx for coming," she said in Bahasa so the Indonesian milisi, listening in, would understand everything.

"It's a matter of pride. We must find your son. Tho' I've never met the child, I can't imagine what you are going thru."

"Been 8 months now. And I discover he's been incarcerated not far from here. I feel terrible."

"Clever on the part of the abduction team. These jails are crowded and, sadly, sometimes officials can still be bribed."

"Not much different from before Purity and Virtue – the golden age of corruption."

"Standards, as they say, are slipping," said Jembrana in English, with a wry smile. "But I don't think we've sunk to the depths of the distant past ... not by a long way."

They sat and Jembrana poured her a cup of tea from an attractive ceramic pot. She smiled at him as she reached for the cup and saucer. "So. I don't qwite know where to go. Every time I'm within grasp of Todd, he's gone, moved by these people. What do they want from me? Only one communication that says wait for instructions. I can't wait."

Jembrana shrugged. "That's why you're here."

They ate a light supper of chicken dumplings followed by rice pudding, delivered by a butler, talking about ways and means of tracing people in the region. Jembrana was much more interested in the chemTrace of the sheens than she, and said he'd send it for further analysis.

Jembrana cheered Madrigal up with his careful optimism. "You'll find him in the end. I'm happy to help with anything. Just let me know." But he added: "I know there's an army of teks out there waiting for the moment of connekt, but somehow I think your opponent is a very slippery customer."

"Don't I know it."

"They will contact you. Don't worry. Somehow, somewhere you have somethink they need."

"True that."

She looked at his concerned face, the deep intelligent eyes. An ex Prince of Bali. She was not guarded when alone with Jembrana tho' she knew she ought to be. He always had a hundred agendas, running at the same time. But then, she usually had quite a few as well, some intertwining with his.

Now she had only one mission. It wasn't the time or place to talk politics. The evening went well and she left cheered that she had such a powerfully alive friend.

HIATUS FOUR

When William Blake wrote of mind-forg'd manacles, he could never have envisioned how bad these digital chains would become, enticing us, clamping us, one and all. How to bust each link, one by one? I will tell you all for the last time.

Meine letzten Äußerungen (My Last Ever Utterances) 2035, Ulli Kalk

THE devil came to town. Finally had the guts to front her and talk.

She was in her corner on the rooftop terrace. It was 2am and warm. Again she'd decided against the sleeping pills because she knew, when the Frisky arrived in its package, there would be a call.

Warm traces of light rain were starting to fall and she felt them on her face. But she was focussed on the voice of her enemy, not the view. She and Pearl had run thru the script 100 times.

"Do the right thing," said the low voice thru the tiny blue Frisky.

"I'll need proof of life."

"Start the Bellingslodes. Two a week to Kyoto arcPoint."

"I will, when you show me proof of life. Can't risk my son."

She and Pearl had researched and reviewed the historic record of old cases, when abduction was an extant crime. They studied the dance steps, the deals, the deals that people made with evil to retrieve their loved ones. Proof of life was a legitimate demand of the kaptors. They knew it. She knew it. Was the abductee still alive?

"What proof?"

"Real time vidVision."

"Hard to manage without Centrl tracing the source."

So they knew about Centrl, eh.

"I need you to prove to me he's alive. In fact, if you want consignments to continue, you'll need to keep me happy with regular proof. That's my bargain. I won't consign power for nothink. For some phantom belief. You must understand my proposition. If it were your kid, you would want confirmation. All realWorld deals are based on proof of somethink. Buy an item – where's the cash? Trade an item, have you got the object? You can do it. Everything you send me is cloaked. This trace is no doubt scrambled to oblivion. You know we've been unable to chase you down. You are very clever."

There was a pause to let the flattery sink in. The devil wasn't buying it. She knew he wasn't.

"Keep the Frisky. Will text a linkLine and a time. You can see your boy for a minute. After that, you will have 7 dayz to start the consignments from your powerFarms ... 7 dayz."

"Proof of life. I need to know the vidVision is not a recording. Have CNN on a teev in the background or somethink?" she reiterated as the deep voice was replaced by the expected fuzz of a scrambler. As she walked thru the glass door of her boardroom, out of the rain, she thought, *now we can hunt.*

MOSS

What you do is much more important than who you are ...
   Meine letzten Äußerungen (My Last Ever Utterances) 2035,
Ulli Kalk

THE Old Man hobbled down a path, gripping his stick. His private garden. On either side was a carpet of moss. The moss was so thick it ran up the boles of nearby trees and coated rocks, then up the side of the wooded hill beyond, a soft green pelt. A private place where he often retreated to think.

He wasn't thinking. He was bursting with terror.

The pain of his anxiety was so acute he was groaning aloud.

The daughter, his favorite – tho she angrily spurned him – had scoped with an update saying there'd been an event. A new event. She'd been excited, convinced she was close to retrieving the boy.

She said kidnappers had contacted her, demanding regular power lodes for, of all places, Kyoto, for the return of the boy. Power lodes! Same as the Like Minds. The demands of those men who he thought were his friends.

Maddy said the voice who'd demanded the Bellingslodes was scrambled to buggery down the tubes of the Virtual, so there was no IDing them, but a new link was being set up. So she could have proof that the child lived, like one of those hoary old films of the golden age.

"We are nearly there," she said excitedly.

When the Old Man had heard the demands tho', his eyes, well, his eyes had rolled like madman's eyes. But he never said anything. Didn't blurt, but nodded dumbly and managed to say "good result." She must have thought him surprized about the breakthru, rather than freaked into 1000 little jangly pieces.

His heart was pounding out of his ribcage tho and it was still racing, there on the bench among the soothing moss.

The same demand.

The Kyoto Bell.

The same crew.

A business deal was one thing, but clearly, clearly, the boy had been held in reserve for criminal extortion if that deal fell thru.

Were the Like Minds that desperate, he thought, to sacrifice a boy for Kyoto? And he decided: Yes, they were.

He felt like a horrible conspirator, being dragged into the midst of a terrible crime.

Around him, in the dark garden grotto, there was a smell of decay and wet wood. The trees arched in tortured shapes, he could see that now. Arched and twisted with wire to form the sweet balance.

A week ago, he'd failed to clinch the Kyoto deal for the Jap/Tais thru Ben Jexen. Ben, as chief representative of the Mantle, had demanded a fair return for the Bellingslodes. Quite rightly, really. It was an unusual and unconscionable business deal, cheap, a demand for almost free power.

His own people back at Phipps Industries never came thru, even after his angry recriminations. Jex and his daughter said no. Now it had come to this. The Old Man felt he was teetering on some ledge. Some thin ledge. Wasn't he supposed to be retired, without a care. Yet his vain boast at the Ninomaru Palace, with its whispering nightingale floors, had triggered a sequence of terrible events.

A cascade of understandings and conseqwences followed his daughter's revelation. He'd leapt up, and gripped his stick, and almost staggered into the garden, the garden that gave him so much solace. Finally, he'd deflated on the moss garden seat, head in hands.

So why hadn't Madrigal put 2 and 2 together?

Mebbe she had.

Mebbe she was being kind to him?

No. He shook his head. She had never been kind to him. But even so, she must *trust* him, to tell him these updates.

"Why, why, why didn't she ask? She hates me, but she trusts me," he said qwietly, in English. "This is ... so terrible."

He sat in his chair overlooking the moss rocks and twisted bowers, away from the watchful eye of Nozomi. *Aieee*, he'd been taken for an old fool. He'd been led well and truly up the garden path.

The Silvery One was a slippery fish in the end, no doubt of that. Somehow, always wanting to prove his superiority. His lifelong rival. What was it the Silvery One hated about him most? Why, it must be the old Jap/Tai deal.

But that was a sweet deal, done legally. Long time back.

Still with a way to go, tho'.

The abduction of the grandson was not a "deal" – it was a crime. Still his daughter was parlaying the whole catastrophe, like a deal, and because she was his daughter, the end result would be Todd's return home. He knew his daughter was a ferocious adversary. He'd trained her. The Like Minds would be hunted down. And the whole catastrophe for Kyoto would be realized.

No more Bell. The Bell lodes would be redirected by the Imperial Power Company and this moss garden, for example, would die. This masterpiece of a thousand years would burn down in a heatwave, or cop so much rain it would rot. No gentle rain from heaven anymore, as they'd enjoyed. No more soft seasons, clement weather.

The Old Man sobbed.

Even worse for him, even when he realized who the culprits were, he'd said nothink to his daughter. No background explanation of the links between him, his foul boast, and the Silvery One's dark methodologies.

He could have told her everything right there and then.

But he'd kept his silly old mouth shut simply because he didn't want her to think he was taken for a fool.

*

Madrigal meanwhile had stomped from the scope and up to her roof terrace, muttering, "He'll keep". She sorely wanted a glass of fine shiraz, but needed to stay in her *clear head, clear purpose* state of mind, and grabbed a bottle of water instead.

"No time for the dilettantes. Not yet."

Plan A was underway. Pearl was directing the operation. C-ops Daniels was on the job back at the Spokes, looking forward to his long desired conclusion. Two killCrews were assembled. The teks and analysts were gathering under her roof. Hoppers at the Perth drome were prepped.

So Madrigal'd kept her tongue from lashing her father, in case the foe was listening.

She presented to the listening-in, eavesdropping, covert, prying world a clean and valid communication with her flawed father, informing him the evil had finally contacted her.

Wasn't going to press him for evidence about the whys'n'wherefores of his shadowy mates who wanted those extra "JapTai" Bellingslodes. Not yet. Probably would have to front the old bast'd personally about them. And that'd be fine with her.

Madrigal took an angry slug of water, straight from the bottleneck.

The Old Man could have given up his coConspirators, right then, over the scope, but hadn't. Mebbe he'd understood that she was closing in on them and didn't want to give anything away, but she doubted it very much. He had turned into a coward but not a stupid one.

She was done with him.

She'd let him know that she knew his culpability in the whole string of catastrophik events. Putting his grandson thru hell and mortal danger. And Todd's friends. She knew his actions would have been unwitting, as he'd never deliberately harm the boy. That he was old, vague, captured by malevolent people.

But no uncertain terms, she'd tell him what she thought when the op was all over.

He'll keep.

PROOF OF TODD

In fact, is identity actually necessary? Let us part with this silly concept once and for all.

Meine letzten Äußerungen (My Last Ever Utterances) 2035, Ulli Kalk

THIS was it? Bulging hologram of men in white uniforms? Hygienic coveralls? Globe eyes, disguised. They looked seriously sinister. The men, bout threeqwarters their real size, moved across the room, tugging a small version of Todd into place in front of a wobbly screen somewhere. Her boy was still trussed, like the doubled over figure from the vidVision in New Jakarta. He raised his head, kept still, and the holo was crisper. He had a white bandage across his face, over his nose, but also the dark obstinate eyes, the set lips.

Madrigal managed to choke on a wail, and kept her blandFace on.

A bandage! What had the bast'dz done? Two guards stood, for effect no doubt, at the back of the projection plot. Todd was out on his ownsome, at the front, staring, looking crestfallen. A small screen in the background, beside one of the men, showed rolling CNN commentary on 'phoon damage across Vladivostok. Her homescreen somewhere behind was the same vision. Couple of secs out of sync with the transmission, but parallel and live. The 'phoon had wrecked parts of Port Vladivostok 12 hours back.

Madrigal's team were situated in the Big Room of her house on the ground floor. It was the only one that would fit everyone and everything: a holo projection with the necessary trace gear and all the personnel.

The music gear, tables, comfy loungeBags had been cleared away. Now benches ran along the back. Cables and router heads. Behind the unfolded projection, a gaggle of teks were qwietly moving joysticks and pressing eqwipment, but the abductors couldn't see this. Neither could they see the 2 large vehicles out the front adding firepower to the trace, unless they had someone on the spot. Drone finders had screened the 'burb and found no unusual tracking or surveillance devices in, or on, any of the buildings or streets. Even so, someone might be lurking, but the evil musta been confident of their scramble.

Room lighting was dim, except for Madrigal's face, the only thing visible to the kaptors. Hers was a straight vid back. Madrigal was standing and feeling xtremely tense. She tried to relax the choking in her throat. Find the correct tone to deal with the people at the other end. She composed her very best Courier blandFace. She was not going to give them the pleasure of a melt.

Toddy was bent forward, sitting on his calves and thighs, kneeling on a tatami mat. Wrists strapped and folded too, on his lap. The strap was obviously very tight and he was wriggling his hands, clearly in severe discomfort. Otherwise, Todd sat still, and looked straight ahead at what was no doubt a vid. The bandage on his face wasn't too big, really. What had happened?

This view of the boy was for full identification. Faces of the 2 white clad men behind him were hidden behind the white masks. They were burly. Some black hair poked out from behind one mask, but that was the sum of bodily bits she could see. These people were not going to look her in the eye. They knew they would be somewhere in a bioMetrik system.

"Ok, Dr Phipps," said a disembodied voice patched into the silent scene before her. "That proof enough?"

Voice had some sort of geoFluid accent.

"We're expecting your weekly lodes over a period of time. The boy stays with us. He's being fed and watered. Bit of a pet, really."

Her long gone son. Even with the bandage, he looked alive and grim. She held her nerve, inside a flush of anger, looking at the bluish images in front of her crew, blandFace holding up.

"What's with the bandage?"

"His little friends in Baru. When they killed the pip in his sinus, they left a dirty little hole. Don't worry. We've cleaned it up. It's healing. He's taking the meds. Still, lost his tastebuds tho."

Hmmm ... on probability, this was correct. The charge coming out of the pip would have made a mess. She wasn't going to crack on about it, tho, could have been worse, like damage to the frontal lobes. But her boy looked satisfyingly surly. Staring forward.

She moved on and said: "Why can't you just buy the power from us? $New50,000 a lode. Not a lot."

"No more funds. Government's changed. They have no commitment to our sacred city. Jap/Tai has other priorities and denied us the wherewithall. These lodes must be sent – your son already understands that this is a qwest on a spiritual level." The dispassionate voice had cracked somewhat.

Madrigal ignored the ridiculous comment.

"Can't some of your illustrious residents pay up? My father, for example. He has his income. Along with those other retired plutocrats who enjoy the calm inside the Bell," she said in an eqwally dispassionate voice. "I'm with the Jap/Tais. This level of powerLode would be better deployed elsewhere. My stockholders'll be pissed if I give it away."

"Don't f'k with us, Dr Phipps. Our terms are final."

"How many lodes a week was it?"

"Two replenishments a week to the Kyoto arcPoint."

"Two a week? A Bellingslode is a big unit of power for an arcPoint. You need a full powerSoaker set up. I'm reluctant to supply without the tek."

The voice was irritated. He knew Madrigal was dikking around with him, extending the narrowcast. "There's a soaker for the specific purpose of the Bell. Tell your networker to relay the light there. This is imperative, so there is no break in transmission. Jap/Tai is going to simply supply general power needs from henceforward, which, as you may know, is a breach of commitments for the preservation of our sacred precincts. Since the Great Wars of the 20th century, Kyoto was protected. Now you are the protector of Kyoto, and we shall protect your son. In the end, he sees it our way, as one of the enlightened."

Her own teks and the experts from Centrl were behind the screen and shaking their heads and thumbing down.

Whatever links the extortionists had set up made the scope untraceable, bouncing thru satellites and space. What's going on? Madrigal thought. We've the best tekHeads in the world. We should have their sourcePoint in the bag. She kicked herself mentally for letting Andaman Marko leave on his idiot boat. Madrigal continued to stall.

"Again!" she demanded in a sharp tone. "I need to know the Kyoto arcPoint is set for a pure Bellingslode. It's a wham of a surge which is usually soaked thru the Tokyo soakers first. You have the storage to cope?"

"All has been organized. Our plutocrats, as you call them, funded the soaker years ago."

"So be it. And when can I be reunited with Todd."

"Within a year. Within a year. After all, you haven't seen him until now for nearly 10 months. I'm sure you've got used to it. As you see, apart from his self inflicted injury, he's fine."

"Can he speak to me?"

"We have no sound on him. You are seeing a live image, but we wouldn't want him shouting coordinates, would we? He's the sort of young pup that would blurt. He's led us on a merry dance, as you know."

Todd was still struggling with his wrist ties, looking angry.

Madrigal applied some annoyance to her otherwise modulated tone: "Send me an edited soundByte, please. Today will do. His voice to tell me he is well and properly fed. I'll know his voice, so don't try tricks. And I'll know he's telling the truth. Then I'll authorize the lodes. I have no other choice. What we have here is the old-fashioned crimes of extortion, blackmail and ... and ... piracy." She was desperately looking for things to say now.

"Xtreme measures are demanded," said the dispassionate voice. "You are rescuing, as I said, a sacred Japanese precinct. The very air here is preserved for the gods."

"Enough of that nonsense," snapped Madrigal. "Next Thursday. 10am Kyoto time. First Bellingslode. If you are ready."

She glanced at Lissa and Narmon, hidden in the shadow. Lissa nodded. Narmon went thumbs up.

While she just wanted to stare at her trussed son forever, her head said: *Madrigal – break the link. Don't let them play their psycho game anymore. You take the initiative.* In the game of power, her headThought won over her heartThought.

Madrigal cut the feed. "Well?"

"He's in Sri Lanka," said Lissa.

"In some villa up a hill," said Narmon.

Lissa referred to notes on her clamB screen, which she'd been filling with wordz while she watched Todd's fingers and wrists talk to her from the start of the link. He'd been most verbose in a Stümmery way, altho' to his kaptors and Madrigal alike, it looked as if Todd merely was attempting to twist the uncomfortable straps to find some circulation in his hands. Narmon went oldStyle and had written notes longhand.

Prior to the link, Madrigal had said: "If he signs, I want 2 versions. See if they match. No room for error."

Lissa cleared her throat: "Todd's hands said: *Kandy.* He spelt the letters out. *In the hills above Kandy. Southward. Big white house at end of winding road, I think tamarind ... big tree next to the gate, 2 pink shed out the back. At nite, I'm locked in the lefthand shed. Two on me at all time. At nite under lightScreen.* Don't know what that means. *Think me, power unit for the whole set up is in other shed.*"

Narmon said: Did you catch that bit where he signed: *The kaptors speak English* and, I think, *Tajik or Turk?*

Lissa nodded. "I got Tajik too."

Narmon was perplexed. "Why Tajik?"

"I think I can guess," said Madrigal. "Thanx, Lissa. Thanx, Narmon. Nice work." Her voice was as dispassionate as that of her tormentor. "He's one of a kind, my boy."

Lissa felt xtremely pleased with herself. She thought: *For once in the universe, Stümmer sign language was genuinely useful.*

She reached out and sqweezed Narmon's hand in silent triumph.

*

Worst thing for Todd was the floor of the dark hut. A steel hut with a smooth hard concrete floor. When the air was warm outside, the hut was sweltering.

Here he was, a chatty guy and he was alone. No Narmon, no Abdurramn, no one to talk to. Worse still, the wound from the pipKiller wouldn't heal. It had blasted a small, pus-weeping hole in his face and infected his tongue as well. Alone and sore. He kept touching the lump on his tongue hoping the pain would go.

The guards had been dressing the wound – after all, he was a tradeable item. Didn't want him dead yet. But he'd lie on his blanket of a nite, on the floor, and when his eyes were shut, the pain in his face felt 10 times worse. They pulled him out during the day and walked him round the verdant green lawn, past the giant tamarind tree at the front of the house, so shady, up to the palms and bushes at the back with their brightly coloured red and orange flowers.

Clearly, he was in South Asia with the abductors. He finally asked the stupidest guard, and the guy wouldn't deny they were in Sri Lanka, middle of the island. Meant to Todd they were close to Kandy (he knew his geography).

The stupidest guy would light him a durrie. When out of the shed, his hands would be manacled, but he could still lift the butt to his lips and smoke and it was a pleasant interaction with a fellow human. Smoking and enjoying the small talk that took his mind away from the pain. He could look across the lawn, see a steep hill, and way across the valley more mountains. Or he would be allowed to sit in a chair reading some crap book from the old mansion's library, amazed the paper hadn't rotted away in the heat.

The stupid one would witter on. Other guards would be monosyllabic. Stupid started to talk about how he missed his kidz.

"Got 3 kidz," he said. "Back home with wife tho' I can't tell you where home is. Boy, 2 girlz," He was as bored as Todd. The other guards allowed no revelations about themselves. Stupid one laughed with Todd, almost conspiratorially. Todd respected the discipline of the others, and egged the stupid one on. Encouraged him to splurge his wordz in case there was a factoid to be had.

Mebbe dumbo was smart and it was all falseFront. Who knew?

Todd could only hope that Liss or Narmon had watched his hands during the short taping session and now knew where he guessed he was, and that they were coming.

The shadows were lengthening, black blots on the dark green lawn. Sun dipping now, orange and misty. He knew soon he'd be pushed back into the shed and the hot hard dark.

*

On a highly scrambled feed, in a cruiserV that was hurtling to the Perth drome, Madrigal was talking to Premier Jembrana. They'd acted fast after Lissa and Narmon had interpreted the lokation. Within 15 minutes the retrieval crews were hitting the Phipps Industries hopper.

As it was only a 10 klik haul to the drome in the fastest car, she'd planned a qwick update scope to the Premier. She watched the coast whizz past, the big houses at the mouth of the Swan, the commuteTrains, other V's whooshing along the beltway back toward the city.

"They can't afford to kill their bargaining chip," he was saying on her screen.

Madrigal knew she'd grown some sort of shell, now. A thick carapace. Had anyone talked about toying with her son's life a few months ago, she'd have wept at the thought.

Jembrana stopped himself, tho', and apologized for being so flip.

"I'm very sorry I said that. They'll keep Todd alive as long as he's useful to them ... years mebbe. And, seriously, this criminal scheme must be about more than 2 lodes a week into the Kyoto soaker?"

"At the moment, I can only take them at their word, Jembrana. If they say it's about protecting Kyoto, I can only work on that premise. You know that."

"Well, I don't believe them. Think they'll ask you for more payola once you bend to their demands. Blackmailers always up the ante, Maddy, but you can only work with what you've got..."

He continued: "Let me tell you this: in the end, it will be to do with money. Lots of it. All crimes like this are. They have stolen the only vulnerability in the Phipps eqwation, namely your son, and the heir to the company. If they are trying to ransom him for somethink, mebbe also for another reason? They could brainwash him? Or excuse me for this, they could possibly ... kill him. To send your business into a spiral without a future, so others can dominate East Asia."

"Don't you think I haven't rolled these scenarios thru my mind ... again and again," Madrigal said. "Ben Jexen is an excellent wargamer. We've spent evenings at it. Now they want sustained Bellingslodes for the life of my boy."

"This foolish nonsense 'bout the Kyoto Bell ... this affair is more than that, surely? That's not to diminish what a disgraceful waste of power the Kyoto protection arrangement is, when so many Japanese people are suffering."

"The Japan-Taiwan Nexus decommission the Bell this week," Madrigal said. "That is their formal policy. I have spoken to their PM directly and my CEO Ben Jexen has verified they will use the power that once charged the Bell, for other industry and housing. It's why they've revealed their hand. They've run out of time. The voicc on the vid ... I tell you, was playing on the top string of desperation. Don't know if the tone was genuine or not, tho'. I suspect a ruse."

Madrigal paused and looked at the soft and kindly face of her friend. Balinese to his boots, like an old Buddha, he was, she thought. Jembrana appeared quite huge on the screen as he bent toward the camera, his eyelids half closed as he thought thru their discussion.

"When I spoke to the Japanese PM yesterday," Madrigal continued, "he told me that up until now a majority of senior Japanese politicians, and Cabinet, supported the protection of the sacred city. He was deeply angry about the arrangement, and now he's in charge, says that Japan has to grow up and grow out of sentiment over the past. He actually said: *These mawkish connektions to old traditions that are no longer relevant. The Singular Enemy has become too strong. The past must be cut so we can deal with the future.* Pretty hardLine talk.

"His oppositional colleagues in the Japanese Diet had cited precendents around the globe, pleading for the dome to be continued. They said many smaller scale light shields are deployed across the world, stopping the weather from ...""

Jembrana burst in: "Their ridiculous dome covers an entire prefecture. You know that Maddy! It's 100 times the size of other secure places. Light shields are used primarily in small doses, supported because they protect power plants, or single valuable buildings."

"I know. And so does the Japanese PM. They need the power elsewhere. He admitted it. The 4 seasons have fizzled out everywhere else in Japan. It's hot wet stormy summers and hot dry winters now, with nothink in between unless you're in the mountains. So the Bell will be decommissioned this week, Kyoto will be unprotected, and the kidnappers have no choice – they are desperate and are now forcing the issue."

Jembrana said: "So what are you going to do? With their threats?"

Madrigal said: "Buckle. For Todd. I have no choice either."

*

Pearl, sitting beside her boss in the back of the cruiser, nodded approvingly as Madrigal closed down the conversation.

Madrigal almost smiled back at her. Almost.

Most people, Pearl knew, couldn't lie to help themselves. Such an honest world.

And no matter how scrambled, a scope on-the-go would have been skimmed and skanned, and given the info was direct to the Premier of Capricornia, the foe may be pleased with Madrigal's news.

No one would dare lie to a Premier. Would they?

HEART OF THE ACTION/ACTION OF THE HEART

A no-one who does something, is far better than a someone who does nothing.

Meine letzten Äußerungen (My Last Ever Utterances) 2035, Ulli Kalk

ALONG the lake's edge with its bright, yellow brick "tooth" wall, Lissa leant against one of the teeth and talked to some kidz. A girl and boy were trying to sell her small silk bags and she was asking who made them? The kidz said, "Us". And how much? "20 Sri Lankan rupee, not much, lady! Very cheap."

Reflected in the water behind were the dark verges of parks interspersed with pink buildings. The only wrinkles on the glassy surface were caused by paddling ducks.

While Lissa feigned friendliness, she was tense, attuned to her earbug, waiting for instruction. She knew the raid was about to happen in the hills, but as casually as possible she reached into her bag and found cash and the little red and purple patched satchels were given to her by eager hands.

"Thankyou, kind lady!" said the kidz, skittering off.

After midday, the air had baked up and it was excruciatingly hot, the sky yellowish. Way high in the stratosphere, lightning flickered in the cloudlessness. A close to the eqwator phenomenon ... almost permanent lightning in an otherwise clear sky.

Somehow Sri Lanka and South India were spared prolonged baleful incursions by the Cloud as it spun around the Earth with its whorls and cyclones, thrown akimbo by the coriolis force. Every so often tho', a few months apart, Sri Lanka and Tamil Nadu would cop a tailFlick from an exceptionally big mid-Indian Ocean event and everyone would head for the shelters from Galle to Chennai to Kerala. SouthAsian metHeads theorized that countervailing confluences around the Himalayas further north, had an eqwally powerful exertion, diverting high jetstreams. These had a protective effect on South India. The exact function of the new jetstream patterns were still being studied.

Others in South India believed they were being protected by the Gods.

Kandy was a sacred Sri Lankan town in the hills, and hadn't changed much over the past few centuries. Holy Buddha's reliqwary was still there in a temple, where one of his teeth was held. In boxes within boxes. The tooth was in the last tiny box!

Lissa loved the thought.

She'd found the town ancient and affecting. She'd never been anywhere so different. The Sri Lankans in her hotel were friendly and interested in her – she'd told people she was a student, which was true, in Kandy to study the religious importance of the Temple of the Tooth to South India, which was false. She'd actually made scope appointments with a couple of scholar monks and an academic in Colombo to prove her reason for visiting, and was feeling bad because the appointments would never happen.

Of course, she wore a wig, chosen by Pearl, with slight facial prosthetics – lobe lifts and a nose dimple – to fool any biometrik skans by her exKaptors, who'd no doubt logged her partikulars when she'd been abducted.

Early the previous day she'd wandered down past the Bogombara cricket park which was the pickUp point, when the rescue raid was over. Once a stadium, other bigger sports and cricket arenas had since been built and, while the temperature was early morning cool, the old park was filled with young Sri Lankan boyz and girlz playing cricket, with parents on the sidelines. The grounds were surrounded by beautiful big trees and the park was wide and green.

Lissa had smiled at all the kidz. Sri Lanka and India were 2 of the big International Cricket teams along with AuZ, tho New Zealand still claimed its own international team, a key point during the constitutional merger after The Grief. Sri Lankans, and Indians, were mad for cricket and the Bogombara parks fairly buzzed, with little kidz swinging bats, and the crash of balls in nets along the edges of the playing fields.

She'd then retraced the route to town to learn it, then sat on the hotel terrace for most of the rest of that day. She spent the following morning at the hotel terrace café, looking out for landVs belonging to owners of the villa further up in the hills. At times, she'd been filled with dread that she'd stuff things up. Watching, waiting. Scared she'd miss somethink. The villa where Todd was held was not far away. Todd was over the shoulder of the hill behind. Her friend.

The Pearl and Madrigal, who'd dropped her in Colombo 2 days before, were adamant. Watch and report. No intervention without direct orders from The Pearl. A serious test she had to pass and a bit stressful therefore.

Lissa chuckled to herself at The Pearl's new, superhero style definite article. After the fitness regime, she'd privately become The Pearl whenever Lissa and Madrigal discussed her.

It was The Pearl chatting thru her earbug – in a sporadic way – that gave Lissa courage, tho' in the planning stages she'd pretended to be collected and focused in the meetings. Joining in. Looking pro. Underneath, if she thought about Todd stuck in some shed, and her task, she was jelly.

Three days prior, as they'd hurtled toward Colombo, one of the HighEyes run by Centrl had picked out the tag numbers of the 5 vehicles that came and went from the villa compound. These tags, Lissa had memorized. She'd waited a day in Colombo doing student activity like museum visits, then caught a train to Kandy to be on the spot. Sri Lanka was easier to travel around in than she'd imagined, as everyone spoke English.

*

Madrigal had been reluctant to use Lissa on the ground.

The hour before departure from the Perth drome, Madrigal had looked the young woman with the flame red hair up and down critically and become concerned. "She's not ready," she said.

Lissa was kitted up, on The Pearl's instructions. Madrigal had second thoughts, eyes clouded. "Could put her in danger. Minnie-Tuton would …" She couldn't even finish the sentence.

The Pearl had disagreed.

"This kid has great instincts, don't you think? She's smart. Been in the heart of the action from the start. No one on the ground will see her as a player. Looking like a kid is an advantage. She deserves this one!"

The Pearl, a warrior, saw somethink kindred in Lissa.

Madrigal rolled her eyes. The Pearl kept on: "An undercover task gets her there, but keeps her out of the firing line. Just waiting, observing, mebbe to neutralize some of their firepower. All easy."

"I s'pose," said Madrigal. "I don't want her hurt." She turned to Lissa and sounding much like a mother said: "Just do what The Pearl tells you. Stick to the script."

"She won't get hurt. I'll be with her every step," The Pearl said. "And I'll brief her. Let's go."

*

As promised, at every step, The Pearl had been in her ear.

Earlier that morning and with some trepidation – but enjoying her first real surveillance task – she'd placed herself on the cafe terrace above the road to watch the traffic pass. The hotel driveway emptied onto the same road that passed by the villa up the hill. The villa where Todd was trapped.

A big mottled-grey cruiserV from the target compound had swung past the driveway and the tagtracer on her knee pinged with the red numbers and letters XN55. A 7 seater vehicle with tinted windows.

When XN55 pinged, Lissa had leapt from her seat, grabbed her backpack and ran down the steps to the Vpark. She hopped on a taxiBike she'd booked thru the hotel, behind the driver, a small Sri Lankan guy, and they'd buzzed after the target at a distance. The cruiserV circled into the town and eventually parked outside one of the modern looking multiStorey offices, close to the lakefront. The modern tower was very out of place with the rest of the old buildings and ancient shopScape.

"Thanx," she said to the bikeV rider with a smile. He was an almond eyed young man about her age, dark skinned, graceful. The lad cheekily asked for her Frisky code so he could call her later and go for a walk along the lake. "Can show you round the town. Good clubs," he said.

She declined sweetly. He laughed, and sped away.

"Shoulda taken up his offer," the listening Pearl said with a laugh in her earbug.

Lissa ignored The Pearl's suggestion and reported: "Two guys and a bloke with shiny silver hair heading out of the car, into the big building. Looks like an office blok. The driver is still in place in the vehicle. S'pose he's waiting for them to come out again."

"Do they look like guards?" The Pearl asked.

"Two of them are big, securitizors mebbe, and the driver is still in the V."

"That's 4 doops outa the compound. Good to go!" said The Pearl, probably to the others in earbugshot.

Lissa strolled up the opposite side of the street in the full sun, trying to look normal and casual, but craning her neck at the same time. She felt sweat trickling down the back of her shirt collar, and saw hot mist rise from the bitumen. She crossed over into the shade of the buildings.

"Liss. Does the driver look security too?" asked Pearl.

"Yes. He's sitting in the car, so not totally sure, but ... he's big."

"Ok, got the item?"

"Yep."

"You know what to do."

The crab. They'd walked her thru with the crab multiple times. Trek past the V and fix the crab to it. Walk slowly. Appraise the V. If anything else looks untoward, then just keep walking and report back. Those were the instructions.

With a deep breath, and heart pounding, she moved into an alley adjacent to the big building. The alley was narrow, in deep shade, with high walls on each side. Thankfully, it was empty, but grubby with litter and dirt. She skanned the walls both sides and saw no surveillance vidz on the alleyway walls, but that didn't mean there were none. Lissa turned the shimmer device on in her backpack. She felt no different but the charged photons around her engaged with the general ambience and she was now invisible to both the naked eye, and any vidVision in the building.

"Proceeding," she said.

She remembered The Pearl's dictum. For shimmers to work well, walk slowly, so the charged photons can merge with the ambient photons. If you hurry, make sudden qwick moves, your feet or hands may be revealed.

"Your urge will be: get it done fast," said The Pearl, "but stay slow."

She emerged from the other end of the alley, returned round the blok. Street was full of people walking, shopping, smoking in huddles. Behind the photonik veil nobody saw her. She stared at XN55's windscreen, which she approached carefully. The driver was fiddling with the control panel, switching things, probably fixing music. The man never looked up and wouldn't have noticed the lump of reAnimated light in front of him. Lissa stopped and carefully bent and placed the crab, a small round disc with 6 thick antennae, under the front wheel cavity near the engine, and locked it on gently by pressing a button. Then she kept going, slowly. Only a dog avoided her, looking up in fright, and skittering across the road.

The fixed crab would already be activated by Madrigal's teks, back in the hopper, high to the west and ready for the raid. The reroute device would hack thru the cruiserV's electroniks and, at the appropriate minute, suck the electriks dry. When the raid happened up the hill – imminently – this meant at least 3 security people and bossDooper wouldn't make it back in time to assist. Extraction would be less cluttered, complicated and bloody.

Lissa knew hers was a peripheral task, but she was part of the action all the same. A reward for being on the job, helping Madrigal track Todd from the start. At the same time, she was kept away from what could be hardArm kinetik.

Team Phipps were finally fighting back! Ha!

And now she'd neutered some doops. After all the travail she'd experienced, it felt great.

Lissa ambled to the lakeside under the shimmer, walked into a small publik toilet block which was empty, and turned off the mechanism.

She emerged visible, into the landscape, feeling clammy from the humidity.

Then all she could do was await further instructions. She walked a little way and took pix of the view. She watched the ducks. She had hovered in the shade until the little purse sellers spotted her and approached her. While they were saying hello, she spotted an elephant moving up a street, which was as wondrous as anything she'd seen, ever.

The elephant was large, grey and carried a whole bunch of sticks in its trunk. A man sat on its back while bikeVs on the street behind were attempting to overtake. She watched the elephant's progress, fascinated, and took pix.

"Woah! Is that real?" she asked a little girl, amazed: "Is that a real elephant? I thought elephants went extinct in the 2030s."

The little girl laughed. "That's Nusra. It's a majjiGlow of a real elephant that used to work in the hills around here a century ago. The glow walks down the hill once every 2 hours for the tourists."

The little boy, very serious face: "No, there are no more elephants in Sri Lanka. Or anywhere."

Lissa could see now that the bikeVs weren't passing the elephant, but just driving straight thru the glow, spoiling the effect. Artful touch for tourists, tho, she thought. And she felt sad for the lost elephants.

They talked for a little while about how awesome elephants were, and how they all wished there were some in the zoo, or the wild, and then Lissa had bought the purses and the kidz spotted another possible buyer, an old couple taking pix further along the lake, so they peeled off.

She started heading to the pickup point.

Not long afterward, the bug in her ear emitted Pearl's voice. It was loud and she was startled. Urgency was in Pearl's voice.

"Ok Lissa, you head back to the pickUp point now. Don't dawdle!"

Lissa was already walking thru steaming morning heat, away from the lake and the Temple of the Tooth. She walked briskly, this time to the Bogambara cricket park, a little further round the lake.

*

Lissa thought about Todd and felt the lurch inside again. The feeling that had been there ever since the terrible trek over the desert. Todd was just up the road, mebbe in the hopper already. She felt that it was right she was there, at the end of the journey. She'd suffered and he'd suffered and he deserved her focus. So she banished those familiar thoughts – where she and he embraced – and kept up her brisk pace.

Lissa's counsellor and psychMedik, Miss Svensonn, was bemused when she'd asked whether she had pleasant daydreams about sexing, to counter the Pepperbeard nitemares, and she'd calmly replied that she thought about Todd a lot.

"I thought Narmon was your steadyBoy," Miss Svennson had said with a strange tone, so Lissa left it there, but it was true. She was now qwite used to happily daydreaming about Todd when she lay tucked up in her bunk.

"I suppose if it helps you past those terrible nitemares," Miss Svensonn said after a pause, "then it's healthy."

Lissa banished that funny exchange with Miss Svennson, and focused again on following The Pearl's orders, and getting to the park. She'd given up hoping to stay cool. She was soaked in sweat.

*

The long grey oblong aircraft swung up over the distant ridge out of the green hills, like a sausageBlur. Lissa watched it from the edge of the cricket field.

For some reason she'd felt followed, but constant checks behind showed general traffik cruising up and down the main road past the park and the fenceline. None appeared to be tailing her. Still, she'd picked up her pace to an almost jog, and entered a side gate at quite a clip. Not sure where the hopper would hover, she waited.

The blur thickened into the shiny grey hopper.

Powered by rotors, not jets, it swooped qwickly toward her, dipping down to the playing fields. Now she'd worked out its target – beside the main play pitch – Lissa started running on the springy green turf toward the aircraft before it had even touched down vertically. The engine was qwiet, but the rotors clattered and she pushed against the downdraft as The Pearl had taught her. The front slider opened. She saw the big guy they called Dante standing on the lip of the hatch. The Pearl had said at the briefing: "No time for steps – you gotta jump."

Lissa leapt and grabbed Dante's wrist in the trapeze hold, and was almost flung in, as he said "Go" in his mic, and slid the door shut.

"Well?" asked Lissa.

"He's in the back, chook," said Dante. "With the doc. Y'can go see him."

RAID

Peace and love go with you all.

Meine letzten Äußerungen (My Last Ever Utterances) 2035, Ulli Kalk

CrewA had never thought it'd be easy to get behind the wall.

Dante led crewA for *incursion*; Pearl led crewB for *extraction*.

A mad tekHead, Dante had fussed with his gear all the way from AuZ thru to their first landfall in Colombo. A furtive drop by the Phipps hopper had seen his team insinuated in Kandy. Went kinetic from there.

*

The day before he'd trapezeGripped Lissa into the hopper, he and his 2 crewmen cautiously approached the villa in the hills behind Kandy, one by one, in a staggered pattern, thru the thick of traffik. The tamarind tree at the gatehouse was huge and threw a cool shadow across the front lawns. The gardeners had braced it against the power of 'phoons with scaffolding up the front stone wall, hidden from view so people on the villa's verandah would just see the big tree and not the steel braces.

Dante's eWash reader showed the air fibrilated with a light shield – light that would max the pain to anyone crossing thru, and set off security alarms to warn the guards. They had no chance of sending a bee thru the shield without the tiny drone exploding so they used opticals, from a reconnaissance position up the hill, to watch figures come and go in the main house. All day Todd had had a close guard and was kept mostly inside. Other guards were posted at the front and some did perimeter security around the villa, while 2 pink sheds were perched further up the back slope. Behind them, another tall stone wall.

Dante wrote his note and snapped the info to a pijjeon – a small homing cylinder – which flew back on subpower to the anonymous hopper, looking benign on the parking apron at Colombo airport among the other private hoppers and scoops. Pearl and Madrigal read the handwritten report and nodded. No radio contact yet. Nothink to break the silence that could be picked up by local skanners in the compound.

Dante scratched his chest thoughtfully. He knew the tree was the way in. He skanned the thick foliage and large branches. Somewhere, further up in its branches the shield would be thinned to accommodate botanic movement. It was a newby fail. A pro would have a taut poweredUp shield in clear air, but no one wanted to chop trees these days. Even crims.

When nite fell, Dante ordered the weediest of his crewmen to dress in old grey clothes, like a poor gardener, and walk the perimeter testing strengths. The crewman held a rake over his shoulder, and walked stiffly up the hill past the house. The rake had sensors. They downloaded the rake at about 1am, and found serious patchiness above the first big branch of the tree, strengthening again just after the scaffold.

That was the trouble with light shields. They had to be thrown as a neat circumference or sqware for the geometric integrity. There was no room for kinks in the airspace, like trees, which interfered with the width of the photonik sponge. You could adjust areas of a shield, but not bend them round big objects, and why it hadn't been set further up the lawn puzzled Dante.

"We'll sqwirm in," said Dante, as he and his men knelt at the back of adjacent rhododendron bushes, looking askance at the readout. "We'll have to use the shimmer to mellow the area above the branches, but there's not enough power in it to raise the alarm. Thin as chopchop paper."

And a half hour later, that's what they did. Shimmers set to low – they may've thrown the odd glimpse and shadow, but it was dark, and so were their clothes. One by one, crewA reached above the wall, threw their shimmer off momentarily, and turned on the function to mellow a patch of the shield. Then up over the branch thru the shield, higher into the tree and thru, then down a cord to the back of the old tamarind bole. The 3 crewmen tacked along the inside wall till they were up behind the 2 pink sheds.

Dante's eWash reader picked up the impressive amount of power that was throwing the shield from the lefthand shed. Todd was secured in the other shed and a subsidiary shield was thrown across his prison. With a 24 hour standing guard. These guys weren't taking any chances with the boy, the re-cidivist escapee. Clearly, he was far too valuable.

So far, with various skanning instruments they'd clokked 8 people around the compound: 7 hostiles, one Todd.

From under thick shrubbery, CrewA watched.

Every so often the perimeter doop would wander across and chat to the standing guard outside the shed where Todd was held – the infrared heat bean on the screen didn't move much – and the guards'd smoke chopchop, or change jobs and keep on canvassing the grounds. To Dante, the men appeared rea-sonably relaxed, but he could see their weapons were ever-Ready, and most times, their eyes were skanning. Everyone on duty was a pro.

The next morning, when the 2 pax and the senior man in the cool suit waited at the front door while the cruiser was brought round from the Vstation, Dante thumbed up to his team. There was a bit of bizz as the cool suit doop gave the guards on duty some instruktions, and then the cruiser hummed hard and looped down the circular driveway and out the electronik gate. Dante nodded but they'd muted all komms for the time.

He thought if that Lissa kid was any good whatsoever, she'd ping the cruiserV and check in with Pearl, and then it'd be on. The girl'd been attentive enough in the briefings on the way over. Asked good qwestions. She'd clok the cruiser, he was sure.

Now there were only 3 guards to deal with. And the potent screening gear in the lefthand shed.

How these dirty skulks pulled enough power off the Sri Lankan grid to build all this shield security was beyond Dante's ken. However they did it, they'd use a few subBellingslodes, he thought.

So they waited as the hour passed.

*

The V crossed Lissa's path.

Lissa hit the V with the crab.

Was on.

CrewA waited until Dante heard a click in his earbug, sent by the sparksman in the attack hopper.

It was 11am. He gave his slotter crew the point, relishing the rush of adrenaline, and they moved forward, into the sunlight. A crewman slapped a neutralizer on the lefthand shed. As soon as the hopper was adjacent, they blew the generator in a great sparky blast, and that was that. Things were kinetic. Dante moved up the steps in a rush as the shed went up behind him, and into the house where a guard stood frozen with terror in front of Todd who was drinking a beige coloured shake in the kitchen.

"Down," said Dante. Todd and the skulk dropped. There were a couple of shots in the garden. Only 2. Dante kneeled on the guard's back and slapped a wrist restraint on him and pulled the man's komms kit from his face and threw it into the waste disposal in the sink, turning it to crunch. He exhaled.

"How'y going kid? Your mum's out in the garden if you'd like to join her," he said to Todd who was still face down on the floor. Todd laughed once, stood up and shook Dante's hand.

"I'd better go and give her a hug then, heh?" the kid said.

In the garden there was a bloody mess by the side of the house which Todd glanced at, then elected to turn his head away with a shudder. It had once been a human. The other guard was trussed on the lawn, face down, like the guy in the kitchen. Two huge people, a man and a woman, whooshed up the steps of the villa past Todd, in a screaming hurry and almost knocked him flying.

Pearl and Madrigal stood on the lawn by the hopper, while Pearl's crewB were engaged in dismantling the powerNub in the shed and stripping the house of evidence.

"Toddy," shouted Madrigal.

Finally they could hug and they did, but it was a brief cloud of body warmth and affection. Todd was too anxious to cry, and Madrigal was shaking with relief.

Pearl didn't let up on the situation, scoping the grounds, watching the crews. As soon as the extraction team came out of the house with guns, clamBs and drives, she hurried the Phipps family along.

"Gotta go, Ma'am," she said, gazing impassively at the mother and son. "The targets in the cruiserV will only be delayed, not neutralized. I want to avoid another kill."

"Of course," said Madrigal, wiping her wet cheeks with a palm.

"Thanx, Mum," said Todd.

They hauled themselves into the hopper, followed by Pearl.

Dante and the crewB people were already back and in. That qwick. They were *that qwick*. To Todd it had happened in a blink and he was free. All boarded the hopper and within a minute, airborne and out.

*

When Lissa hurried back to the hopper's exec area and saw Todd buckled into the flight seat, she threw herself on him. She gave him a fierce glorious hug feeling the comfort and utter relief of his live warm body against her. She refrained from kissing him, especially in front of Madrigal, who was fondly smiling like a mum. A kiss would have given Todd a fright, too, probably. But she wanted to.

"Liss, Liss, you're alive," said Todd, holding her face in his hands, looking in her eyes.

"I am!" She hugged him again and then, feeling a bit embarrassed under the gaze of Madrigal, composed herself. "I never thought I'd see you ... it's miraculous."

He sported a look of wonder, that his friend was there. Last action between him and Liss was his shouted, *"Run"*, in the Scorpion Claw waterhole. He'd spent months wondering whether she'd died in the desert. Now she was here, light as a bird. Bright green eyes, hair bunched behind in a teflite hoodcoat, excited to see him.

"Buckle in, Liss!" snarled Pearl from behind, but she didn't hear the command. The white bandage was gone from his face and there was a big scabby scar from the bridge of his nose to under his eye.

"Are you okay – with the injury?" She gently touched the good skin beside the wound.

"I'm having terrible headaches still. Doc'll do tests when we get back."

The hopper lurched to one side and Lissa fell sidewayz from Todd's seat, bodySlammed against the bulkHead and bounced into the companionway with a gasp. She grabbed an armrest and struggled into an adjacent seat as the hopper tilted back the other way, and put her harness on with shaking hands.

"Lock in everyone," shouted Pearl thru the door, "Incoming! GroundLaunched rangeBanger!"

Somehow the cruiserV that Lissa had stalled with the crab device had hoarded a bruteForce weapon. Clearly the skulks had got to an open place in sight of the fleeing hopper, pulled it from the V's boot, armed it and launched. A slim missile had shot past the weaving hopper and was turning back on its kill-Course.

"No!" said Madrigal. After all that effort, she suddenly had a terror of being blown to smithereens high above Sri Lanka. She had a mindFlash of Minnie-Tuton's sad face at an imagined funeral.

The rangeBanger detonated at the edge of the hopper's photonShield which the copilot instantly activated, and the blast bucked the bubble, with the aircraft inside, further into the air. Lissa gasped. There was an age, more like 80 seconds or so, of troubled tumbling as the pilot applied jets and fought for control. Slowly, the corkscrew effect flattened to circling, and a horizontal velocity was brought to bear.

Madrigal shouted: "Are we all okay?"

"Yes," said the various passengers.

"No more Bangers?" she shouted thru to the front section.

"No, Ma'am," bellowed Dante's voice. "None on screen. Outa range."

"Righto. I'd better get on the scope and explain myself to the Sri Lankan defence force," said Madrigal, unclasping her harness. "We've been rude and discourteous, busting thru Sri Lankan security and causing a ruckus, but I know General Dissanayeke from the old days. He may forgive me ... and then we can avoid their airForce which, no doubt, is being scrambled as we speak." She slid from her harness and slipped into her workSuite at the back of the hopper.

Todd smiled, his nose too sore to snort. He knew most mothers would never have been able to find and free him. He knew of no other person in the world that could say somethink like that about General Dissanayeke. He also knew, these dayz, the big Hegs generally did as they pleased, as poorly funded milisis and other militaries were otherwise engaged in rescue and reccovery work. When Phipps Industries wanted to assert above and beyond a sovereign law, they were no different to other Hegs.

Todd looked sidewayz at his buckledIn friend. His hand found Lissa's.

*

The hopper lifted to high altitude to weave home thru an atmospheric knothole in the cloud above the Maldives. The velocity slowly steadied, and for a while, the buffeting died away and Todd calmed and tried to sleep beside Lissa, propped on the seat beside him, her head resting on his shoulder. She snored gently.

Every time he closed his eyes tho', he saw the dead man, head shot off and half leaning against the house wall. Half a glance! That's all he'd had time for on the way down the steps. Half a glance and out to the hopper on the lawn, but that's all it took for a mind-fixed picture. Like his eyes had taken a vidShot. Couple of stillz. He had to keep his eyes open.

Before, when his kaptors allowed Todd to sit in the garden and read, that same man would amble over. The wittering guy with the half beard. With a family. They'd smoke chopchop together. Todd'd never trusted the bloke, in case the wittering was him being tricksy. The man'd never introduced himself. Still, they'd shared a joke. Wondered at the weather. He'd called Todd "kid" in a foreign accent, and asked how he was going ... like some sort of dodgy dad.

Now Todd couldn't sleep, what with the image of the the dead man's brains, and his own perpetual pain caused by the wound in his face.

He listened to Lissa's little snores and thought of her terrible rape, those bruises which had now faded from her neck, and decided: *We're both messed up.*

When the cabin lights came on several hours later, and as they crossed the northern vestiges of the northwest Capricornia coast, he was facing Pearl and Lissa, and finishing a kopi. Adrenaline spent, he was exhausted. He'd blurted that he had no sleep at all because of the horrible wakeful vision.

"His face wasn't there ... just like like minced fish," he said to them. Lissa looked qweasy, but Pearl shook her head.

"Kid. He took a shot at the hopper as we landed. We shot back. Some things are ..." she looked for a word, "not negotiable. You know what I mean? You have to retaliate."

"Easy for you to say," he said.

Pearl said: "Phipps Industries was hardly going to send those Bellingslodes to Japan for free, and you would have been at existential risk if they'd worked that out. Dr Phipps played them. Thanx to your immaculate directions over the vid, we found you."

"Yes, but," Todd was still distressed, "I smoked chopchop with the dead guy."

"You smoke chopchop?" blurted Lissa, horrified.

"Yizz ... I was in prison for 4 months. You smoke in prison to pass the time and be social. But," he added, "prison's nothink like ... like what happened to that guy. Talked with him about his family. He has 2 daughters and a son," said Todd.

"I know. I know," said Pearl as gently as possible. "But when it comes to the realWorld. Your realWorld ..."

She looked at the distressed young man and felt another unusual emotional pang. "Oh Todd, if the memory or spirit of that man haunts you, see a psychMedik, but realize this: one day, you will be a powerful HegBoss. And serious corporations cannot let anyone take advantage – you must hit back. Your mother understands this. Now you do too."

Lissa also listened intently to The Pearl's dictum.

"Some of the world out there still floats on the dreams of Purity'n'Virtue, as much as it can, but some of us don't. And HegBosses float on the reality of the bizz. See a medik. Get some sleeping pills. Talk until you lose the sharpness of the pic in your brain."

Todd nodded, looking at the big woman's concerned face. He could see Pearl's was a genuinely heartfelt speech. Lissa was looking at Pearl as well, mouth slightly open, slightly shocked. Todd, tho he'd been thru 10 months of personal hell didn't qwite understand, but somethink about the experience, on the path to a hardMarked destiny, was beginning to dawn.

TEKSPRATS

Names don't matter. Names are for suckers.
Meine letzten Äußerungen (My Last Ever Utterances) 2035, Ulli Kalk

JUST after the raid, thousands of kliks away at Centrl, in the Spokes HQ deep under the Tasman Sea, a tekSprat lifted his head in surprize. He was one of around 40 so-called tekSprats on a 24 hr surveill of those new traces that Andaman Marko had passed on.

*

The Spokes was a facility in the Southern Ocean that radiated long pipes ranging all directions into the deep ocean. The pipes delivered cool deAcidified water from The Spokes giant filter factory. The factory was vital to planetary ocean health, specifically the South Pacific and Southern Ocean, one of only 3 deAcidification filters in the Southern Hemisphere. It was a massive deepwater treatment plant. Taking advantage of its incredible importance – its inviolability – AuZgov had also strategically stationed their most secret security base within the factory infrastructure.

The massive filter engines relentlessly pulled the ocean waters thru catalysts, and blew salty ph neutral water back down the spokes of pipes which allowed krill to form healthy shells and start the foodchain. If ever there was war, it was critical environmental infrastructure, unlikely to be hit. Currently, the war with the Singular Enemy was far too time consuming to worry about international clashes ... AuZgov administrators who gamed conflict would put the likelihood at an "outside of all probability event". But if things got tense again, and nation turned on nation, no sane leader would torpedo the Spokes. Fish stocks, krill sustainability and human survival depended on less acid in the subAntarctic.

It always made Madrigal's head spin, how planetary health and national security were tangled up in one piece of machinery, built on the southern lip of AuZtralia's continental shelf. In the maze of laboratories and secure rooms of the security base, the junior security personnel, known as Sprats by everyone, had for weeks been tracking the leads Andy'd passed onto the Spokes. The Sprats watched carefully for any transactions ticking within the various identified accounts owned by the putative kidnappers.

*

The Sprats leader, deputy tekAnalyst Dr Vu, had been delighted when Andaman Marko passed Centrl the link to his vast toolbox of ancient codes, laid out in the methodical Marko way.

"Hey, Dr Vu," he'd said on an uncharacteristic scope.

"Mr Marko," she'd answered, beaming with pleasure. "Long time, no chat!"

Of Vietnamese descent, Dr Vu was still the same – friendly, patient, and earnest. And she'd liked Marko even tho', when they worked together, he'd been sneaky, and not truthful about the extent of his capabilities, not so much lying to her, but holding out.

"Have you missed me, Dr Vu?"

"Oh, not really," she said honestly to the weatherbeaten face in the scopeScreen. Boy, he looked older.

She remembered when he was held prisoner in the Spokes, his reluctance to provide full access to his genius harpoon program. Much of his illegal enterprise was based on historic malware, which he'd refashioned. For weeks, he'd refused to properly explain his strokes to her, an official of AuZgov! His intransigence could have been characterised as sedition.

"You well know I found you most frustrating during your time here, but we are grateful for your recent help. My young tekSprats will learn much from your repository of knowledge."

"This is our collective history," said Marko cheerfully. "The collective history of tekSprats and masters. These are the codes that made our world."

Dr Vu asked whether he was well, and he told her about the boat, and how he planned to disappear again.

"I'd qwite like it if Centrl forgot about me," he added. "In return for the help I've provided. I won't bring any harm on anyone, but I can't help you anymore either. You have my core knowledge now, in the socket sets I have sent. You don't need me."

"I can talk to my superiors," Dr Vu said solemnly. "Ask them to beg off."

"Y'don't qwite understand. I am formally surrendering. All the knowledge is with you now so I'll never need to be suborned again. You have it all, Dr Vu. You can't imagine how painful it was for me to be brought ashore. Please tell them. I just can't stand being ... followed," he pleaded.

There was a pause as Marko looked at her, a little frightened now.

"But you are a person of interest," she said, without a hint of menace. He just was.

"Not anymore. I have nothink interesting left to give." But he knew his plea was futile. Centrl would still keep tabs on him, and on Flick, because it was a national sickness. A bureaucratic disease. They never let go.

"Do your best, Dr Vu," he added.

"Well, keep well, sail safely ... is that what you say?" she said.

"Thanx. Will do. Bye," he'd said. "The knowledge is all yours now. Have fun."

*

"This is wonderful," Dr Vu had exclaimed to her interns as they explored the material.

"How were all these screeds still there?" asked one of her followers. "That LINUX is quite neat."

"After The Grief, this knowledge was ignored. Not forgotten. It just faded away," Vu said. She was a small intense woman. "SubAtomic programming was perfekted just before The Grief. We didn't need these older structures. We let them go. Marko didn't forget. Kept his box of tricks. He's somethink else."

Over a week, her team parsed each ancient program one by one and compared to programs the Stümmers still used. The PRSFL program from the 2030s stood out. Dr Vu shook her head, amazed that the old screeds still interfaced into later formats.

"Some clever person interfaced this stuff back in the 50s and 60s. We'll never know who the authors were tho. But I'd thought this info would be Moonshot ... left to gather moondust."

During the climate stepChange, The Grief, everything known to humanity was placed on solarPowered servers in subLunar warehouses in the Moon's Sea of Tranquillity. A giant data horde. Worst case scenario was a complete wipeout of Earth – a dystopia where men and women hoarded petrol and solar panels and fought for water and fuel on busted vehicles in a blasted landscape. If they survived at all. Was unimaginable to Dr Vu.

The climate stepChange was brewing worse than everyone imagined and at that time, Govs were unable, in the modeling, to guarantee their people's survival. Thus, they collaborated to ensure that the wealth of human knowledge would at least be preserved, accessible to any survivors, who could either scope it down, or physically reach the moon from one of the 2 planned human colonies in space.

In the end, that early collaboration to save human knowledge led to global management of The Grief that was often brilliant, sometimes unsound, but nevertheless countries were able to lean on each other, and those leaders saved humanity.

Afterward, as a young man, Marko had found the keys to the past virtual codes and told no one. Found them not thru MoonScopes, but in the Codex Library at Queensland University when he was a student.

*

So, hours after the raid in Kandy, one Jurvel Kinsey, the surprized tekSprat, was trying to trace a payment just gone – in Kyoto, Japan – to one of the opaque accounts connekted to the cash cluster that Marko had found. An inactive cluster that had paid some $New thru to the Stümmers old funding account more than a year ago.

He knew the legendary Dr Phipps had put them on surveillance a month back. Industrious they were, on 3 x 8 hour watches at the Spokes, full 24/7 coverage. And, thanx to Andaman Marko's historic cache of ancient programs, the Sprats were learning heaps about arcane money deliveries, as they watched the various accounts.

The opaque account that had just transacted was blessed with around $New5000 for some reason, but there'd been no signature. The $5000 had been drawn from a private account – a huge amount of $, and shifted thru a Government one. However, the transaction made the opaque account more accessible.

"Kor," said Jurvel aloud, to his screens, "the recipient's name is very familiar." He looked it up in a wikilog, and found a spray of information. "Why would he be getting a fat dollop of money? He's loaded to the gills!"

Jurvel intejered the desk scope and contacted his supervisor, who was having dinner a couple of floors above in the staff restaurant. The supervisor said: "Stay on it. Be there in a tick."

Within 10 minutes the same dollop of $New5000 had been redirected to a more publik account owned by one Sylvester Artarkan. The wikilog also had a long spray on the Artarkan guy. His life as a head honcho for Central Asia Energy until retirement 5 years ago and now ensconced in Kyoto. Mmmm, thought Jurval. Opaque account pays out, and same sum flicked back qwick but to an identifiable account. Wonder if Mr Opaque and Mr Artarkan are joint owners?

Jurval was only 23 and a keen tekHead. He studied financial investigations rather than those multivarious subAtomic screeds beloved of most tekHeads. Rather than being thrilled up about the tek, Jurval obsessed about why crimes occurred, and what motivated people. Well, he knew the screedTek too, but anyone could work that out. Other tekSprats would have kept following data screeds while Jurval looked up biographies. When the supervisor arrived, the young man rattled off a qwick debrief. Jurval'd been practising in his head, as each lump of info accumulated, and the supervisor nodded appreciatively.

"Unusual, possible. But theories are all very well. We gotta prove it now ... but I'll let Dr Phipps people know."

CONSEQWENCES

This is now a global movement. Millions now know there is nothing but exposure and loss if they engage with The Man. And shame. Now we retreat, and not before time.

Meine letzten Äußerungen (My Last Ever Utterances), 2035, Ulli Kalk

"THE hiGlow meeting in the scope room was clear … you could see the participants' reactions?" Madrigal asked, toying with her chilled shakeGlass.

"Like they were sitting pat in the room, right alongside. Love that tek!"

"Yeah … but you can't smell the fear, can't smell the anger," Madrigal added. "Or the disappointment."

"True that," Jexen said.

She and Ben Jexen were in the entertainment alcove of the corporate boardroom high above the city. Perched on a stool next to the juice bar, Madrigal was rid of her Green teflite uniform with wool trim, and instead flaunted a simple bright pink, red and gold frock, enjoying the feeling of air on her arms and legs. Ben Jexen, as usual, was in a cool suit, his face all salt and pepper and chiseled.

Jexen was bent across the exec juice bar, clean sun on his face, briefing his boss on the awkward meet he'd had earlier that day. The hiGlow duality feed meeting, with a dozen participants. Madrigal had elected not to attend.

During a gritty session thru the duality feeder, Jexen had presented the damning evidence of conspiracy. The feeder allowed himself and Courier Rox, plus Mrs Soong from the White Lady Heg, plus the Imperial Power Company execs, the police and the Jap/Tai Minister for Energy Replenishment, to sit virtually round the same table, tho' they were on different continents. With 3D, full definition quality. As the photonik energy network supplier, Mrs Soong had invited herself along, because she was nosy and Ben Jexen never could say no to her.

"So the Jap/Tais are grudging, but on our side?" Madrigal asked.

"Woah! Couldn't qwite say that," said Ben Jexen. "Those sunnyboyz and sunnygirlz up in East Asia are not happy. Criminal events are rare, and rarer still when exposed by foreign authorities. Jap/Tais were a hot mixUp of angry and sqweamish. And being mainland Chinese, Lulu Soong who sat with me at the top of the hiGlow table, was happy to poke them all with a metaphorikal stick!"

"She's a sadist," said Madrigal, sucking shake thru a straw.

"Thing is, when the Imperial Power Company were first briefed months back by your father's Kyoto colleagues, they spruiked up their legitimate first gambit to the power company – on behalf of Kyoto's tradition of sanctuary, to power the Kyoto Bell. Said your dad would swing a cheap deal from Phipps Industries, blah blah blah. Was pointed out by Sylvester Artakan who was at the meeting (not your dad, mind) that this might be a contract variation that could change the original core cost agreements for all Jap/Tai power we supply. At that point, the Imperial Power Company's sunnyboyz were happy to dud Phipps Industries and wriggle out of the original terms of our long contract. They'd even promised to help the Like Minds with continuity of lodes for the Bell, at least on the tek side."

Madrigal noisily sucked more shake thru the straw, and continued to listen.

"But the Imperial Power Company knew nothink about fallback plan B – the abduction," Jexen continued. "When we laid it out on the table, the abduction, and the havoc created by the killTeam in Jakarta, and your excursion to Sri Lanka, they were horrified. Should have seen their eyes."

"Thought so," Madrigal said, shaking her head, wrinkling her nose.

Jexen told her the police representative at the table had announced that the criminal party they sought, "Silver" Sylvester Artakan, former CFO of Central Asian Energy, had vanished from his rangeHouse in the Kyoto prefecture, a house located in the hills, just within the edge of the Kyoto Bell."

Madrigal'd seen the recorded glows of Artakan, and he certainly wasn't the senior doop leading the team in Kandy, tho pix of that partikular skulk had been passed to Northern Hemisphere policing and her milisi. Artarkan was being sought by the Japanese National Police. The other soughtAfter party, the Imperial Power Company executive, Jarman Kailikeri, had been arrested.

She'd watched his hostile reactions on the police vidz when they busted into his flash house, but didn't catch the Japanese curses.

Jap bizz now. Madrigal had withdrawn her resources and let others capture Artakan and Kailikeri. Japan had to deal. Their crime. Their criminals.

*

Mrs Soong had sat at the far end of the table during the Virtual Roundtable meeting. She'd gazed implacably at the Japanese delegation.

Phipps Industries paid for this expensive hiGlow connekt because Jexen wanted to make his point forcefully, wave his hand around, and eyeball the Imperial Power Company execs to project his displeasure.

Displeasure at abduction, conspiracy to commit fraud, collusion with criminal elements (a big no no in the Jap/Tai nexus, with their longtime visceral fear of organized crime). And the hard fact was that the Imperial Power Company had unwittingly assisted Sylvester Artakan in committing a crime thru one of their senior finance doops, Kailikeri.

The 4 Jap/Tais at the meeting, one after the other, adamantly complained that Dr Phipps own dad seemed to be involved in the conspiracy as well.

"Dr Phipps own father was a member of the so called Like Minds and attended the shadowy meetings where he and Artakan and Kailikeri conspired," said the IPC CEO.

"Not qwite. Mr Phipps was architect of our 25 year contract. Yes, he had involvement, but was clearly a pawn for the conspirators. An old, muddled fool. But I know one thing – he was proud of his original deal and was clear on its fixity," Jexen began.

"He was a superdupe," shouted the Jap/Tai Energy Minister, interrupting Jexen. His 3D image distorted slightly as he waved his hand angrily.

"Mr Yashimoto," said Mrs Soong qwietly, firmly, from the end of the Virtual table, "the Imperial Power Company would have done very good business from the breach of contract. Don't forget that!"

The Energy Minister was very angry about what he saw as favorable treatment of Old Man Phipps.

Jexen was severe in his retort.

"All ties between Mr Phipps and Phipps Industries were cut more than 10 years ago when he became a Japanese citizen,"

Jexen had said. "Your police should talk directly to Mr Phipps about his role in this."

The senior police at the meeting accepted this, and said they'd be charging him with collusion.

Mrs Soong, who was very fond of Old Man Phipps, looked a little bit upset, but said nothink.

*

Prior to Jexen linking the Virtual Roundtable thru the hiGlow connekt, Madrigal had instructed Jexen directly. She'd been been furious and firm. *I want you to leave my father to his fate. No exception. He could have told us much more. Much more. Left me dangling. He put 2 and 2 together 'bout Toddy, way before me.*

Madrigal was convinced, also, there was a 90 percent chance her dad could wheedle his way out of any charges because he was the supreme operator. Jexen thought she was being most severe, and far too optimistic about the muddled old man's capacities, but didn't say so.

Jexen finished the private boardroom brief. He summed up outcomes – police arrests, original longterm Phipps contract still intact, police interviews with Old Man Phipps in the offing.

And that was that.

Jexen and Madrigal looked at each other with a mutual admiration borne of years of hard corporate slog. Jexen remembered Madrigal when she was a little takker in her dad's office. Madrigal remembered Jexen when he was younger and genuinely handsome without the help of rejuves and gym fanaticism.

She patted his hand.

"Serious outcome, Ben. You handled it well. Saved profits for the company and all the partners 'round East and West Cap. I trust my dad will wriggle his way out of his mess."

Ben Jexen said he hoped so too, and hid his doubts.

Madrigal walked behind the juice bar, threw the empty shake cans in a sink, and dug out a bottle of Launceston Grange Shiraz 2107, then got busy pulling the cork. A 35 year old Grange. Nice, she thought. A true reward for us both.

She poured a good chug in their glasses, then settled herself down on her barstool again.

"By the way – how much would those goddamed Tajiks at Central Asian Energy have made if Sylvester Artakan had succeeded?"

"Billions of $New. If they'd smashed our old contract and negotiated a freshy. They'd have made 35 ... mebbe 38 billion, over the remaining 18 years. And the Jap/Tais would have saved the same. Without that, we continue to clean up. But I'm now on the lookout for other attempts on the fixity of your dad's deal."

Madrigal wrinkled her nose again.

"Tawdry, eh?" Ben said. "All for a contract. Playing off the new Government's decision to turn off the Kyoto Bell, against the genuine sentiment and worship of Kyoto's ancients. Stealing your boy."

"As I said Jex – took us a while to work it out – mebbe even too long – but proper job. Proper job."

*

At 7am, the morning after Ben Jexen's hiGlow connekt, 3 policeV's rolled onto the Old Man's raked driveway in the Kyoto hills and a group of immaculately uniformed senior officers knocked on the 19th century oak door.

The Kyoto Bell was now decommissioned. The air was suddenly hot, with gusts from the southeast. With no protective photon shield, there was immediacy with the stratosphere, which flickered ominously, as it did in most quadrants around the world. The policemen were sweating. The sky looked like warm rain.

A valet opened the door and waved them inside.

The Old Man was expecting them.

The police were taken to a spacious room with a raised tatami mat platform at the back, and were ushered to a chunky teak table. They waited, standing, until the Old Man sheepishly entered the room followed by Nozomi. He presented a polite half bow and handshake to each officer.

While still standing, the Superintendent apologized and the Old Man was then formally arrested and a pip was inserted thru a stainless steel straw into his bony wrist, to allow authorities to trak him. Once a bandaid had been placed on the small wound, and more apologies were uttered, the police party sat at the table. Due to his venerable age, and strong spiritual links with the community, they interviewed him respectfully in his own home.

All officers, except the Superintendent, were from the Kyoto prefecture. Local police, to a man and woman, supported the protection of their homes from the Singular Enemy. Because of potential bias, Superintendent Chokan had been hoppered down from Hokkaido to lead the investigation. He had no sympathy with the accused and was regarded as neutral.

"I returned the money back to Sylvester Artakan, soon as I received it," the Old Man said to Chokan. This was true. Chokan had the skanned transaction accounts on a chip, provided by Ben Jexen.

Chokan knew the Old Man's act of returning the funds immediately to the chief conspiracist was an exercise in finger-pointing. The boomerang of funds had alerted the AuZgov authorities to Artakan's identity. What puzzled Chokan was that Mr Phipps never directly told his daughter, Madrigal, the culprit's name. Or even alerted her to the reverse transaction.

Perplexed, Chokan asked Phipps San why he didn't communicate the information directly with Dr Phipps, who was investigating her son's kidnapping.

The Old Man was dismissive.

"My mess. I took responsibility. Knew she'd sort it out. Didn't want another fight with her. No, I did not."

"Tho it related to your missing grandson? Missing for some months?"

"She's smart. Taught Madrigal everything she knows, I did. She worked it out." The Old Man was stroppy, irritable at the qwestion. Qwerulous.

"I see," said Chokan carefully, not wanting to spoil the interrogation before it properly began. "So how did you identify this man Artakan. That he was responsible?"

"I woke up to the fact," said the Old Man, "that these 2 people, Artakan and Kailikeri, so called Like Minds in our esteemed group, really cared naught for Kyoto, our sacred city. The man Sylvester Artakan was nurturing an ancient grudge match with me! He wanted to bust open my golden deal with the Jap/Tai's Imperial Energy Company. A longterm deal that will continue for another 18 years, to the benefit of the company I established. Artakan tried, thru his various attempts at duress, to force a variation on a contract by making Phipps Industries provide extra Bellingslodes and this would have revoked my original deal. Nullified it. Not on. Not on."

Chokan nodded without any understanding. "Your deal?"

The Old Man rolled his eyes in exasperation which was not a good move.

"Look, officer," he began, "more than 12 years ago, before I retired, I nailed down – nailed down with big hard nails – a 30 year contract with your monopoly power provider, the Imperial Energy Company for photonikally transmitted power, generated in AuZtralia, to cover the entire Jap/Tai marketSphere. It was an expensive arrangement for them, but I have to say a remarkably reliable supply and isn't that what we all want these dayz? Reliable power."

Chokan nodded.

"My deal was that Phipps Industries would supply a steady pulse of Bellingslodes for one moderate price. Almost 30% of Jap/Tai needs. The kicker was, when other domestic power stations lost output, we would provide extra pulses at a higher price. My company's high profits depended on a slow failure of the Japanese and Taiwanese networks.

"When this deal was struck, I knew that the Jap/Tai infrastructure was heading for senescence. Old and unreliable — like me nowadayz. I also knew that the Singular Enemy would strengthen further in your qwadrant of the world. Storms and cloudOuts would make solar generation difficult and new publik power generation expensive. My company made a fortune, even in the first few years of the deal."

Senior Superintendent Chokan nodded. "Sounds like a smart call," he murmured.

"My commercial rivals never forgave me. They were locked out of one of the best commercial deals in East Asia, ever. Ever! The Japan-Taiwan nexus has been immensely prosperous. Phipps Industries generated the power, my friends at the White Lady Heg in South China provided network. A beautiful thing. Artakan never forgave my insights, my foresights, my professionalism. My powers of persuasion."

"Obviously not," murmured the policeman, astonished at the Old Man's verbal acuity in Japanese. And his gigantic hubris!

"Artakan and Central Asian Power conspired to force a contract buster and then they would re-bid at a lower rate. First they tried the power of persuasion, cheaper power directed at the Kyoto Bell soakers, using me as some sort of Trojan horse.

"So on behalf of his old company Central Asian Power, Artakan worked on me, trying for a cut price lode to take over when your Government abandoned the Kyoto Bell. He spent months emoting me, nagging me, trying to get me to persuade my former company to change the contract. And I was very upset that Kyoto could become vulnerable ... wasn't I, Nozomi? I succumbed to his pleadings."

Nozomi watched the performance impassively, amazed the Old Man was oblivious to her own role at the behest of the Silvery One.

"Because you and your friends were desparate to protect Kyoto?"

"My friends ... me ... Nozomi here ... had no idea of Artakan's plans."

"We know this," said the Superindendent. "Many of the men you eat and pray with are highly revered across our nation."

"Yes, I understand that. And to be frank, I agreed to go ahead with Artakan's plan also. I promised to try and get cut-Price lodes. I didn't think thru the conseqwences. I was so anxious to save our beautiful life."

"I see," murmured the Superintendent.

"So, ultimately, my successors at Phipps Industries, my daughter and Mr Ben Jexen, correctly spurned my overtures, tho' I did feel hurt and frustrated at the time."

The Old Man sipped green tea from his cup, wetting an overworked throat. Then he returned to the conclusion:

"Finally, they used their secret weapon. The kidnapped boy. In return for my grandson's life the power was to be supplied free. As the Kyoto photon soaker was part of the Jap/Tai infrastructure and tied to the Phipps Industries contract, it would have been a changed contract. A variation! Can't you see? Once the original contract was busted, then the offer would have come from the Tajiks at Central Asian Power, for a different deal. The Japanese and Taiwanese Governments would have dissolved my contract in the courts, freed to follow this up. And somewhere along the line, my grandson would have been qwietly released. I can tell you that the Imperial Power Company would be delighted if my deal was breached. But as a national entity, bound by international powerVending agreements, they could never be part of the conspiracy."

"Certainly not," the Superintendent murmured.

"Still, when my daughter informed me that my grandson was abducted, I still didn't see clearly that he was part of a broader threat. Not only do the eyes fade with age, Officer Chokan, so do the instincts!"

"You thought they were separate events, you mean?"

"I had no idea Todd was the ultimate bargaining chip. To force my daughter's hand in providing the power supply, if I couldn't come thru with the variation in the Jap/Tai contract. Except, my daughter found the boy first. When he was rescued, Artarkan then sent me a 'payment' hoping I'd bank it as part of some faux agreement, even tho I severed ties with my old company years ago. And he also thought it would ensnare me in his plot. This was his last desperate gambit. He thought, hoped, that this would float in a court of law as a contract variation. A desperate ploy on his part. Futile. I sent the money straight back. That's when I knew that they were after my sweet deal!"

"So, then you understood he was after a change of contract, rather than the integrity of the Kyoto Bell. And you realized he was also behind the abduction of your grandson?"

"Yes," said the Old Man. "At that point."

"And he used your grandson as bait?"

"As a threat. To force my daughter to ..."

"What?"

At this point the Old Man raised the silk sleeve of his robe to hide a tear rolling down his face. After a moment, composing himself he lowered the sleeve. The Old Man was feeling very tired. Nozomi, sitting dutifully in the corner, watched the conversation and knew her husband was slumping, but her respect for police authority, and a desire to hear her husband's excuses, prevented her from intervening.

"Have you ever met your grandson?" Superintendent Chokan asked.

"Once. To attend the wedding of a very old friend, I returned to AuZ, and met the little fellow then. The boy and my former wife, Netta, were very close."

"I see," said the Superindendent, unimpressed at the Old Man's lack of devotion to family. In the briefing, he'd learnt the boy was now 17.

"I've failed," said Old Man Phipps, sniveling. "Failed them all."

At that point he stopped talking, and Nozomi was forced to intervene and make another interview appointment for the following day.

"He is very old," she said apologetically. "He has no energy left."

The policeman bowed to her formally, said that Mr Phipps was under house arrest and could not leave the boundaries of the property, and then disappeared with his associates into the policeV.

From the door, Nozomi watched the car crawl down the drive. She was frightened by the thick humidity that settled over her face.

PARTY

Peace and love go with you all.

    Meine letzten Äußerungen (My Last Ever Utterances) 2035, Ulli Kalk

WITHOUT Peet's thin and insistent voice, The Philosophikal sounded wrong, but they played anyway. The muzos made the musical braids work and enjoyed the old bond of performance. Narmon asked a muzo friend, Gazz, to sing. Gazz'd helped build The Philosophikal's sound tek early on.

Gazz sang because Narmon couldn't sing, Worse, Todd's burnt tongue was still not working either. Jaim'z who was shy, claimed he was too young, and Lissa was playing a reed instrument so her lips were unavailable. Gazz was 21 and his warble was more mature, a less reedy voice than Peet's. To the original band members it was hard to get used to, but to the listeners the band sounded smooth and professional.

Todd, Lissa, Narmon, and Jaim'z keenly missed Peet, their bruzz, but the remaining muzos made a pact to perform to both the ear and the dots, and do it perfektly to celebrate their freedoms. They'd practised seriously and were rewarded.

*

Todd stood on the raiser, playing his old simalcrum, listening to the braids, and watched his fellow performers. He remembered the hopper landing at the Perth drome, and Jaim'z bursting into tears and hugging him to the point of strangulation when Todd and the team traipsed down the steps to a large welcoming party. The crowd had clapped the rescuers, but Jaim'z had grabbed his cuzz and gripped him hard, tears streaming down his cheeks. Now, Jaim'z head was down, percussing with a new gusto. Since the big crazy welcome, his cuzz had been practising, wanted to make the evening zing'n'zigg. Todd smiled as he played on.

The crowd was jjigging along, some sedate, others more kinetic. The rehearsals'd been fun, better than their qwiet jjams in the Hermitory courtyards the previous year. But because they'd played often in the Hermitory, they weren't far off pitch perfekt during the performance.

Gazz had the biggest challenge. It was a steep curve to memorize the wordz (he didn't like reading off a screen) but he was no slouch, and he made the evening.

Todd's gaze rested on Narmon, his heavy browed, mop headed bruzz concentrating over the music, playing the braids thru his elegant old guitar and thought, this is the concert we shoulda played that nite at the Club Karribee. With the Peet-Man.

But all had changed. Todd felt it sorely. But after each song, Narmon would rate them as "delish", as he used to, and give Gazz the big thumb. He looked so happy.

The ensemble entertained the Phipps Industries staff who'd been involved in the hunt. Rox was there in a spangly frock. The Jexens. There were family, schoolmates and Madrigal, of course. WestBased AuZgov personnel were there too. TekHeads and pilots. Langer had been invited by Todd to scope from his Swiss study to enjoy the performance. Todd could see his dad in the screen on the sill of the small stage, sitting back in his comfy chair with a whisketty, tapping a finger.

After the Philosophikal's set was played, the crowd spilled onto the terraceTop where it was hot, but at least the air was fresh. MistMakers kept the temp down. Aides wandered round with trays of fizz. Todd said bye to his dad and signed off, and was followed out by Szygy the kelpieDog – the hound had stalked him from the moment he'd walked in the door.

After concentrating on the music, Todd moved entirely to some other mindPlace. He was happy to be home, but still dis-combobulated by his experiences and in pain around his face and nose. He wasn't ready to study again. No wayz. He'd run thru The Philosophikal practises to try and find some peace, and he'd found some relaxation with his friends, doing this joyful thing together. The room of dancing people'd lifted his spirits, just then.

But still, there was an underlay of the gloomz.

Todd strolled to the edge of the balcony and watched jags of lightning in the dark north and could hear Narmon and the muzo guy, Gazz, and Jaim'z continue to jjam gently with their new stuff, sounding fantastik.

Could he fall back into that groove, with the muzos? He was finding it tricky. Things still haunted him. How vulnerable he'd been. How he'd failed and people had died. PsychMediks made it clear he was not the actor, the impetus that caused such events, and others were culprits. But ... he'd been the bunny. All the lethal eventualities had followed him.

Overall, the endGame was taking on a Phipps Industries re-sponsibility. Things his mum and The Pearl had said about his future made it sound fixed already. But he'd also watched his mum in action, and it hadn't seemed that nice. He wasn't sure he wanted that life.

The gloomz turned to his biggest gloom of all: his bruzz Peet, up north with Curl, dealing with the silence. How could

Peet ditch them, his friends? It was beyond Todd's imagining that such a raffish livewire, whose wordz tumbled from his mouth and onto the screen, could absent himself, and live among the Qwietude.

Pearl caught him in his thoughtStream. "Howz'ya, Todd?" she asked.

The Pearl was in a dress! The gloomz evaporated with this revelation. A red Chinese floral pattern. Silk. It was like she was in disguise or somethink. She was still very, very tall and scary. And held a glass full of soda. No alcoholik drink would ever addle The Pearl.

"Yowz! You look great!" Todd blurted.

The Pearl, in a proper voice said, "Thank you. And are you doing that catchup study, Todd?"

"Yeah. But I missed the biskit. Liss and Narmon got thru to uni for the half year start, but I was too late, so I've gotta wait til November. But, study's hard. My brain's sorta fuddled up after everything that's gone past. Trying to kickstart a normal life is difficult." Didn't say it sadly – just matter'o'fact.

"Understandable," said Pearl.

"Kept alone in a dark shed for that month like some cheeky dog," he said, "that was the worst. At least in the Baru Jakarta prison I had a bruzz or 2 to talk with." He made a repeat mental note to somehow find Abdurramn again. Thank him, without getting him into trouble, for the help he extended. Help that ended in yet more disaster, more death.

"You were detained for a long time. All sorts of ways," Pearl said.

"I'm out now, thanx to you and Mum."

"Don't mention it. My job." Pearl raised her glass of soda in salute. "And don't forget your friend, Lissa. She had your interests front and centre from the moment we found her. Her crabwalk in Kandy, killing that engine. Wow – she was pure pro!"

Todd smiled. He looked around for Lissa who was talking intently with Cinzia Jexen further up the terrace. Liss'd walked away from the jjam too. Was clear both he and Lissa were now less commited to The Philosophikal, while the other muzos couldn't get enough.

"I should go thank her again," said Todd to Pearl, wondering at the big woman's insistence 'bout the worth of Lissa. He wandered over. Szygy stood, and followed at Todd's heels. Lissa was in the middle of an explanation about *stupid Stümmers in the gorge* and what music they had wanted The Philosophikal to play.

"Wave music … my lord!" Lissa said, rolling her eyes. "Awful, awful dull." Liss had made it her business to attack the Stümmers, wherever and whenever.

"Well, young lady," said Cinzia smoothly, "I prefer wave music when I'm lulling. When you meditate, it is so very gentle and harmonious. Takes me to another place entirely."

"Sorry, Mrs Jexen, it may sound lovely, but it was too dull for us," said Todd.

"Never mind. You played xcellently there. Party music. Not dull. Very appropriate," and Mrs Jexen moved on to another group, unwilling to be corrected any further by the very young.

Lissa smiled at Todd in what he thought was a strange way. With a little glint in her eyes. An extra crinkle. She had nice teeth, he noticed again.

"You ok?" he asked.

"Sure am. Good party."

"Suppose so. I keep thinking of what happened to us. What happened to you, because of … me." The gloomz started gathering again.

"So, will you press those charges against Leader of Women?" Lissa the babyLawyer asked, who'd gone'n informed herself about the shades of limited consent and illegalities of vertical hierarchy abuse in organizations.

"No," said Todd, "you know I'm not. I knew exactly what Leader of Women was up to. I told Mum it was ... nothink. I'm just really embarrassed."

"But Todd. You were shaken, afterward. You warned me about elders sexing with us in the Hermitory. And then it happened to me."

He knew Lissa wanted the Stümmers brought down and Peet brought home. He also knew Lissa's experience had been brutal, way worse than his own. Worst he could say about his sexing with Leader of Women was "awkward ... embarrassing, now" because once he committed, he wanted it. At that time he was sexing with lots of the girlz at the Hermitory. In fact, he admitted to himself the actual sexing session with the older woman had been a revelation to him tho he'd felt a bit odd afterward. But he didn't feel used. In his case, he couldn't work out what the fuss was. Lissa's case was very different.

And he was now 18, like Lissa.

"I'm sorry. You got really hurt."

She patted his arm.

"Well, there's what the psychMediks call 'closure'," she said, "with Pepperbeard dead and that. But I still can't sleep very well. I push thru the dayz ... like it's one big trek ..."

Todd looked closely at her and saw tears start to form in her eyes. Still wobbly, he thought. And fair enough. He shouldn't have been so flip about Leader of Women just then, cos what she'd done had been wrong. Todd gave Lissa a long, heartfelt hug, gently holding her head to his shoulder. He was starting to finally beef up and she was small. Lissa gripped him with both arms round his waist. Small, but *strong,* he amended.

"I'll be here. Narmon'll be here," he said in her ear, which was very close to his lips. Lissa's hair smelled sweet. She snuggled into him.

"When he's not off to practise with Gazz and Jaim'z, or look-ing for rare 20th century instruments," said Lissa qwietly. "Or editing his latest tune for the 500th time."

Todd suddenly felt awkward once more. He wasn't sure where Liss was aiming her wordz. He found a smile, and stepped back from the clasp.

"It's his thing, Lissa. At least Narmonics understands his own world."

"That's true," she said, and reached out to hold her second best friend's hand.

*

Madrigal Phipps watched her son and Lissa from the corner of her eye.

At least sparx were happening between those 2, even if the dog didn't look pleased.

Madrigal was leaning on the balcony rail, her thinking spot in the corner, wineglass on bricktop, party buzzing around her. Madrigal'd been in deep conversation with Peet's dad. Back to the bizz – the terrible toll of the abductions, and the one last set of anguished parents.

She didn't tell Peet's dad that the whole fiasco was because another power generating Heg wanted to force a contract vari-ation on her company. What a tawdry farce! The enemy had pressed hard, but she'd won in the end, thanx to the kidz. All of them.

And then the poor kidz became part of a weird deal to re-plenish a gene pool for desperate colonists in the middle of nowhere. Plucked and abducted as newDNA donors for the gorge families, to please the Qwartermaster, to keep him sweet. Ohhh, even for Madrigal it was all too obscure, not in her para-digm of understood behaviours.

She should tell Toddy about the gene legacy matter. And Liss, being snatched with Todd, was a victim of the Qwarter-master's filthy agenda. Big time. She could still hear Dan

Monthly parroting Pepperbeard's wordz: *The presence of these young men and a young woman for a time – well, the chance is there for us to take advantage of the situation.*

But she'd swerved away from explaining the gene pool agenda to the parents. They'd been told the events of the past year were purely an extortion attempt for money (which was true) and that the extortionists had wanted to hide the witnesses (which was slightly true). Madrigal had made good with promises of funded tutoring, assistance at the university, possible job starts, everything that she could do to help the parents and kidz get their lives back to normal.

But Peet's parents were another matter. They were bereft.

This qwiet conversation between Peet's dad and Madrigal had canvassed possibilities of retrieving Peet, and Peet's dad had promised to keep her informed of any weakening of his son's resolve. Had been an animated chat, and Peet's dad looked happier for it. Peet's mum had been too upset to attend the party, surrounded by Peet's visible, Perthside friends, as well as Lissa's mum, Minnie-Tuton, and Narmon's parents.

As Peet's dad walked off to scope his wife with a Peet retrieval update, Madrigal thought about the scope call Peet'd made a couple months back. He'd sounded anguished: "Dr Phipps, you have to tell him. Toddy's girl Bangle is having a baby. Toddy's the dad!"

Madrigal's head'd swum when Peet had uttered the wordz.

"And Little Bones too. She's pregnant. Like, very pregnant. Starting to look like a balloon. You have to tell him. The girlz say Todd was their only partner at the time of conception. Leader of Women tricked us. She was telling the girlz to sex with us, but she lied to the girlz and told them the boyz were taking the antiFecundities when she knew they weren't. So the girlz weren't to know. Not their fault. Not Toddy's either ... I know it's not a good sitch. Will you tell him?"

Madrigal said: "Yes. Yes. Your news is very troubling. Is Curl pregnant too?

"Yes ... that includes my Curl too," Peet had said uncertainly. "She's 7 months in."

Madrigal waited to hear if Leader of Women was also pregnant, but Peet didn't say, and Madrigal didn't dare ask.

After the pause, she asked if Peet was okay about it.

"Of course. We'll manage," he said confidently, "but you make sure you tell Toddy."

That was more than 2 months back. The babies were probably born, and she'd be a grandma, like Netta.

As he knew he was going to be a dad, Peet immediately told his parents and they hadn't told anyone! Even during that private chat with Peet's dad, no way was he revealing their Stümmer grandchild.

"So untoward," she thought.

Peet's parents kept their counsel, and Madrigal kept hers.

*

Todd was a licensed Oncer, which came thru when he'd turned 16. He'd known this. Now he had fathered 2 children thru adolescent exuberance between him and 2 girlz she knew not, because of slimy, slovenly trickery on the part of the Snake Gorge Qwietude. The Leader of Women was a worm. Unwittingly, Todd'd broken the strikt fecundity laws of AuZ.

She shook her head, bemused, thinking of the important obligation of parenthood in AuZ generally, and in their own Indijj community. Those babies needed, in time, to understand their 100,000 year old inheritance. Was no doubt in Madrigal's mind, because in the end she did things properly, always ... while Stümmers defied the laws that kept society sustainable and peaceful, and got away with it.

She'd stopped Todd from talking to Peet. Just said he was a silent one now, and not to blight his friend's commitment. What if Todd found out about his babies right now? Right now? He was so *confused* still. Coming to terms with being back in Perth, for a start.

Good thing was, the bond between Todd and Lissa was tightening, and this pleased Madrigal. Lissa was a smart, driven, self-sufficient, canny young woman.

Madrigal'd watched them clinging together like lovelocked limpets. All Lissa's homeTraining and encouragement was working her and Pearl's way. If Lissa found out about the babies, would the bond growing between her and Todd be broken? Madrigal hoped not.

Peet's news presented a huge conundrum that so far she'd kept to herself.

DyNAst was hard and fast about the fecundity rules. Kidz out of qwota was a crime. Tho' Todd was an innocent victim, his qwota was done and doubled. She knew the Stümmers would never trumpet anyone's identity and the Stümmer babies wouldn't even have names, just general descriptors. They wouldn't be regarded as Phippses by anyone in the Hermitory.

Unless someone told AuZGov, DyNAst would never find out. But Toddy was liable and there was no way round the DyNAst lawz.

What were the chances? What should she do? She certainly regarded the babies as Phipps family, her grandkidz, with ceremonial responsibilities to follow – they hadn't even been smoked into this world by Elders. Nothink!

She'd half considered talking to Langer about the babies, discuss whether she should tell Todd, and when was the right time ... but Langer was a goddam f'king ethicist. She knew what Langer would do – directly scope their son and tell him. So she ignored her ex, as per usual, for the moment.

Madrigal emerged from her pondering, and skanned across the swirl of chattering people on her terrace, pleased to see the happiness was back, once again. Lissa was still holding Todd's hand and they were laughing uproariously. Young Narmon was in the boardroom making his beautiful music with Jaim'z and the others, oblivious to the change in Lissa's heart.

Madrigal knew that the rebalancing of Lissa's, Narmon's and Todd's hearts would work out, with a little bit of help.

But the babies thing? Todd was only 18.

Soon she'd tell him, very soon. And work out a way to carry on. His exams were coming up, and he was still recovering from his ordeals – the deprivation of liberty, the faceWound, the entire trauma where he feared he'd die, the torture of solitary, and being a witness to several murders. Now was not the time. Not yet.

After the exams.

Madrigal'd found Todd after almost a year's anguished separation, and she would continue to protect him.

For a little while longer.

DEATH POEM

Rather than you, let the State taste oblivion.
Meine letzten Äußerungen (My Last Ever Utterances) 2035,
Ulli Kalk

July, 2142

WAY north, xtreme storm J/2142/5, the fifth category 7 'phoon born of the Northern Hemisphere's summer Cloud event, had curved up from the China Sea. The supercharged thermocells swept into the East Asian Qwadrant across Wakayama prefecture, over Koyasan, over Nara, and proceeded to obliviate the now unprotected Kyoto Prefecture.

The protective Bell, summarily decommissioned by the Face the Future Government, had been switched off some months back. Just like that. The shell of photons was there one moment, gone the next.

The Bell's infrastructure – lode soakers and arcs – were shifted to areas that needed basic power upgrades, mostly the wareFactories along the urban sprawl that was 22nd century Japan. The newly elected Government had had enough of the decades of indulgence, and had bet on there being a couple of years clear of anything more than Cat5. They wanted to steelDrip Kyoto's homes and buildings, to move people out of risk areas, divert rivercourses and modify the many ancient gardens to protect sacred trees with smaller, intermittent shields.

The raw power was desperately needed elsewhere – for civilian powerlodes – as 2 ancient nuclear reactors were being shut down. Both from the early 21st century – dangerously beyond their core safety margins. And as communities went subterranean, power for extractors and cooling was more and more in demand.

But in hindsight, the climate hardening in Kyoto should've been done first.

Kyoto's residents had had no time to take protective measures in the face of J/2142/5. The 'phoon was relentless. The wind shrieked at 1000 decibels. The power of the superheated air hammered the very rocks and hills.

Kyoto prefecture's trees, which had greened up with new leaves in the artificially induced Holocene spring, were stripped bare, broken and then toppled as the 'phoon passed over. Meters of rain soaked into the hillsides and mudflows started fluming down the river like a tidal wave of brown vomit, thru the inadeqwate drainage systems, including thru the prettiest section of the city – the Gion distrikt – which was submerged under meters of water for a time, drowning hundreds of people.

Buildings were crushed, and, apart from one or 2 of the temples that had small photon shields paid for privately by devotees who huddled together inside, 1000 year old pagodas and Torii gates were knocked over as superCyclonic tubes worked their way thru the ancient town.

In the modern part of the city, underground Vparks filled to the brim with mud, and windows smashed as debris flew like projectiles thrown by nebulous giant madmen. The people who hadn't evacuated to Osaka shelters hid, terrified, in substandard bunkers, some of which didn't hold against the pressure. Whole families perished together.

Tragically, the Jap/Tai Infrastructure Adaptation Division had set the ¥New aside in the forward budget and calculated on an 18 month construct window to strengthen Kyoto's reserves, but they'd miscalculated. The Singular Enemy continued to intensify across the globe with its conveyor belts of 'phoons mostly heading east to west in the Northern Hemisphere, and west to east in the Southern. They'd given their ancient city no time.

It seemed ridiculous to consider but, to many Japanese cowering in their homes in the far south, or in Tokyo and other cities to the north, watching the realTime vidz of the destruction of their ancient capital, it was almost as if the Singular Enemy well knew that the coast was clear, that Kyoto's protection was gone. That it was free to destroy the very last relik of the Holocene.

*

Nozomi found the Old Man slumped in the Garden Pavilion, with its golden gables and teak beams. He was half buried under a pile of pale green leaves, wetBlown in from the maples and cherry trees which were now upended. The leaves were delicate adornments to the black silk pattern on his robe. She flicked a few of them off with her fingers and then stopped. She was not going to tidy him up, ever again.

A gale still blew, and the warm rain continued to dribble from the eaves of the pavilion. The structure was surprisingly intact. Some of the ancient carved facing was wrecked, but the beams, with their massive primitive wood joins, had stayed together. She'd thought it would be the first structure to go. Instead, it was her husband who had collapsed.

In the middle of the tempest, when the roof of their house was coming asunder, when she was calling for help, he'd gone missing. Nozomi knew there was nothink a person so feeble could do in the face of the 'phoon and she feared their whole home would crash around them. They'd been huddled with the servants who lived with them, in the room with the downstairs *onsen,* before the eye passed over. When the Old Man departed during the minutes of calm, she'd expected his return.

Prior to his flight, she'd told the Old Man they were all in grave danger and the fault lay on his head. He'd failed with the Bell. Failed Kyoto. She said it with force. The strengthening 'phoon had frightened her terribly and she had screamed at him in panic and fury, and he'd disappeared. While the wind howled, she'd been too fearful to go upstairs and search the house. The 5 servants who were with them refused her order to go outside and find him. She decided he'd wandered into the garden somewhere, but couldn't follow, terrified of the lethal debris, crashing and crushing, hurled by the terrifying wind. Several hours on, as the storm died away but while the rain still poured thru like a torrent, she'd put rubber boots on and anorak, and ventured into the grounds. She'd been fearful of what she might find.

In the aftermath, the garden was in a terrible mess of broken branches and mud and uprooted trees. As she walked in her teflite trackpants and anorak thru the thinning rain, carefully stepping over or avoiding debris, she saw with a sinking heart a 500 year old maple tree fallen in the pond. Round the side of the house, only the Zen garden with its stones was unscathed, tho underwater.

Finally, she'd picked up the courage to walk the sodden pathway and enter the Pavilion at the end of the property. The Old Man's blood was comingled with the wet brown leaf matter, the blade of his stupid precious sword under his knees. He'd tied his knees together so not to fall in an undignified way.

"He was no samurai," thought Nozomi. "What was the idiot thinking?"

The evisceration had been done with a single slice across the stomach with a tanto, a small, exceedingly sharp, 2 bladed knife. Then he'd cut his wrists to qwicken the end. The stomach wound was hidden, thankfully, with only the hint of a pink intestine poking out over his sash. The gashed wrists were visible. The wrist where the pip had been implanted was almost cut off, as if he'd tried to angrily pick it out with the end of the blade.

What a mess. What a waste.

She found the Death Poem, in Japanese, in his robe.

> *My precious gardens are a ruin*
> *stripped and broken branches, blighted buds, as fallen*
> *as my name, my fortune, my transient honour.*
> *Only the Zen Garden with immutable stones and rocks*
> *Sits sullen, puddled, and unmoved.*
> *I am not like those rocks.*

Nozomi snorted. *Bad poetry*, she thought. *And anyhow, it was my garden, not his.*

She was engulfed in another flare of anger. Nozomi, a Shinto traditionalist, was obliged to mourn and honour the Old Man. Would be humiliating. How he'd failed his community was beyond the pale. He had failed Nozomi, and failed their friends. He'd failed the spirits and the temples. Worst, he'd failed his young grandson, Todd, who was an important obligation. *What was he thinking?*

An act of *seppuku*, an honourable suicide, was just like him and his silly whims. Just what he'd do, so romantically bonded was he to ideas of Japanese culture and the old ways which he *entirely misunderstood*! Old ways were iron-hard. Dishonour was dishonour after all. She looked down at the slumped figure and the blood soaked floorboards. His grey wispy hair.

In that, *seppuku* was a fair choice, but far beyond his social station. Only warriors, samurai, were properly entitled to this ritual. He was but an Old Man who had borrowed beliefs, but which, she admitted to herself in that dripping pavilion, she'd helped cultivate.

The corpse in front of her had lived long, way beyond his natural time.

Nozomi realized she would have to contact Dr Madrigal Phipps and inform the Old Man's daughter of the death. This displeased her too, and she tutted. She disliked Dr Phipps intensely.

Looking at the ponded blood and the wet leaves, she decided that whether beyond his station or not, what he'd done in this pavilion was, in his muddled way, the proper act. Nozomi knew she'd never forgive him, or bring herself to honour the Old Man's memory in the shrine. Not in the way she honoured her long-passed parents and late first husband, who had been much kinder and less erratic than the second and would be, without doubt, more likely to look after her from the spiritworld. She would always honour them.

As the 'phoon hurled out of the ocean and across Wakayama Prefecture, then smacked into Kyoto with full force, Nozomi knew he'd seen her face of thunder, heard her sharp wordz, and he'd understood the enormity.

Nozomi turned from the small slumped body in the blossom silk robes, with his withered old feet sticking out like chicken claws. She returned up the long path thru the mud without looking back, rubber boots sqwelching at each stepfall. On approach to her damaged house where half the roof was gone, the handyman and the gardener were flinging ropes and ordering each other around to qwickly cover the missing tiles in orange tarpaulins.

Life continued. Men were busy. The wind was dying down.

She walked up the ancient teak steps and inside, out from the wind, to scope and inform the local milisi of the suicide.

And then burn the Old Man's stupid poem.

NOT A JOT

Breach and broach the Quiet – truly, I shall speak to you no longer.
   Last line in: *Meine letzten Äußerungen (My Last Ever Utterances)* 2035, Ulli Kalk

AS for Andy and Flick, Centrl never tagged them again.

Sure, on departure they'd thrown their only scope overboard. Was to be expected. And Andy Marko'd found and crushed the 2 tracking pips some AuZgov smartass had stuck between *The Kingdom's* decking, even after his plea to Dr Vu to allow them to disappear in peace. He'd expected nothink less. He'd also ditched the ClamB that Madrigal'd handed him, so no joy with those coOrdinates.

But there was always an expectation that either a hard sighting of the boat itself, or a detected dip into the Virtual where Marko's savant fingerprints were recognizable, would pin them for a fleeting moment of time.

Whether they were gone north forever, in the warm Baltic seas, or mebbe along the Greenland Arables, or whether they'd risked one too many crossings and perished, wasn't known. Andaman Marko's file stayed open for many a year, but no administrator added a jot to their record after they'd departed the Hi Top Marina, Fremantle Sound, in early April 2142.

Proving the effluxion of time was, as ever, the greatest purveyor of anonymity, *The Kingdom* was finally written off as *Lost* and its crew as *Deceased*.

Acknowledgements

Novels are a big undertaking, it goes without saying, and *The Kyoto Bell*, its prequel *The Capricorn Sky* and my favourite action plutocrat Dr Madrigal Phipps and her fractious family would never have been fully manifested without help and encouragement from a range of wonderful people.

My long-term writing group consisting of Hannah Holland, Sue McIntyre, Peter Wheatley, the older and wiser Colin Campbell and Philip Kirby whose advices, chapter by chapter and then full manuscript reads kept me focused and believing. Also, a big thanks to Steve Rouch and Michael Martin for taking time to read and sail with me under the auspices of the Canberra Ocean Racing Club to get a sense of Flick Allenby's obsessions. My brothers, Steve and Graham, lifetime collaborators who have aided me in all sort of ways. With *The Capricorn Sky*, David Vernon at Stringybark Press also was a great guide through the pitfalls of publishing. The wonderful Stephanie Smith edited both novels and set me straight. Also, thank you to Martin Shaw.

Most of all I'd like to thank my wife Alice Roughley who has provided immense support in getting the two novels out, and my daughters Esther and Alex for throwing themselves into the job as constructive critics and proof editors.

Once, in Australia's deep North, Colly Campbell was a journalist, sometime playwright and musician. He moved to Canberra in the '90's working for the Federal Labor Party as a Senior Media Advisor. For a time he was Communications Director at the Australian Institute of Criminology.

Pacey crime and speculative fiction intersect in Colly's Venn diagram of *Imagineering. H*aving worked around government and travelled all over Australia, the future holds an endless fascination and deep concern.

Colly is now a full-time writer.